Rashemen . . .

The mysterious homeland of the barbarian Fyodor, ruled by the wychlaren, who hide their strange powers behind elaborate masks.

Shakti . . .

Drow priestess of Lolth who lurks in the shadows of the Underdark, burning with an implacable hatred of all things that walk the surface of Toril.

Liriel Baenere

Now the drow princess must decide if she will return with Fyodor to his native land. There she will face the ultimate test of her courage and will glimpse for a fleeting moment that which she has sought all her life—a home.

Windwalker

by Elaine Cunningham

Songs and Swords
Elfshadow
Elfsong
Silver Shadows
Thornhold
The Dream Spheres

Starlight and Shadows
Daughter of the Drow
Tangled Webs
Windwalker

Counselors and Kings
The Magehound
The Floodgate
The Wizard War

Evermeet

FORGOTTEN REALMS®

Wind Walker

Starlight &
Shadows
3

Elaine Cunningham

Wizards
OF THE COAST™

WINDWALKER

Cover art by Todd Lockwood
First Printing: April 2003
First Paperback Edition: April 2004
Library of Congress Catalog Card Number: 2003111911

9 8 7 6 5 4 3 2 1

US ISBN: 0-7869-3184-1
UK ISBN: 0-7869-3185-X
620-96535-001-EN

U.S., CANADA,
ASIA, PACIFIC, & LATIN AMERICA
Wizards of the Coast, Inc.
P.O. Box 707
Renton, WA 98057-0707
+1-800-324-6496

EUROPEAN HEADQUARTERS
Wizards of the Coast, Belgium
T Hofveld 6d
1702 Groot-Bijgaarden
Belgium
+322 467 3360

Visit our web site at **www.wizards.com**

ACKNOWLEDGMENTS

With appreciation to Todd Lockwood, a remarkable visual storyteller. Thank you for trying to see Liriel as I did and for succeeding beyond any expectation. I'll never be able to look at the cover of *Tangled Webs* without experiencing a momentary shock of recognition!

Thanks to Bob Salvatore, whose generous spirit and gracious support made venturing into dark elf territory a little less terrifying than it might otherwise have been.

Finally, thanks to the readers who over the past few years have written requesting the finale to Liriel's tale.

DEDICATION

This story is dedicated to the memory of my grandmother, Franceszka Cwitovzska, a reader of dreams and singer of old tales, a kindred spirit then and still. She would have been very much at home in Rashemen. Dzienkuje, Babka.

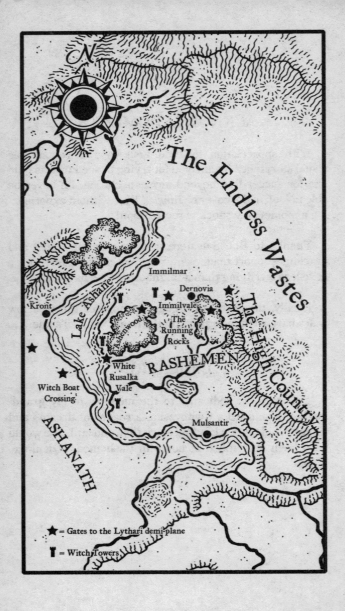

The Endless Wastes

The High Country

Immilmar

Dernovia

Immilvale

The Running Rocks

Ashenwood

Kront

Lake Ashane

RASHEMEN

White Rusalka Vale

Witch Boat Crossing

Mulsantir

ASHANATH

★ = Gates to the Lythari demi-plane

♜ = Witch Towers

PRELUDE

THE BLUNT SWORD

The Battle of Immil Vale,
Rashemen, DR 1360

The ruins of an ancient tree guarded the western border of Immil Vale. Its massive trunk, blackened by long-ago fires, was as thick as a wizard's keep, and storm-twisted branches, winter-bare and sharp as spears, encircled it with the determined air of mountain elk standing antler to antler against an onslaught of wolves.

Warm mists swirled around the base of the tree, and high overhead, faint light spilled from an arched portal half-hidden among jagged spires of shattered wood. Framed in that doorway stood three black-robed figures: witches of Rashemen, guardians of a land besieged.

They looked out over a place of exceptional beauty, a deep narrow valley that ran along the northern side of the mountain range known as Running Rocks. Rashemen winters were long and stubborn, but in this place eternal springtime ruled. Hot springs bubbled and steamed in small rocky enclaves. The grass grew thick and soft, and the scent of meadow flowers sweetened the warm air. Swift-running streams chattered excitedly, telling boastful little tales of journeys down rugged mountainsides. The witches who kept this tower usually went about their business to the accompaniment of birdsong. Today, no bird flew, no songs were sung. Even the whitewater streams seemed oddly subdued. The valley, like the witches, awaited Death in silence.

In the center of the trio stood Zofia, a plump, aging woman who in some other land might be mistaken for a cheerful village crone. Here in Rashemen the Othlor—elders among the witches—drew magic from the land itself. Springtime held potent promise, but no Rashemi denied either the power or the beauty of winter. Zofia held herself like the queen she was, as did the two Hathran with her: competent witches in the late summer of their lives. The three formed a powerful sisterhood, ready to combine their magic into a single force. Other, similar bands stood ready on mountain ledges, their robes dark slashes against the snow.

Zofia scanned the battle-ready company below with keen, bright blue eyes. All was as it should be. War bands had come from many villages, and each *fang* gathered under its own bright banner. Berserker warriors took the forefront, as was custom, but today all were mounted on shaggy, rugged Rashemaar ponies. The wild, running charge of screaming berserker warriors, so effective in melting an enemy's courage and resolve, was of limited effect against the Tuigan riders. Today the warriors of Rashemen would meet cavalry with cavalry.

The huhrong himself commanded the forces. Zofia's gaze went to him, and she noted with a pang of sadness that the Iron Lord had become a graybeard, his once-massive shoulders stooped with age. She brought to mind his broad, weathered face, lined with the passing of time and the scars of battles fought and won.

On impulse she slipped one hand into the bag tied to her belt. She fingered the ancient rune-carved bones, tempted to see if the old warrior had one more victory in him.

No. Though Hyarmon Hussilthar might lead the fighters, she was Othlor here. Ultimately the battle was hers to win or lose, and any witch who sought to know her own future was courting ill fortune.

Zofia quickly drew her hand from the bag and spat lightly onto her fingers, then fisted and flicked her fingers sharply, three times. The other witches showed no reaction to the little ritual. To the Rashemi such things were as commonplace as children's laughter or winter coughs.

The warding didn't quite banish Zofia's unnamed fears. Her eyes flashed to the place where the berserkers of the Black Bear lodge gathered, all of them mounted on sturdy, coal-black ponies. At the head was Mahryon, the *fyrra* of village Dernovia, a bear of a man as dark and shaggy and fierce as his half-tamed war pony.

A surge of pride warmed the old witch's heart. Though she was an Othlor among Rashemen's witches, her thoughts turned to Mahryon, her only son, whenever she tallied her contributions to the land. How swiftly the wheel turned, how soon boys became warriors! Her child was a grizzled veteran, and his own son rode beside him. The boy—Fyodor—was not yet twenty, but he had been counted among the berserkers of Rashemen these past four winters.

Zofia's lingering unease deepened. She had heard Fyodor's name spoken of late. The first stories recounting the young berserker's exploits were told with gusto, which was soon flavored with awe. The last few tales that had come to Zofia's ears were tinged with apprehension, an emotion that Rashemi were slow to acknowledge and slower to admit.

Her gaze clung to her grandson as a distant rumble, like the muted cadence of war drums, began to swell. The berserkers lifted their own song, a musical invitation to the battle rage. As the song increased in power and size, so did the men who sang. Their faces burned blood-red, and dark hair writhed around their fierce faces as if stirred by sudden winds. The illusion granted by the magical battle frenzy extended even to the ponies, lending them the daunting size and solidity of a knight's armored mount.

The huhrong lifted one hand high, holding back the swelling tide of battle. Zofia knew his strategy: Once the charge began, the witch whips would flail the advancing enemy from behind, cutting off escape, unhorsing many of the enemy and forcing them to fight with their feet on Rashemaar soil.

A grim smile curved Zofia's lips. These invaders would soon learn that the Land was Her own best defender.

The enemy came into view, and the witch's smile faltered. A large battalion of infantry roiled forward, well in advance of the mounted Tuigan warriors.

Strange, that so many warriors went afoot. The Tuigan and their horses were nearly as inseparable as the two parts of a centaur. Though the tundra-bred horses lacked the ferocity of a Rashemaar pony, they had proven to be intelligent, loyal beasts that would stay with their riders until death.

The truth came to Zofia suddenly.

"*Dierneszkits*," she said softly, glancing at the witches on either side. "The Tuigan are bringing the spirit-fled against us."

The two women paled. In this land, zombies were seldom encountered and greatly feared. Quickly they took up a singsong evocation. Zofia joined them in a plea to the spirits that inhabited the streams and trees and rocks of this enchanted vale. With one voice the witches importuned the spirits to quit their homes for a short while, to inhabit the bodies of slain enemies and bring them under the witches' control. Their magic reached out into the valley, entwined with the seeking mists, ruffled the springtime meadows.

However, the spirits, who for more than two years had been growing increasingly capricious, did not answer at all.

The undead hoard shambled steadily forward. The riders pulled up, staying within the parameters of a large circle of winter-brown grass that scarred the land like a fading bruise.

Zofia's voice faltered first. "How is this possible?" she murmured. The location of magic-dead spots was a secret closely guarded. The Tuigan were said to be skilled at torture, but it seemed remarkable to her that a Rashemi would yield this information under any circumstances.

Fraeni, the youngest of the trio, pantomimed the sprinkling of salt in a semicircle before her, a warding against evil magic. "The Time of Trouble," she intoned, "when the Three were silent, and long-dead heroes walked the land. Our power has not been the same since."

The Othlor dismissed the obvious with a sharp wave of one hand. "But the rest of the valley wasn't touched by the magic-death. The place spirits—the *telthors*—are here. I can feel them. I just can't *reach* them."

"It is like trying to sing in tune with our Sisters on the Rookery Peak," the third witch said, nodding toward the farthest outpost. "We see them, but we cannot hear them or they us."

"Just so," Zofia agreed grimly. "Let's get on with it. Command the whips!"

Scores of weapons—many-headed hydras fashioned from magic and black leather—emerged from the empty air. The broad, metal-fanged tips lifted, arched back, and whistled forward. Sharp cracks, like lightning and thunder combined, echoed though the valley and bounced in fading echoes from peak to peak. Each whip tore deep, bloodless furrows into the advancing enemy.

The zombies kept coming.

The witches joined hands and shouted a single ringing word. Steam erupted from the land in killing geysers. The stench of rotten meat filled the air, but the zombies' advance did not falter.

Dark wings filled the air as ravens answered the witches' summons. They swooped down upon the undead carrion, their talons raking and their beaks diving deep into sightless eyes. Feathers flew as the zombies batted the birds aside. Finally the ravens yielded the fruitless battle, leaping into the air to circle and scold.

Still the undead warriors came.

One of the witches on a nearby ledge loosed a stream of magical fire at the undead warriors. The weapon never came close to its target. A dense cloud of mist, dragon-shaped, exploded from a stream, jaws flung wide. It lunged at the flame, swallowed it whole. Wisps of steam rose from its nostrils as it sang back into the waters.

"Fool," muttered Zofia. "You cannot defend the land by attacking it. Are we wizards, to create what we want by destroying what we need?"

"These monsters are not of the natural world or the spirit world," argued Fraeni. "How are we to fight them?"

The old witch nodded toward the impatient berserkers. "This is their battle now."

At that moment the Iron Lord waved his men into battle. Several *fangs* kicked their mounts into a running charge.

Zombies went down under thrashing hooves and flailing swords.

They did not die as men did. They pulled the horses down with them, and bony fingers clung and burrowed and tore even after the body and limbs were hewn asunder. Many a warrior urged his mount up and forward, unaware of a severed hand making its way, spiderlike, up a pony's withers toward the rider.

As Zofia watched, the huhrong's sweeping sword caught one zombie below the ribcage and severed it neatly in two. The upper body went spinning off, arms windmilling in wild search for a handhold. The half-zombie caught a fistful of long flying mane then managed to drag itself up and fling its arms around the pony's neck. Its teeth began to gnaw, and its head shook savagely as it tore out the animal's throat. Meanwhile, the lower body and legs kept plodding forward, its gray entrails dragging behind, directly into the thickest part of the charge. One of the black ponies plowed into the half-creature and stumbled. Its rider went down and quickly disappeared under a swarm of undead.

Everywhere Zofia looked this scene was being re-enacted in endless, grim variation. She shaded her eyes and squinted toward the far end of the battle. The tuigan riders stayed where they were, in the magic-dead stretch of land where no witch whip could venture, no spell could reach. She had anticipated that this might occur—by accident if not foreknowledge—but had thought it no matter for concern. After all, the spirits could walk where they willed.

Why, then, were they silent?

She felt Mahryon's horse stumble, felt her son go down before her eyes actually found the place that received his spilled blood. His sword lifted again and again, a bright flash among the writhing, seeking limbs of the soul-fled monsters who had dragged him down. The man himself she could not see, but his flame burned bright in her heart and soul.

And like a wind-snuffed candle it was gone.

A wail of soul-deep anguish burst from the aged witch, a keening lament for Mahryon—her firstborn, her baby, her heart's own! The younger women laced their arms around her waist, supporting her as they matched her cry and turned it into power.

A sudden gale lifted a score or so of the undead creatures and sent them hurtling back. The berserkers they had been assailing picked themselves up and charged forward, unaware of their wounds.

Zofia beat back the wave of her grief and looked for Fyodor. He had not yet been unhorsed, and his scream of rage and fury carried on the wind, as alike her own as if it were a mountain-cast echo. His pony wheeled and kicked and bit as Fyodor beat aside a knot of zombies. Horse and rider broke through and rode for the fallen warrior at a gallop. The boy leaped from his mount before it could break stride and hit the ground at a run. The pony veered away; Fyodor stooped and seized his father's sword.

Lofting it high, he let out one fierce roar and burst into a charge. He ran forward, scything through the undead warriors like a farmer harvesting rye. To Zofia's astonishment, he emerged from the deadly gauntlet and kept running toward the waiting riders.

"There is courage!" exulted Fraeni. "But what can one sword do?"

As if he heard the witch, Fyodor slammed the sword into the sheath on his back and kept running. He seized one of the ineffectual witch whips from the air and hauled it back.

All three witches caught their breath. Their astonishment was mirrored throughout the valley as witch and warrior beheld the inconceivable. For a moment time stopped. . . .

The many strands of black leather flashed forward in a single gray blur.

Fyodor's first strike took a Tuigan rider, wrapping around his body with bone-cracking force. When he pulled the weapon away, it came dragging long strips of flesh. The horse shied away from the thunderous crack and the sudden fountain of blood, sending its owner's body pitching into the next warrior.

Fraeni exhaled on a curse and made the sharp, slashing hand gesture reserved for those Rashemi who flouted the cardinal laws of the land. When she caught Zofia's incredulous stare, she said defensively, "The boy is mad! It is death to wield a witch whip!"

"Yes, he is mad," Zofia agreed, "and yes, it is death—and may the Three be praised for it!"

By now other berserkers had broken through, dodging their way past Tuigan swords and stampeding horses. Fyodor continued on his suicidal path, lashing at the invaders, tearing them from their mounts and urging the horses into panicked flight.

Once unhorsed, the invaders could do little against Rashemen's battle-mad defenders. The *fangs* of Rashemen drove them away from the magic-dead circle, deeper into the valley. The witch whips awaited them there. They joined in deadly song with Fyodor's whip, lashing the Tuigan toward Imiltur and the army that awaited them there.

When it was over, Zofia dismissed the witches to go among the wounded, to find and help those who might yet be saved. It was grim and dangerous work, separating the wounded from the dead, and the dead from the undead. Nor would they work alone: The skies were already black with ravens, and the hungry cries of wolves rose from the darkening shadows of the Ashenwood.

Zofia quickly slipped into a witch's trance, sliding into the gray overworld that linked the living and the spirit realms. She reached out to the Sisters guarding the Watchtowers of Ashane. They must know what was coming their way.

She quickly touched the minds of the first Guardian, the witch who stood at the portal to the overworld, and conveyed without words what needed to be said. When the tower had been warned, she moved to the next and to the next. At the third tower, no entranced witch guarded the portal. Instead Zofia encountered a chaos of displaced spirits—

And a burst of power that threw her across the room.

The gray world exploded in a white burst of pain, and there was only darkness.

Zofia didn't hear the warriors come in, couldn't have said who had the effrontery to pour a swig of *jhuild* down her throat. She came to herself choking and sputtering, and her first words were a few choice phrases she'd learned in her days in the warriors' lodge.

A thin but still-strong hand captured hers and hauled her to her feet. "Save it for the Tuigan, Zofia."

She focused on the face of the aging huhrong then glanced at the white-faced youth who stood a pace to the side and two behind. Her gaze returned to the huhrong's face.

"We have won another battle, Hyarmon Hussilthar. Perhaps we should all have another drink."

"The time to celebrate has not yet come," the huhrong said coldly. "Young Fyodor broke ranks and should be dealt with accordingly."

Zofia let out a derisive laugh. "Broke *ranks?* Has your eyesight so faltered, Hyarmon, that you mistake our berserkers for Cormyr's Purple Dragons? The men of Rashemen do not march into battle like ants."

The old man's face mottled. "Wolves attack with more discipline and order!

"And with less ferocity," she countered. She nodded toward Fyodor. "That young warrior turned the battle. You know it."

"That young warrior is dangerous, and *you* know it. He is not his own master. What man in control of his wits would lay hands upon a witch whip?"

The Iron Lord reached over his shoulder and drew a long, dark weapon from the baldric slung there. This he threw onto the floor. It landed on the stone floor with a deep ringing clatter, like the bass-voiced bells that tolled a warrior's death.

"I will not deny that young Fyodor did his duty," the huhrong said in more tempered tones. "Now I must do mine, and you, yours."

It was the law of the land, born of stern necessity, and Zofia had no argument against his demand. She gave a curt nod that was both agreement and dismissal. The Iron Lord inclined his head and strode from the room.

She stooped to pick up the weapon. With both hands she held it at arm's length, sighting down the blade. It was straight and true, as well made as any weapon of Rashemen. It was also heavy—even in the strength of her girlhood, she could not have held it so for more than a moment. Such swords were nearly impossible to wield in battle except in the throes of berserker frenzy. It had no edge. It was a bludgeon, not a cutting weapon. A berserker raging out of control was a danger to himself as well as others, and it was the greatest dishonor for any Rashemi to die by his own hand, his own sword.

She turned to the young man and saw the bleak acceptance in his eyes. Before she could speak, a dark cloud of magic shimmered in the far side of the tower room, then took silent, solid form. The bodies of three of Rashemen's witches—the women whose death had nearly been

Zofia's—had returned to the nearest fastness.

Zofia dropped the black sword and hurried to her fallen sisters. Her mind refused to catalogue all their injuries, acknowledging only that they had been horribly slain. Two of them still wore the black masks that witches donned when traveling and sometimes when spell casting. The third witch wore her mask tied to her belt. Her face was untouched by her violent death, and it appeared young, fair, and very familiar. It was the face that Zofia had seen when as a girl she had looked into a clear pool or a silvered glass.

Her heart breaking, Zofia dropped to her knees and untied the mask. The woman's face changed to the aging face of Zhanna, her twinborn sister. Zofia gently smoothed aside a strand of gray hair and whispered a prayer to speed her sister's spirit on its way.

A lifetime of duty pushed aside this new pain. With steady fingers Zofia tied the mask to her own belt. Later she would call Fraeni to her, give her the mask, and send her to hold the Watchtower. Zhanna was one of the most powerful witches in the land, and she had been the guardian of many treasures. In addition to the Mask of Danigar, she had been entrusted with an ebony wish-staff and the task of ferreting out the ancient power hidden in the Windwalker amulet.

A deep foreboding filled Zofia, and she slid one hand beneath the high collar of his sister's robes, her fingers seeking the chain. It was gone—taken by the wizards who had slain her sister.

Gone, too, was her sister's dream. According to the old tales, in the Windwalker lay the power to bind and to break, to heal and destroy. Zhanna had been certain that it had a role to play in the restoration of Rashemen's magic.

The burden of grief was suddenly too heavy for Zofia's

shoulders. The tower room spun and blurred, and her own spirit strained at its life-tether in a yearning to follow its twinborn self.

"Grandmother?"

The tentative question, voiced in a deep, resonant bass, jarred Zofia back to herself. She rose to her feet in a single smooth movement, schooled her face to a mask of calm majesty, and turned to face Fyodor.

The young warrior was pale and haggard, weaving on his feet. It was a marvel he could stand at all. The sickness that fell over Rashemen's warriors after a berserker rage could be as devastating in its own way as the killing frenzy.

Pride and grief mingled in the old witch's heart as she beheld her kinsman for the last time. Fyodor was his father's son—a strong man, a fine warrior. Young as he was, there had been talk about making him leader of his own *fang*. With a heavy heart, she took up the dull black sword, holding it so it lay flat across her two hands.

"You have brought honor to Rashemen," the witch said softly. She marveled that she was able to speak the ritual words without wavering. Even so, she had to swallow hard before she could speak the last words. "In honor go to your last battle."

He took the weapon from her, accepting without hesitation his sentence of death. An honorable death, yes, but death all the same. Zofia lifted one hand to give the blessing bestowed upon the dead and dying, but try as she might, she could not form the ritual gesture.

For a long moment the old witch and the young warrior stood in frozen tableau, then Zofia's hand dropped heavily to her side.

She had had too much of death.

The bag that held her augury stones shifted, as if the ancient bones within stirred of their own accord. She reached in, drew out a handful of the engraved stones, and cast them to the floor.

They landed in a precise circle around the young man. Instantly he was surrounded with translucent, rapidly shifting images, too many and too fleeting for Zofia to perceive. The one that seized her attention was a raven with golden eyes, wearing about its neck an ancient amulet, a rune-carved dagger of dull, weathered gold.

"The Windwalker," she said aloud, and heard the power that filled her words like strong winds passing through winter trees—the power of Sight. "You will find the Windwalker. She will bind and break, heal and destroy. You will bring her to Rashemen, and she will bring you home."

The images around Fyodor faded, and the witch's summoned power receded like a departing storm.

"The Windwalker," Zofia repeated in her own voice, responding to the puzzlement on her grandson's face. "It is an ancient artifact of our people. You must find it and return it to me."

The warrior responded with a bleak smile. He lifted the black weapon, gripped the blade and drew his hand along it, then showed her his unmarked palm.

"I have been declared *nydeshka*, a blunt sword. By Rash-emaar law, I am a dead man."

"That excuses you from obeying the Othlor?" she demanded tartly. "If I say you will go, you will go."

Fyodor's lips thinned. "I accept our customs and tradition. Any berserker who cannot control his rage has earned death," he said evenly, "but what dishonorable thing have I done, Grandmother, that you condemn me to exile?"

"Consider it *darjemma*, then," she said, naming the journey all Rashemaar youth took in early adulthood.

"No youth has gone on *darjemma* since the Tuigan

invaded. Would you have me abandon Rashemen while she is under attack?"

"Have I not said so?"

He acknowledged the command with a nod. For a long moment, however, he waged a silent battle against pride.

"I am willing to die," he said at last, speaking his plea with quiet dignity, "but let me die at home. Do not condemn my spirit to walk lands it cannot know, like the fallen Tuigan."

That startled her, for she thought none but witches perceived these unquiet exiles. "You can see these ghosts?"

He hesitated. "Sometimes, yes. From the corner of my eye. When I look straight upon them, they are not there, and when I speak to them, they do not answer."

These words described with distressing accuracy the situation with the spirits, as well. So Fyodor had the Sight, Zofia noted. That was no great wonder, seeing that men of their clan were counted among the *vremyonni*—the Old Ones, the rare magically gifted males who crafted weapons of magic and fashioned new spells. Zofia considered telling Fyodor of the state of Rashemen's magic but decided that he had burdens enough to bear.

"I will enchant your weapon so that the blade will cut, but only those who are not of Rashemen," she said. "So armed, you have as good a chance as any man of completing your task and returning to Rashemen with honor."

"And if I fall?"

"I will send a Moon Hunter to find you and bring you home," she suggested. "I promise you, by the word of an Othlor witch and by the power of Mother Rashemen, that whatever comes of your quest, your bones will rest beneath the skies of your homeland. Will that content you?"

Despite his situation, Fyodor's winter-blue eyes brightened with the wonder of those whose deepest joy was the hearing and telling of tales. "Moon Hunters truly exist? I had thought them to be legends! Do you truly know such a creature?"

"Have I not said so?"

He pondered this marvel for a moment, then he let out a long breath and shoved one hand through his dark hair. The smile he gave her was wry and far too old for his years.

"These are strange times, indeed! A blunt sword is sent on a witch's quest, and a Moon Hunter stalks a dead man. What is this about, Grandmother? *Truly* about?"

"I cannot tell you," she said with total honesty.

His regarded her for a long moment. "With all respect, Zofia Othlor," he said softly, "it seems to me that the reason you cannot tell me is that you do not know the answer."

Oh yes, he saw too much, this son of her blood and her spirit.

"Find the Windwalker," she repeated. "With it you will find your destiny and perhaps that of all Rashemen."

REPRISE

Unconquered Foes

Skullport, DR 1361

In many a Waterdeep tavern, ballads are sung of an ancient city doomed by the evil of its inhabitants. According to the song, the city was swallowed by rock and sea, and the gods raised a vast headstone to mark its grave.

Most of the revelers who join in drunken refrain have no idea they are drinking in the shadow of this "headstone," which is in fact Mount Waterdeep. Few realize that the city of Skullport lies directly beneath them and that it is far from dead.

Skullport's streets and shanties sprawl untidily through a series of enormous stone caverns, and networks of tunnels delve throughout the north-lands and under the sea itself.

In a remote corner of one of these warrens, a dark figure floated along the ceiling of a narrow stone passage. His drow magic kept him aloft, well above the magical wards and alarms that would betray his approach. He pulled himself from one jagged handhold to the next, moving carefully toward the moment that had filled his dreams since the day he'd first met Liriel Baenre.

Gorlist, the warrior son of the wizard Nisstyre and second in command of the mercenary band Dragon's Hoard, struggled to tune out the alluring clash of weapons echoing through nearby stone corridors as drow fought drow. The enemy whose death he desired above all others would not be among the sword-wielding priestesses of Eilistraee.

A warning heat began to kindle in the drow's left cheek. He slapped a hand over the dragon-shaped tattoo emblazoned there with magical ink—a talisman that warned of nearby dragons and indicated with faint, colored light the creature's kind and nature. No telltale glow spilled through his fingers. There was a dragon ahead, but it was a deepdragon, a creature of darkness.

The drow scowled. Of course that would be Pharx, for what deepdragon would allow an interloper so close to its lair? Pharx was a powerful ally. Any battle the dragon joined would be short and decisive. Victory was important, of course, but Gorlist had his own vengeance to consider.

With an impatient flick of his ebony fingers, Gorlist dispelled the levitation magic holding him aloft. He swooped toward the tunnel floor like a descending raven and hit the stone floor at a run. The time for secrecy and stealth was past.

Gorlist raced toward his father's hidden sanctum, leaving in his wake blinding explosions of magical lights and alarms that keened like vengeful banshees. The wall ahead shifted, and a ten-foot, two-headed ettin broke away from the stone. The monster rose up before him, blocking the passage with menacing bulk and a spiked club. Gorlist ran through the utterly convincing illusion as easily as a pixie might flit through a rainbow.

The tunnel traced a curve, then ended abruptly in solid stone. Gorlist sped around the tight turn and hurled himself at the wall, leaping high into the air and snapping both feet out in a powerful double kick. The "stone" gave way, and he crashed through the hidden door.

Wood shattered, and spellbooks tumbled to the floor as the concealing bookshelf gave way. Gorlist rolled quickly and came up in a crouch, a long dagger in each hand. With a swift, practiced glance he took in the small battlefield.

His father's study was empty.

It was also a disaster. Cracks slithered up the stone walls. Artwork hung askew or lay broken on the mosaic floor, which had buckled and heaved until it was little more than a pile of rubble. Part of the ceiling had given way, and chunks of it lay in heaps against one wall. Dust still rose from the recent stonefall, and water released from some tiny, hidden stream overhead dripped steadily onto the rubble.

Gorlist nodded, understanding what had happened. As he'd anticipated, Liriel Baenre had come to reclaim the magical artifact Nisstyre had taken from her. The wizard had responded with a tiny, conjured quake—a canny move on Nisstyre's part. There were few things the people of the Underdark feared more than a stonefall tremor. There no better way to send the troublesome wench scurrying out into the open—to a place that offered Nisstyre every possible advantage.

Bloodlust sang in the warrior's veins as he picked his way through the ruined chamber and sprinted down a tunnel leading to the dragon's hoard cavern. Pharx would be there, ready to protect his treasure. Surely this was the battlefield Nisstyre would choose!

Gorlist was nearly there when a shriek of terrible anguish seared through the air. Without slowing his pace, he seized the flying folds of his cape and drew the magical garment around him in a shield of invisibility.

He burst onto a walkway encircling the vast cavern, squinting into the bright torchlight—or so it seemed to his sensitive drow eyes—that filled the hoard room with flickering shadows. Pharx's lair was dominated by an enormous heap of gold and gems. The hoard glittered in the light of several smoking torches thrust into wall brackets. The object of Gorlist's deepest hatred climbed this pile, moving with a dancer's grace over the shifting treasure.

Liriel no longer looked the part of a pampered Menzoberranzan noble. The erstwhile drow princess was clad in simple black leathers, and the sword on her hip was serviceable at best. Her elaborate braids had been undone, and thick wavy hair tumbled down her back like a wild, whitewater stream. Gorlist could not see her face, but it was emblazoned in his mind: the patrician tilt of her small, stubborn chin, the catlike amber hue of her scornful gaze. For a moment Gorlist could see nothing but Liriel, and his thoughts held nothing but hatred.

His sharp eyes caught an anomaly: a smooth wash of gold amid the jumbled treasure. Beneath the acrid dragon musk lay the stench of burned flesh — a not uncommon scent in a dragon's lair but under the circumstances, ominous. Gorlist caught sight of the dying drow embedded up to his chest in cooling, molten gold.

There was no mistaking Nisstyre, despite the ravages of a heat so furious that it could melt coin as if it were butter. A large, glowing ruby was embedded in the seared forehead, and its magical light dimmed with the swift ebbing of the wizard's life-force.

Liriel plucked the gem from Nisstyre's forehead and gazed into it like a seer contemplating a scrying stone—which, in fact, the ruby was. She greeted the unseen watcher with a smile such as a queen might give a vanquished rival or a hunting cat use to taunt its prey.

"You lose," she said.

Crimson light flared as if in sudden temper, then abruptly died. Liriel tossed the lifeless stone aside and half-ran, half-slid down the pile.

So do you, Gorlist silently retorted, noting the dragon-shaped shadow edging into view against the far wall.

The dragon staggered into the cavern, and Gorlist's lips shaped a silent, blasphemous curse. It was not Pharx after all but a smaller, stranger creature: a two-headed purple female. Obviously the dragon had seen battle, and her presence indicated that she had prevailed over Pharx — but not without price. From his position, Gorlist could see the deep acid burns scoring the female's back.

Liriel could not see the wounds, and she greeted the dragon with a fierce smile. They exchanged a few words that Gorlist could not hear. The dragon seemed about to say more, but its left head finally succumbed to injury. Enormous reptilian eyes rolled up, and the head flopped forward, limp and lifeless.

For a moment the right head regarded the demise of its counterpart. "I was afraid of that," the half-dragon said clearly, then the second head crashed facefirst into Pharx's treasure.

Liriel threw herself to her knees and gathered the dragon's left head in her arms. "Damn it, Zip," she said in tones ringing with grief and loss.

The right head stirred, lifted. "A word of advice: Don't trust that human of yours. An utter fool! He offered to follow me into Pharx's lair and help in battle if needed. In return, he asked only that I kill him if he raised a sword against any of Qilué's drow. Best deal I was ever offered."

The dragon turned aside, and her fading eyes held a conspiratorial gleam. "You're on your own now."

Gorlist followed the direction of the dragon's gaze, and his crimson eyes narrowed. A young human male strode swiftly toward Liriel, his black sword naked in his hand and his concern-filled gaze fixed upon the mourning drow.

"He lives," Gorlist muttered flatly, disgusted at himself and Nisstyre for allowing the human to survive. When last they'd seen this man, he had been sprawled beside a dying campfire. The drow mercenaries had seen only what Liriel had wanted them to see: the distraction offered by her unclad body and the lie of the human's "death." The truth had hidden behind the dark elves' fascination with the deadly game—known among drow as the "Spider's Kiss" in honor of the female spider who mated and killed—that Liriel had tacitly invited them to contemplate. Gorlist granted the female's devious little ploy a moment's grudging admiration.

All of Liriel's cunning seemed to have vanished with the dragon's death. She cradled the enormous purple head in her lap, rocking it tenderly, all but oblivious to the crescendo of approaching battle.

The drow warrior sneered. So that was the princess's weakness. If the loss of a dragon could so distract her, imagine her state when her pet human lay dead at her feet!

Anticipation sped Gorlist's steps as he unsheathed his sword and crept, silent and invisible, toward the unwitting pair.

Liriel gently put aside the dragon and rose. She jolted back as she found herself nearly face to face with her companion. Her astonishment turned to rage, lightning quick, and in full drow fury she hurled herself at the man, pushing him toward one of the exit tunnels.

"Get out of here!" she screamed. "Stupid, stubborn . . . *human!*"

The young man easily removed himself from Liriel's grasp and turned toward the main tunnel. The clamor of swords announced that battle was almost upon them.

"It is too late," he said in bleak tones. As he spoke, magical energy crackled in a nimbus around him—an aura faintly visible to the magic-sensitive eyes of the watching drow warrior. Before Gorlist could blink, the human began to take on height and power.

The drow caught his breath. Once before he had seen this common-looking young man transform into a mighty berserker warrior. He remembered little of the battle that had followed, for the memory had been seared away by the healing potions that had brought him back from defeat and near-death.

No fighter had ever before bested Gorlist with a sword. For a moment he burned to erase this insult in open combat.

Liriel brandished a familiar gold amulet—the Windwalker, the artifact that Nisstyre had considered so important. She snatched a battered flask from the human's belt, pulled the cork free with her teeth, and tipped the flask slowly over the golden trinket.

Shock froze Gorlist in mid-step. Nisstyre had coveted the Windwalker for its ability to hold strange and powerful magic. With the help of this treasure, Liriel had brought her undiminished drow powers to the surface, something few drow had been able to accomplish. Could she possibly be willing to throw away this hard-won gain?

It was unbelievable, unconscionable! What drow would willingly surrender such an advantage?

For a moment Gorlist was torn. He yearned to reveal himself, to defeat the human, to gloat at the pain the man's death would inflict upon Liriel. Then the human began to sing in a deep bass voice. Gorlist could not understand the words, but he sensed the power of ritual behind the song.

Any delay would put his main prize at risk. Better to dispatch the male quickly and savor the second, more important kill. Still shrouded with invisibility, Gorlist darted forward, his sword high.

The human's transformation ended with a surge of magical growth, one so sudden and powerful that it sent him stumbling forward. The stroke that should have cleaved his skull dealt only a glancing blow, but Gorlist noted the swift flow of blood and knew that, unchecked, it would suffice.

The ritual song stopped abruptly, but the man's fall was slow, astonished, like the death of a lightning-struck tree. Liriel caught him in her arms, staggering under his weight. With difficulty she eased him to the ground. A small cry escaped her when she noted the white flash of bone gleaming through the garish cut.

Gorlist flipped back his cape, revealing himself and his bloodied sword. "Your turn," he said with deep satisfaction.

Liriel went very still. The eyes she lifted to him were utterly flat and cold, as full of icy hatred as only a drow's could be. In them was no grief, no loss, no pain. For a moment Gorlist knew disappointment.

"Hand to hand," she snarled.

He nodded, unable to contain his smirk of delight. The princess was not as unaffected as she pretended to be. If her heart had been untouched and her head clear, she would have never agreed to face a superior fighter with nothing more to aid her than steel and sinew!

The stupid female closed the Windwalker. She rose and pulled a long dagger from her belt.

They crossed blades. The strength of Liriel's first blow surprised Gorlist—and unleashed a wellspring of fury.

He slashed and pounded at her, raining potential death

blows in rapid, ringing succession. Gone was his yearning for a slow death, a lingering vengeance.

But the princess had learned something of the warrior's art since their last meeting. Liriel was as fast as he, and though she could never best him, she was skilled enough to turn aside each killing stroke. Her strength, though, was no match for his, and Gorlist drove her steadily, inexorably, toward the cavern wall. He would pin her to it and leave her there to rot.

Through the haze of his battle rage, Gorlist noted the tall, preternaturally beautiful drow female running lightly along the far edge of the cavern. Qilué of Eilistraee had arrived, and fast behind her came a band of armed priestesses! His victory must come quickly or not at all.

The newcomers paid little heed to the furious duel. Lofting a silvery chorus of singing swords, they rushed to meet the mercenaries that yet another band of females herded into the open cavern.

Liriel had also noted her allies' arrival. She made a quick, impulsive rush toward them, in her relief forgetting the uneven floor. She tripped over a jeweled cup and stumbled to one knee. Gorlist lunged, his sword diving for her heart.

The drow princess was faster still. She rose swiftly into the air, and the warrior, deprived of his target, found himself momentarily off balance. Before he could adjust, she spun like a dervish and lashed out with one booted foot.

To his astonishment, Gorlist felt himself falling. The floor of the hoard room seemed to drop away, throwing him into a maelstrom of faint, whirling lights and magical winds.

Before his heart could pick up the beat stolen by shock, he was flung out into cold, dark water. He fought off the urge to take a startled breath and began to swim for the surface.

It was all too clear what had happened. Somehow Eilistraee's priestesses had learned of the magical gate hidden beneath the dark waters of Skullport harbor. They must have waylaid some of the Dragons' Hoard mercenaries and stolen the medallions that granted passage through this portal. Liriel knew this, and she knew just where to find the hidden magical door. Her "retreat" from his assault had been calculated, every step and stumble of it! This knowledge pained Gorlist nearly as much as the burning of his air-starved lungs.

Gorlist burst free of the water and dragged in several long, ragged gulps of air. He dashed the back of one hand across his eyes and squinted toward the bright light of a battle.

The situation was grim. A small crowd of drow children—valuable slaves bound for a dark elven city far to the south—huddled together on the dock. Their wary, watchful red eyes reflected the light of the burning slave ship.

Gorlist's second ship was still intact, but that was the best he could say for it. His minotaur boatswain slumped over the rail, his broad, brown-furred back bristling with arrows. The crow's nest flamed like a candle. The drow archer stationed there had tried to leap free and had become entangled in the rat lines. His garish crimson leathers identified him as Ubergrail, the best archer in the Dragon's Hoard. He hung there, slain by his own red arrows—Qilué was known for her disturbing sense of justice—like a bright insect caught in Lolth's web. Other, nameless dark shapes bobbed in the water around Gorlist, silent testament to his band's defeat.

Nonetheless a few males still stood and fought. Heartened, Gorlist swam steadily for the ship. He seized one of the anchor lines and hauled himself up out of the water. A burst of levitation magic sent him soaring over the rail.

He dispelled the magic and dropped to the deck beside a comrade.

As Gorlist rose from his crouch, the "comrade" whirled toward him. A black fist flashed toward his face and connected with a force that snapped his head to one side. He instinctively moved with the blow, using the momentum to add distance between himself and the traitor. Drawing his sword as he turned, he blinked away the stars that danced mockingly before his eyes.

This opponent was a tall, silver-haired drow male who crouched in guard position, waiting for Gorlist to gather himself for battle. The stranger's foolish chivalry and silvery hair proclaimed him a follower of the hated goddess Eilistraee.

Gorlist's lip curled in a sneer, and he made a contemptuous beckoning gesture with one hand.

The silver-haired drow lifted his sword in challenge. "For the Dark Maiden and our lady Qilué!"

The mercenary fisted his beckoning hand and twisted it palm down, releasing a dart hidden in his forearm sheath. Immediately his opponent shifted his sword to deflect the projectile. It exploded on impact, sending a slick of viscous black liquid skimming over the blade.

In less than a heartbeat, the metal of sword and hilt melted and flowed into a steaming, lethal puddle—too quickly for the drow defender to understand his doom or to toss aside his blade. Flesh and bone dissolved along with the molten steel, and the drow stumbled back, staring in disbelief at the ragged shards of bone protruding from his still-smoking wrist. His back hit the aft mast hard and he started to slide down it.

Immediately Gorlist lunged forward and thrust his sword between two ribs—not deep enough to kill, but enough to hold the wounded drow upright. His victim didn't even seem to notice this new injury.

"Look at me," Gorlist demanded softly.

Stunned eyes flashed to his face.

"Isn't it enough that we must answer to the females of Menzoberranzan and their accursed Lolth? What male would cast off this yoke, only to worship Eilistraee?"

"Elkantar," the drow said in a fading voice. "I am Elkantar, redeemed by Eilistraee, beloved of Qilué."

These words filled Gorlist with fierce joy. He slammed his sword forward, felt it bite into the wooden mast behind the traitorous male, then wrenched it free.

"That was a rhetorical question," he told the dying drow, "but thank you for sharing."

"You! Drider dung!" shouted someone behind him, delivering the insult in strangely accented Drow.

Gorlist's moment of dark pleasure shattered. He spun to face the speaker, who strode toward him, sword in hand. The warrior was furious, female and—as if those things were not trouble enough—*faerie*.

Gorlist held beliefs foreign to most of his Underdark kin, but he shared in full measure their hatred of surface elves. This particular faerie elf was tall, with moon-white skin and sleek ebony hair—a bizarre reversal of drow beauty. Her eyes were a strange shade of golden green, and a streak of silver hair, most likely the mark of Eilistraee, hung in a disheveled braid over one shoulder.

Gorlist ran a few steps toward the female. He stopped suddenly, letting her close the distance between them, then delivered a high feinting jab. She ducked and answered with a lunging attack, a quick move that sent her silvery braid swinging forward. Gorlist parried the darting sword with a circular sweep of his blade, catching her weapon and moving it out wide. He seized the faerie elf's braid, determined to rip it from her scalp.

A dagger appeared in the elf's other hand. Up it

flashed, severing a few inches of braided hair. The lock in Gorlist's hand flared with sudden light and flowed into a new and deadly shape. Suddenly he was holding a small viper. Its tongue flashed like miniature lightning as it tasted the drow's scent, and its head reared back for the strike.

Gorlist hurled the tiny monster to the deck. It landed with a splat, breaking apart into a hundred tiny silver balls. These rolled together and reshaped into a tiny dragon. The diminutive monster hissed, catlike, and leaped into flight, hurtling straight for the tattoo burning silver-bright on Gorlist's face.

The drow refused to be drawn by either distraction. He kept his sword in guard position, swatting the little dragon aside with his free hand. It let out an indignant soprano squawk and flapped out of reach.

Gorlist and the elf exchanged a few blows, taking each other's measure, testing defenses. The female was tall—nearly a head taller than he, with a reach that exceeded his. Worse, she seemed to understand the ever-shifting patterns of drow swordplay. She met each attack with a casual, almost contemptuous ease.

For several moments they moved together in perfect coordination, like light and shadow. All the while the silvery dragon circled them.

Suddenly the dragon faded into mist, which expanded into a bright, hazy cloud. This settled down over the embattled pair—a deliberate and mocking reversal of the globe of darkness that drow often employed in battle. The last thing Gorlist saw with any clarity was the smirk on the faerie elf's face.

He squinted into the too-bright mist. The elf's outline was still visible, and her sword reflected the diffused light as it dived for his hamstring. Gorlist leaped high above the blade, throwing himself into a spin to gain distance from the second, third, and fourth attack that any drow would surely have planned and ready.

This impulse saved him. A second, unseen weapon scraped along his leather jerkin, and the stroke that would have disemboweled him merely drew a stinging line across his backside.

Gorlist landed and lunged in one quick, fluid movement, but his sword plunged through shadow without substance. The elf was gone, leaving an illusion behind. The drow over-extended, but instead of adjusting his footing, he threw himself several steps forward in hope of outpacing the bright globe. His abysmal luck held: the Lolth-bedamned light clung to him.

A dark form appeared in his path. Gorlist pulled up short, nearly toe to toe with a drow male.

Instantly they fell apart, snapping into guard position with mirror-image precision. Gorlist recognized one of his mercenaries. The other drow's eyes widened with horror as he realized he faced his commander. He lowered his weapon and dropped to one knee, tilting his head to one side and baring his neck as a sign of submission.

Gorlist also turned away. Holding his sword with both hands, he whirled back, putting all his strength into the blow. The blade hewed through flesh and bone, and the mercenary's head tumbled across the deck. Before the body could fall, Gorlist snatched the medallion from the severed neck.

"Surrender accepted," he muttered as he draped it around his own neck.

He bolted for the side of the ship and vaulted over the rail. The globe of light followed him all the way to the water. He dropped into the darkness and was swept into the magical passage.

Gorlist emerged in a familiar stone tunnel and immediately kicked into a run. The ships were lost, but perhaps the mercenaries he'd left behind were faring better.

He ran through several passages before he heard the song: a jubilant paean to Eilistraee voiced by Qilué's priestesses.

Fury surged through him, speeding his steps into a headlong sprint, but even as he ran, Gorlist acknowledged the truth: The Dragon's Hoard band was defeated. He was alone, without resources or allies. Everything Nisstyre had built over years of effort was gone.

Or nearly everything.

Gorlist veered off into a side passage, one that led to his own private stash. It would provide a new start. One way or another, Liriel Baenre would die. He would leave no means untested, scorn no alliance—*no* alliance, no matter how deadly or distasteful.

Suddenly Gorlist knew what he must do. As soon as he could, he would return to the hoard chamber. He would find Nisstyre's ruby, and he would seek out someone who hated Liriel nearly as much as he did.

In the Abyss, time did not exist. There was no day or night such as the surface dwellers knew, no magical timepiece enchanted anew at the midnight hour. The drow female stumbling through that gray place could not know that the slim crescent moon that shone on the night of her defeat had since grown smug and big-bellied.

The same moon had waned and waxed several times since the battle of the Dragon's Hoard and the death of Nisstyre, her valuable and reluctant ally. The drow knew nothing of that, either, nor would that knowledge have mattered. Her purpose, her entire being, was focused on the hunt for

Liriel Baenre. What was the passing of spring and summer to a drow of the Underdark, and what did it matter if the hunt took place in Menzoberranzan or across the seas of the surface world? Hatred, like the Abyss, knew no limits of time and place.

Only that hatred fueled Shakti Hunzrin, traitor-priestess to both Lolth and Vhaerun, and kept her pressing on in her search for escape.

To the exhausted drow, it seemed that both of her deities had abandoned her. She had viewed the Abyss through the scrying bowls employed by Lolth's priestesses, but none of her studies had prepared her for the reality.

Fetid mists rose from the ground, which was sometimes strewn with sharp rocks and sometimes so soft, so indistinct, that it hardly seemed solid at all. Bizarre fungi grew to huge size. More than once the famished drow had attempted to break off a piece of giant, malformed mushroom only to have some strange, slumbering creature come awake roaring for blood.

So far, Shakti had been equal to all these battles. Hatred always made her stronger. In the Abyss, hatred was the natural element, and Shakti breathed it in as a fish breathes water, but though her spirit burned ever stronger, her physical form was weakening. She could not continue in this manner for much longer.

"I can save you."

The words were spoken softly, seductively. Shakti whirled toward the sound, her hand instinctively flying to the handle of her snake-headed whip.

Too late, she remembered that the snakes were dead, slain in battle with Liriel Baenre. It was a marvel that she could forget this for even an instant, since the stench of rotting snake flesh had followed her for what seemed an eternity. It clung to her robes still, even though all that remained of the once-proud weapon was five slim chains of bone and cartilage held together by dried sinew. The rotting weapon had been a constant torment and a danger as well. The Abyss, like all places of the dead, had its scavengers, and the smell of carrion drew them. Yet never once did Shakti consider discarding the weapon. It reminded her that she had been a high priestess, heir to House Hunzrin. She would die with her whip in her hand as befitted a noble of Menzoberranzan.

"I can save you," the voice repeated, more insistently this time.

Chagrined by her wandering thoughts, Shakti forced herself to focus on the swirling mists. A dark, lithesome figure stepped from the gray shadows like a dream taking on substance.

The newcomer was quite simply the most beautiful drow male she had ever beheld. Except for the glittering *piwafwi* draping his shoulders, he was as naked as a newborn rothe calf. His eyes held none of the disdain that high-born males usually turned upon Shakti, nor any of the veiled resignation she was accustomed to seeing on the faces of those males under her power.

"You are weary," he crooned. "Too weary to find your way out of this place. There is a way, you know. You can find it, if only you rest a while, clear your mind, and ease your body."

A courtesan, Shakti reasoned, wasting his afterlife the only way he knew how. She reached into her empty coin bag and turned it inside out. "You're wasting your time," she said shortly. "I can't pay."

He looked genuinely shocked. "Anything between us would be a gift given two ways! You are most beautiful, and I have been too long alone."

Beautiful? Shaki's lip curled in disdain. All her life she had been plump and graceless, as close to homely as it was possible for a drow to be. Moreover, she had lived her life in the dangerous shadow of a physical defect: weak, near-sighted eyes. Terrified that squinting might betray this imperfection, she had compensated by holding her eyes wide open, which caused her to blink rather too frequently and lent her a pop-eyed, frantic appearance. This habit had persisted long after the two deities she served granted her perfect vision.

"You don't believe me," the stranger said in wondering tones. "Here—look for yourself."

He gestured to the mists, which parted to reveal a shallow, stagnant pool. The surface silvered, and in it Shakti saw reflected a perfect image of the handsome male. Before she could think better of it, she took a step forward and gazed at her own reflection.

"Lolth's eight legs," she swore softly.

The face and form reflected back to her were familiar, yet different enough to cause her to wonder, briefly, if the male had magically altered her reflection.

As Shakti gazed at her image, she saw the truth. The Abyss had hardened her, burning away the dross and leaving behind only the drow essence. Her black face was not just thinner but reshaped. The rounded, sullen countenance now boasted a sharply angular form, a dramatic slash from wide cheekbones to narrow, pointed chin. Determination had focused her crimson eyes, changed her wild expression into one of imperious dignity. Her mist-sodden robes clung to her, revealing a newly lithe form.

"You see?" the male said. "So very beautiful." He took two gliding steps forward, one hand reaching out to her.

Shakti's first response was irritation. Before she could crudely suggest that the male attempt to procreate without benefit of partner, her robes shifted and parted as if in anticipation—a telltale bit of magic she had experienced once before.

Terror and loathing swept through Shakti in chilling waves. She seized her treacherous garment and tugged it back into place, crossing her arms over her chest so that one hand was hidden beneath the folds. A quick glance at the reflecting pool assured her that her expression of lofty disdain had not faltered.

"Be gone," she said coldly. Her hidden hand began to shape the warding that repelled unwanted advances of seductive demons.

The crimson eyes of the drow-shaped incubus tracked the subtle gesture and filled with rage. An inhuman roar exploded from the creature's throat as it leaped, changing form in midair. A hideous winged demon hit Shakti full force and bore her to the ground. They hit the silver puddle together, shattering the mirrorlike surface into a thousand watery shards.

"I can save you," the creature gloated in a voice that was like a chorus of the damned. "You were a high priestess once. Shall we enact the ritual anew?"

Shakti writhed and kicked, raking the now-scaly skin with her nails. "I am a priestess of Lolth, and you, whatever else you may be, are *nothing but a male!*"

As she shrieked out the last words, a jolt of power seared through her. Something stirred between them, and suddenly the incubus was rearing back, shrieking in agony.

Shakti scrambled away and staggered to her feet. To her astonishment, a skeletal snake head rose to regard her, black eyes glowing like living obsidian in the once-empty sockets. The snake's fanged jaws parted, and it spat.

The priestess regarded the bloody trophy, then threw back her head and laughed with triumph and delight. She raised her whip high and lashed forward. All five skeletal heads dived in for the kill, their fangs bright, sharp, and eager in their bony jaws.

She worked her whip until her shoulders sang with pain, until the incubus huddled and cowered before her, flayed of every inch of its hide.

"Death," it pleaded.

"This is the Abyss," Shakti said coldly. "We're already dead."

She turned on her heel and marched off, feeling better than she had since her defeat at Liriel's hands. In that battle, Lolth had chosen to honor the Baenre brat, but the pleasant rasp of bone as the undead snakes wound themselves around her was like a hymn of dark redemption. Her priestess whip had been restored to life—or something close to it. Surely that was a sign of Lolth's favor!

Drunk on this triumph, the drow passed a giant mushroom without giving it much heed. She did not notice until too late that the thing crouched and clenched itself like a hideous fist. The cap suddenly unfurled, and greenish spore exploded toward the drow in a noxious, stinging cloud.

Mushroom spore burned down her throat and into her chest, searing her like droplets of black dragon venom. Shakti fell to her knees in a paroxysm of coughing. She fumbled for her whip and silently commanded the reptilian skulls to tear the mushroom to shreds.

They rose but did not strike. As soon as she could, Shakti wiped her streaming eyes and struggled to her feet.

She immediately fell back to her knees.

The "mushroom" had taken new form. A tall creature resembling nothing so much as a column of melted wax regarded her with blood-red eyes the size and shape of dinner plates. It possessed no other recognizable features, but the fluid, rippling undulation of its body suggested that it could take any form it fancied.

"Yochlol," Shakti breathed, naming the creature that served as handmaiden to the Spider Queen. Their appearances were few and usually limited to the great priestesses. Never in her life had Shakti aspired to this honor. So far, her death showed far more promise!

You are not dead.

The yochlol's voice sounded in Shakti's mind, feminine and somehow familiar. She recalled vaguely a theology class at Arach Tinileth, the priestess academy, concerning the nature and origin of yochlol. That had been an academic debate, something of little interest to the practical Shakti. Now she wished she had paid closer attention.

"I am in the Abyss," Shakti said carefully, not wishing to openly contradict the handmaiden. "I challenged another priestess and lost. If I am not dead, what am I?"

Here, the yochlol responded. *You are here, no more or less. Even in the Abyss, there are many ways of being or not being. Before you stands the glorious form to which a priestess of power and prestige might aspire!*

Beneath the proud words lay a level of irony, and beneath that, despair. Shakti's suspicions hardened into certainly.

"You are not long dead," she ventured. "You still remember your life and your name."

In time, all this will fade, the yochlol recited. *The priestess will be forgotten. Only Lolth will remain.*

"Her name be praised and feared," Shakti said, adding slyly, "as is the name of the House she honors above all."

The yochlol's form shifted and flowed, taking on an oddly wistful expression—and the faint outline of the face it had worn during its mortal existence. The next moment, its countenance snapped back into a formless glob, and its red eyes reclaimed their intense focus.

You did not destroy the incubus. We wonder why, when

there is pleasure in destruction—pleasure, and the blessing of the goddess.

"There is little pleasure of any kind to be had in this place," Shakti said curtly. "I would just as soon put my efforts toward a better result."

The incubus might seek vengeance.

"It is more likely to seek refuge," Shakti retorted. "Such demons know the way to and from the Abyss, and given its weakened state and vulnerable flesh, it is likely to flee the scavengers that haunt this place. When it goes, I will follow, like a hunting lizard who has a taste of its quarry's blood."

She lifted her hand, showing the magical symbol traced there with the demon's blood—a spell that would enable her to follow the wounded creature wherever it went. It was one of many spells she had made a point of learning during her hunt for Liriel Baenre.

A cruel and far-sighted plan, the yochlol observed. *Lolth is pleased.*

Shakti's gaze dropped to her skeletal snakes, which were wrapped companionably around her arms and waist. For a long moment she struggled to contain the central question of her existence. It burst out of her, regardless.

"If Lolth is pleased, why did she favor Liriel Baenre over me?"

A lesser goddess has shown favor to this girl. That, Lloth cannot abide.

A shiver of dread raced down Shakti's spine. After all, she herself had a foot in two divine camps! As she considered this answer, however, it seemed that the whole story had not been told.

"Other drow follow other gods. I have never heard that Lolth pursues and rewards these heretics. Why grant such gifts to Liriel, when better, more loyal priestesses would gladly receive them?"

The yochlol's face twisted in unmistakable scorn. *Do you think the goddess answers your prayers out of love? Like most priestesses, you crave Lolth's power. Liriel Baenre does not. Indeed, it is a torment to her.*

Understanding began to edge into Shakti's mind. Underlying the cruelty and chaos of the drow was a certain grim practicality. Whatever else a drow's actions might be, they were certain to be self-serving.

Suddenly Shakti knew the true reason for Lolth's interest in the runaway Baenre princess.

"So Liriel has been chosen to bear Lolth's power because she is willing to relinquish it!"

And what of you? the yochlol countered. *Destroying the incubus would have been a pleasant diversion, yet you resisted in favor of a larger goal. What more would you be willing to relinquish?*

A merchant bred and born, Shakti knew better than to hand a blank note to any drow, living or dead, mortal or divine. "What does Lolth ask of me?" she parried.

Your burning desire to destroy the Baenre princess—could you bear to subject that to the will of Lolth?

For a long moment Shakti stood silent as pragmatism battled mightily against hatred. Her snakehead whip unwound itself from her and writhed about in a frenzied dance, giving silent testament to its mistress's agitation and indecision.

Finally the skeletal dance subsided, and the priestess lowered her head in submission to Lolth's handmaiden.

"Speak," she said grudgingly, "and I will do."

CHAPTER ONE

Liriel stood at the rail of *Leaping Narwhal*, the sea breeze on her face and her white hair streaming behind her. The sunset colors had all but faded, and a rising moon silvered the waves. Her friend Fyodor was at her side, his back to the rail and his keen-eyed gaze following the on-duty crew as they prepared the ship for the coming of night.

"Lord Caladorn seems a capable sailor," he observed, nodding toward the tall, auburn-haired man lowering the foresail.

The drow reluctantly dragged her attention from the splendors of the sea to the human nobleman. "Hrolf didn't trust him."

"True, but Hrolf believed Lord Caladorn to be an enemy of the sea elves," Fyodor reminded her. "Had the captain lived, he would have learned his error."

She shrugged this aside. The pirate known as Hrolf the Unruly had, in a very short time, become more of a father to her than the drow wizard who'd sired her. Hrolf's death was a wound too new and raw to bear the weight of words.

"Ibn likes this Caladorn well enough. At least, he likes the color of the man's coins and the 'lord' before his name! It's lucky for us his lordship wanted passage to the mainland. Ibn never would have bestirred himself on our account."

Fyodor nodded and turned a troubled gaze toward *Narwhal*'s new captain, a man of middle years and narrow mind, hunched over the wheel with a grim concentration that reminded Liriel of a duergar "enjoying" his morning gruel.

Though Liriel would never admit it, she shared Fyodor's unspoken concern. Ibn had been Hrolf's first mate, and he'd been a pebble in her boot from the moment they'd met. Most Northmen were wary of elves, but Ibn, despite his years aboard Hrolf's ship *Elfmaid* and the assistance of the sea elves who'd watched over the jovial pirate, distrusted all elves with a fervor bordering on hatred.

Well, there was no help for it. Fyodor had pledged to return the Windwalker to the witches of Rashemen. Liriel had promised to accompany him. It was an impulsive decision that she had questioned many times during their westward voyage, but Fyodor had steadfastly assured her that she—a drow and a wizard—would be accepted in a land that hated both. Before they faced that particular battle, they would have to survive a journey that spanned hundreds of miles inhabited by surface dwellers who had reason to fear and hate dark elves. Considering the larger picture, what was one elf-hating sailor?

A subtle movement caught the drow's attention—a slender blue hand edging over the rail. Liriel watched in fascination as a peculiar creature slid soundlessly onto the ship.

Elflike in feature and lavishly female in form, she was none-theless as alien as any creature Liriel had ever beheld.

The newcomer's skin shimmered with tiny aqua scales, and her long, silvery blue hair undulated as if in a gentle current. She wore ropes of pearls and a short, wet, cling-ing gown. Liriel's sharp eyes noted the weapon sheaths cleverly hidden among the wet folds. Her native curios-ity, however, was stronger than her impulse to shout an alarm.

Liriel watched as the creature's blue-green eyes scanned the ship, settled upon the man at the wheel, and took on a predatory gleam. She started toward Ibn purposefully.

The drow elbowed Fyodor and nodded toward the creature. "A water genasi," she said, speaking just above a whisper. "I've never actually seen one before. Drow keep trying to breed them. You don't want to know what we get instead."

"Is she a friend?" Fyodor asked, eying the beautiful creature uncertainly.

"That depends. Does your social circle usually include other-planer half breeds?"

Fyodor, his gaze intent on the genasi, let that pass. "She's after the captain," he said, noting the creature's approach on the unwitting Ibn. He placed one hand on his sword hilt and started forward.

His determined stride faltered after a pace or two, and he stood watching the genasi with fascination. Several other men left off their chores and drifted closer. Their wonder-struck eyes drank in the beautiful blue face. Several of them darted envious, even murderous, glances at the unsuspect-ing Ibn.

A charm spell, Liriel surmised, eyeing the blue female with new respect. For a moment she was tempted to let the genasi's enchantment run its course. Liriel's people had a thousand ways to weed out the foolish and the weak, and the ship would probably be the better for a cleansing battle. That accomplished, she could subdue the blue wench and restore order—and, not incidentally, put a more congenial captain in Ibn's place.

As she settled back to enjoy the show, a small voice in the back of her mind inquired, *Yes, but what would Fyodor think of this plan?*

Irritation swept through her. Such intrusions on her drow practicality were becoming annoyingly frequent.

"At the moment, he's not thinking at all," she muttered. "At least, not with anything that lies between his ears."

Fyodor, the voice said implacably. *Honor.*

The drow hissed in exasperation then gave way with an ungracious shrug.

"Hoy, Ibn! Who's your lady friend?" she sang out, pointing. "Nice legs. Too bad about her choice in men."

The captain's head whipped toward the genasi. He let out a yelp of outrage—proving, no surprise to Liriel, that his bigotry was stronger than the genasi's magic.

"Another damn sea elf! Git off my ship, you long-eared fish!"

Astonishment froze the genasi in mid-slink, and fury twisted her azure face.

"Now you've done it," Liriel murmured happily. According to drow lore books, a sure way to infuriate any genasi was to mistake it for a "lesser creature."

A sly smile curved the drow's lips. There would be no avoiding battle now!

The genasi threw both arms high in a dramatic spellcaster's stance and let out an echoing call that rose and fell like the song of a whale. It danced over the undulating sea, gathering power as it went—more power, unfortunately, than Liriel had anticipated.

She swept both hands wide in a circular pattern as she whispered an arcane phrase. A silvery sphere, a barely visible enchantment that resembled the ghost of a giant soap bubble, soared toward the genasi. The creature touched one blue finger to the conjured sphere of silence, and the magical ward dissolved like the bubble it resembled.

Liriel took note of the genasi's powerful spell resistance. She'd do better to concentrate on the creature's magic rather than the genasi herself. She mentally listed the spells she had ready to cast, and, since no sensible drow went into battle without every possible advantage, she strode over to Fyodor and stomped sharply on his instep.

The warrior drew in a startled gasp and shook himself like a man abruptly awakened from a dream. His gaze flicked from the genasi to Liriel, and an expression of deep chagrin crossed his face.

"Things could get interesting," Liriel warned him. "I might need time and space for spellcasting."

His only response was a grim nod. Knowing him as she did, Liriel understood the source of his dismay. Fyodor regarded Liriel as *wychlaran*, a position of highest honor in his homeland, and himself as her sworn guardian. Even though no harm had come of it, he would view succumbing to enchantment as a failure of duty.

A conscience, noted Liriel, could be as irrational as it was inconvenient.

At that moment the genasi's spell ended in a keening wail. The sea stirred, and a small wave rose and swept toward the ship like a dark hand.

Liriel sped through the gestures of a midday mist spell, a handy bit of magic that transformed a targeted water source into cool, harmless vapor. Magic collected between her hands, forming a globe of sparkling lights. This she hurled toward the rushing water.

Her globe struck the water and expired with a damp sigh and a scattering of stardust. A few wisps of mist spiraled toward the moon, but the wave came on.

The drow hissed a curse. She wrapped one arm around the mainsail mast and seized Fyodor's belt. He enfolded her in a protective hug and raised his voice in a shout of warning to the besotted sailors. His words were drowned by the magic-summoned wave.

Icy water dashed over Liriel, leaving her gasping with shock. When it had passed, she wriggled free and took stock of the situation.

Ibn had managed to hold onto the wheel, but the sailors who'd been drawn by the genasi's spell were nowhere to be seen. Their whereabouts, however, was no mystery—startled oaths rose from the sea as several men awoke from the enchantment to find themselves paddling in the cold, dark waters.

Fyodor shot a glance at Liriel. "Can she do that again?"

"Not if she's busy elsewhere," Liriel said with dark glee. Forsaking the notion of a spell duel, she launched herself into a running charge.

The genasi spun toward the sound. She reached into her skirts for a weapon, decided there was no time, and presented her nails instead.

Liriel batted aside a raking hand and went for the genasi's throat. The blue flesh was cold and slippery, and Liriel's small hands couldn't get a grip. Changing strategy, she fisted both hands in the creature's flowing blue hair and let herself drop to the deck.

The genasis tumbled with her. For several moments the two females grappled and rolled, a tangle of flailing blue limbs and small, deft black fists. Finally Liriel managed to pin her opponent, straddling her and holding her arms over her head. The beautiful creature continued to buck and writhe, emitting small plaintive sounds that brought to mind a weeping seal pup.

"You're breaking my heart," sneered Liriel. "Where I come from, females have more pride."

The genasi quieted instantly and sent Liriel a fulminating glare.

"That's better," the drow approved. "Now, let's discuss who you are and why you're here."

In response, the genasis emitted a trilling call that managed to convey both disgust and exasperation.

Liriel gave her a shake. "One way or another, I intend to get an answer. If you *can* talk, now would be a good time."

For a long moment the genasis stared at the drow with hate-filled eyes. "I was called to battle," she admitted in a voice like wind and water. "Before the appointed time and against my will."

"Called to battle?" Ibn echoed incredulously.

The drow shot a glance over her shoulder. The captain stood over the females, his face red with fury. "Battle? What battle? This your doing, you damned elf?"

Liriel blew a lock of hair off her face. "First, I'm a drow, not a damned elf. Second, *if* I'd called this thing, don't you think I would be the first to know?"

The captain puzzled this over for a moment, then his eyes widened with panicked understanding. "The men in the water!" he bellowed. "Pull 'em in, and step lively!"

Several sailors charged to the rail and threw knotted ropes into the sea. Every rope but one fell ominously slack. The sole successful rescuer pulled his rope in, hand over hand and with frantic speed.

Not fast enough. A shriek of pain rose from water. Two more men seized the rope and hauled. A thin young man slammed against the rail, a sun-browned boy with a fragile wisp of mustache. He shrieked again with the pain of impact, and kept howling as a pair of sailors lifted him over the side—a task complicated by the wicked spear impaling his thigh.

"Hold him," Ibn said grimly. He seized the barbed point with both hands and tugged. The youth screamed as the shaft slid through his leg. He slumped, mercifully silent, between his rescuers. The two sailors dragged the unconscious lad into the shelter of the aft castle. One man stood guard over him with drawn cutlass. The other returned to the deck to join his battle-ready mates. Fyodor stood with them, his black sword resting on one shoulder as he awaited the fight.

Liriel intoned a minor spell designed to hold the genasi in place. Once again, magic slid off the creature like drops of water.

The drow shrugged off this failure, made a fist, and drove it into the genasi's face. The creature's sea-blue eyes rolled up, and her head lolled to one side.

Liriel sat back on her heels and looked to Ibn. The genasi obviously had powerful defenses against magic, yet something out there possessed magic strong enough—or unusual enough—to circumvent these wards.

"What summoned Princess Blue?" she demanded, tossed her head toward the unconscious genasi.

"You'll see soon enough." With a curved sword, the captain pointed to the night-black sea.

Liriel rose, took a harpoon from the rack, and came over to the rail. Her eyes were keener than the sailors' and more sensitive to subtle differences of light and shadow. She studied the large, dark shape swimming just below the moonlit surface. Something about its movements was disturbingly familiar.

The creature reared up in a sudden surge, sending moonlit waves skittering off like startled spiders. A large, bulbous green head broke the surface, a hideous visage that resembled a giant frog.

"Kua-toa!" Liriel breathed, naming an Underdark monster and vicious foe of the drow.

"Bullywug," corrected Ibn grimly. "They got a shaman. Where there's a shaman, there's a swarm."

Several more heads crested the waves, and suddenly the monsters were leaping for the rails. The sailors rushed to meet them, weapons high.

Liriel ran toward the nearest bullywug, hurling her harpoon as she went. The monster lifted its spear like a quarterstaff and blocked, a quick twirl that sent the barbed weapon clattering harmlessly across the deck.

The bullywug whirled its spear once again and then snapped it into attack position: shaft level, point leading. Liriel skidded to a stop and danced away from the creature's long-armed lunge. Her arms crossed over her forearm sheaths and flashed open. Twin daggers gleamed in her hands.

From the corner of her eye Liriel noted a crablike object, inexplicably airborne, spinning toward the bullywug. The monster's long tongue snapped out reflexively. Tongue and crab reeled in, and the bullywug's eyes bulged. The drow, knowing what was to come, let out a peal of wild laughter and darted around behind the doomed creature.

Another bullywug clambered over the nearby rail. Liriel faked a stumble, drawing the monster's attention. It leaped to the deck and waddled toward her with astonishing speed, its spear poised for what appeared to be an easy kill.

The "crab" burst free of the first monster's gullet, tearing through flesh and bone and continuing its interrupted flight. The magical weapon whirled over Liriel's head and spun directly toward the charging bullywug. Barbed legs bit deep into the sharkskin armor covering the creature's rounded gut. For a moment the monster stared down in surprise, then the animated weapon began to burrow. The bullywug tore at the weapon with frantic fingers only to have its entangled hands follow the "crab" in its inexorable path through armor and flesh.

A bullywug distinguished by a weirdly patterned black and green hide charged the drow. Liriel sent her daggers spinning toward this new foe in two quick tosses. The creature slapped aside the first weapon. The second dagger caught the huge, webbed hand and pinned it with deadly precision to its throat.

The drow kicked the feet out from under the dying monster and leaped onto its large, prone form. From there she could reach the web of rat lines. She climbed these and hung there, silhouetted against the rising moon, as she took in the battle.

At least a dozen monsters were still standing, fighting with distressing tenacity. She sought out Fyodor. With his black hair and light skin, he was easy to spot among the roiling melee of giant frogs and fair-haired, sun-browned Northmen. He stood with his back to the mast, his black sword tangled with the many-notched spear of a monster standing nearly seven feet tall.

With relief Liriel noted that her friend seemed to be holding his own and that he had not summoned his berserker frenzy. Fyodor was no longer prisoner to unpredictable bouts of battle fever, but she'd seen his berserker transformation rage out of control too often to welcome its return.

The drow worked her way across the web of lines toward Fyodor, planning to drop to the deck behind his monstrous opponent. As she fell, she saw yet another bullywug launch itself toward Fyodor in a powerful, deck-spanning leap.

Two things happened in one instant: Liriel's boots

touched the wooden planking, and a long black tongue slapped onto her face.

The drow recoiled, but not before she felt the wet, muscular thing curl around her neck. She reached for her sword, knowing that a quick jerk would break her neck—knowing, too, that she would not be fast enough to stop it.

Another "crab" whirled past, severing the bullywug's tongue. Liriel stumbled away. She ripped the twitching thing off and handed it to the stunned monster. While the bullywug stared in bemusement at the object in its hand, she slammed her sword between the laces of its sharkskin armor.

Before the monster could move, she leaped up and planted both feet on its chest. Pushing off with all her strength, she described a half flip and landed lightly on her feet, sword in hand. The bullywug staggered back, stumbling toward the waiting cutlass of the pale but grim-lipped boy who stood, once again, supported by two fellow sailors.

Liriel sent the wounded lad and his comrades a curt nod and a fierce smile. These Northmen understood something of retribution and knew much of courage.

She whirled in her rescuer's direction. A slender male sea-elf stood a few paces away, his green eyes taking in the chaos of battle with a warrior's measured gaze. Xzorsh, her erstwhile apprentice and Hrolf's self-appointed guardian, had returned—if indeed he had ever left her.

Another throwing spider, one of several magical weapons Liriel had given him, was ready in his webbed hand. Seeing no immediate threat, he shifted his gaze to the troubled waters. His head bobbed slightly, as if he were taking a tally.

"More?" she demanded.

"Thirty, at least," Xzorsh responded in grim tones. "Too many."

Liriel shook her head and reached into a bag attached to her belt. She showed the sea elf a large, perfect emerald, part of the trophy she'd taken from the deepdragon's hoard. Xzorsh's eyes widened, then sparkled in anticipation. His tutelage with the drow had been brief, but they'd spoken of such wonders before she'd exhausted her scant supply of patience.

Xzorsh pointed toward Fyodor, who was tugging his sword from the body of the seven-foot bullywug. "That was Karimsh, shaman and swarm leader. He called the genasi, he commands the others. I could probably repeat his summoning call—not perfectly, and it would lack magic, but a bullywug in battle frenzy might not notice any lack."

Liriel responded with a nod and a predatory smile. Lofting the emerald, she began to chant in a soaring, eerie soprano. Xzorsh threw back his head and emitted a call—a strange sound that began on a low, rattling croak and leaped into a series of gulping staccato notes mingled with rapid clicks.

The bizarre elven duet rang above the clamor of battle, and in moments the ship began to rock as dozens of large webbed hands gripped the rails. Deep, booming chuckles rolled from the bullywug swarm as they celebrated the prospect of a quick slaughter and a good meal to follow. Sailors lurched across the rolling deck to meet this new threat.

Nearby, Ibn swatted aside a spear and slashed his curved sword across a swelling green throat. He rounded on the elven pair, shaking his bloodied weapon.

"You're dead, the both of you!" he promised.

In response, Liriel threw her emerald at his feet. The captain scuttled back and let out a startled curse as the gem began to grow. In a heartbeat, a living statue stood before them—a beautiful half-elven female, green as emerald, dressed in a simple tunic and trews and crowned with an ancient headdress.

Liriel frowned. "That's odd. She's supposed to be a sea elf. And goddess knows, I dressed her better than *that!*"

"She's perfect," Xzorsh breathed, his gaze fixed upon the tall, glowing golem.

The bullywugs also seemed impressed. Roaring with battle frenzy, they threw themselves at this new challenge. The golem eyed them with disdain as they jabbed at her gem-hard form. For several moments, the booming calls of the giant frogs mingled with the click and clatter of spears against emerald. So fierce was their death-frenzy assault that the bullywugs did not notice the faint green glow spreading across the deck. When it encompassed most of the creatures, Liriel shouted a command word.

The emerald golem disappeared, and the bullywugs with it.

Every warrior left behind—sailors and frogmen alike—stood gaping with astonishment at this unexpected end to battle. The resulting silence was so profound that it pressed against Liriel's ears like a physical thing.

After a startled moment, the surviving monsters readied themselves for a renewed assault. Spear butts thumped the deck and defiant battle-croaks made grim and empty promises. The sailors answered with ready steel, and a few pairs of weapons clashed and tangled, but the battle was over, and all knew it. In moments the last few bullywugs broke off the attempted rally and leaped into the waves.

Liriel twined one arm around the sea elf's waist and met Ibn's scowl with a falsely sweet smile. "Wasn't it lucky that Xzorsh happened to be swimming by? Without him, I'd be dead. Without me, *you'd* be dead."

Several of the sailors—many of them longtime members of Hrolf's crew—sent up a tired cheer, raising Xzorsh's name to the listening stars. But the red-bearded captain continued to glare.

"Hrolf is gone, and *Elfmaid* with him. Any debt between you two is long since paid," he told Xzorsh coldly. "As for me, I'm not needing a web-fisted shadow."

Liriel elbowed the sea elf. "Humans have so little appreciation for irony. Have you noticed that?"

Xzorsh's lips twitched, but he inclined his head to the captain in a dignified bow. "If that is your wish, I will return to the sea as soon as my business is completed." His gaze shifted to the drow.

Ibn noted this, and his eyes shouted reluctance and distrust, but his men had been Hrolf's men, and many of them owed their lives several times over to these mismatched elves. "Make it short," he said grudgingly.

Liriel sent a look toward Fyodor, and the three friends withdrew to the far side of the ship. Xzorsh shrugged a sealskin bag off his shoulder and took from it a tightly rolled tapestry. The drow's heart leaped and fell in a painful thud. She did not need to unroll the tapestry to know what it was: a beautifully crafted horror depicting the torture of captured sea elves. What made the tapestry even worse was the knowledge that it was more than just a twisted piece of art. The spirits of the slain elves had been trapped within the threads.

"None of your priestesses could free them? Or priests?" she added as an afterthought, recalling that surface elves didn't limit themselves to an exclusively female clergy.

Xzorsh shook his head. "This is a thing born of dark magic, something foreign to our sea-elven gods. It must be undone as it was made."

A great weight seemed to settle in the pit of Liriel's stomach. Darkness was her native element. Who better to unravel the tapestry's mystery than she? Still, the prospect of delving into this vile magic chilled her, as did the choice it implied.

She glanced at Fyodor. He nodded slightly to indicate he understood her dilemma. If she had the power to do good, was she obligated to do so even if it meant trafficking with evil? Liriel had dared to hope that the need for such decisions had been left behind on Ruathym. The expectant, trusting expression on Xzorsh's face told her that it had not.

"I'll handle it," she said shortly. "You'd better go. Ibn is looking this way, and something tells me he's imagining a bright red harpoon target painted on your backside."

"First, there is something you must know," Xzorsh said with quiet urgency. "The Regent of Ascarle is seeking you everywhere. The seas resound with her agents and messengers."

"Really. In that case you can easily find a way to send her *this*," Liriel said, lifting one hand in a rude gesture.

The sea elf smiled faintly. "A difficult sentiment to express with webbed hands, and just as well. I'd rather not alert the illithid's minions to my location and yours. I just came here to warn you."

"And perhaps to remind me of my promise?" she suggested slyly.

"When have I ever offered you such insult?" he protested. "You said you would find another wizard to teach me the art of magic. In my mind, the thing is as good as done."

Liriel huffed and slid an arch glance at Fyodor. "He doesn't know much about the drow, does he?"

"He knows you," Fyodor said, sending an approving nod toward the sea elf.

The drow rolled her eyes. "I'll find someone in Skullport and send word to you through the Relay," she suggested, naming the efficient underwater alliance that sped messages throughout the northern seas.

"It would be better to keep your location as quiet as possible, even after you arrive in Skullport," Xzorsh advised. "Whatever your captain says, I plan to stay with the ship until you reach port. In these troubled waters, you will need my eyes and my voice."

"Your voice," repeated Fyodor thoughtfully, his gaze shifting from the drow to the sea elf. "If word of Liriel's passage is widely spread, it is likely that goodly folk will also hear of a sea-going drow wizard, and mistrust her intentions. She may need someone to speak for her."

Xzorsh acknowledged this with a grimace and a nod. "My people have heard. Many are deeply concerned."

"What about the sea elves we freed from the prisons of Ascarle?" Liriel pointed out. "Some fought at Ruathym. They will speak for me!"

"They will speak of a drow priestess, and more than a priestess," Fyodor said soberly. "You did not see yourself soaring above the battle, black fire spilling from your hands and burning in your eyes. Those who saw might well believe they have reason to fear you."

The memory sent a surge of despair racing through the drow. She quickly gathered herself and pushed both memory and emotion aside. Casting her eyes skyward, she threw up her hands in feigned disgust.

"Sell your soul to the dark powers on behalf of goodly folk, and this is the thanks you get," she said flippantly. "Oh, yes, I definitely see the allure in a life of service."

Xzorsh looked shocked, and doubly so when Fyodor chuckled. The warrior clapped the sea elf on the shoulder. "It is only her way of speaking," Fyodor assured him. "All will be well."

The elf nodded uncertainly. He vaulted over the rail and

slipped into the waves without sound or splash. Fyodor watched him go, and the expression in his winter-blue eyes did not match his reassuring words.

All will be well, Liriel repeated silently. She had never once heard this sentiment expressed during her years in Menzoberranzan, but humans seemed inordinately fond of it. Some of them actually believed it to be true.

The bleak look on Fyodor's face proclaimed he knew better.

She twined her arms around his neck and let him gather her close, marveling anew at the comfort in a simple embrace. Before he buried his face in her hair, Liriel noted his troubled expression. Most likely, she surmised, he was concerned that his words to Xzorsh shaped a pledge he could not keep. She could think of few things more likely to trouble her friend. Drow promises were like the thin wheaten sea biscuits that formed a staple of the seafarer's diet: easily made, easily broken. To Fyodor, a promise was as immutable as sunrise.

It occurred to Liriel, and not for the first time, that humans led incredibly complicated lives.

CHAPTER TWO

A WOLF IS ALWAYS A WOLF

The drow and the Rashemi stood together for a long moment, entwined in each other's arms. After a while Fyodor stepped back and attempted a smile.

"This is thoughtless of the others. A long sea journey is hard enough on a man without such reminders of what they cannot have."

Liriel's white brows shot up. "If you're feeling generous enough to suggest sharing the wealth, forget it. You're more than enough for me."

"Words I have heard from many a fair maiden," he said lightly.

"Really? How many?"

He sent the drow a questioning look.

She shrugged. "Just wondering how many human women I'll have to kill once we get to Rashemen."

Fyodor's jaw dropped. "Little raven, I was speaking in jest!" he sputtered.

The drow let out a crow of laughter. "You really thought I was serious?"

"Sometimes it is hard to tell," he said carefully.

She considered that and found it reasonable. "I suppose it would be."

They fell silent, sharing the moonlight if not their individual thoughts. After a while she glanced up at Fyodor's profile and gave him a teasing poke in the ribs.

"You're wearing your storyteller face," she observed, referring to the far-off, pensive expression that preceded one of his tales. Her people's few storytellers existed to extol the victories of the ruling matrons and their warriors. She found an odd appeal in the notion that guidance and wisdom could be found in ancient legends. Not that she would ever admit to this, of course.

He absently captured her hand in his. "Storyteller face? What does such a thing look like?"

"All serious and tight, like you're trying to hold in a sneeze. Must be the mold growing on those old tales of yours."

Fyodor met her teasing with a somber stare. "A story, yes, but not one of the old legends."

He released her hand and propped his elbows on the rail. "A few years ago, my sister Vastish found a wolf pup in the forest, an albino runt that would never have survived in the wild."

"I know of these wolves," Liriel interrupted eagerly. "Beautiful and fierce they are said to be! A drow I killed a while back gave me some lorebooks about the surface world. I didn't kill him for the books," she added defensively, noting the incredulous expression on Fyodor's face. "Forget it. Say on, and I'll be silent."

"The villager elders counseled Vastish on her folly," he continued. " 'A wolf will always be a wolf,' they said. 'It will steal chickens, chase the children at play.' Vastish was never one to take any counsel but her own, and so the wolf stayed. She named the pup Ghost for its white fur. Ghost was as fond and loyal to Vastish as any dog could be, but always the villagers watched him with narrowed eyes."

Fyodor fell silent for several moments. Liriel's gaze searched his face. "This story makes you sad. It's not finished, is it?"

He turned to face her. "Time passed, and a child was born to Vastish, a son who grew up with a wolf at his side. One day the boy was in the forest gathering mushrooms when he came across a den of wolf pups in the hollow of a bassilia tree. The mother returned. She defended her young." His bleak expression spoke of the child's fate, but the way he regarded Liriel suggested that this tale was not, first and foremost, the story of a lost boy.

"What happened to Ghost?"

"He was destroyed," Fyodor said. "The villagers feared that another child would learn to trust and would forget caution."

Liriel nodded. "Smart." Her eyes widened as she made the connection. "So you're telling me that if your people fall afoul of a drow, any drow, I'm the next Ghost?"

For a long time Fyodor didn't answer. "Not while I live," he vowed.

"Ah, then all will be well," Liriel said lightly, hoping this foolish human sentiment might tease the troubled look from his eyes. "You're very hard to kill—Lolth knows *I've* tried!"

Her blasphemous jest brought a faint smile to his lips, and again he reached for her hand, but before Fyodor could touch her, Someone else did.

A sudden and profound chill fell over Liriel, freezing her, body and soul, like the embrace of a malevolent spirit.

After the first shock, Liriel recognized a familiar presence, one she had welcomed during her short stay in Arach Tinileth. Back then, the young drow had looked upon Lolth with affection. The goddess listened to prayers and rewarded devotion with gifts of magic. This was a level of attention and generosity beyond anything Liriel had experienced. She knew the goddess better now. Lolth was no loving parent; Lolth was a power that corrupted and destroyed.

A jealous power.

Liriel's eyes darted to Fyodor's face, and in her mind's eye she saw again a devotion common in Menzoberranzan: a priestess walking swiftly to Lolth's altar, holding in bloody hands a tray bearing the still-beating heart of her lover. Such was the dedication Lolth demanded. Whenever lust's smoldering embers threatened to flame into something pure and bright, a drow's heart-fires were extinguished in blood.

She struck aside Fyodor's offered hand and backed away, her arms wrapped tightly around herself and her head shaking from side to side in frantic denial.

Fyodor instinctively took a step toward the drow. She shied away from him, flinging one hand toward him in vehement rejection.

"Get away. Get *away!*" she shrieked.

He watched as she continued to back away, her eyes wide with horror and fixed upon the deck. With the sudden surety of Sight, Fyodor realized that she was not fleeing something, so much as leading it away.

It was then that Fyodor saw the shadow—an enormous spider with the head of a beautiful elf woman. The rising moon was directly behind Liriel, and the shadow stalked her, moving with her as if it were her own.

Acting on impulse, Fyodor drew his sword and thrust it into the shadow-spider's heart. The blade bit deep between the deck's planking. Before he could release the hilt, a spurt of power—cold, dark, and angry—shot up through the sword and sent him hurtling backward through the air. He hit the ship's rail with a bone-shaking thud.

"Run," Liriel pleaded, "or swim. Anything, but stay away!"

He could not understand the anguish in her voice, but neither could he leave her to fight this battle alone. He pushed himself off the rail and came back in at a run. Instead of renewing his attack, he took Liriel in his arms, sweeping her aside and standing so that their combined shadow covered that of the Spider Queen.

"You have no hold upon Liriel," he said softly, speaking directly to the lurking evil. "You have broken with her and she with you."

Faint, mocking laughter rang through his head. *Once a wolf, always a wolf,* taunted a too-beautiful female voice, speaking in a strange language that he somehow understood.

Liriel covered her ears. "*She* was listening to us," she said in a despairing whisper. "Fyodor, leave me now."

"No."

"You don't understand! No male comes between a priestess and her goddess and lives!"

"What of it? You are no priestess."

"I was," Liriel said, "and She's not going to let me go."

"She has no choice," Fyodor said firmly. "No god, no goddess can force worship upon a sovereign soul. You wish to be free of her?"

"Yes!"

"Tell her so."

"I *have*."

"Again," Fyodor urged, "then one time more. Repudiate a god three times, and all ties are broken. All the old stories promise this."

It seemed worth a try. Liriel nodded and took a deep breath. "Lady Lolth, I am your priestess no longer. Mother Lolth, I am your child no more," she said in whisper.

The chill intensified. Liriel noted the pallor of her friend's face, the blue-gray hue that touched his lips. Her fear for him returned, and she tried to wriggle away. Fyodor shook his head and tightened his grip, then drew his cloak around them both. The warmth they shared coursed through them both, pushing back the darkness and cold.

The drow and her sworn guardian clung together for several moments, breath abated as they awaited the dark goddess's response.

Moments passed, and there was nothing but the sounds of the crew at work and the slap of water against the ship.

Liriel slipped from Fyodor's arms and stepped away. The moon-cast shadow before her was her own—an image of a small, slender drow with shoulders squared and head thrown defiantly back.

She resisted the temptation to wilt with relief and sent Fyodor a wan grin. "Next time I tease you about those moldy tales of yours, remind me of this moment."

"Better that we both forget," he countered. "These things belong in the past, and there they will remain."

"Will they?" she said, her voice suddenly serious.

"You must make it so. Do not speak that name. Do nothing to invoke Her return."

"Hoy, First Axe!" shouted a rough male voice.

They both turned toward the call. For a short time, Fyodor had held this title and acted as a war leader on Ruathym. Some of the men who'd fought beside him sailed on *Narwhal*.

A few of the sailors stood idle, gazing toward the drow and her champion quizzically as they tried to make sense of Liriel's latest, inexplicable outburst. Most, however, were busily employed with tending the wounded, rolling dead bullywugs over the rail, or swabbing the gore of battle off the decks. One man stood apart, his bloody mop raised to point at the moon. Fyodor recognized him as Harlric, a grizzled veteran of sea and sword. Winging across the moon was a dark, avian form, one he also knew.

"A raven?" he murmured.

Liriel came to his side, one hand shielding her eyes from the bright moonlight. This was a mystery, one that lay close to them both. Fyodor's fond name for her was "little raven," and in her time on the surface she'd learned enough of these intelligent, uncanny birds to appreciate the comparison and to understand the oddity of this sighting.

"Don't they fly only by day? And aren't we still two or three days from land?"

He nodded. "This is no natural creature."

"Full moon," one of the men observed sagely. " 'Tis the time for strange visitations. Killed me a werewolf once, and at the full of the moon."

"Full moon or no, it's an omen," muttered another man. His fingers shaped a gesture of warding, and he cast a suspicious glance at the drow. "An evil omen!"

"Not according to the First Axe's stories," insisted Harlric. "The way he tells it, the raven carries messages twixt one world and t'other. Must be important news to bring a land-loving bird so far out to sea."

"Must be," agreed the slayer of werewolves, his eyes following the messenger's spiraling descent. "It's a-comin' in. Who here's on speakin' terms with a raven?"

No one moved forward. The bird banked sharply and veered away in a rising circle. Fyodor caught sight of the pale streak on one gleaming wing.

"The mark of Eilistraee," he said quietly, pointing.

Liriel's eyes widened as she noted the silver feathers. She lifted a clenched fist high, bracing her forearm with her other hand. The raven promptly swooped down and landed on her wrist. From there it hopped to a nearby barrel and bobbed its black head in greeting.

"I come from the Promenade Temple and from its Lady, the High Priestess Qilué Veladorn," the raven announced in shrill, slightly raucous tones. "I bear a message for Liriel Baenre, daughter of the First House of Menzoberranzan."

Liriel darted a glare around the circle of curious men who'd gathered to witness this wonder. Her gaze lingered on Lord Caladorn. Something in his face—the watchful intelligence in his eyes, the considering mien of his pursed lips—set off alarms in her mind. Drow deathsingers wore a similar expression when they witnessed feats of treachery and mayhem, weaving tales of dark glory while the deed was still in the doing. This Caladorn sang tales to someone, of that Liriel was suddenly very, very certain.

"Do you mind?" she snapped. "This is a private conversation."

"Not on my ship, it ain't," Ibn retorted. "No message comes or goes without my say-so."

The raven turned its bright black gaze upon the red-bearded pirate. "In that case, captain, I urge you not to land in Waterdeep. Danger awaits. You must come directly to Skullport."

A faint flush suffused Ibn's sun-browned cheeks. Liriel's eyes narrowed. "Wait a minute—isn't that what we're planning to do?"

"Changed my mind," Ibn said shortly. "Last trip to Skullport went bad and ended worse. No one knows that better'n you. 'Twas a near escape for us and not something the folks thereabouts will soon be forgetting."

"Now we've got a different ship, and a different captain,"

Fyodor pointed out. "It seems to me the bigger risk lies in ignoring Lady Qilué's warnings."

Caladorn Cassalanter clicked his tongue in a small, dismissive sound. "With all respect due this drow priestess, you are far more likely to encounter trouble in the underground city than on the streets of Waterdeep. I will be met by considerable strength at the docks, and we do not anticipate trouble."

So here it was, Liriel thought grimly: Caladorn's interest in this matter. It would be like Ibn to deliver her up for ransom, and who better to arrange terms than a Waterdhavian lord?

However, if they thought she would be so easily taken, they had little understanding of the dark elven talent for creative mayhem!

Liriel kept these thoughts from her face and gave the Waterdhavian nobleman a puzzled smile. "Skullport is not without its moments of excitement," she agreed, "but if what you say of Waterdeep is true, why did Qilué warn me away?"

"I would not presume to know her mind, but of this I can assure you: Waterdeep is a lawful city," Caladorn said firmly.

"Maybe, but I'll wager that you don't see many drow there," she pointed out.

Ibn took the pipe from his mouth. "Man just said it's a law-abiding city. The rest goes without saying."

Liriel scowled at this interruption and flung one hand skyward in a sharp, impatient gesture. A cloud of noxious smoke billowed from Ibn's pipe and clung to him in a faintly glowing green globe. He lurched toward the rail and hung his head over the sea.

"I hope Xzorsh isn't following the ship too closely," Liriel commented.

Fyodor gave a resigned sigh and turned back to Caladorn. "If drow are uncommon in Waterdeep, Liriel's arrival will be noted, and word of her presence will spread."

"So? Has she any need to conceal her presence?"

"Survival is a priority to me," Liriel shot back. "Call it a quirk."

The nobleman shook his head. "A dramatic assessment, but not an accurate one. I assure you, all will be well. I and some of my associates are paying the expenses of this ship's passage, and steps have been taken to ensure the safety of all. The decision is mine, and the captain's." He sent an inquiring glance toward Ibn. The rank smoke was drifting away, but the captain still clung to the railing. A distinctly green hue underlay his sun-browned face.

"Not Skullport," Ibn said, faintly but firmly.

"What of the raven's warning?" pressed Fyodor.

"Waterdeep is a lawful city," Caladorn repeated. "If the drow does no wrong, she need fear no harm."

Fyodor's jaw firmed. "If you are mistaken, Lord Caladorn, if danger awaits Liriel in your Waterdeep, who but me will fight for her? You? Your 'associates?'"

The nobleman crossed his arms. "You seem very certain that there will be fighting."

"I have reason," Fyodor said flatly. "Can you truly claim that the good folk of your lawful city will smile and wave as a drow passes through? Once the ship reaches port, Liriel and I will stand alone in a hostile place, and you know it well—you, and perhaps also your associates, who, as you say, will be meeting you at the dock with considerable strength."

For a long moment the men faced each other down. Finally Caladorn faltered before the accusation in the Rashemi's glacial stare. "I mean the drow no harm, but perhaps there are others in the city who might," he conceded.

"You will speak for her?" Fyodor pressed.

"I cannot," Caladorn said flatly, "for reasons I do not care to discuss. Do either of you know anyone in Waterdeep? Anyone who can help her pass through unnoticed if possible, and speak for her if needed?"

A memory popped into Liriel's mind: a chance-met encounter with a human male. He'd been clever enough to take her measure without alerting his vapid companions that the "noblewoman in drow costume" was in fact the genuine article.

This man knew a way to Skullport, and he knew of Qilué. Perhaps he was even one of Eilistraee's followers. During the dragon's hoard battle a few moons past, Liriel had noticed a few humans and even a halfling among the priestess's band. At the very least, surely this man could send Qilué a message.

"There might be someone," she said slowly. "We met at a costume party in the meadowlands outside of Waterdeep. I was not told his name, but I can describe him. Fair hair, gray eyes. Caladorn's height. He was quick to smile and jest. I saw him playing an instrument with strings on the front, and a wooden back so rounded that the thing looked as if it were about to give birth."

"A lute," Fyodor supplied.

Caladorn considered Liriel's description with a wary expression that suggested he knew the man of whom she spoke and heartily wished he did not. "What colors was he wearing?"

The drow shrugged impatiently; she had yet to understand the human preoccupation with the color of things.

"If you are speaking of the color of his clothes and gems, then the answer would be green," Fyodor supplied. "If you are speaking of heraldry, I noticed that one of his rings appeared to be a heraldic image: a unicorn's head with a raven."

Exasperation flooded Caladorn's face. "Naturally," he muttered. "Should Judith ever wish to find her brother, all she need do is hire a diviner to seek out the nearest impending disaster!"

"You know this man," Liriel observed. "Name him, and his house and birth order—or whatever other thing passes for rank in this law-abiding city of yours."

"Rank and wealth are closely related. Waterdeep is ruled by her merchant families," explained Fyodor.

The nobleman shook his head. "The noble houses do not rule the city," he corrected. "The Thann family is richer than any three gods combined, granted, but Danilo is a younger son. The youngest of six sons, I believe. Danilo is amusing enough, but that's the best can be said of him."

Liriel privately disagreed and adjusted her opinion of Caladorn accordingly. Among the drow, younger siblings concealed their ambitions, and sometimes their abilities as well, until they were ready to take their desired places.

"Can you get word to this Danilo of House Thann?"

Caladorn hesitated. "I can send a messenger once the ship docks."

She shook her head adamantly. "Not good enough. I won't let the ship reach the harbor unless he meets Fyodor and me at the dock, bringing enough muscle and magic to ensure our safe passage through Waterdeep. Assure him that I can and will reward him for this favor. Just to make sure there are no misunderstandings, tell him that the drow repay betrayers with their own coin."

For a long moment Caladorn stared toward the faint, silvery border between sea and sky, his face carefully neutral—at least, neutral by human standards. Liriel watched with fascination as emotions chased each other across the man's face. Finally he turned back to them and gave her a curt bow. "Very well. I will do as you ask."

Liriel and Fyodor watched him stride away. The raven cleared its throat. "Your response, Princess?"

The drow's gaze snapped back to the avian messenger. "Tell Qilué what was said here, and assure her that we will come to her with all possible speed."

Black wings rustled as the raven lifted off into the night. Perceiving that the show was over, the sailors drifted off to their duties or their rest.

Fyodor waited until they were alone before speaking his mind. "It seems to me that Lord Caladorn will do as you ask, and more beside."

The drow lifted one eyebrow. "You noticed that, did you? If he can send word to this man before we reach the harbor, he can alert others, as well. Well, let him. We could use a bit of excitement."

At that moment a scream, furious and female, rose from the rear of the ship. Liriel watched with amusement as Ibn grappled with the revived genasi, shouting colorful warnings at his men to stand aside as he carried the struggling, cursing creature over to the side of the ship. Closer at hand, two sailors stumbled by, dragging a bullywug carcass by the feet. Fyodor helped them heave the dead monster over the rail.

That accomplished, he sent a wry smile toward the drow. "I am most interested to know, little raven, what you would consider excitement."

Liriel drew near and told him, in a sultry whisper and with considerable detail. When she paused for breath, Fyodor shook his head in half-feigned astonishment.

"The midnight watch begins in four hours. Is there time for all that?"

She sent him a sidelong glance and strode toward the hold. "I don't know," she said casually. "So far, no one has survived the first hour."

The Rashemi chuckled, but his laughter faded after a moment passed and Liriel did not join in. "You were jesting, were you not?" he called after her.

No answer came from below decks. After a moment, Fyodor shrugged and started down the ladder. The night was young, the moon was bright, and there were many worse ways to die.

CHAPTER THREE

DEEP WATERS

In the waters far below *Leaping Narwhal*, Xzorsh swam eastward, intent upon ensuring that the drow's journey continued on a relatively sedate course. All around him, however, was evidence that his chosen task would not be an easy one.

Bullywug carcasses drifted lazily downward, and blood spiraled out into the dark water. The sharks would soon gather, harbingers of slower but even more fearsome scavengers.

Human sailors knew the surface of the sea and understood something of her moods and caprices. The depths were a mystery to them, a vast and unfathomable place described in song and story as the "silent halls of Umberlee." The sea Xzorsh knew was far from silent. Bubbles murmured and popped on their path toward the stars. The subtle swish of current-tossed sea grass gave a precise report of tides, currents, depths. Fish clicked and squealed as they schooled through the dark waters. A low chorus of grumbling croaks, fading in the distance, marked the bullywugs' retreat. Whale-song from a distant pod rose and fell in a haunting, plaintive melody. A discreet clicking pattern, almost inaudible above the complex murmur of the sea, warned Xzorsh of the ambush ahead.

He loosened the weapons on his belt: a fine knife, fire-forged by land-dwelling elves, and one of his precious throwing crabs. Seizing the element of surprise in his own webbed hands, he pulled his spear and dived toward a thick stand of sea grass.

Several sea elves erupted from their hiding place, scattering and then regrouping to surround Xzorsh. One of them, a large female whose head was shaved to better display her skin's dramatic green-and-silver markings, was known to him. He noted the trident in her hands, the grim purpose on her face.

Xzorsh tipped his spear skyward in a gesture of peace. "Greetings, Coralay. Do you seek me in particular, or did I swim into the wrong trap?"

The female lowered her trident but kept it at the ready. "A bullywug swarm gathered and sang songs of war. Why didn't you summon help?"

"None was needed," Xzorsh said.

Another elf swam to Coralay's side, a young male with a sea-going swagger and a spear still unblemished by battle. "What need has Xzorsh, the great sea ranger, of our help?" he said scornfully. "What need for sea elves at all, when Xzorsh counts every monster of the deep among his friends?"

Xzorsh stiffened at this sneering reference to Sittl, his long-time friend and partner, recently revealed as a deadly traitor to the Sea People. Sittl had been a malenti, a mutant of the evil sahuagin race. Like all malenti, Sittl hid a dark heart beneath the fair form of a sea elf.

"If you accuse me of treason," Xzorsh asked coolly, "you speak at cross currents with the Council of Waves. The court has heard the matter and declared me blameless."

"The malenti made a fool of you," persisted the youth.

"He fooled us all," Coralay said in a tone that demanded an end to the matter. She fixed a steady gaze upon the scout. "We're not here to swim yesterday's tides."

Xzorsh nodded, encouraging her to continue.

"Many bullywugs attacked that ship. Only eleven returned to the sea, dead or alive. You are known as a friend to human folk. You would not have left one of their ships in the hands of those monsters while you could still stand and fight."

"For those words, I thank you," Xzorsh said cautiously.

"Yet here you are."

For long moments they faced each other. "The bullywugs were defeated," he said at last.

"That many?" she said incredulously. "What manner of humankind sails that ship?"

"Northmen pirates, for the most part. With them sails a warrior from a land far to the east, and a powerful wizard."

The female's face hardened. "Speak of this magic user."

Xzorsh spread his hands. "The battle was won. What more need be said?"

"I have heard wordier tales told of another battle recently won," Coralay countered, "a battle fought on the shores and seas of Ruathym. There was magic there, as well. Tell me plainly: Is the drow priestess of Ruathym aboard that ship?"

"Why do you seek this knowledge? What use will you make of it?"

Coralay's eyes narrowed. "A strange response from a ranger, whose duty it is to inform the People."

"To inform, yes, but also to protect," Xzorsh added. To

ensure that his meaning left no room for doubt, he lowered his spear back to guard position.

Astonished rifts of bubbles burst from the sea folk. "You would defend an evil drow against your own people?" one of them demanded.

The sea elf ranger turned his gaze toward the speaker. "Have you ever met this dark elf?"

The other elf blinked. "No."

"In that case, I respectfully suggest that you are in no position to judge her. Liriel is a princess in her land, trained since childhood in the ways of magic. She is a proven friend both to the humans of Ruathym and to the Sea People. It might interest you to know that she too was raised on stories of evil, deadly elves, with one difference: The villains of her childhood tales were the fair-skinned elves of the sky and sea!"

Coralay scowled. "It is not the same thing."

"Isn't it?" persisted Xzorsh. "People are not always what they seem. Night-black skin does not prove an evil heart any more than a fair, familiar face offers guarantee of friendship. The malenti Sittl wrote this lesson in runes of blood."

The elf war leader regarded him in silence for a long moment. "We will consider your words. Will you also consider mine?"

Xzorsh inclined his head respectfully.

"As you say, people are not always what they seem. We often see what we expect to see, or what we *wish* to see. Perhaps you are right about this drow. She has fought at your side and given you weapons of magic. It is even said that she promised to teach you the Lost Art." She lifted one green eyebrow quizzically.

"That is true," Xzorsh admitted.

"Fine things all," she agreed. "Perhaps we are wrong to look upon this dark elf and see only evil, but is it not possible that you see only the good things she has offered and refuse to swim the depths beneath?"

Xzorsh wanted to deny these words, to reject them utterly. Perhaps he might have been able to do so had he not seen the battle on Ruathym's shore.

"It is my duty to protect," he said slowly, "and it is possible that the best service I can do the People is to guard Liriel well. While I live, no harm will come to her—or *from* her."

At last Coralay lowered her trident. "That is all I wished to hear. Go, and do."

A fair-haired young man, green-clad in garments of fine summer silk, whistled a popular tavern ballad as he sauntered toward Blackstaff Tower. The rounded black keep was a Waterdeep landmark, an ancient marvel of smooth black stone unmarked by either windows or doors.

The visitor walked straight toward the tower as if he intended to pass through solid stone. He hit the wall hard and staggered back a few steps, clutching his head with bejeweled hands and cursing with great vigor and imagination.

His next few attempts were more tentative—a prod here, a careful kick there. Finally a slim feminine hand thrust out of the wall and seized a handful of his tunic. His guide tugged him through the invisible door.

Danilo Thann looked down into the indulgent face of Sharlarra Vindrith, an elf wizard apprenticed to Khelben "Blackstaff" Arunsun. He removed her hand from his tunic, gazed into her eyes—violet with flecks of gold, he noted—and raised her fingers to his lips.

"Lovely Sharlarra," he murmured, "once lauded as the most beautiful elf in Waterdeep."

Still smiling, she lifted one brow in challenge. "Once?"

"Well, naturally." Danilo gingerly touched his forehead. "Since I'm seeing *two* of you today, you'll have to share the honors."

The elf laughed and tucked her arm into his. "I assure you, there is no one else quite like me," she purred.

"Pity. The possibilities were, to say the least, intriguing."

"Are you both quite finished?"

The question was spoken by a deep male voice made familiar by a slight burr and a certain irritation of tone. Sharlarra let out a startled gasp and spun to face her master.

Khelben Arunsun was, or appeared to be, a powerfully built man in late middle years. His dark hair was touched with gray and a streak of silver divided his neatly trimmed beard.

"The potions?" he reminded Sharlarra, pantomiming a stirring motion with one hand.

The elf bowed and hurried off to tend her duties. Danilo watched her go with a smirk that loudly bespoke masculine appreciation. The moment she left the room, however, his smile dropped away.

"What is it, Uncle? The urgency spell affixed to your summons nearly set the parchment afire."

"This came from the harbor merfolk." The archmage lifted one hand, snapped his fingers, and plucked a sealskin parchment from the air.

Danilo took the offered document and skimmed the message. After a moment, he raised incredulous eyes to his mentor's face.

"Apparently you made quite an impression on this visiting drow wizard," Khelben said in a sour tone.

The young man smiled complacently. "Women have

frequently described me as an unforgettable experience."

"I've heard the same said of camp fever and the galloping flux. You will not meet the drow at the harbor."

"I won't?"

"No. Do not challenge me on this matter, Danilo. There is more at stake here than you know."

"There usually is," he murmured. He folded his arms and leaned against the wall. "Just for novelty's sake, would you care to enlighten me?"

The archmage linked his hands behind his back and began to pace. "Caladorn Cassalanter sails with the drow. He was very displeased by your involvement with the drow, and none too flattering in his assessment. I thought you two were friends."

"So we were, and so we will be again," Danilo said easily. "But Caladorn was sniffing around Judith, and I responded as any younger brother might. Any brother who possessed knowledge of magic," he amended, "and one whose spell components included an ample supply of saltpeter." He cocked his head and considered his words. "Small wonder Caladorn went to sea. Until the spell wears off, he'll have nothing better to do."

"A good lad, Caladorn is, with a sharp eye and a sense of responsibility that you'd do well to emulate," Khelben scolded.

"They also credit Caladorn as the chief arbiter of style," Danilo said with mock gravity. "I expect that nautical attire will be all the rage this season."

Khelben shot a glare at the young man. "In addition to the message before you, Caladorn sent word of *Clipper*'s fate. You may recall that name as one of the Waterdhavian ships gone missing this season. It was set adrift as a ghost ship, with barrels aboard containing the bodies of over a dozen sea elves preserved in brine."

The young man's face darkened. "The Northmen are no friends to the fair folk, but I hadn't realized matters were in such dismal state."

"Northmen and elves," Khelben repeated. "When are matters ever so simple as that?"

"Until you get hold of them?" his nephew suggested helpfully.

"Do you want to hear this, or not?"

Danilo lifted one hand and traced a circular flourish that indicated the archmage should go on.

"According to the Harple thesis on Underdark cultures, the destruction of the surface elves is a guiding principle of drow life, second only to the domination of the underground realms."

Danilo pushed away from the wall. "You believe that our pretty little wizard is joining forces with the Northmen to this end? That she was a partner in the deaths of those sea elves?"

"Truly? No. I don't see the First Axes of Ruathym making more than a passing alliance with any elf, of any color, for any reason. As an old Northman saying advises, If you use a wolf to hunt a wolf, keep two arrows near to hand."

"Charming sentiment, catchy rhythm. I must set that to music straightaway," Danilo murmured. "Assuming there is no such alliance, what, in your opinion, is she about?"

"Therein lays the problem," grumbled Khelben. "I have no idea what motivates the female."

A feminine chuckle informed the men that they were no longer alone. Laerel Silverhand leaned against the doorpost, her arms crossed and her eyes bright with amusement.

The archmage's lady, herself a mage of legendary power, was fully as tall as her lord. Though the day was young, she was clad in a scant, silvery dancing gown the precise hue of her hair, which spilled in lustrous waves down to her knees.

"Are we discussing females in general, or did you have a particular one in mind?" she inquired.

"I was speaking of the drow."

Something in Khelben's voice stole the humor from Laerel's face. "If you are speaking of my sister Qilué—again, I might add—you might wish to amend your tone."

"Let's not plow this furrow again," the wizard said testily.

"Does this mean you have no interest in my latest family visit?"

Khelben's face turned even more somber. "You've been to Skullport again?"

"Yes, I've only just returned. Qilué is very concerned about her young friend. Someone is looking for Liriel, someone capable of casting a very large net. My sister intends to help Liriel safely to her destination."

"There you go, Uncle," Danilo broke in. "Problem solved."

"It is my observation," the archmage said darkly, "that Qilué solves fewer problems than she creates. She might be Mystra's own, but she is drow to the core: impulsive, temperamental, vengeful, and illogical."

"She speaks well of you, too," Laerel said with exaggerated sweetness.

Khelben refused to be baited. "Tell me all."

The lady mage paused for a long-suffering sigh. "Qilué said that inquiries have been made, bribes paid. She believes the search for Liriel has spread to Waterdeep. Have you been listening to the tavern songs, Dan?"

"Yes, but I don't understand all I hear," he admitted. "There appears to be a very impressive bounty on someone named Raven. I couldn't make out more than that."

"That's enough to tell the tale." Laerel sighed again and tucked a silver lock behind one ear. "Qilué's young friend will be sought by every unlawful faction in Waterdeep, not to mention every scoundrel looking for a way to pay his gambling debts."

"Not to mention those folks who consider battling evil, which by most lights would include all dark elves, to be their righteous duty," Dan put in.

The woman grimaced. "I was hoping no one would mention them."

"Waterdeep's well-intentioned are the least of our problems." Khelben took a small mesh bag of gems from a hidden pocket in his sleeve. "This is part of a deepdragon's treasure hoard, used by Liriel to purchase the freedom of *Elfmaid*, a Ruathymaar pirate ship owned by Hrolf the Unruly. Since these gems were in the drow's possession for several days, they can be enspelled to seek her out. More than that: They can show us who also seeks her by means both magical and mundane."

Danilo watched intently as Khelben sped through the gestures of a spell. In moments there floated before the archmage a wondrous map, a miniature landscape showing the islands and coastal lands of the northern sea. Khelben produced a vial from his bag and took from it a pinch of sparkling powder. This he tossed over the map. Tiny, falling lights twinkled down over the illusion, releasing a complex aroma into the tower chamber.

The young man studied the illusion, watching as threads of silver raced across land and sea. He pointed to a particularly bright web connecting Luskan and Ruathym.

"The recent sea invasion, I would imagine. What is the connection between these two old enemies and our new friend?"

"The captain in charge of the assault was Rethnor," Khelben said, "one of the Five Lords of Luskan."

"Captain Rethnor," Danilo said thoughtfully. "He is said

to be subtle and devious, the sort of man unlikely to accept blame for his failures. And what better scapegoat than a drow?"

"Waterdeep," Khelben said, as if Danilo's question had sought an answer. "Even now, he spreads rumors that Ruathym has made powerful and dangerous alliances—alliances that justified this attempt on their sovereignty. Rethnor claims that Ruathym is allied with dark elves and that Waterdeep gives tacit approval, perhaps even support, to their dark schemes. Liriel set sail from Waterdeep. If she is accepted back into the city and allowed to go her way, we give credence to his words."

"That's absurd!" Danilo protested. "Who would believe such reasoning?"

Khelben let out a derisive sniff. "Since when did logic govern the path of rumor? If a thing is said often enough, there are fools aplenty who will believe it to be true."

"So what do you propose to do? Turn Liriel over to Captain Rethnor?"

"There are many who would gladly sell her, and not just to Rethnor." Khelben intoned another arcane phrase. Silvery threads filled the sea like fishermen's nets and sank deep into soil and stone.

"The Kraken society," Danilo reasoned, nodding toward the sea, "and the underground network, I suppose, would be the drow. It would seem that Liriel has been busy."

"Would that she had stopped there." Khelben tossed another pinch of powder, and the map took on yet another aspect.

Several translucent spheres overlapped, the images overlaying each other like multi-layered rainbows. Threads streamed from all these planes of existence and converged in a shadowy tangle in the sea just to the east of Waterdeep. The overall shape resembled a spider's web.

"This can't be good," the young man muttered.

"It could hardly be worse! This divination suggests that our young wizard has drawn the special interest of a certain drow goddess."

The ire faded from Laerel's silver-green eyes as she met Khelben's somber gaze. "You're saying that wherever Liriel goes, Lolth is likely to follow."

"That is my fear," Khelben agreed. "It has been long years since the drow goddess turned her attention to the surface world. Liriel must be followed and if necessary stopped."

"Very well." Danilo took a deep breath and squared his shoulders. "Allow me a hour or so to pack, and I'll be off."

The archmage shook his head. "Not you, Dan, not this time. The elves of the Pantheon Temple have an agent of their own."

Khelben turned his gaze toward the chamber door. His apprentice appeared in response to his silent summons. "Bid our guest attend."

In moments Sharlarra returned, a tall female elf at her side. The newcomer was raven-haired, clad in well-worn leathers and a chain-mail vest and armed with sword and bow. Her long black hair was loose except for one silver lock, which had been gathered into a neat braid.

"This is Thorn, a champion of Eilistraee, lately come from Ruathym," Khelben announced. "You will leave this matter in her capable hands."

"As you say, Uncle," Danilo agreed. He turned his most charming smile upon the newcomer. "It's a great relief to know that Liriel has made friends among Eilistraee's own."

"As to that, I could not say," the elf responded in a husky, oddly accented voice. "I never met her."

"But you have come from Ruathym?"

"What of it? She is a quarry, not a comrade." The elf's strange eyes, a color more gold than green, narrowed at him. "Most humans outgrow the need to ask endless questions when they leave childhood behind. Or perhaps it just appears to be so because the inquisitive seldom survive for long."

"You say that as if it were a warning," Danilo observed.

In a lightning-quick move, the elf swept her bow off her shoulder and sent an arrow spinning toward the young man. It dived between his boots, piercing the ancient oak planking and quivering fast enough to produce an audible hum.

"That," she said, "was a warning."

Danilo took a careful, belated step backward. "What bard or diplomat in all of Waterdeep could match elven subtlety?" he said in admiring tones. "Obviously, the good archmage is quite right: I must not meet our drow friend at the harbor. Lady Huntress, my Lord and Lady Arunsun, lovely Sharlarra, I bid you all a good day."

The rainbow layers of the illusionary map filtered over him as he bowed deeply, first to the elf warrior then to the wizards. As he strode from the room, he gave Laerel a friendly kiss on the cheek and Sharlarra a kiss that was friendlier still. The elf girl watched him go, then sent an inquiring glance at her mistress.

Laerel sent her apprentice off with an absent-minded wave and turned her attention to the warrior. "It has been long years since the Dark Maiden took a champion."

"You know the history of the People," Thorn observed. "You must also know that an equal amount of time has passed since Lolth granted the powers of a Chosen to any mortal."

The color drained from Laeral's face. "You don't mean to suggest that Liriel . . ."

"I do not suggest," the elf said coldly. "I *know*. I *saw*. Her path led to Skullport then out to sea. I followed until my ship was captured by sea ogres. Those aboard who were not killed were imprisoned in the undersea realms of Ascarle. A band of sea elves freed the prisoners and led us through a magical gate to Ruathym. We joined the battle between the Northmen of Ruathym and Luskan. I saw this drow channel the power and fury of Lolth against the invaders."

"Then Caladorn did well to persuade the captain to dock in Waterdeep," Khelben said. "Lolth's power will be considerably stronger in the underground city."

Laerel's eyes widened. One slender hand flew to the cheek Danilo had kissed.

The archmage noted her chagrin. "Problem?"

"You might say that." Laerel lowered her hand, fist clenched. "Liriel will go straight to Qilué. We must get word to my sister at once!"

Khelben frowned. "You know that isn't possible. It takes hours for a mere message to bypass Qilué's wards and magical diversions. No one can teleport directly into the Promenade Temple."

"I can," Laerel said grimly, "using the ear cuff my sister gave me—the cuff I was wearing just moments ago." She unclenched her fist. Her hand was empty.

The archmage's brows knit in puzzlement then flew up as he realized what had happened. "Danilo said he would not meet the drow! Goddess knows the boy has his faults, but he has never gone back on his word."

His lady cast her eyes skyward. "He agreed he would not meet the drow *at the harbor.* Khelben dearest, you really must learn to speak Rogue. Consider this: Where is your powdered essence of sky, sea, and stone? Where are Liriel's gems? Where is the missive the merfolk brought from Caladorn's ship? Where are all the things that will enable one wizard to find Liriel's ship—and ensure that another wizard cannot?"

Khelben's gaze darted from the writing table to the scrying platform. The delicate vial was gone, as were the bag of gemstones and the sealskin parchment.

He uttered a single word—a barnyard epithet delivered with great force and little regard for the dignity of his high rank.

"The boy's gone straight to the ship! Damn and blast it! Why did I entrust Mystra's Art to such a hopeless fool!"

Laerel fingered the unadorned curve of her ear. "Now that you mention it, I probably shouldn't have taught him those pickpocket tricks, either."

"It would seem that your overschooled protégé has a few lessons yet coming," Thorn announced. She plucked her bowstring, which sang like a battle harp.

Khelben's irritation disappeared, chased from his face by a flash of paternal panic. Power rose like mist around him, creating an illusion of an imperious, elf-blooded wizard, ancient and mighty beyond words—an illusion that held more truth than his familiar form.

"Whatever comes of this, the boy is to be spared," he demanded in a voice ringing with power.

The elf champion shrugged, unimpressed. "If possible," she said. As she strode from the room, she repeated, "If possible—and provided he doesn't annoy me overmuch!"

Khelben's enhanced image dissipated like a sigh, leaving his mortal façade looking old and careworn. He sent a troubled glance toward his lady. "Do you suppose she meant those terms quite literally?"

"Well, she does seem give her threats a bit more emphasis, but how many elves have you met who don't mean precisely what they say?"

The archmage nodded as if he'd expected this response. "In that case," he muttered, "the boy's as good as dead."

Laerel shook her head as another thought occurred to her. "Sharlarra has been getting restless of late."

Khelben stared at her as if she had gone moonmad. "And you mention this because . . ."

"I go to Skullport from time to time. I *need* to, and not just for the information I can find there."

He nodded, acknowledging the side of his lady that he did not share and could not quite understand.

"Did I ever tell you where I met Sharlarra?"

"Lady Sharlarra of the Vindrith clan? I had assumed Evermeet, but something tells me that would not be the correct answer."

She laughed shortly. "Hardly. We met in Skullport."

"No! A gold elf, in that cesspool of a city? What the Nine bloody Hells was she doing there?"

"Surviving," Laerel retorted, "and doing a damn good job of it. She lifted my purse. The thing was magically warded, and she *still* almost got away with it."

The archmage huffed indignantly. "That convinced you to bring her to my tower as an apprentice?"

"Why not? Talent is talent. For that matter, Sharlarra isn't a gold elf. But we're getting sidetracked. Sharlarra stood right over there while your light-fingered nephew robbed us blind. If she hasn't gone to reclaim the goodies, I'll shave my head."

Khelben lifted one brow. "It has not escaped my attention that you spoke of Sharlarra's boredom. Will you place the same wager that your Skullport protégée will return these stolen items at first opportunity?"

Laerel took a thick handful of silver mane in each hand and draped it over the archmage's shoulders. She entwined her arms around his neck and gave him a lascivious wink. "You should probably bear in mind that it would take me two hundred years to grow it back to this length."

A reluctant smile tugged at one corner of Khelben's lips. "In other words, no deal."

The wizard sighed and lowered her bright head to his chest.

"Afraid not."

CHAPTER FOUR

DARKNESS VISIBLE

Stalker Lemming lurched down the narrow Skull-port street, his peg leg clicking briskly against the ragged cobblestone and sloshing through fetid puddles. Though he was almost home, he affected the air of one who had miles to go and scant time to get there.

A small man in his youth, he'd been further diminished with every lost battle and each mis-spent year. Hunched and potbellied, the native swarthy hue of his skin faded to ash by long years of underground living, he was occasionally mistaken for a duergar dwarf. Stalker did little to discourage this misapprehension. Indeed, he grew a straggly beard to heighten the illusion. Ruffians who would consider a pudgy, one-legged human easy prey might think twice before attacking a deep dwarf.

Stalker dodged a particularly unpleasant puddle and impatiently waved away the underfed and over-painted courtesan who stepped into his path. Hair like straw, he noted with disdain, and skin the color of a fish's underbelly. In his land, the women were pleasantly rounded, and they had melting black eyes and sun-warmed skin. The thought quickened his step, as if such a woman might be awaiting him in his hovel.

He dreamed, from time to time, of returning to southern lands as the dashing, wealthy captain of his own pirate ship. More often his dreams were simpler, almost wistful: to feel the sun on his face, to see the vivid purple and gold of one more sunset. Just that, and he could die a happy man.

Well, maybe not *happy*. The way Stalker saw it, there wasn't much about life to inspire happiness, and he didn't expect death to improve matters much.

Fact was, there was no returning to the surface. Stalker figured he'd left behind at least three mortal enemies for every one of his scars, and he had a lot of scars. Enemies could be killed, but assassins cost money and lots of it. A Skullport official earned a paltry wage, with the understanding that theft and extortion would make up the difference. Given Stalker's lifelong bend toward venality, he should have been able to put enough away to hire a band of assassins—or even the legendary Artemis Entreri—to kill all his enemies and most of his friends. Making money in Skullport was one thing. Keeping it, quite another.

The clamor of a street battle increased as he neared his home. As he rounded the final corner, he noted the small, roiling crowd blocking his front door and the adjacent alley, a narrow pass roofed by the leaning, two-story hovels on either side.

A fleeting, lop-sided grin slinked across his gray face. If he hurried, he could lose himself in the small melee, the goal of which appeared to be the communal dismemberment of a kobold pickpocket.

Stalker closed the distance with a lop-sided gallop. Yowling with pretended bloodlust, he hurled himself into the fray.

A few confused and painful moments later, he staggered out the other side of the battle and into the alley beyond. He leaned against the tipsy building he called home to catch his breath and take stock of his injuries. Blood trickled from his nose. One eye was already swelling shut. The knuckles of one hand stung, and the circle of dents on his forearm was undoubtedly the mark of teeth.

Stalker grunted in satisfaction. Could have been worse. Usually was.

He swung aside the loose board that served as a secret entrance and ducked into the dark shanty. Steel and flint hung from the rafters on two convenient cords. His seeking hands found the lamp and pinched back the wick. A quick, practiced click of steel on stone produced a shower of tiny sparks.

Wisps of malodorous smoke drifted upward, then the wick caught flame. A feeble circle of light pushed against the darkness. Stalker blinked once to adjust to the relative brightness.

In that tiny moment of time, the lamplight changed to an eerie violet, a deep and unnatural color that was somehow more ominous than total blackness.

Stalker's body reacted before his mind could catch up. He whirled to scan the room for the source of this mystery.

Two dark figures were seated at his only table. He squinted into the purple shadows. When he perceived the identity of his visitors, he staggered back, screaming like a halfling girlchild.

Somehow, the drow known as Gorlist had found him! With him was another drow, a male who wore his thick white hair in a multitude of tiny braids that, to Stalker's terror-struck eyes, appeared to writhe like small, hungry snakes.

The stranger turned an ironic smile to his associate. "Friend of yours, I take it?"

Gorlist snorted. "Who befriends a duergar? This one is a weasel and a coward, even by the measures of a deep dwarf."

"That's harsh," the other drow commented. "Some duergar are capable of dying well. Not all, of course, but enough to make killing them worth one's time and trouble."

He rose from the table. With a theatrical flourish, he flipped his cloak back to reveal the magically animated emblem pinned to his coat. A tiny ivory skeleton appeared to beat upon a drum while its bony jaw worked silently and rhythmically.

Stalker swallowed hard. This drow was a deathsinger!

"I see that you are familiar with my art," the dark elf commented. "Perhaps you've heard my name, as well? Brindlor Zidorion of Ched Nasad? No? Well, never mind. As you surmised, my current task is to witness and immortalize great deeds of vengeance. The question before us is this: What part will you play in this tale of dark glory?"

The drow's voice was as sonorous as the sea, and he smiled pleasantly at the terrified official. Somehow Stalker found Brindlor's studiously pleasant mien more fearsome than Gorlist's lowering scowl.

He felt rough, damp wood beneath him and realized that both his knees and his bladder had given way.

"I'll do anything, say anything," he babbled.

"Liriel Baenre," Gorlist said curtly. "A drow female, cohort of the Eilistraee priestesses. She paid you to release a confiscated ship registered to Hrolf of Ruathym."

Stalker's first impulse was to deny this out of hand-

standard procedure where any charge of corruption was concerned. He knew from painful experience, however, that this drow was not inclined to settle for partial answers and half truths. So he cudgeled his memory until he knocked loose the required information.

"It was a while back," he remembered. "Seems to me it was early spring Above. Musta been four, five moon cycles past."

"She paid you well?" Brindlor inquired.

Greed momentarily edged aside terror. "Well enough," he said cautiously.

"I don't suppose she mentioned that the payment came from a dragon's hoard." The deathsinger sent Stalker a smile that chilled him clear to the bone. "A deepdragon, to be precise. The hoard was taken from a nearby cavern, in fact."

Panic rose in Stalker, dragging a wave of bile in its wake. Dragons were notorious for knowing their treasure down to the last brass button and for hunting down anything stolen.

Brindlor sauntered over and gave him a friendly pat on the shoulder. "The dragon is dead. You needn't fear another surprise visitor any time soon. All we want is the girl."

The girl, Stalker repeated silently and bitterly. That made the job sound right simple, as if he could turn over the drow female and another dozen like her before his breakfast porridge cooled!

Any drow was trouble, but this wench was also a wizard. She'd told Stalker exactly what would happen to him if he turned on her, and gave him reason to believe she possessed both the will and the magic to back up her threats.

"Hard to find a drow in these tunnels," he hedged.

"Not for a weasel like you," Gorlist said coldly. "The princess spent much of her share of gems and coins bribing fat, lazy officials. You're very familiar with 'those tunnels.'"

Stalker began to see the path ahead, and his knotted shoulders relaxed just a bit. Dragons hoarded magical items. So did drow, and for that matter so did wizards of any race. The female had made off with something these two wanted.

"She paid in gems," he said, which of course is what they'd be seeking. Gems held and transmitted magic better than almost anything a man, dwarf or elf could make.

Gorlist sat bolt upright. "Was a ruby part of the payment?" He held up one hand, thumb and forefinger apart at a distance approximately the size of a ripe fig. "About this size?"

The man nodded avidly. "Oh yes, I remember that stone well. Flat on the top, sharp point on the bottom. A bloody caltrop, it was."

"You *remember* it," Gorlist repeated. "Where is the stone now?"

"I sold it," the man said hastily. "The same day, or the one after. I don't recall which."

"Let us hope, for your sake, that you recall the buyer."

Despite his situation, a feeling of wonder suffused him. "Never will I forget! The buyer was a woman, taller than most men and slender as a willow. Her face was like music, and her hair held the silver of moonlight on a quiet sea."

"A poet," the deathsinger observed, lifting one white brow into a supercilious arc. "I've heard it said that poets generally find acclaim only after their deaths. Tell me, Stalker Lemming, do you hear the siren call of immortality?"

Terror returned in waves. "No! I don't hear a thing. Really! I don't seek immortality—I want to live!" he babbled frantically, if not logically.

"Easily done. Tell us more about this vision of female perfection," Brindlor suggested.

"I don't know her name, but I kept every coin she gave me, and the bag they came in! I'll give 'em to you! All! You could find a wizard to trace her."

Stalker looked hopefully at Gorlist. The drow nodded, and the official scurried to his safe. He took out a small bag fashioned from pale blue silk and handed it to Gorlist.

The drow glanced at the coin bag and tossed it to his deathsinger companion. Brindlor traced one finger over the rune worked in silver thread. Stalker knew what he felt—a faint crackle of power.

After a moment, the deathsinger looked to Gorlist and smiled like a hungry dragon. The warrior's sword hissed free of his scabbard and slashed toward Stalker.

Time seemed to slow, and the sword's leisurely arc seemed to gather and hold the strange purple light. Stalker remembered the bright clouds of his homeland, and his foolish notion that a glimpse of one last purple sunset would allow him to die happy.

Not gonna happen, he realized. A man can't *die* happy who never learned how to *live* that way.

Gorlist cleaned his sword on the dead man's tunic and turned his attention to the blue coin bag. "That's a sigil, isn't it?" he demanded, naming the unique magical symbol that wizards adopted as signature and talisman.

"Indeed. Wasn't it kind of this lovely wizard to leave so clear a trail?"

His irony was lost on the warrior. Gorlist sniffed derisively. "Wizards are arrogant. Either she's warning us off or daring us to track her down. Can you do it?"

"Me?" Brindlor shook his head. "I can do minor magic, but spells of seeking are beyond my sphere."

Gorlist claimed and pocketed the bag. "No matter.

Merdrith will see to that," he said as he strode toward the back door.

The deathsinger grimaced and fell into step. "Are you sure this is wise? The others dislike this alliance with a human wizard."

"They will become accustomed to it in time," Gorlist replied tersely.

"Perhaps, but time is not your ally."

This was, in Brindlor's opinion, a masterly understatement. Time was in fact running out for the warrior. The Dragon's Hoard mercenaries were growing impatient with their leader's obsessive quest for Liriel Baenre.

For months now, Gorlist had been stymied by her sea voyage. His own ships had been destroyed, his seagoing minions slain in battle with the Promenade priestesses. After several attempts to replace his ships, Gorlist turned his efforts to spinning a web of informants, and waiting, spiderlike, for the female's return.

In Brindlor's opinion, while Gorlist's mercenaries might have many fine qualities, patience was not foremost among them. They had gone without the catharsis of battle for far too long. They could not endure in this state much longer.

The deathsinger followed Gorlist into the street. "The mercenaries grow restless," he pressed. "This long period of inactivity is dangerous."

"Inactivity?" Gorlist snapped. "The hunt should keep them fully occupied. If it does not, they are not working hard enough. See that they understand this."

The deathsinger shrugged and subsided. Gorlist would hear this song sung in time, whether he wished to or not.

A sharp, tingling heat flared along the palm of Shakti's hand. She couldn't see the incubus, but she could sense its movement. Her exhaustion forgotten, she strode quickly through the swirling, gray mists.

With difficulty she turned her attention back to the Handmaiden. "With your permission, of course."

I will accompany you.

This was not what Shakti had expected, but she gave a quick nod and set off briskly. To her relief, the yochlol kept pace, its fluid form oozing along like a giant snail under a speed enchantment.

Before long they came to a stone arch pierced by eight rounded portals. In the center of each floated a peculiar skull. As they slowly rotated, they revealed the remains of not one but three sets of features. The six eye sockets of each skull glittered with crimson light. For a moment Shakti marveled that she could have missed so bright a landmark. Curious, she took a single step back. The arch disappeared in the gray mists. Quickly she stepped forward, fearful of loosing the portal she had sought for so long.

The yochlol's form shifted and flowed into two armlike appendages. Over one was draped a fine spidersilk robe, over the other, a glittering *piwafwi.*

Clothe yourself as befits a matron heir, the yochlol commanded. *Then you will take the priestess back to Menzoberranzan.*

Shakti quickly stripped off her tattered clothing and replaced them with the new garb. "As Lolth commands, I do. But tell me this: Why is Liriel so important?"

The answer lies in the light. It is your task to find it.

One of the yochlol appendages flattened, like a hand spreading out palm-up. On it rested a translucent bubble.

The drow's eyes widened with astonishment. This was a soul bubble! She had heard of them but never expected to see one. The crafting of them involved complicated spells and many layers of cruel necromantic magic. Such devices could contain a soul for centuries, be the captive alive or dead, and return the soul to mortal life at will.

Shakti's lips curved in a wicked smile. So she was to bring Liriel back alive or dead. No need to ponder *that* choice overlong! Moreover, she could think of few things that would be of greater torment to her nemesis than imprisonment. Shakti would have to let Liriel out eventually, but she would savor each moment of her captivity.

The yochlol shifted once more, this time into a thick gray mist. This flowed toward Shakti as if it were being sucked into the bubble. Swiftly the yochlol disappeared, and the small globe turned dull and cloudy. There was no sense of weight within, but Shakti could feel the malevolent energy.

For a moment she regarded the bubble, not sure what was going on. Perhaps Lolth did not trust her to deal with Liriel. Perhaps, Shakti admitted reluctantly, with good reason. With a yochlol at her side, she would be more than a match for the princess.

Well?

The yochlol's voice sounded sharply in Shakti's mind. She stepped through the portal. . . .

. . . And found herself in a place stranger than she had ever seen or imagined.

All around her were tall, dark, thin structures that moaned and creaked and rattled. The air here was cold and swift-moving, and small papery things drifted down from on high and collected in drifting piles underfoot. Shakti looked up, past the tall things and beyond to the sapphire sky. Bright pinpricks of light brightened it, the "stars" that were said to inspire faerie elves to insipid orgies of dance and song.

A familiar panic gripped her, that strange vertigo she had experience upon the humans' sea-going ship. It was not natural, these vast distances. At least her gods-granted eyesight swiftly adapted to the new conditions of light.

Light.

Shakti's head snapped toward the blood-bright smoke staining the edge of the sky. She hissed a curse, the vilest and most hated word in the drow language, that which named the horror that surface dwellers called the Sun.

She looked wildly about for shelter. The soul bubble was a magical construct. It would dissolve with the coming of day. The yochlol's soul would return to the Abyss, and she would be entirely alone. Her whip, her new cloak, her carefully hoarded spells—all this would dissipate.

Gathering up her robe, she began to run. There were rocks ahead, large chucks of her homeland no doubt spat up by some long-ago tremor. Now she perceived the swift run of water, getting loud enough to hear over the rustling underfoot. It was said that mountains, like inverted caverns, often housed caves, and caves offered portals to the Underdark.

Her foot caught on something hard and fibrous, hidden beneath the drifting papery bits. She pitched forward, too fast and too hard to twist aside or prepare her fall. She saw the scattering of rocks awaiting her then saw nothing at all.

Some time later, Shakti stirred and groaned. Her head throbbed, and her eyes burned as if she'd been staring into candlelight. Moments passed before she could manage to open them.

A scene of utmost horror was stretched out before her.

The sun had risen, sending punishing golden light through the strange place. The little papery things seemed to glow with that light, showing every color from crimson to russet, from amber to a brilliant yellow-red shade Shakti had never seen. Even brighter were those bits still affixed to the tall structures, like scales on a molting dragon. The cries of unseen creatures filled the air with mocking laughter. Small, winged demons, some of them brightly feathered, hopped along the intertwined walkways overhead, no doubt casting some fell and foul spell. Small marvel the incubus was drawn to such a place!

Shakti dragged herself to a sitting position and took stock of her situation. There was a large lump on her forehead and a bit of dried blood. Her body felt battered and bruised, but that was to be expected. She'd had five long chains of reptilian bone wrapped around her when she hit the ground.

Her whip!

Its familiar embrace was gone. She pawed frantically through the bright debris in case it had dropped away during her fall. In a moment she could no longer deny what she knew would occur. The whip was gone—destroyed by the wicked sun.

A wave of desolation swept through her. The badge of a high priestess, the mark of Lolth's favor. It might be years before she would be granted another, and never would she have so wondrously macabre a weapon!

Something rustled through the piles of fragile scales. Shakti pulled the knife from her belt and leaped to her feet, whirling toward the sound.

Her head spun, and for a moment she was certain that the sight before her was nothing but a manifestation of her recent head injury. Slithering toward her, its five skeletal heads moving this way and that like the fingers on a dancer's undulating hand, was her snake-headed whip. The central head was held high, and draped limply from its bony jaws was a plump, soft-furred creature. This it lay at her feet.

Shakti sank to the ground and plunged her knife into the small beast. She swiftly slit and peeled back the hide and sliced off a strip of still-warm flesh. For several moments she cut, chewed, and swallowed, savoring the first real nourishment she had had for many days.

As her hunger ebbed, astonishment took its place. The snake whip had hunted for her. Never had she heard of such a thing!

The deeper marvel was that it *could*.

Shakti snatched up a handful of her new cloak. It glittered in the bright light, a brilliant black in which danced colors she had never dreamed possible.

A priestess's whip, a *piwafwi*—such things should have disintegrated with the coming of the sun! What in the name of Lolth's eighth leg was happening?

Carefully she removed the bubble from the hidden pocket of her robe. It fairly hummed with life, the malevolent energy undimmed. Gone, however, was the murky gray. The tiny globe was translucent again, and a tiny storm seemed to be raging within. Shakti held it up and gazed inside. A tiny dark figure whirled and danced in wild exultation. As if it sensed Shakti's scrutiny, it came to a stop, splayed tiny hands on the inside wall of the bubble and leaned close. The miniscule lips moved, but the voice sounded directly in Shakti's mind.

The magic held! crowed the former yochlol. *It held! Gromph's little bastard wizard-bitch actually did it!*

Shakti's keen eyes made out the details of a familiar face, one she had never expected to see again. "How is this possible?" she whispered.

Wild joy shone in the tiny crimson eyes. *No questions, traitor-priestess! The Handmaiden bade you to take Lolth's priestess back to Menzoberranzan. Why do you wait?*

A shimmering oval of magic appeared before Shakti, quivering with power and impatience. Filled with foreboding, Shakti stepped into the portal.

The whirl of magical travel engulfed her. Shakti savored it as the most peaceful moment she was likely to know for a very long time. Although she was not sure what had just happened, of one thing she was very certain.

This was likely to be a most unusual homecoming.

The waves sparkled with the early morning sun, and tiny, blinding rainbows of light danced toward the merciless horizon. Liriel bore it as long as she could before retreating below decks to the cabin she and Fyodor shared.

The small chamber felt stuffy and hot without the sea breeze to cool it. For a moment Liriel was tempted to create a porthole to let the air in and cloak it with magical darkness to keep the light out. Practicality overruled comfort. Unseen enemies sought her, and hoarding her spells ensured she could offer the next foe an appropriate magical greeting.

Fyodor settled down on the cot and closed his eyes. His shipboard duties included late watch, and he always slept while Liriel studied her spells. By unspoken agreement, one of them stayed awake and alert at all times.

"Why do you trust this nobleman?" Fyodor asked suddenly.

The drow looked up from her spell book. "He can help us get to Qilué."

"Perhaps he can. You seem very certain that he will."

"He did once before," Liriel reminded her friend.

"Yes." Fyodor opened one eye and sent her an equally lopsided smile. "Through the sewers of Waterdeep."

Her expression darkened at the memory. "There's probably another way in, a better way. Chances are, he didn't trust us enough to reveal it."

The Rashemi propped himself up on one elbow. "The path of your thoughts runs alongside mine, little raven. I have often wondered why Lord Thann offered aid to strangers. He had little reason to trust us."

"Especially considering that one of us is a drow," Liriel said, giving voice to his unspoken words.

As she spoke, the air in the cabin shifted and stirred, and a faint shimmering of light began to coalesce into human form. Liriel had her daggers out—then sheathed again—before her friend noted the magical intrusion.

A tall, fair-haired man appeared in the chamber, a young man probably within a year of so of Fyodor's twenty summers. He held out his long-fingered hands and flipped them palms-up in a gesture of peace.

"To the contrary, I think rather highly of drow," Danilo Thann announced in his lazy drawl. "Say what you will about the dark elves, they're seldom boring."

Liriel's eyes narrowed. She drew her dagger and leaped at the invader in one cat-quick movement. Seizing a handful of fair hair, she yanked the much-taller wizard down to eye level and pressed the point of her blade to his throat.

"They're seldom stupid, either," she snarled. "Who are you, and what have you done with Danilo of House Thann?"

For a long moment the wizard stared at her. "Just for future reference—assuming of course I *have* a future—how did you know?"

"Your hands," Liriel said curtly. "The man whose form you're wearing played a stringed instrument. There would be calluses on the tips of his fingers."

The wizard sighed. "The demons hide in the details, don't they?"

They might as well have been discussing a bottle of wine, for all the concern the pretender displayed. Liriel was not certain whether to be impressed or irritated. She turned to Fyodor, who stood with sword ready.

"I'm going to strip away the cloaking spells. If there's anything you don't like about this idiot's looks, kill him."

She stepped back and flashed through the gestures that would dispel magic. The green-clad nobleman disappeared, and in his place stood an female elf with skin the color of blushing pearls and long, red-gold hair.

A faerie elf.

Deep-seated fear and loathing bubbled to the surface of Liriel's mind like acid. Liriel spun to Fyodor. "What are you waiting for? Kill it!" she shrieked.

The Rashemi stepped between the two females. "Perhaps you should explain," he told the elf.

"I'm Sharlarra Vindrith, apprentice to Laerel Silverhand. She's Qilué Veladorn's sister."

"Qilué sent you?" Liriel demanded, peering around Fyodor.

"Indirectly," the elf said, also leaning to one side. "She sent word to you, and you sent word to Danilo—"

"And he sent a faerie elf in his place," the drow said in disgust. She crossed her arms and glared at Fyodor. "You were right. He wasn't to be trusted. Go ahead and gloat."

The Rashemi shook his head and turned back to Sharlarra. "Does Lord Thann know you are wearing his sword?"

She glanced at the jeweled weapon on her hip. "He may have figured it out by now. Chances are he's still fuming over the loss of the gems and magical items, but he'll get over it." She shrugged and smiled. "They always seem to."

Fyodor turned to Liriel. "In my land, the witches have spells that allow one person to appear as another. To do so, you must carry a weapon used by the person whose form you wish to wear. Perhaps Lady Laerel taught her apprentice such a spell."

"I picked it up on my own," Sharlarra said, "but otherwise you've got it right. Can we get on with this?"

The drow gave a cautious nod. Sharlarra took a silver cuff from her ear and held it out. "Danilo stole this from Laerel, and I stole it from him. It'll take you both right to Qilué."

Liriel took the little hoop and examined the intricate carvings. The markings were familiar and unmistakably drow in origin. The spell they shaped was indeed a variation of a powerful travel magic. Entwined among the magical marks was Qilué's personal sigil. No wizard but she could carve that mark without courting swift magical retribution.

She slid the cuff into place on her ear and spoke Qilué's name. An oval of magic shimmered into sight, a gossamer fabric that was at once black and silver.

"Do you need anything else?" the elf asked.

For a long moment Liriel studied the faerie. "Why are you helping me?"

Sharlarra shrugged. "Danilo could have done it, but he'd end up paying for it."

"And you won't."

"Let's just say I was ready to move on, anyway."

"So you did this for him," the drow said, still trying to understand.

"And for me. Life was getting a little slow in Blackstaff Tower. I was ready for something different."

Inspiration struck. "Here's something that might suit you," Liriel said dryly. "A sea elf named Xzorsh follows this ship." She pronounced the name carefully, a sharp click followed by a lingering, sibilant sweep. "He wants to learn the Art. I suspect his talent is small, but he has the sort of dedication that ignores limitations. Can you find him a teacher?"

"A sea elf mage," Sharlarra mused then shrugged again. "Why not? Consider it done."

A faint tapping came from the other side of the hull, a rapid, rhythmic pattern that shaped a jaunty tune sung on nearly every ship asail.

Liriel's eyes widened. "The merrow alarm!" she said, naming the signal for impending attack—and the monsters that approached the ship. "Xzorsh was right on the mark about the illithid's messengers!"

"Sea ogre *messengers?*" murmured Sharlarra. "Assassins, more likely."

"See?" Liriel retorted. "You got the message already."

"Oh. Good point."

"There will be battle, and soon," Fyodor said glancing reluctantly from the magical gate to the cabin's door. "We cannot in good conscience leave the ship now."

Sharlarra waved them toward the gate. "Go along. I'll stand in for you. Really," she said, responding to the Rashemi's dubious frown. "It'll be fun."

Drow and elf exchanged a quick, cautious grin. "Her I think I could like," Liriel told Fyodor. "Let's go."

The gossamer gate shimmered as they passed through, and their next step fell heavily on solid stone. Liriel, accustomed to the tumble and whirl of drow magical gates, seized Fyodor's arm to keep from stumbling. Her gaze swept over vaulting stone walls and a multilevel maze of connected walkways.

"Impressive," Liriel murmured, referring to both the magical transport and the Promenade temple.

The ground under their feet suddenly gave way, and they were sliding down a steep, smooth passage. Before Liriel could catch her breath, they were dumped unceremoniously into a small, brightly lit chamber.

She shielded her eyes with one hand and gathered her

feet beneath her. Dark shapes surrounded her and Fyodor, and the searing torchlight glinted off a circle of ready weapons. She made out the shape of a large, low bowl on a stone pedestal—a scrying bowl, no doubt, armed with spells that watched the temple parameters and captured whatever ventured into the bowl's "sight."

Liriel spread her hands, palms-up. "We're friends," she began.

"Of course you are," chirped a little-girl voice. "Enemies are seldom received so graciously."

A relieved grin crept over Liriel's face. "Iljreen," she said, naming the drow battlemaster. "I'd say it's good to see you, but I can't. See you, that is. Do you mind dimming the lights?"

The unseen priestess snapped her fingers, and the leaping flames ringing the small stone chamber sank low into the wall torches. A small female clad in silvery party clothes and sparkling gems lifted one finger to her forehead in a grave military salute. To those who knew Iljreen, the gesture held no irony whatsoever.

"Expecting hostile drow visitors?" Liriel asked, blinking away the lingering stars.

The tiny female shrugged. "Most of them are."

"We have many enemies among the drow," observed a lilting, low-pitched female voice, "and so, my young friend, do you."

Liriel squinted in the direction of the speaker. Her vision focused on the beautiful dark face of the high priestess.

A faint smile curved Qilué's lips, but sadness seemed to linger in her eyes—a familiar sadness, one that Liriel had learned on Ruathym. For a moment the pain of Hrolf's loss engulfed her, a wave of loss and regret so strong that she could hardly draw breath.

"You lost someone," she observed softly.

"Elkantar," the priestess responded. "He was slain aboard ship during the dragon's hoard battle."

Liriel's brow furrowed as she tried to remember which among the drow males bore this name. "Your *parzdiamo*," she said sympathetically, using the drow word Menzoberranzan females employed to refer to male playmates who did not officially hold the title of House Patron.

Outrage flamed in Qilué's eyes, bright and brief, then the sorrow returned. "He was my beloved, and he is dead. I cannot speak of it without pain. Instead, let us talk of the drow who killed him."

Liriel responded with a cautious nod. It was clear that she had offended, but she was not certain how.

"The mercenary known as Gorlist survived the battle," the high priestess continued. "He blames you for all that he has lost. He has become obsessed with vengeance. To that end, he has rebuilt the Dragon's Hoard band beyond its former strength. They seek you throughout Skullport and beyond. The tunnels between here and Rashemen are not safe."

Liriel laughed without humor. "Where the Underdark is concerned, 'safe' is never the first word that comes to mind. If the tunnels are as bad as all that, we'll go overland."

"That path is no better," she cautioned. "There are among the humans those who will spill blood for gold, and care little whose blood is spilt or whose gold they pocket. Such men are watching for you in Waterdeep, and they will follow any path you take."

"Bandits and ruffians," Fyodor observed.

"That is not the sum of Gorlist's forces," Qilué cautioned. "He has gathered a band of drow warriors who have grown accustomed to life on the surface, followers of Vhaerun. He has also enlisted the aid of a wizard."

Liriel shrugged. "I've fought wizards before."

"Human wizards?"

A stern glance from Qilué stole the sneer from Liriel's face. "Do not underestimate this foe," the priestess cautioned. "Drow magic is powerful, but it is not the only magic. A small dagger that you do not anticipate will kill you more quickly than the sword you see."

Liriel nodded thoughtfully. "The ancient rune magic is very different from anything I learned in Menzoberranzan."

"Just so. This wizard is Merdrith, a reclusive, little-known wizard of considerable power who makes his home in the High Forest. The Dark Maiden's priestesses have reason to know and fear him. Gorlist, knowing Merdrith's hatred for Eilistraee's own, has persuaded him to Skullport. His magic seeks you even as we speak."

"Not the tunnels, not the surface," Fyodor repeated. "How, then, are we to travel to Rashemen?"

Qilué turned her gaze to the warrior. "That is why I called you here. By the grace of Eilistraee, I can call moonbeams to take you to the borders of Rashemen. No farther can I send you—the witches who guard that land employ spells against such intrusion. My sister Sylune learned of such spells during her time among Rashemen's witches. We use similar enchantments here to ward our temple. Speaking of my sisters, I see that you have something that belongs to one of them."

Liriel removed the ear cuff and handed it over. "You can call moonbeams?"

"A spell granted Eilistraee's followers. Shall we begin?"

In response, Liriel held out her hand to Fyodor. Their fingers entwined. At a nod from Qilué the warriors left the chamber, passing through unseen doors. The torches snuffed out abruptly. Darkness and silence ruled absolute.

The priestess began to sing, a soft haunting melody that

was more like wind than music and that might well be lost on a night wind.

Soft white radiance filled the chamber as slender beams of moonlight streamed down from an unseen sky. The thick ceiling of soil and stone seemed to fade away, and motes of mundane dirt whirled and danced in the moonbeams like stardust. In the center of this summoned magic, Qilué danced.

The voice of the priestess—and the magic of the Dark Maiden — flowed through Liriel like strong wine. Almost without realizing it, she too began to sway and circle in time to the music.

Listen to the moonsong, whispered Qilué's voice, mind to mind. *Whatever land it touches sings with joy, and each song is unique. Find the song of Rashemen. Listen, and follow.*

"And Fyodor?" Liriel asked aloud.

Your destiny and his are entwined. This he knows. You are the song his heart hears. Go, and he will follow.

The young drow reached out through magic's web, much as she had when she sought the great oak known as Ygg-drasil's Child. Her senses caught the distant tune, a simple melody that seemed to follow the cadence of Fyodor's ancient tales. Liriel gave herself fully to the music, letting the silvery magic of Eilistraee flow through her swaying limbs.

A deep chill shimmered through her, stopping her in mid-whirl. Liriel froze, and for a moment she relieved the horror of the Abyss and those few moments when Hrolf's ship *Elfmaid* passed through Lolth's realm on its way to safety.

The memory passed, but the horror did not. Liriel stared in disbelief at the dark threads streaking down along the conjured moonbeams. Spiders the size of house-cats dropped into the chamber and skittered off through the invisible doors and out into Qilué's carefully warded sanctum.

Low, mocking laughter filled the chamber, echoes that welled up from unfathomable depths. Dark threads snapped together to form a web, which lowered slowly toward Liriel.

Mine, exulted the voice of the goddess—a terrible sound that mingled the shrieking of chill winds and the multitudinous voices of the dark-elven damned. *This one I claim now. The rest we will take soon enough!*

Qilué shook off her moment of stunned inaction and seized the silver medallion bearing her holy symbol. A quick tug snapped the chain, and she held the disk aloft. Again she sang, and again she danced.

A soft haze of moonlight flowed from the medallion, slowly pushing aside the darkness of Lolth. Again Liriel joined in the dance, desperate to help push away the unwanted Presence.

Qilué whirled toward her, her face grim. A graceful leaping kick dealt a blow that sent the younger drow reeling to the chamber wall. Liriel hit hard enough to knock the breath from her body. For long moments she sat on the cold stone floor, struggling for air, helpless to do anything but watch as the high priestess called upon one goddess to banish another.

Finally the terrible Presence faded away, and so, more slowly, did the silvery light surrounding Eilistraee's priestess. Qilué strode to the scrying bowl. She gripped the rim with both hands and leaned in. After a moment she straightened and raised a haggard face to Fyodor. "Come, Rashemi, and tell me what you see. The battle took more of my strength than I had thought possible."

He came to the priestess's side and gazed over her shoulder.

"Goblins are coming from the tunnels below," he said crisply, a warrior giving report. "There's a kobold horde nearing the postern gate. Small bands of drow fighters converge from these three tunnels. Those humans there—I've seen similar tunics worn by Skullport bounty hunters."

The priestess spun away and shrieked for her battlemaster. Iljreen appeared suddenly. Her gaze snapped to Liriel and then returned to the high priestess, taking in the situation. "The wards?"

"Down."

Iljreen nodded crisply. "I'll see to the battle. You'll have your hands full elsewhere."

"Tell me what I can do to help," Fyodor offered.

The battlemaster's delicate face hardened, and her narrowed eyes again flicked to Liriel. "You can take that Lolth-loving bitch out of my stronghold before she kills us all," she hissed.

With that Iljreen was gone, as suddenly as she had appeared.

Sick understanding filled the pit of Fyodor's stomach. Somehow, he knew not how, Liriel had once again invited Lolth's touch. He glanced at his friend. Her eyes, enormous in her stricken face, mirrored his fears.

"How is this possible?" she whispered.

"Isn't it obvious?" spat Qilué. "Liriel is bound to the Spider Queen. You shouldn't have come!"

Liriel's spirit returned in a sudden rush. In one swift movement she was on her feet and in the priestess's face. "You told us to come. Or was your talking raven lying through his beak?"

"You should have sent word of this!"

"We didn't know."

"Didn't you?"

The searing accusation in Qilué's voice snapped Fyodor out of his horror-struck daze. Liriel was *wychlaran*, and while he lived, no one would accuse her of such treachery.

"Liriel has turned away from ways of her people and given up the evil goddess," he said with quiet certainty.

"That doesn't mean that Lolth has given up on Liriel," Qilué retorted. She whirled on Liriel in magnificent wrath. "Do you know how many years of work, what a fortune in magical resources, went into warding the Promenade from Lolth's view? All that, undone! You have turned this place over to Lolth and her evil followers. Have you any idea what that means?"

The young drow's bravado faded. "Of course I know," she whispered. "How could I not? I was born in Menzoberranzan."

"A place not easily left behind," Fyodor said softly. "You yourself said that Liriel was pursued. I swear to you, she gives no more invitation to the huntress than the hare gives the hawk."

The bright heat of Qilué's fury faded away, and her shoulders rose and fell in a deep sigh.

"I can do nothing more for you but show you a quick way to the surface. I will send word to my sister Laerel. She will see you safely out of Waterdeep. Word of a traveling drow will reach the Dark Maiden's followers. If you are stopped and questioned, show them this. It will grant you safe passage."

The priestess handed Liriel a small silver talisman, an engraving of a slender elf female armed with a bow and accompanied by a wolf. Both hunters lifted their eyes to a rising moon.

"Thank you," Liriel said fervently.

Qilué's stern gaze softened. "A servant will guide you through the tunnels. Go, and may the Dark Maiden watch your path."

Fyodor bowed and took Liriel's hand. They disappeared together through one of the hidden doors.

The moment she was alone, the high priestess sank to the floor in exhaustion. Her battle against Lolth's intrusion had drained her strength to the point of exhaustion. She thought it unwise to show the extent of her weakness before one the Spider Queen had so obviously claimed as Her own.

No matter how reluctant Liriel might be—and Qilué did not doubt the young drow's reticence—where Liriel went, the eyes of the goddess would follow.

Perhaps it would be different on the surface, Qilué mused. The power of Lolth could not reach the lands of light. The central tenant of her faith was that darkness was destroyed by light, not rendered invisible. So it had always been, and she had no reason to believe that it would not always be so.

Why, then, could she not dispel the sense that the world had shifted beneath her feet?

CHAPTER FIVE

WIZARD'S APPRENTICE

The illithid known as Vestriss paced the mosaic floor of her throne room, which until recently had been a treasure trove in the submerged ruins that long-dead elves had called Ascarle. Only a few of these ancient treasures remained: large statues for the most part, or golden objects too heavy for the illithid's fleeing slaves to carry away.

Vestriss herself was decidedly worse for wear. Her amethyst rings had been stripped from her four-fingered hands. The silver circlet that had adorned her lavender head was gone, as was the medallion bearing the royal crest she had assumed as the self-proclaimed Regent of Ascarle. Her fine robes had been torn by frenzied, thieving hands, her sensitive facial tentacles bruised. The only reason she still lived was that the slaves had thought her already dead. Liriel Baenre's immobilizing magic had seen to that.

The illithid was not, however, feeling the least bit grateful.

Vestriss's seeking thoughts perceived her genasi slave's foot-dragging approach. Facial tentacles twitched and writhed as if the illithid tasted the air, but Vestriss read the story of the genasi's mission in the emotional storm creeping toward the throne room. Rage the genasi knew in plenty, and frustration, failure, and fear.

Fear. Oh, yes. There was reason for fear.

Vestriss settled into her throne and turned her empty white eyes toward the door. In moments a lithe, blue-skinned female entered the room and dipped into a deep reverence. Purple bruises mottled her face, and one eye was nearly swollen shut. Hatred for the drow who had done this swirled through the genasi's mind, and her overwhelming desire for revenge sang in concert with the illithid's own, similar fury.

Vengeance is the reward of the competent, the illithid "said," projecting a regal, feminine voice directly into the genasi's mind. *You, Azar, have failed me.*

The genasi's lips thinned, and insulted pride rolled from her in pungent waves. "If I have, mistress, it was because I lacked the necessary magic," she said in petulant tones. "You said the drow was a wizard. You did not know how powerful."

Did I not? Liriel Baenre stood in my presence. Were I so inclined, I could list every spell in her quiver. I gave you all the magic you needed to stave off her attacks. One tentacle stabbed toward Azar like an accusing finger. *What cause have you for complaint? It wasn't magic that marred your face.*

The genasi hand lifted to the swelling around one eye. "Even so, lack of magic was the mission's undoing. I intended to follow the ship and slip up on the drow unobserved, but a bullywug shaman sent me into battle, and I had no defense against his call. This I must have."

The illithid dismissed her slave's concern with a flip of her purple hand. *Bullywugs are vile monsters, to be sure, but their magic is of little account. They surprised you once. You will not be caught a second time.*

"I wish that were true!" the genasi wailed. "The shaman's call—I can hear it still! It is not fitting that the Regent of Ascarle's servants must heed a lesser's voice. Is there nothing you can do to loosen these degrading bonds?"

After a moment's consideration, Vestriss inclined her bulbous head in assent. *Quiet your thoughts as best you can. It will make the process less painful for you, and what is far more important, more convenient for me.*

The illithid rose and glided toward the slave, who dutifully knelt and tipped up her battered face. Facial tentacles enfolded the genasi's head as Vestriss's innate mental magic probed her slave's mind. She slipped past Azur's roiling thoughts with the ease of a halfling pickpocket, past word-shaped thought, past all emotions the genasi acknowledged and understood, moving swiftly and directly to the mind's hidden depths. There Vestriss found a hard, hateful knot of compulsion. With a mental touch as sure and delicate as a harpist's fingers as she loosened the threads—

Her concentration shattered suddenly, completely. Vestriss staggered back, staring in disbelief at the dagger's hilt protruding from between her lower ribs.

For the second time in her life, the illthid's mental voice was silenced—not by a drow's magic but by the white-hot pain pulsing from the blade.

"No more compulsion," Azar hissed. She rose to her feet, and her blue hand seized the dagger, twisting it. "No more slavery. Only vengeance. Do you still find me incompetent?"

The truth came to Vestriss slowly, beating at her dazed mind like the sound of distant surf. Azar hated the drow, loathed the bullywug shaman. That was real enough, but the mental clamor of these new indignities had cloaked her first and most bitter resentment.

Vestriss threw her will against the terrible pain, forcing it aside long enough to shape a final, important thought:

And the drow?

A sneer twisted Azar's bruised face. "Even now, you assume I'll do your bidding! The drow bested me, yes, but she bested you as well. In my mind, this settles all scores. Know this: You will die and she will not. If that pains you, I am content."

The genasi jerked the dagger's hilt downward and shoved the blade in high and hard, a brutal thrust that quested deep into the illithid's chest. Muscle resisted briefly, painfully, then the blade sank into something soft and pulpy.

The genasi tore the weapon free, and suddenly Vestriss was drowning. Ichor bubbled from her tentacles and welled up in her eyes, spilling down her face in scalding green tears.

The marble floor sped toward her. Vestriss did not register the impact, but she gradually became aware of a new and distant pain. Horror flooded her as she realized its source. Azar's dagger was slicing through a facial tentacle.

The genasi tossed one twitching appendage aside and reached for another. "Despite all, the bullywugs were an instrument of my freedom. This will be their reward," she explained. "As the drow will soon learn, I settle all scores."

The tapping on the hull of the ship grew more insistent. Sharlarra frowned. "Perhaps I should have asked for the answering code," she muttered.

With a shrug, she stepped over to the wall and rapped out an echoing quatrain of the unmistakable rhythm of "The Mermaid," one of the bawdiest tunes sung in Skullport taverns. That seemed to satisfy the unseen scout. Now it was time to pass the warning along.

That presented a problem. According to Khelben, Caladorn Cassalanter was aboard this ship. Sharlarra didn't know him well, but they had been partnered at the last Winterfest ball. There was a distinct possibility that he had figured out what happened to his jeweled cloak pin. No one would suspect one of Khelben Arunsun's apprentices of thievery, but she was far from Blackstaff Tower. In her close-fitting dark clothes, with a nobleman's jeweled sword on her hip, she looked suspiciously like a halfling second-story artist after a good night. Only taller. And sober.

Inspiration struck. Calling to mind Fyodor's face and form, she cast the illusion spell over herself and her gear. She examined the result in the bronze mirror over the washbasin and winced at the unfashionable image he presented: leather jerkin, linen shirt, dark wool trousers tucked into low, worn boots. Her gaze dropped to her "borrowed" sword, which now appeared to be a thick black weapon decorated only by the crudely carved bear's head on the pommel.

She started for the door, drawing the sword as she went. A hum of magical energy jolted through it, and a baritone voice broke into fervent song:

"Who draws the sword commands my voice;
My song pours forth at your command!
Let evil bleed and good rejoice
While hymns of victory speed thy hand!"

Sharlarra let out an exasperated curse. She kicked shut the door and prayed that no one had heard. "A singing sword! Damn and blast that man!"

"I don't command perdition's gates,
Nor can I hurl a blasting fire;
Yet mortal agony awaits
The man who dared arouse your ire," the sword sang apologetically.

"Thanks ever so much, but we're in disguise today," she told the sword. "That means no singing."

She felt a dimming of power, uncannily like a human sigh of disappointment, then the magic again blazed bright. The sword switched from song to oratory.

"No melody shall sing thy praise,
Yet ringing meter I'll declaim!
In spoken verse my voice I'll raise
That quaking foes may know thy name!"

Sharlarra gritted her teeth in frustration and glanced toward the ceiling. The scuff of boots on the deck had the leisurely pace of men at ease. The sailors had not yet perceived the coming threat. Time wasted now meant blood spilt later.

"One more word, and I'll have you melted down and recast as a chamber pot. Got it?"

"Hmm hmmm-hm hmm—"

"Sweet sodding Mystra!" she exploded. "Why couldn't Danilo have purchased a Sembian sword? Those weapons know how to take a hint! Listen: No singing, no declaiming, no humming, no idle chit chat. Just kill things. Quietly."

At last the sword subsided. Sharlarra hurried down the narrow corridor and scrambled up the ladder. She drew the disguised weapon and pointed it toward the sea.

"Sea ogres approaching, lads! Let's give them a proper welcome!" she roared, doing her best to imitate Fyodor's Rashemaar accents.

Several of the sailors stopped and looked at her quizzically. Belatedly, the elf realized that her illusion did not extend to her voice—she still spoke in her own sultry elven tones. She'd forgotten to steal one of the berserker's weapons. Without it, the illusion was incomplete.

The sword in her hand chuckled softly.

Sharlarra was saved by a shout from the crow's nest, and the clatter of men gathering weapons to meet yet another foe.

A pair of huge, webbed hands slapped onto the rail. One of the pirates ran forward and slashed down with his cutlass, but another hand thrust forward and caught the man's wrist, halting the blow with ease. A quick twist disarmed the pirate and sent him to his knees. He rolled away a second before enormous feet thumped onto the deck.

The creature crouched in guard position was like no merrow in any lorebook Sharlarra had ever seen. Its head was fishlike, with a spiny standing fin starting at the crown and running down the length of its back. Two large side fins resembled exaggerated elven ears, and its large round eyes were as black and hungry as a shark's. The hideous head was split by an enormous mouth lined with stiletto-like fangs. A sea serpent's tail—long and sinuous and ending in a double row of spikes—flowed from a heavily muscled humanoid torso. Four thick arms, each armored with a ruff of elbow spikes, flexed in preparation for battle.

"Sea devils!" shouted a stout, red-bearded man. "Sahuagin aboard!"

A ringing battle shout burst from Sharlarra's sword, and it fairly leaped toward the crouching monster. The elf followed as best she could, muttering a bloodboil spell as she went.

The sahuagin batted aside the attacking sword with an open-handed swat. One of its upper hands seized Sharlarra's tunic and jerked her up to eye level. Another hand closed around her sword arm with bone-crushing force, and the gaping jaws spread in anticipation.

The black eyes turned glassy, and a fetid steam hissed and swirled through the monster's bared fangs. All of its hands began to tremble violently as its body cooked from within. Sharlarra wrenched her sword hand free and killed the monster quickly, a belly slash that spilled steaming entrails onto the deck.

She carefully sidestepped the mess and spun to survey the chaos around her. A dozen or so of the creatures fought with weapons salvaged from the sea: ancient pikes and rust-brown swords with pitted edges. The pirates held them off easily.

Perhaps too easily.

The elf edged her way out of the melee, parrying sea devil thrusts and jabs as she went. When she was free of the tangle of flailing weapons and cursing pirates, she sprinted toward the aft castle and climbed the ladder to the platform.

From this vantage she had a clear view of the entire ship. As she suspected, on the opposite side of the ship several sahuagin climbed quietly over the rail and made directly for the hold.

Not for these monsters the rough, forgotten weapons of drowned sailors. They were armed with spiked halberds carved from sea ivory, and they wore weapon belts heavy with fine daggers. On every belt hung a net.

They were hunting, and apparently they wished to take their captive alive.

Sharlarra's brow furrowed in consternation. In moments the sahuagin would discover that their quarry was gone. From what she'd heard tell of them, they would kill every man aboard just for sport.

She glanced down at the sword. "Do you think you could imitate Fyodor's voice?"

"Not without talking," it observed rather snidely.

Sharlarra let that pass. "Just shout out an occasional battle cry, an encouraging word, a warning—that sort of thing."

"It's better than nothing."

"Very gracious of you. Let's go."

As she leaped from the platform the sword let out a terrible roar—a blood-chilling sound that brought to mind the charge of a wounded bear. Two of the monsters—and Caladorn Cassalanter—instinctively turned toward the sound.

A third sahuagin darted toward the distracted nobleman. Sharlarra pointed the sword toward the new danger, and her rapidly chanted spell was swallowed by the warning shout pouring from the weapon.

The monster stopped just short of Caladorn, its raised weapon clanging sharply against a miniature wall of force. Sharlarra dispelled the barrier with a quick gesture—just in time to allow the man's answering strike to pass through.

She spun to the right, following the impulse flowing from the sword. The blade tangled in the spires of a rusted trident, bringing her much closer to a sahuagin's fangs that she had ever hoped to be.

The sahuagin grinned horribly and punched the enjoined weapons toward the elf's face. Instinctively she ducked, ignoring the sharp pain in her shoulder as her sword arm was forced back. She pulled a knife from her boot with her free hand and thrust up, throwing all her weight into the attack.

Thick hide resisted the blade longer than Sharlarra would have thought possible. It gave way suddenly, and the hilt slammed into the monster's belly. The sahuagin shrieked in pain and drew back, leveling the trident for another attack.

One of the well-equipped sahuagin strode over and shoved the wounded monster aside, planting himself in front of Sharlarra and leaning menacingly toward her. To her surprise, the creature did not strike, and it held one hand high overhead. The monster let out a call, a series of loud, chittering clicks that seemed to resound through every plank on the ship.

All over the ship, the sahuagin fell away from the fight and stood with weapons at guard. Something had changed in their manner. Even though the fighting had ceased, the monsters suddenly looked more menacing.

"Where is the drow?" the leader hissed.

"Do you wish to answer, or shall I?" the sword enquired softly.

"Tell them we'll never yield her," Sharlarra prompted. In Fyodor's voice, the sword shouted the response.

"The hell we won't," retorted the red-bearded pirate. "I'm captain here, and I say take her and be you gone!"

The hideous head snapped toward the speaker. "Where are you hiding her?"

"Hiding her?" the captain said incredulously. "I wouldn't spit on her if'n she was on fire."

"Chivalrous sort," Sharlarra murmured.

"Traitor! Coward!" the sword translated loudly.

"Bilge water," the captain snapped at "Fyodor." "Any man

what takes up with a black elf has no call to name another man 'traitor.' Yield her up, or I'll kill you myself."

A gleaming trident whirled through the air and sank into the deck at the captain's feet. All eyes traced the weapon's path back toward the sea.

Balancing lightly on the rail were a dozen sea elves. A tall green-skinned female, her shapely head shaved to show off her exotic markings, sent a contemptuous glare toward the captain.

The elves leaped nimbly to the deck and hurled themselves at the equally eager sahuagin. For a long moment the sailors hung back, uncertain. Sharlarra noticed the battle warring on their captain's face—a conflict as fierce as that between the sea elves and their mortal enemies.

Finally the captain lifted his curved sword. "It's our ship, lads! We need no scrawny elves to hold it for us! Heave to!"

The pirates surged forward, and Sharlarra followed them—or more precisely, followed the sword. The thing had gotten fully into the spirit of battle and was roaring out some Rashemaar battle hymn. She fell into place at the sea elf's back, and though her sword tangled with a sea devil's pike, her cold gaze warned the captain to hold his distance. From what Sharlarra had seen, she would not be the least surprised if an elf or two took wounds from something other than a sahuagin's blades or talons.

Not today. Where she came from, elves of all kinds stood together.

Not far away, a male sea elf battled one of the net-wielding sahuagin. The monster employed a spiked flail with which it attempted to herd the elf into position, but though it whirled and cast the net again and again, each time its quarry slipped away, darting and dodging with astonishing grace.

The sahuagin advanced steadily on its smaller opponent, backing the sea elf toward the rail between two roiling clusters of fighters. The net spun out full, dropping toward the elf like a jellyfish intent upon surrounding its prey. There was no place to go, and the sea devil's skull-splitting grin celebrated victory.

A silver blade slashed up, tearing through the net as if it were slicing a ripe pear. The sahuagin's head tipped slowly back then rolled to the deck. Its smile was still in place.

Magical knife, observed Sharlarra. This must be the Xzorsh of whom Liriel spoke.

Her attention was seized by the sword's eager shout. A four-armed sahuagin rushed toward her, brandishing a shining weapon in each hand.

Sharlarra cast a hold-person cantrip on the charging sea devil, freezing it in mid stride. She finished the creature off with a quick thrust. Not exactly sporting, but in her opinion, neither was having an extra pair of arms. In any event, she had her hands full with the monster coming hard on Four Arms' heels.

For many moments Sharlarra stood and fought the sahuagin, her disguised blade singing merrily as it clashed, clattered, and scraped against the monster's rusted sword.

The sea devil worked the singing weapon down low, then lifted a taloned foot and stomped on the blade. The weapon was wrenched from Sharlarra's hand.

She dived away from a lunging strike, rolled aside, and came up wielding the first weapon that came to hand, a long, slender lock pick. The sahuagin stood like an ugly black statue, frozen in the act of delivering a wicked backhand slash.

Xzorsh strode past, toppling the immobilized sea devil with a casual shove. The monster rolled to the deck, still frozen in attack position.

"My first spell," the sea elf said proudly. "Liriel taught me this herself. Where is she?"

He spoke softly, but Sharlarra heard him clearly. She noticed that the battle had died down to a few skirmishes. The ship was nearly empty of both sahuagin and sea elves. Most likely they'd decided that the humans didn't matter and had taken their battle back to the seas.

The sea elf's eyes narrowed. "There is a haze of magic about you, more than the berserker rage could summon. You might look like Fyodor, but you are not he."

Sharlarra smiled. "Liriel was right about you—you do seem to have an inherent gift. She asked me to find you a teacher. Maybe we should continue this discussion in private."

A delighted smile lit the elf's face. "Your voice is elven."

"So's the rest of me," she purred, "but I'm not going to show it to you up here."

The sea elf chuckled appreciatively and led the way down into the hold of the ship. They went to the cabin shared by the drow and Rashemi and shut the door.

The elf quickly dispelled the illusion, and stood before Xzorsh in her own form.

"I'm Sharlarra Vindrith, and I've recently left an apprenticeship with Khelben Arunsun, also known as Blackstaff, archmage of Waterdeep. The drow asked me to find you a teacher. In the meanwhile, I'd be happy to pass along some of the things I've learned."

"A gold elf teaching the Lost Art to one of the Sea People!" he marveled.

"Not a gold elf," she corrected him, and shrugged. "I'm . . . something else, though no one I've met can tell me precisely what."

He accepted this with a nod. "When can we begin?"

"As soon as our two friends are safely to their destination, or at least well on their way, I'll send for you. Can I get word to you through the harbor merfolk?"

"Yes, of course!"

"Wait for my word." The sea-elf looked hesitant, so Sharlarra took Liriel's little mesh bag of gems from her bag, spilled one into her hand, and handed the rest to the sea elf.

"I need one jewel in order to follow Liriel. Take the rest as my bond."

Xzorsh accepted the bag and watched as Sharlarra summoned a magical gate and stepped through it.

"Someday," he said wistfully, "I will be able to do that and more!"

He watched as the gate began to fade, the iridescent colors sliding along the surface like the captured rainbow of a child's soap bubble. Like that imagined bubble, it peeled away. A tall, raven-haired female elf stood where the gate had been.

"Where is he?" the female demanded in a low, rather husky voice.

"Whom do you seek?" Xzorsh asked.

"Blackstaff's apprentice."

The sea elf stood silent, considering this new puzzle. The Blackstaff's apprentice had demonstrated an ability to change form, but Xzorsh had assumed that the apprentice truly was a beautiful elf maid with red-gold hair and violet eyes flecked with gold. In truth, he knew nothing about Sharlarra but the name she had given him. It could have been invented. Even her voice might have been the product of magic. Liriel had told him more than once that he was too trusting.

Yet the stranger knew of his wish to learn magic, and she had entrusted him with a fortune in gems.

The elf woman's gaze followed his to the coin bag, and she snatched it from his hand.

"He was here," she confirmed grimly. "A rampaging green dragon leaves a more subtle trail!"

"Those gems were given me in trust," Xzorsh said quietly but firmly. "I will not relinquish them to you."

The elf looked at him with measuring eyes. "The drow can be traced through these gems. Possession of them might bring trouble."

"Let it come. I never thought that the Art would be an easy thing."

"So be it." She tossed the gems at Xzorsh and waved him away from the door. He moved aside, and she wrenched it open.

A thin line of moonlight streamed down from the open hold. The elf woman splayed her fingers wide and reached out for it. As the light spilled between her fingers, she simultaneously began to shrink in size and rise toward the moonbeam's source. In a heartbeat she was a glowing mote among the dust swirling through the faint light, then she was gone.

Xzorsh watched with shining eyes and a heart filled with longing. He gazed at the stream of light long after the elf had disappeared, as if the secret to this marvel might be whispered by the swirling dust motes.

He dropped his gaze to the little mesh bag in his hands. With a reverent finger he traced the gracefully swirling rune that was the mark of a mage.

Someday he would have such a mark. Someday he would step through air bubbles into distant seas, and follow moonlight wherever it went.

Such dreams filled his heart as he quietly climbed the ladder and slipped, unnoticed, into the sea.

CHAPTER SIX

A DRAGON'S EYES

Merdrith the Mad, formerly a zulkir among Thay's Red Wizards, pensively scratched his beak of a nose and studied the little silk bag he held at arm's length. Unlike Brindlor, he did not touch the wizard's sigil embroidered on it.

Gorlist sent a quick glance toward the deathsinger. The drow lounged elegantly against the opposite wall, his arms and ankles crossed and his expression politely interested. At his side was one of the young warriors who seemed to shadow the handsome male's every step.

As a general rule, followers of Vhaerun preferred the company of other males. Brindlor wanted nothing to do with females under any circumstances. That suited Gorlist well enough. Brindlor suited him well enough, too—except, of course, for his subtle but stubborn disapproval of the human wizard in their midst.

Gorlist had his reasons for including Merdrith

in the band. The wizard might appear to be as dry and wizened as a treant, but the flame of his hatred burned bright. Gorlist was not inclined to trust anyone of any race, but in his opinion obsession granted a singularity of purpose and purity of heart. Merdrith's hatred was one that Gorlist understood well.

"This is the sigil of Laerel Silverhand," the wizard announced. "Haven't seen it for a good fifty years. Not that the past fifty years have been particularly good, mind you."

Gorlist considered these remarks in the light of the description that Stalker Lemming had given of the mysterious lady wizard. Humans aged appallingly in fifty years, yet in the dwarflike human's eyes this Laerel had been young and lovely. He voiced this observation.

"Laerel Silverhand will be as beautiful as she wants to be when your whelp's whelps have turned to dust," the wizard said flatly. "Wizards of great power such as myself find ways to cheat death for a few decades. Laerel has seen centuries come and go. Most likely anyone attempting to follow her path will run into magical traps that could hold a lich prisoner throughout this eternity and the next. You don't want to meddle with her. Mystra's mounds, *I* don't want to meddle with her!" He tossed the bag to the table, where it landed with the solid *chink* of many coins.

"I want that gem," Gorlist said resolutely. "Find another way."

The wizard thought this over, stroking the thin, artificially crimson braid that passed for a beard. "These gems were part of dragon's hoard, yes? A dragon never forgets treasure. Scry for the treasure through a dragon's eyes."

"Through a dragon's eyes," Gorlist repeated, in the manner of one who prompts further response.

"Precisely. Ask the dragon," Merdrith said slowly, as if explaining something patently obvious to a rather slow child.

"The dragon is dead," Gorlist returned in kind.

The wizard's aged face crinkled with impatience. "Your point would be?"

Brindlor pushed away from the wall. "I believe I see where this is going. We require a necromancer, one who can speak with dead dragons. Come along, Falail, and bring a dozen stout lads with you."

The young warrior gave the deathsinger a salute and wheeled off.

"Congratulations on your promotion to commander," Gorlist said with cutting sarcasm.

The deathsinger merely smiled. "I'll try to be worthy of the honor. Shall we?"

Gorlist bit back a retort and followed the deathsinger out of the cavern that served as the wizard's study. His father, the wizard Nisstyre, had never employed a deathsinger and had nothing but scorn for those who did, but Nisstyre, for all his claims about building a new drow kingdom, had been far too timid and furtive. He, Gorlist, would wave Liriel Baenre's scalp, both literally and metaphorically, and let the enslaved drow males know that no female was sacred, none beyond the reach of their swords or the power of their Masked God. For that, he needed Brindlor.

There was a limit, however, to what he would accept from Brindlor. The deathsinger had swiftly found comrades among Gorlist's ranks. As long as he did not attempt to build a more far-reaching power base, all would be well. The moment any drow hinted that his loyalty had shifted, however, would be the last moment of Brindlor's life.

A small band of drow awaited them outside the wizard's lair. Gorlist told them what they needed to know and set off at a brisk pace through the tunnels leading to Pharx's lair.

The vast stone chamber was dark and empty, silent but for the steady dripping of water from some antechamber, haunted by the memory of battles fought and lost. The treasure had been claimed, hauled away by Qilué and her cohorts. Not a single coin remained.

They found Pharx's body in an adjoining chamber. There wasn't much left of it. A few dull scales draped well-picked bones, lending the massive corpse the appearance of a skeletal knight moldering in plate armor.

The drow set to work with swords and axes. After a long and sweaty interval, they wrestled off the skull. It took all thirteen of the warriors to carry the massive skull. With six to a side and one bringing up the rear, they looked like pallbearers on their way to a crypt.

They struggled down a series of tunnels, each one a bit narrower than the last. As they neared the necromancer's cave the drow were reduced to pushing the skull along, tipping it this way and that to move it through the tight passage. Bone screeched against rock, setting up a vibration that sent small stones tumbling down the tunnels walls and onto the laboring drow.

A wild, piercing yell cut through the racket, and a tall elf exploded out of a hidden cave. He spun toward the drow, arms and legs flailing wildly.

All fourteen drow drew their swords in deadly unison.

The elf gyrated closer, but Brindlor held up a restraining hand. Gorlist noticed that the "elf" was taller than most humans and covered with a faintly green, scaly hide. His wild eyes were golden and bisected by vertical pupils, like the eyes of a goat.

Or a dragon.

"A half-dragon," murmured Brindlor, as if responding to the warrior's thoughts. "Crazy as a gasinta bug but gifted in necromantic sorcery. You couldn't find a better mage for the money."

"What are we paying him?" Gorlist inquired.

"We're not."

This logic did not exactly inspire confidence, but before Gorlist could protest, Brindlor presented their request to the half-dragon. The mad necromancer nodded and placed a reverent hand on Pharx's remains. A glowing mist began to rise from the titanic skull. In moments, a wraithlike image of a deepdragon swirled through the air, circling the skull and weaving in and out through the empty eye sockets like a cat curling around the legs of its favorite human.

"Pharx's spirit," Brindlor said softly. "You can ask it four questions or make four demands. Chose carefully. The dead tend to favor oblique answers."

Gorlist stepped forward, glad that his search had yielded the magic gem's name. "I seek the Ruby of Chissentra. Tell me where it lies."

The massive skull swiveled to face him, but the voice came from overhead, where the dragon wraith circled. "How should I know? The Chissentra Ruby was not in my hoard."

"One point for the dragon," murmured Brindlor. He met Gorlist's murderous stare with a smile and gestured toward the skull.

"It was added after your death," Gorlist specified, "and taken from the hoard chamber along with gems you knew. Can you sense familiar gems alongside a large, magic-laden ruby?"

"Yes."

The deathsinger sent Gorlist a wry glance. "That would be two. Care to rephrase that last question for your third attempt?"

Gorlist gritted his teeth, then tried again. "Describe the stones that accompany the ruby, and tell me where I may find them."

The ghostly dragon faded into shadow as if drifting off to seek the gems. After a while, it flared back so swiftly that it seemed, just for a moment, to take on solid form.

"The Nssidra diamonds," it mused. "A full score of them, trapped in silver filigree. They frame the gem you seek. I see it gracing an elf woman, a red-gold torch flaming behind walls of black stone."

"Black stone," muttered Brindlor, looking not the least bit surprised and none too happy. "Tell me this: Does this black stone mark the tomb of ancient dragonkind?"

The dragon wraith looked to the deathsinger, and ghostly fangs flashed in a smile. "You know the answer to that already, deathsinger, or you would not have asked the question. Farewell to you. Sing our story well."

With those words, the wraith faded away. The half-dragon, too, drifted back into the cave. His wild babbling subsided into an odd, angular little dirge sung in a language Gorlist had never heard.

He spun toward the deathsinger, his face hot with fury. "Only four questions, and you waste one of them on something you knew already?"

"Perhaps I was hoping to be proved wrong," Brindlor said with a wry smile, "but given the wizard we seek and the clues Pharx's spirit yielded, our destination is appallingly clear."

It was not at all apparent to Gorlist. For a moment, the drow envied the deathsinger his knowledge of the human world, his ability to take on the appearance of other races and mingle with strange people in strange places. Such things gave knowledge, and with knowledge came advantage.

But Gorlist was a warrior, not a deathsinger. He would fight the battle, not stay to the side and compose songs about deeds done by better drow!

"You were hired by the Dragon's Hoard for your knowledge of the Night Above," he said shortly. "Earn your pay, and speak plainly."

Brindlor swept into a bow. "As you command. Legend claims that the city of Waterdeep was once a dragon stronghold. The bards of many races sing songs referring to this city as the tomb of ancient dragonkind. In this city is a famous wizard's keep fashioned of black stone. Thus, it appears that we're off to Waterdeep to besiege Blackstaff Tower and spirit away the red-haired elf who lives within. That feat, once accomplished, should justify my pay."

Blackstaff Tower, repeated Gorlist silently. He was no expert on Waterdeep life, but even he had heard of this tower and the mage who ruled there.

Justify his pay, would it? If Brindlor could find a way to accomplish this marvel, all the treasure the deepdragon's hoard had once held might be accounted a fair reward!

Not far from the cavern where Pharx's headless bones lay in repose, Liriel and Fyodor waded through a rat-filled tunnel, moving carefully on high wooden stilts. The footrest stood nearly three feet from the ground, and the wood below had been greased to deter the rats from climbing. Even so, the ravenous vermin swarmed wildly around them, climbing over each other in their frenzy to reach the living flesh just out of reach.

Liriel grimaced as she picked her way along. "I'm starting to get nostalgic for those sewer tunnels. With a little thought, I'm sure I could find an interesting way to rid the tunnel of these vermin."

Her companion teetered, steadied himself with a hand to the low rock ceiling. "No magic," he reminded her. "Lady Qilué's command."

"Command?" Liriel repeated. "What gives you the impression that we're under any obligation to follow her orders?"

"This is her territory," he pointed out. "Her servant told us what to expect in this passage and gave us what we would need to pass through."

The drow kicked away a particularly persistent rodent. "For that we should be grateful? Besides, where's the harm? There's a world of difference between clerical magic and a wizard's spells."

"I don't know what harm might come of it," Fyodor admitted, "but in this matter I am content to remain in ignorance."

Liriel didn't press the point. Qilué's miscast teleportation spell, the resulting intrusion of the evil drow goddess into Eilistraee's stronghold—this was too new and disturbing.

Suddenly the rats scattered, squeaking in terror. Fyodor dropped to the stone floor and drew his sword. Liriel also tossed aside her stilts but called upon her innate drow magic to keep herself aloft. She pulled a pair of knives from hidden sheaths and waited.

There was a whispering rush, and a spider the size of a hunting dog darted toward Fyodor.

Liriel froze in mid throw. For a long moment she hung there, trapped in a nightmare of immobility as the taboo against attacking a spider warred with the need to protect her friend.

Fortunately Fyodor had no such scruples. He swung his black sword and batted aside the stream of venom the monster spat in his direction. He dived aside, then changed direction and rolled back so that he lay directly under the spider's front pair of legs.

The spider's beaked mouth stabbed down. Fyodor thrust

his sword between the two mouthparts and twisted himself to one side. The spider flipped onto its furred back. Eight furious legs beat the air as it tried to right itself.

The Rashemi leaped to his feet and leaned in, sword leading. One of the spider's legs curled around the weapon while another encircled Fyodor's wrist. A single powerful tug tore the weapon from his hand and sent it spinning away.

A silvery streak dived toward the spider, and one of Liriel's knives buried itself up to the jeweled hilt. The creature hissed but continued the struggle to regain its footing. The missile had missed a vital spot.

Liriel bit her lip. She was far from being a master of dark elf swordplay, but her aim with thrown weapons was as good as that of any drow she knew. She hadn't missed a target since before her blooding ceremony!

She was not certain which troubled her more: the knowledge of this failure or her suspicion that she hadn't really missed at all.

Fyodor made good use of the weapon she gave him. Gripping the dagger with both hands, he pulled it savagely across the furred body. The flailing limbs stilled, and the rounded body deflated like a broken wineskin. Hundreds of tiny spiders skittered away from the corpse, infants freed by their mother's death.

The warrior rose and wiped his face. He looked to toward Liriel. To her surprise, there was no accusation in his face, no sense of betrayal.

"In my land, there are many troublesome and mischievous creatures," he said softly. "The Rashemi might be better off without them, but not one among us would lift a sword to them. It is not our way."

For a moment she gazed down at him, moved beyond speech. She had seen many marvels since leaving her homeland but none so wondrous as this man's ability to see into her heart. Shortly after they'd met, he'd given her a priceless jewel, an ancient spider trapped in amber. Though he'd assured her that such things were common in his land and not at all costly, Liriel knew that her pendant would be the envy of every priestess in Menzoberranzan. How could he know this? How could he understand things he had never seen?

The drow nodded her thanks and floated down to his side. She glanced down the tunnel ahead, and her golden eyes widened. "I've never killed a spider, but I might not have a choice," she murmured. "Look."

She snapped her fingers, and a small globe of blue light appeared. A gesture of one hand sent the magical thing floating down the stone corridor.

Thousands of delicate strands glowed in the azure light. Fyodor caught his breath and let it out on a Rashemaar oath.

Layers upon layers of webs blocked the tunnels. In them lurked the infant spiders, already the size of ravens and growing fast.

Liriel squeezed her eyes shut for a moment. She drew her sword with one hand and conjured a firebolt in the other.

Fyodor caught her wrist before she could hurl the flaming weapon. "Look at the webs. See how they glisten?"

She considered his words. Spider webs, even natural ones, were incredibly strong and resilient. These were no natural spiders, and no doubt the webs were preternaturally strong. A fire large enough to destroy their new-spun webs would most likely suck the air from the tunnel.

A smaller fire spell might do some damage, but the lethal babies were fleet of foot. Most of them would scamper away from the small blaze and bide their time. Liriel glanced at Fyodor and weighed their chances against the hundreds of lurking monsters.

A small, grim smile curved her lips as a solution presented itself. "Climb up on that boulder," she told Fyodor, nodding toward a pile of rocks that rose well above the damp floor. "Whatever comes, don't touch the wall."

She slammed her sword back into its sheath and let the firebolt fall to the floor. It sizzled out in a scum-covered puddle, unheeded by the drow who had summoned it.

Again Liriel summoned her levitation magic. Floating, she began to chant. The damp and fetid air stirred, and a small, jagged flare of light scratched a path against the darkness. The drow seized it and hurled it like a javelin toward the glistening webs.

Blue light flared and sizzled its way along the spider web, darting from one web to another. The drow flung her head to one side, squeezing her eyes shut against the blazing destruction, clapping one hand over her nose to mute the stench of burning spiders.

Hours passed, or perhaps moments. She felt Fyodor's hand close on her ankle and pull her down. She wriggled out of his comforting arms and strode forward, not sparing a glance at the charred bodies. Fyodor followed without comment, as if he understood that the breaking of a life-long taboo had left her emotions so brittle than a touch, even his, might shatter her composure.

The rest of the trip passed without serious incident. Within the hour, they found the shaft Qilué's servant had described and managed to climb its deceptively smooth walls.

Liriel clung to the last handhold and tapped on the wooden ceiling. The hatch swung away. A beautiful elf face, framed by red-gold hair and backlit by thoughtfully dim candlelit, thrust into the opening.

Sharlarra greeted the drow with a comrade's grin. She seized Liriel's wrist and pulled her up with surprising ease.

The drow took stock of her surroundings. They were in a small room walled and floored with dark wood. The yeasty smell of ale permeated the air. A tavern, most likely. Another human, a burly, balding man who wore a publican's apron over a warrior's bulk, helped Fyodor into the room.

Liriel shoved a handful of soot-laden hair off her face. "How did you find us?"

The elf showed her a large, well-cut gem. "This came from your share of the dragon's hoard. With it I was able to trace you to the ship then follow your path here to the Yawning Portal Tavern."

The drow's eyes lit with interest. "I'd like to learn that spell."

"Another time," Sharlarra murmured, glancing at the older man. "The first order of business is to get you two out of the city. I brought gloves to cover your hands, fashionable cloaks to pull over your heads. I have a spell that will change your appearance to that of a human lady, and Durham—our kind host and the proprietor of this fine establishment—has two horses, saddled and provisioned, awaiting you in the stable behind this tavern."

"Horses," Liriel said with distaste.

"Well, I thought that giant lizards might be a tad conspicuous," Sharlarra said with a quick grin. "The road out of the East Gate crosses a stream. After the bridge, veer north and follow the stream to its source, a spring in the hills of a small forest. I'll meet you there and see you on the next part of your journey."

Fyodor came to Liriel's side and offered his hand. "Come to Rashemen," he said softly. "If it is adventure and friendship you seek, there is no better place to find it."

The elf, looking oddly touched, took his hand in both of hers. "Safe home," she bade them.

The pair nodded to Durham and slipped quietly out the back door. The innkeeper turned a somber gaze upon the elf.

"Your master the archmage isn't going to like this."

She sent Durham a hopeful smile. "Does he have to know?"

"He always seems to."

Sharlarra sighed. "Good point. In that case, I'd better revise the terms of my will before I pack. You'll be remembered in it, have no fear of that."

The man chuckled and gave her cheek a fatherly pat. "Off with you."

He waited until Sharlarra had left before easing the heavy wooden cover back into place and carefully filling in the crack with powder from a sack he carried on his belt.

The substance seemed to melt into the wood, obscuring any trace of the hidden opening. It was a gift from Waterdeep's archmage, a long-time friend who had never quite approved of Durham's self-appointed role as guardian to the gates of Undermountain. Khelben Arunsun would certainly disapprove of his apprentice's sponsorship of the pretty little drow and her Rashamaar companion.

Durham, however, understood this impulse perfectly. In his day, he would have done much the same thing.

Come to think of it, his day was far from over.

Perhaps, Durham mused, his old friend Khelben could wait awhile before learning about this night's adventure.

CHAPTER SEVEN

HOMECOMING

Shakti paused at the gate of House Hunzrin. Wrapped in her new *piwafwi* and cloaked in invisibility, she gazed at her childhood home and her inheritance.

The family mansion lay on the outskirts of Menzoberranzan, close to the fields and pastures whose care was the business of House Hunzrin. The estate was not as large as many of the city's mansions, comprising only three large stalactites, a few connecting bridges, and a number of rather ramshackle outbuildings.

Even so, pride filled Shakti. It was not an imposing estate, but it was hers, or soon would be. Judging from the individual standards that draped one of the crosswalks, her older sister had finally succumbed to that mysterious wasting disease. The banner bearing her mark—a ridiculous thing showing the silhouette of a rothé against a circle meant to depict a wheel of cheese—no longer hung in second position. In its place hung a banner emblazoned with Shakti's symbol, a pitchfork flowing with magical energy. She was now her mother's heir, a high priestess in the full favor of Lolth. In many regards, her future looked deliciously dark.

But first she had to sort through the puzzling secret that had been entrusted to her. It would be rank foolishness to show herself at House Hunzrin before these matters were settled. She had a younger sister who would not hesitate to exploit the weakness that Shakti's uncertain state presented.

Still wrapped in invisibility, Shakti walked through the city to the Baenre estate. As she neared the outer wall, she flipped back her concealing cloak and revealed herself to the guards. Magical wards surrounded the house like a moat, and it was better to come openly than to be caught approaching in stealth.

A squadron of guards surrounded her at once. They listened with narrowed eyes to her demand for audience and sent a runner to carry this message to the Matron Mother. In moments Triel's response arrived: a floating disk meant to convey a visiting priestess with honor.

Shakti settled down on the conveyance and held her head high as she progressed through the several gates that warded the residence. She had no doubt that Gromph would hear of her arrival within the hour.

Resolutely she put that thought out of mind. She would need all her wits to deal with the subtle and treacherous Triel. Any distraction would be lethal.

The disk brought her to directly to the door of Triel's audience chamber. Shakti dismounted on the driftdisk and began the long walk toward the matron's throne. The chamber was huge, with high-vaulting ceilings and intricately carved walls. Each footstep echoed softly, the sound like that of stones dropped into deep wells. This approach was meant to intimidate, but knowing this did not lessen the effect in the slightest.

Triel watched her approach through narrowed crimson eyes. The diminutive priestess had augmented her mother's throne with a gorgeously carved footrest. Shakti supposed it was less than dignified for a matron's feet to dangle like a child's when she sat in state.

She came to a stop at a respectful distance and sank into a low obeisance. The Baenre matron acknowledged Shakti's reverence with a steady, unreadable gaze, which Shakti met with an equally unwavering stare. Looking directly into the Baenre female's eyes, she announced, "Matron Triel, I have failed."

For a long moment, silence ruled the chamber as Triel plumbed this strange pronouncement for hidden depths.

"You did not bring Liriel with you," she said at last.

"I have not," Shakti admitted, still on her knees. "Lolth has a purpose for the princess that I do not yet fully understand."

The First Matron's crimson eyes narrowed dangerously. "You presume to speak for Lolth?"

Shakti bowed her head. "I only repeat the words her handmaiden the yochlol spoke to me."

She was rewarded with another silence—briefer this time but still potent. "Where did you encounter this handmaiden?"

"In the Abyss."

Triel's eyelids flickered. She gestured for Shakti to rise and take a seat. "Tell this tale from the beginning."

The priestess settled down in the offered chair. "On your command, I gathered powerful allies and pursued Liriel. She also had surrounded herself with strength, and our forces met in a fierce battle."

"Who allied with her?"

"Many. The humans of a distant island known as Ruathym and a band of sea elves."

Triel sat bolt upright. "A daughter of House Baenre in alliance with faerie elves? What foul lie is this?"

"No lie," Shakti maintained firmly. "If I wished to shape the truth to my benefit, would I not tell a tale more pleasing to your ears?"

The First Matron conceded this point with a curt nod and gestured for her to continue.

"Liriel fought her way into the stronghold of an illithid sorceress, ancient faerie elf ruins buried deep in the sea. She released the illithid's sea elf prisoners and led them in battle. I myself would not have believed such an alliance possible had I not seen it."

"You lost a battle to humans and faerie elves," Triel summarized, her voice dripping with disdain.

"No," Shakti responded calmly. "I lost to the power of Lolth."

The matron's tiny hands gripped the arms of her throne. "You have already proven incompetent. Beware of adding blasphemy to your faults!"

Shakti pressed on. "I challenged Liriel to *nai'shedareth*," she said, naming the ritual combat between two priestesses to determine which had the greater favor of Lolth.

Triel settled down, and a sardonic smile curved her lips. "A bold move," she sneered. "You are a high priestess, she is barely an acolyte!"

"She is of House Baenre, and I am not," Shakti said bluntly. "My snake whip was slain, my spells turned aside."

"The girl is not that powerful," Triel said uncertainly.

"On her own, no. But she was made *Zedriniset*."

The heat slowly drained from Triel's face. This word,

one of the most sacred in the Drow language, was seldom spoken aloud. It was an honor and a power that every priestess secretly aspired to attain for herself and feared to see in another.

"You saw this."

"Many did. Lolth's power flowed through the Baenre daughter during the battle for Ruathym."

The small priestess digested this. "Yet you challenged her."

Shakti inclined her head in what she hoped was a suitably humble posture. "I was condemned for my arrogance to the Abyss."

The matron considered these words for many moments, examining them for the layers of subterfuge and hidden intent common to all drow interactions. When she spoke, she addressed the most obvious question.

"Yet, here you are."

"Here I am," Shakti agreed. "I was condemned for attacking a Baenre, yet the Queen of Spiders knows my heart. The priestesses of House Hunzrin have ever been supporters of Baenre. I am your servant. To punish me too harshly might cast an ugly glare of light upon the smooth darkness of your path. Lolth's handmaid tested me, and found me faithful. I was returned from the Abyss with signs of the goddess's favor."

Shakti reached into her robe and drew forth her five-headed snake whip. The skeletal heads rose, and then dipped in obeisance to the First Matron.

"This is the whip you yourself gave me," she explained. "It was destroyed in battle with Liriel and restored by the power of Lolth during my sojourn in the Abyss."

Triel regarded the undead weapon skeptically. "So you say, but any high priestess can animate the dead. You will have to be more convincing."

"Lolth's handmaid also gave me this as a token of the goddess's highest favor to House Baenre and her wish that you prosper above all Houses."

She handed Triel the soul-bubble. The matron gazed into it, but her eyesight was not the equal of Shakti's.

The Baenre matron snapped a command to her guard. The males disappeared, to be replaced in moments by a score of well-armed females. These were Matron Triel's personal guard, hand-picked for ferocity and personally enspelled for loyalty. The females formed a circle around Triel's throne.

At a nod from Triel, all the guards drew two weapons, which they crossed with those of the females on either side. A faint hum resounded through the room as protective magic surged through the ready steel. No magic could be cast from the circle, and none could endure within it.

Triel tossed the globe toward the nearby guard. It shattered before it hit the floor, exploding with a puff of glowing, greenish smoke. The smoke drifted off and stopped just short of the humming swords. Since it could not disperse, it was slow to fade. When it cleared, all gazed in astonishment at a tall drow female standing in the protective circle. Her eyes were dazed and her hair disheveled, but her face was unmistakable.

"Quenthel," Triel said in a strange voice.

It was undoubtedly Quenthel Baenre, a powerful priestess slain years before. It could not be otherwise, for any attempt by any other drow to claim her form would be dispelled from the magical circle. Quenthel had died in battle, and her body had been returned to the city, where it was burned to ash according to the custom for honoring high-ranking priestesses. Lesser corpses were embalmed and stored, a resource to be called upon when nameless zombie troops were needed.

Burned to ash—and yet, here she stood. Quenthel was undeniably alive. There was no denying the clear sign of Lolth's favor. A powerful priestess had been returned to House Baenre!

Lolth's favor, indeed, mused Triel. One Baenre priestess returned from the dead, another favored as *Zedriniset*, a Chosen of the goddess!

With such powerful allies as this, Triel would never need to look far for enemies. And what of Shakti, who had been entrusted with so much honor and information by the Goddess Herself?

The Baenre matron hid these thoughts and dismissed her guard with a sharp flick of one hand. Then she turned to the two watchful priestesses, her gaze moving from one conspirator to the other—for such they undoubtedly were.

"How did you find your way out of the Abyss?"

The resurrected drow priestess stared at Triel for a long moment.

"I-I don't . . . know," she admitted and staggered as if she might faint. With sheer force of will she pulled herself erect. Her face took on something of the haughty mien Triel remembered.

Triel managed a smile, and said the only thing there was to say.

"Welcome home, sisters."

That night, Brindlor, magically disguised as a human dock worker, shouldered his way into a crowded, odorous tavern in the dock ward of Waterdeep. He scanned the crowd, looking for a sun-browned Northman with a red beard and hard, suspicious eyes.

He found the man seated alone at a small table near the kitchen door, his boots propped up on the only other chair at the table and his fierce glare daring anyone who ventured close to try to claim it.

Brindlor worked his way back to the captain. He leaned against the wall and snagged a mug from the tray of a passing wench—a deft bit of thievery that earned an admiring nod from the red-bearded pirate.

"Busy night," Brindlor commented, speaking in the coarse language known as Common and flavoring it with the bluff accents of the wintry Northlands. He nodded at the nearby kitchen. "*Too* busy, I'm thinking, if'n they've taken to seating sea captains so close to the latrine."

A flicker of amusement crossed the pirate's face. "Sounds like you've et the chowder here."

"Tried it. Couldn't stomach the swill." Brindlor patted his artificially ample belly. "Ah, well. This wouldn't be the first time I made a meal of ale. And it's right hungry I am!" He jingled his coin bag and grinned. "If I'm sitting, I'm buying."

The pirate peered into his own mug and swung his boots off the second chair. Apparently he deemed the offer of free ale to be of greater value than the loss of his privacy.

"You know me as a captain," he observed. "What else are you knowing?"

"Not much," Brindlor said easily. "I worked the docks this morn, helped unload *Narwhal*. Saw you with the dockmaster, heard your name spoken as Ibn. They call me Wolfrich," he said, offering a massive paw.

Ibn nodded in satisfaction at the Northman's name and took the man's hand. Neither of them spoke another word until the next round of ale went down, and the one after that.

In truth, Brindlor knew a great deal about Ibn. He was a native of Ruathym, a good seaman who possessed great pride in his heritage and an equally profound hatred for elves. He was a notoriously taciturn man who would never speak three words when one would do the job. There was one exception to this habit: Whenever Ibn came ashore, he indulged in a mug or two. And the more he drank, the more he talked.

"Met one of your boys," Brindlor offered. "Leigaar. Tells a good tale, that one."

A suspicious glare furrowed Ibn's ale-flushed face. "What story's he telling now?"

The disguised drow shrugged. "Nothing I'd credit as money-on-the-barrel truth, but a fine and fancy tale for all that. Something about a tapestry of souls and a sea elf guardian."

Ibn made a sour face. "Sad to say, that's plain truth."

"Is that so." Brindlor took a long, considering pull on his ale. "You know this sea elf?"

"Know him? Only too damn well. Name's Xzorsh. Since the day I signed on with Hrolf the Unruly, the elf's stuck to us like wet knickers. Got some notion about protecting the ship, him and the elves he commands. Hrolf's gone below the waves and his ship with him, but the damn elf's got himself another reason to follow me. A drow wench, if that don't beat all."

"Really." Brindlor signaled for a fresh pitcher and poured them both another drink. "What would a sea elf be wanting with a drow wench?"

"Magic," the sailor said shortly. "He fancies himself to be a web-fisted wizard, if that don't beat all. The drow promised to find him a teacher."

Brindlor leaned back in his chair and stroked his yellow-bearded chin. After a moment of silent contemplation, he sent a sidelong glance at Ibn. "This Xzorsh is nearby?"

"Stone's throw, if'n you got a good arm. Swimming the harbor with the merfolk, last I heard."

"Hmmm. He commands many elves?"

"How many, I couldn't rightly say, but enough to turn a sea battle our way more'n once," Ibn said grudgingly.

"Well, I surely do see your problem."

Ibn earnestly tried to focus his blurry eyes. "You do?"

"A risky thing, handing any kind of weapon to a drow wench," Brindlor observed. "I've had some dealings with the dark elves. They'll all bad, mind you, but the females are the worst of the lot. They don't do anything unless it serves a purpose. Chances are she has a use in mind for this Xzorsh and his sea elf friends."

Ibn continued to stare at him with uncomprehending eyes. The drow suppressed a sigh. Perhaps he'd been over-generous with the ale.

"If it's plunder they want, no pirate between here and Lantan could compete with magic-wielding sea elves," he explained, "and no honest sailor could win a sea battle against them, if it came to that."

Ibn considered this for a long moment.

"Of course, I understand how you'd be wanting to protect the sea elf, seeing how he's a friend of yours."

Ibn was suddenly grimly sober. "No friend of mine. My duty's to the ship, and the men on her."

"And Xzorsh knows your ship," Brindlor concluded meaningfully.

The captain studied him with eyes that were suddenly clear and shrewd. "You seem mighty helpful, even for a man's got a half keg of ale in him. You got a stake in this?"

"I'd like to." He leaned forward confidingly. "I'm looking for a ship to take a cargo to the north Moonshaes. Good money in it for both of us, long as the ship makes port with no questions asked. Might be smart to cut down on the risks where we can, if'n you follow my meaning."

Ibn tossed back the rest of his ale and crossed his arms. "As long as you're buying, I'm listening."

The bells of the Temple of Ilmater sounded the second hour past midnight, releasing the penitents from their painful devotions. They staggered out into the night, indistinguishable from those who made their unsteady way home from one of the many dockside taverns. The soft clanging drifted across the Waterdeep docks and rolled out to sea, where they mingled with the whisper of unseen waves.

Ibn strolled across the dock, hands linked behind him in a studiously casual pose. He nodded to the guard, an elderly sailor nearly as taciturn as himself. Stopping a few paces away, he turned toward the sea and pulled out his pipe.

"Smoke?" he offered, holding out a small packet of the fragrant weed.

The guard accepted it, packed and lit his own pipe. The two men puffed in companionable silence and watched the moon sink toward the sea.

"Had enough of the city," Ibn commented. "A man needs to have the sea close to hand."

"Yep," the guard agreed.

"Can't sleep in them stinking inns, those flat beds. You're a man of the sea. Bet you still sleep in a hammock."

"Yep."

"Mine's on yonder ship, and that's where I'd like to settle for the night. Bends the laws a mite, that I know. Reckon it'll cost me some."

The guard held out his empty pipe to indicate the desired currency. Ibn reached into his jacket and pulled out several small packs of pipe weed. The old man studied them for a moment, then held up three fingers.

"Fair price for a night's sleep," Ibn agreed. The goods changed hands and the pirate paced quietly toward his ship.

He made his way down to the galley, and shouldered open the portal set above the water line. A wooden chest stood just below the portal. Ibn opened it and took out a hurdy gurdy, a peculiar instrument that looked like a lute but was played by turning a crank to vibrate the strings and pressing keys to produce a tune. He thrust it into the water and began to grind out a few measures of "Lolinda, She's a Lusty Lass," a tune accompanied by strange clicks and squeaks that had no meaning Ibn could follow.

It had been Hrolf's idea to use tunes and musical rhythms as signals. The boisterous pirate had had a fondness for a well-sung tale. His own singing, however, had inflicted nearly as much pain as his sword. A rare smile came to Ibn as he remembered.

Then the surface of the water stirred, and a too-familiar face popped up beside him. Ibn tossed aside the hurdy gurdy and reached for his pipe.

Xzorsh regarded the human with astonishment. Never before had Ibn used the summoning song, never had he sought audience with one of the Sea People. He hid his puzzlement as best he could and waited politely for the captain to speak his mind.

Ibn sent a smoke ring drifting toward the open portal. "I've come about the drow wench," he said at last.

The sea elf nodded and waited for the sailor to continue. Ibn seemed edgy, uneasy. Xzorsh put this down to the man's dislike of elves and his reticence to pass along a favor.

"Here," Ibn said at last, thrusting a silver medallion into Xzorsh's webbed hands. "It's about the teacher. This will take you where you need to go. Don't ask me no more questions," he concluded in querulous tones. "What I said is what I know."

The sea elf thanked him and slipped the medallion around his neck.

Immediately the familiar chill of the sea vanished, to be replaced by stone walls and too-dry air. Water puddled on the floor, but it felt thin and somehow unhealthy. Curious, Xzorsh stooped and dipped his fingers into the shallow pool. He tasted it, and his eyes widened with delighted understanding.

"Fresh water!" he exclaimed, marveling that such a thing truly existed.

"Hardly," said an amused, musical voice behind him.

Xzorsh rose swiftly to his feet and turned to face two drow males.

His first instinct was fear, and his hand flew to his weapon belt. He caught himself before drawing steel, and silently chided himself for his reflexive, narrow-minded response. Of course these were the teachers Liriel had promised him. He had not expected drow, but what other wizards was she likely to know?

The two males watched him come, and their flat, cold eyes reminded him of a shark's gaze. Xzorsh's smile faltered, and he came to a stop a few paces away.

"The gems," one of them said.

Xzorsh produced the little mesh bag given him as surety and handed it over. "These belong to Liriel. Since you know of them, I assume she offered them to pay for my tutelage. Although that's kind of her, I would prefer to pay my own way. Will you return these gems to her, and accept my word that an equal value in coin and gems will replace it at first opportunity?"

The short-haired drow responded with a thin smile. "She will get what's coming to her. I can promise you that."

There was no mistaking the drow's meaning. Or, now that Xzorsh considered it, his character. Evil rose from the drow like ink from a squid, filling the too-thin air with an almost tangible miasma.

Too late Xzorsh realized that a terrible mistake had been made. He saw the knife in the drow's black hand, noted the deft toss, the spinning approach. The thud of impact felt more like a fist than anything else. He stared at the hilt buried between his ribs.

His fading eyes sought the drow's faces. "It's true, what they say of you."

"That, and more," hissed the short-haired drow. He closed the distance between them, seized the hilt and began to twist.

The second drow stepped forward and caught his comrade's hand. He looked into Xzorsh's face, and it seemed to the sea elf that his faint smile held sympathy, possibly even warmth.

"I imagine you've heard some unpleasant things about *her*, as well," he said in a beautiful, musical voice.

Xzorsh nodded, and waited for this kind drow to dispel these slanders, to remove the undeserved mantle of evil from Liriel's shoulders.

Brindlor smiled gently into the dying elf's face. "Those terrible things you heard? They're completely true."

The deathsinger watched with pleasure as the sea elf's eyes filled with despair, and then emptied of everything. He looked to Gorlist and winked.

"There is more way than one," he announced, "to twist a knife."

Sharlarra swung herself down from her "borrowed" horse and took the reins in hand. She knew this forest well enough to trust her own footing better than she did the horse's.

She followed the river while the moon rose above the forest, casting flirtatious glances through its leafy veils. The savory smell of roasting rabbit led her to the campsite, which had been set at some distance from the spring.

Liriel was seated by the campfire, studying a small book by the dancing flames. She glanced up at the elf's approach. A sudden dark flame flared in her eyes, quickly extinguished. Sharlarra understood. She'd felt much the same about drow until she'd met Qilué's bunch.

"Where's your friend?" Sharlarra asked as she strode into the circle of firelight.

"Hunting. Scouting. Setting up camp." The drow shrugged, dismissing mysteries about which she knew little.

Sharlarra took the book from her and glanced at the intricate markings. She quickly handed it back, knowing better than to gaze too long upon the magical runes. "Not a familiar spell."

"I should think not! It's drow."

"The script looks a bit like the magical calligraphy used in Thay," she observed.

A shadow crossed Liriel's face, quickly dismissed. "Tell me about the Red Wizards."

"Well, they're bald . . . "

The drow cast her eyes skyward. "Not much of a story-teller, are you?"

"Something tells me you've got a story of your own," Sharlarra stated.

After a moment's silence, the drow nodded. She began to speak of her first encounter with a human wizard. He had been a captured slave, a quarry she was meant to track through the tunnels of the Underdark and slay with steel or spell. In the end, her mentor was actually the one to fight and slay the human. Liriel ended the tale with an insouciant shrug, as if none of it mattered. Sharlarra got the distinct impression that she left out far more of the tale than she told.

"It's a rite of passage," Liriel concluded. "Do you have these in Waterdeep?"

"In a manner of speaking. Young men of Waterdeep go about in groups of three and four to frequent fest houses, get roaringly drunk, and piss into public fountains. I'd have to say that your ritual is, on the whole, far more dignified."

Liriel's lips quirked in appreciation for the dark irony, but her gaze remained steady. "That's not what I meant. What of you faerie elves? How do you mark the passage from childhood?"

The elf averted her eyes. "Couldn't tell you. Each clan or settlement has its own customs."

"But surely—"

"A band of Thayan slavers caught me when I was a child. I was dragged down to Skullport and sold." She gave a quick shrug. "Hard to leave a childhood you never had."

They sat in silence for a moment. "And now you're a wizard," said Liriel.

"I know a few spells, but it's not my first profession." By way of explanation, Sharlarra held up one of Liriel's throwing spiders.

The drow's eyes rounded with astonishment, then narrowed in menace. The moment quickly passed, and she threw back her head and laughed delightedly. "Well done! I'd like to learn that trick."

Sharlarra took a silver flagon from her bag and passed it to the drow. She took an experimental sip, and her amber eyes widened with surprise and pleasure.

"That's *qilovestualt!* How did you get hold of a drow wine?"

The elf spread her hands in modest disclaimer. "You can get anything in Waterdeep, provided you've got deep pockets, light fingers, or disreputable acquaintances. No—keep it," she said when Liriel tried to hand it back.

Instantly the drow's eyes turned wary. Few people, whether they lived beneath the sky or under fathoms of stone, gave something for nothing. Sharlarra smiled a little, understanding the path her thoughts had taken. "Tell me about the drow, and we'll consider the debt paid."

Liriel lifted one snow-colored brow. "What do you want to know?"

"Anything. Everything!"

A small smile curved the drow's lips. She handed Sharlarra the flask and motioned for her to take a sip. At a precisely timed moment, she said, "Well, to begin with, that wine is made from fermented mushrooms."

The elf gave a startled cough, a reflex that sent the potent beverage searing down her throat and spurting from her nose. After a few moments spent coughing and sputtering, she wiped her streaming eyes and gave Liriel a rueful smile.

"Drow humor?"

"A very tame example of it," Liriel agreed with a grin. "There aren't many ways to have fun in Menzoberranzan. Playing tricks is one of them—the more malicious, the better."

"Things tend toward chaos, do they?"

"Of course! How else would the structure be maintained?"

The elf's brow furrowed. "You maintain structure through chaos?"

"There's another way?"

She chuckled at Liriel's genuine puzzlement. "Tell me how that works."

"On the surface, it's very simple. Everyone and everything has a rank. First comes the Houses—you would probably call them families, or clans. They are ranked according to strength, with the matrons of the most powerful houses ruling on the Council of Eight. Within each House is a constant battle for rank and position. It's the same in the schools, the arenas, the guilds, the markets, even the festhalls."

"I think I'm beginning to understand," Sharlarra said. "There's constant competition within a rather rigid structure. That would account for the fine drow weapons and the fabled power of your magic."

"In part," Liriel agreed, "but bear in mind that there are two ways for a sword smith to rise in rank. One, he can work very hard and improve his craft. Two, he can simply kill the better smith." She smiled again, but this time the smile didn't reach her eyes. "That technique also requires good weapons and powerful magic."

"Good point," the elf said. "Don't take offense, but from what I've heard of the Underdark drow, it's safe to assume that the second method is the one most preferred."

Liriel's smile disappeared completely, and her amber eyes turned grave. "Where drow are concerned, it's never safe to assume anything."

"I'll keep that in mind."

They passed the flask of drow liquor back and forth a few times. Fyodor joined them, took the offered flask, and tossed back a swallow of the bitter brew without a grimace or flinch.

"How do you know anything about the Underdark drow?" Liriel wanted to know.

Sharlarra waved aside Fyodor's offer of his own flask. She had very unpleasant memories of a morning after her first flirtation with the potent Rashemaar *jhuild*.

"A wizard from the Harkle clan—eccentric bunch, even as human wizards go—conducted a lengthy interview with a wandering drow from your home city. Harkle wrote a treatise, which has been circulated among city leaders and leading wizards."

Liriel smirked. "Which of these things are you?"

"Both, and more besides," Sharlarra returned with mock gravity.

They shared laughter and passed the flask again. "I've had occasion to speak with Qilué. She told me a few things about the drow."

"How do you know her?"

"Through her sister Laerel Silverhand, the lady—and possibly the sole redeeming virtue—of my former master, the archmage of Waterdeep."

Liriel considered this for a moment. Her gaze shifted to Fyodor, and an expression of hope and contentment lit her remarkable eyes. Sharlarra wondered briefly what message the drow had heard in these words. With a pang of regret, she realized that she lacked the time to find out.

The elf rose to her feet and brushed off her clothes. "If you like, I can summon a gate that will take you to the High Forest and cut days from your travel."

An expression of alarm crossed Liriel's face. She told Sharlarra what had transpired in Skullport. As she listened, the elf pondered the possible ramifications of her involvement in the plight of these two fugitives. But where would she be if Laerel hadn't stood with her when she was ass-deep in sewer snakes? It was time to make good on the promise she'd made to herself that day: to stand for someone who needed her help as much as she had needed Laeral's.

Sharlarra shrugged off Liriel's warnings. "I'm not afraid of Lolth."

The drow's eyes flamed. "Then you're a fool!"

"I've heard that," she said mildly, "but at least I'm a fool who knows some useful spells."

Liriel pursed her lips, considered. "Perhaps you can help me with this."

She unrolled a tapestry and explained what it was.

Sharlarra was doubtful but she gave it a try. Several failed spells later, a simplified legend lore spell yielded one important bit of information.

She shook his head. "This is elf magic. Ironically, it's the one school of magic I know nothing about."

"Faerie elves," Liriel said, speaking the words like a curse.

"Never heard of them," Sharlarra said easily. "We've got moon elves—they're usually ready for a good time—gold elves, about whom the less said the better, forest elves and wild elves—the lines there tend to blur a bit—and sea elves. Legend has it that there once were elves known as avariel, winged elves. There might still be some, for all I know. We've even got lythari, elves who can transform into wolves. But faerie elves?"

"That's what we call all elves who are not drow."

"Well, maybe it's time to learn some new insults," she suggested. "You want to get a moon elf's blood boiling, call him a gray elf. To really flick off a gold elf, call him a moon elf."

Liriel took this in. "There really is that much division among the elf races?"

"Stupid, isn't it?"

The drow was quick. Sharlarra saw the flash in her eyes as she caught the point, the thoughtful gleam as she considered it.

"Elf art and magic has been around for a very long time," the thief continued. "I heard that you saw the ruins of Ascarle. The elves who built it were overcome centuries ago, and the magic that lingered was altered to fit a darker purpose. It is much the same in Myth Drannor. The ancient mythal still exists, and there are many who seek ways to twist it."

"My people among them," Liriel added. Sharlarra saw the drow's quick, rueful smile, and knew that this bit of information had clicked into place. Reluctantly, she rose to leave, and with a start she realized that she really didn't part ways with the drow. Already there seemed to be a bond between them, an easy sisterhood that was compelling as it was unexpected.

"There's a hunter after you," she said bluntly. "A tall elf woman who calls herself Thorn. She's a champion of Eilistraee, which means she's got some magic to back up her weapons. Watch yourself."

"I will walk with you for a while," Fyodor offered.

Sharlarra untied her horse and led it back toward the spring. They paused in the clearing. The Rashemi threw back his head and drew in a long, slow breath.

"There is winter in the air," he commented. "Already the leaves turn to scarlet and gold. In a ten-day, many will fall."

The thief nodded. She remembered enough of woodcraft to realize the difficulty of passing unseen through a denuded woods. The roads would be crowded with caravans carrying goods to far-flung cities and villages, in preparation for the late harvest markets and the long winter that followed.

For reasons she found it impossible to name, the thought of Rashemen stirred something inside her. Almost irresistibly, she found her eyes drawn east. She looked at the Rashemi thoughtfully.

"My offer to open the gate to the High Forest still stands."

"It is a risk," Fyodor acknowledged.

"What isn't when you're traveling with a drow?"

The Rashemi grimaced and nodded. "You understand perfectly. I wished to have private words with you for another reason. This elf you described, this Thorn. She is a Moon Hunter, and it is not Liriel she follows. The witches of Rashemen sent her after me. If I fall in battle, she will see me home."

Sharlarra nodded thoughtfully. "My people feel strongly about resting amid the roots of their homeland's trees. Thanks for telling me."

"Who are your people?"

The question, though reasonable, set Sharlarra back on her heels. "Oh you know. *The People*. Elves," she said lightly.

Fyodor merely smiled. "My offer stands, as well. Come to Rashemen, listen to legends of elf maidens with amethyst eyes."

Her own gem-like eyes grew thoughtful, but she offered no response.

He watched as the elf sped through the complicated gestures of a spell. An oval of liquid magic appeared. Fyodor noted that the trees beyond were faintly visible through it. It was a marvel to him that they could walk through this veil and emerge far away.

This thought brought another to mind. "The horses?"

Sharlarra shook her head regretfully. "Two people, no more. It's the best I can do."

"No matter. We would have to lead the horses through most of the forest anyway. Would you return them to their owners, with my thanks?"

"How do you know they're not mine?"

The Rashemi merely lifted one brow. The elf grinned and swung herself into the saddle. She cantered off, the other two horses close behind.

Fyodor squared his shoulders in preparation for battle and returned to camp. To his surprise, Liriel offered no argument. She swiftly gathered up her things and followed him to the clearing.

They stepped through the iridescent gate—and into an encampment of drow females.

The dark elves reacted like birds startled into flight. Those who appeared to be asleep were on their feet in a heartbeat, weapons in hand. Dancers clad in gowns the color of moonlight dived for their swords. A tight circle formed around the two companions, and beyond that, another.

For a long moment the drow females sized up their captives. *"Que'irrerar stafir la temon?"* inquired one of them.

The language was similar to the drow language Liriel had spoken since birth, but the intonation was different—softer, more fluid, with gentle trills rather than hard, clicking sounds. Judging from their garb, Liriel guessed they were priestesses of the Dark Maiden. She shook her head to indicate that she did not understand and took off the medallion Qilué had given her.

One of the drow, a tall female clad in a filmy gown, strode forward and seized the medallion.

"Whom did you kill in order to get this talisman?" she demanded, speaking in Common.

Liriel bristled at the accusation. "No one," she snarled. "Now ask me whom I'm willing to kill in order to keep it."

The leader swept a glance across her ranks. All but one stepped back. The one who lingered handed the drow a sword.

Fyodor started forward. His progress was halted by a dozen silver blades—and a burst of magic that froze him as surely as a white dragon's breath. Apparently the leader intended to take Liriel's comment as a challenge and would brook no interference or distraction. He watched helplessly as his friend drew her sword and fell into guard position.

"Dolor," the female snapped, naming herself according to the drow custom.

"Liriel."

A strange expression crossed the priestess's face, and her sword lowered just a bit. Sensing an advantage she did not quite understand, Liriel lunged.

The female spun away, light as thistledown, and responded with a lightning-quick riposte. Liriel leaped above the blade, employing her levitation ability to gain height.

A murmur of surprise rippled through the company, quickly taking on angry overtones. Fyodor's heart sank. This simple act, so natural to Liriel, had indelibly marked her as a drow of the Underdark. Few drow could bring their innate magic to the surface, much less retain it for any length of time.

The priestess was not to be outdone. She pointed her sword toward Liriel and flung her free hand toward the moon. A thin stream of light filtered through the trees in a sharply slanting stream and fell upon the drow's bare feet. She slid up the moonbeam toward Liriel, sword leading.

Liriel released her levitation spell, dropping out of range. Her opponent also leaped to the ground and landed in a crouch. She tamped down like a cat and hurled herself at the smaller drow. Liriel fell flat, rolled away. In a quick fluid motion she rose and leaped forward into a deep lunge. The other drow parried.

The moon rose high, and the silent stars watched as the deadly dance continued. Liriel fought as best she could, but the other drow was taller, stronger, more skilled. Some instinct Fyodor did not understand prompted the drow female to keep the pace fast and furious—too fast for Liriel to draw one of her many throwing weapons. Forced to react, she could never make the battle her own.

The numbness in Fyodor's hand gave way to a painful prickling. With effort, he managed to edge it slightly toward his sword. The drow females encircling him leaned in, and the tips of a dozen swords pierced the skin of his neck.

"If you move again, you die," snarled one of the drow.

The threat caught Liriel's ear. She snapped her gaze back toward him, her eyes wide with anguish and denial.

That moment of inattention was all the priestess needed. She lunged, her sword scraping along Liriel's until the hilts met and tangled.

Liriel went for a knife. The other drow seized her wrist. A quick twist disarmed Liriel and sent her weapon flying. A second twist brought her to her knees. Dolor laid the edge of her sword against the vanquished drow's throat.

A throaty growl pierced the expectant hush, and a tall, black-haired elf woman appeared in the clearing. She took in the situation in a glance then threw herself at Liriel's captor.

They rolled together. Liriel scuttled away away from battle and toward her discarded sword. The pale-skinned elf quickly overcame Eilistraee's priestess, though it seemed to Fyodor that the drow didn't put up much of a resistance.

Liriel snatched up her sword and crouched in guard position. "You and me, Thorn," she said, beckoning the elf on with one hand.

The elf woman sniffed and turned back to the priestess. "I can appreciate your concern, Dolor, but this drow is under my watch."

"Your protection?" the priestess said in disbelief.

"My watch," the elf repeated firmly. "If she needs killing—and I'm not convinced that she doesn't—the task falls to me."

CHAPTER EIGHT

UNPLEASANT TRUTHS,
DANGEROUS LIES

Shakti made her way back to House Hunzrin openly
and in triumph. She had been honored by Matron
Triel Baenre. No matter what Gromph Baenre
heard, he would not dare move against her.

Not yet, at least.

A lone priestess paced the courtyard of the Hunzrin compound, glancing toward the gate every few
steps. Shakti recognized her mother and smiled.

The guards at the gate did not immediately rec-
ognize her. She showed them her house insignia
and gave them a pop-eyed glare. They made the
connection and ushered her through.

She approached her mother and dropped to one
knee. "Matron Kintuere," she said formally.

The older drow studied her with narrowed
eyes. "What is the meaning of this long absence?
You left the academy—the city!—without my permission. Now I must learn of your return through
rumors and servants' gossip?"

Shakti rose, also without her mother's permission. "I was removed from the academy by Triel Baenre and sent on a secret mission."

Kintuere sneered. "Aren't we grand. What was the nature of this mystery? Purchasing rothé studs to improve the herd? Seeking out a new variety of mushroom?"

"Quenthel Baenre was restored to life. That is all I can tell you," Shakti said calmly.

Matron's eyes widened then flicked to the snake head whip on Shakti's belt. A tiny movement, but telling. She understood that her daughter and heir was more powerful than she, and in this knowledge she saw her own death.

That was the way of the drow, and for a moment Shakti was tempted to claim her inheritance here and now.

"I am not yet ready to take on the mantle of matron," she told the older female. "I have other tasks to attend. Rule well, mother, and you will rule long."

She strode off without waiting for dismissal and made her way to her old suite of rooms. The servants and guards nodded to her as she passed with greater deference than she had ever been shown. Perhaps the news of her audience with Triel had spread. Perhaps they had merely observed the shift of power that had occurred in the courtyard and adjusted their behavior accordingly.

After bathing and dressing herself in fresh robes, Shakti dismissed her slaves and slid a page of parchment from its hiding place—a slim crack between two dressed stones. This was a page she had taken from one of Liriel's lore books quite some time ago.

She made her way to Narbondel, the heat-filled pillar that marked the passage of time, and awaited the coming of midnight and the arrival of Menzoberranzan's archmage.

Gromph Baenre appeared suddenly at the base of pillar, splendid in his glittering *piwafwi* and fine robes. Shakti watched the enchanting of the magic timepiece, the dramatic chants and gestures that kindled the rising heat anew.

Always before she had seen only the ceremony and the power. Now she understood this ritual for what it was: a short chain that tethered the archmage to the city.

Gromph Baenre finished the casting and spun away. Taking a terrible risk, she wrapped herself in her *piwafwi* and fell into step with him.

I know you're there, announced a mellifluous male voice, speaking directly to her mind. *Why don't you say what you came to say and have done with it?*

"My lord—"

SILENTLY! thundered Gromph's voice. *Think the words you would say. I will hear them plainly enough.*

Shakti nodded, having no doubt that the great archmage perceived the gesture. *Liriel is dead. The amulet she carried is being returned to Rashemen's witches.*

No emotion crossed Gromph's face, not even a reaction to the loss of his talented daughter.

You wished me to return her to you, for her wizardly powers would be valuable. I was unable to do so, but I offer myself in her place.

A faint, sardonic chuckle shimmering through Shakti's mind. *You have become a wizard?*

I am what I ever was, my lord Gromph. A priestess of Lolth.

There is no shortage of priestesses in Menzoberranzan, he observed.

True enough, but how many of them listen in counsel and report to you what they know?

Gromph scowled in her direction. A kobold slave intercepted the glare, assumed itself to be the intended recipient, and gave a squeak of alarm. The wizard made a casual gesture toward the fleeing slave, and the kobold's tunic burst into flame. Shrieking wildly, the wretched creature tore off the treacherous garment and threw it to the ground, stamping out the flames with its bare feet and whimpering with each stomp. The two drow continued without breaking stride.

What you suggest is impossible. Absurd! Triel would rip thoughts of treachery from your mind before they were half-formed.

Indeed she would, if my only shields were those granted me by Lolth, but the mask of Vhaerun is difficult to perceive.

A shuttered expression fell over the archmage's face. *I have no idea what you're talking about.*

Do you wish to find out?

The only response was a profound mental silence. Shakti allowed herself a furtive smile and matched the archmage's mental shields with one of her own.

After a few moments, Gromph shot her a fulminating glare. *Continue, but know that your words will destroy you long before they harm me.*

If you wish to know my thoughts, take them from me.

Gromph turned a look of pure incredulity upon the impudent female. Rage burned in his amber eyes, but the flame faded as her meaning became clear to him.

You can keep me from your mind. Me! he marveled.

Shakti dipped her head. *Through the god's grace, I can. Do you know what I want most from this new power?*

A sour expression crossed the archmage's face. *The usual, I suppose—the early death of your matron mother and a smooth succession, the advancement of your house, a seat on the Council of Eight, the dark pleasures of power.*

"I want to survive," Shakti said, speaking softly but distinctly. "I want to wield power, yes, but I know this city, and I know what I am likely to achieve. I do not want to be driven mad by the limits on the power available to me. Who knows this skill better than you?"

Gromph turned slowly, looking her full in the face. He did not chide her for speaking aloud or for the presumption inherent in her words. For the first time, a flicker of interest lit his amber eyes. After a moment he turned aside.

There is more, she added hastily, reverting to silent speech. *I have followed Liriel's path, and know where the amulet is bound. Therein lies my value to you. If you had interest in Vhaerun, you could seek out others who follow the masked god. If you had need of ears and a voice among the counsel, you could surely find a more powerful priestess to do your bidding, but I alone can promise you the return of the Windwalker.*

He glanced at her. *Promises are easily made. Have you forgotten that Triel also seeks this artifact?*

No longer. I told her that Liriel still lives and that it is the will of Lolth that she stay in the Night Above and continue to wield the artifact to Lolth's glory.

Gromph chuckled softly. *Did my sister believe this?*

A soft and pleasing lie is more readily distrusted. Tell tales that people do not wish to hear, and they are more likely to believe.

The archmage sent her a considering look. *Devious*, he admitted, *but surely that alone did not convince Triel.*

Shakti dipped her head in another bow. *As you say, my lord. Lolth gave powerful evidence of her favor to House Baenre by returning Quenthel to life and to Triel's side.*

Quenthel. Alive, you say?

Yes, Lord Gromph.

There was a long silence as Gromph considered the possibilities inherent in this new shift of power. *That should please Triel*, he said at last.

Who can say? Shakti commented. *I have done what the*

yochlol bid me, except for one thing. By the command of Lolth, I must find a way to repay you for Liriel's loss.

Yochlol. The command of Lolth. These were powerful words, and they hung heavy in a silence that lasted for many steps.

Go to Narbondel, Gromph said at last. *Seek out the trio of flayed illithids engraved on the obelisk. Touch the head of the illithid in the middle three times. After the third touch, a small pebble will emerge from the stone and into your left slipper. Do not take it out. When I wish to speak to you again, you will know. Go to a private place and take the stone into your left hand.*

With those words, the archmage disappeared. However, he did not stop watching. He noted the smile of satisfaction on the priestess's face and her confident stride as she turned back to the pillar.

He watched her search for the flayed illithids among the intricate carvings, run her fingers across it. She shifted her weight to her right foot, indicating that the pebble had found its way into her slipper.

With a thought, Gromph sent out his "message."

A jolt of power coursed through the priestess, startling a yelp of pain from her and sending strands of white hair dancing wildly about her face. She quickly smoothed her hair and strode away, keeping an admirably level pace despite the pain in her foot.

Gromph followed her toward the lake. Several small boats were tied to a dock, ready to ferry workers to and from the island where the rothé cattle grazed. He remembered that the care of these animals, the production of meat and cheese and wool, was under Hunzrin direction. With a grimace, he quickened his pace, intending to intercept the priestess before she could set off for that dreary place.

He seized her arm and forced her into step with him. In

two paces, they stood in his private study.

Shakti tried not to look disconcerted at finding herself so abruptly transported. She carefully edged away. "An honor, one I had not thought would come so soon."

"Call it a test, if you will. I take it my summons was clear?"

"Pelucid, my lord."

"It's well that something is," he grumbled. "Your story was entertaining after a fashion, but your argument defies logic and reason. Matron Triel believes that Liriel is alive, and that it is Lolth's will that her niece continues on the surface in possession of the Windwalker amulet. What do you suppose my dear sister's reaction might be, if I have—and use—this artifact?"

"The goddess is capricious," Shakti said without hesitation. "She favors the devious and the bold. If you have the Windwalker amulet, would it not seem obvious that Lolth's favor has shifted away from Liriel?"

"So many will say," Gromph admitted. "All things that happen under this stone sky are attributed to the will of Lolth. Very well, bring me the Windwalker if you can. I will put a mercenary band under your control."

"Better to have them meet me beyond the city," she suggested. She took a tube from her flowing sleeve and shook out a large map, which she unrolled on the table. "Here are the tunnels under the land of Rashemen," she said, pointing. "This is the homeland of Liriel's human lover. After her death, he claimed the Windwalker. He will return it to the witches who rule there."

"A human?" Gromph repeated with distaste. "Is this true, or is it another of those unpleasant lies that you think can masquerade as truth?"

Shakti's eyes showed a flicker of panic. "Does it matter, as long as the Windwalker is yours?"

Gromph shrugged. "Not really. I will dispatch the fighters at once." He dismissed her with a curt flick of one hand then added, "One more thing."

She turned back. He handed her a tiny crystal vial. "When the time is right, this will speed your mother's demise. Matron Kinuere does not sit on the Council of Eight. Prove yourself as matron mother, and your family's fortunes may swiftly improve. Now go, and serve yourself and me."

The priestess responded with a brilliant smile. Gromph noted, to his great surprise, that she had become attractive. Not beautiful, as Sosdrielle Vandree had been, but few drow could match Liriel's mother for beauty, not even her daughter.

He felt a rare twinge of regret, an emotion quickly banished. He had not thought of his long-time mistress for many years.

Shakti waited politely. Gromph realized that he was staring. "Why do you delay?" he snapped. "You have been dismissed."

The priestess bowed. With a gesture, she conjured a curtained gate. Five skeletal snakes rose from the folds of her robe and ceremoniously peeled the drapes aside. She walked through. The curtains fell then disappeared.

It was an impressive exit, Gromph had to give her that. Not incidentally, it was a reminder that Lolth's favor was with her. In many ways, Gromph was far more powerful, but as the priestess had just demonstrated, true power in Menzoberranzan ultimately came through the goddess.

Perhaps this human artifact, this Windwalker, might offer options he had not previously considered.

CHAPTER NINE

FIGHTING DROW

In a small clearing in the High Forest, the dark elven priestesses of the Wildwinds Coven gathered around the embers of their fire, listening with grim fascination to Thorn's terse recitation of Liriel's recent past. From time to time their red-eyed glances licked like twin flames toward the place where the puzzling young drow and her companion stood, just beyond the range of hearing and under heavy guard.

When the tale was finished, Dolor, the priestess who had challenged Liriel to battle, rose to speak.

"This girl is a danger to us all and to those we serve," she said. Drawing her lips into a firm, straight line, she resumed her seat, clearly signifying that all that needed to be said had been spoken. Her eyes dared the elf woman to challenge her assessment.

Thorn returned the drow's glare calmly. "You are high priestess here. It is your decision whether to help these two or not, but they *will* pass through the forest."

Several of the priestesses shot glares at the elf, but no one challenged her decree. The Champion of Eilistraee was honored by all of the MoonShards. These, the scattered bands of the Dark Maiden's followers, were named for the celestial fragments that followed the moon through the night sky – small points of light scattered through the darkness, isolated yet united in their veneration of the Divine Huntress.

"As Lady Qilué learned to her sorrow, these travelers cannot be sent through moon magic," one of them pointed out, "and it's a long walk to Rashemen."

"Not through my people's lands," Thorn said.

The priestesses fell utterly silent. For several moments they stared, slack-faced, at the elf.

"You would do this?" marveled Dolor. "Why, when none of us—not even Ysolde, not even Qilué!—has been permitted to see your homeland?"

The elf rose. "Perhaps in time Liriel will tell you about it. She's more likely to do so, of course, if you work with me to ensure that she survives her journey."

One of the priestesses responded with a short burst of sardonic laughter. "So we are to fight for an Underdark noble, a priestess of Lolth. I suppose your people will be joining us?" she said in a catty tone.

"I will ask them."

The silence that greeted this response was even deeper and more profound than the last. Those who were charitable by nature had supposed the priestess's comment to be a rhetorical question. Those not inclined to call a spade an entrenching tool more properly recognized it as a bitchy little jab. No one had expected any response at all from the Champion and certainly not this one!

Thorn rose to her feet. "Sound the horns. Send word to Ysolde and the Whitewaters Coven that we three—the drow, the Rashemi, and the hunter—will walk beneath their trees tomorrow before the mornmist fades."

She strode toward the place where Liriel and the Rashemi awaited their sentence. The young drow impatiently shoved aside one of her guards aside. She took a single belligerent stride forward before her way was barred by a pair of crossed swords.

"Took long enough for you to decide whether or not I 'needed killing,'" Liriel growled, tossing Thorn's recent words back at her. She bared her teeth in a semblance of a smile. "If you think *that* was a chore, just wait until you try to *implement* the decision."

The elf woman's gaze skimmed over Liriel and settled on Fyodor's watchful face. "We three will be leaving now. I will take you as far as Lake Ashane."

"The borders of Rashemen," he observed in a wistful tone. He studied the tall elf for a long moment. "You fought for Liriel when I could not. For this, I thank you."

"A bit too much courtesy to give a gray elf," Liriel said, remembering Sharlarra's advice about insulting the faerie elves.

Fyodor looked appalled. "Little raven, this is a Moon Hunter!"

In response, the drow pointed skyward to the waning moon. "There it is. Now that I found it for her, can we go?"

The tall elf merely sniffed. "Where would you go? To Rashemen, yes, but do you know the way?"

Liriel looked expectantly at Fyodor. After a moment, he sighed and shook his head. "It pains me to admit this, but I could not mark our location on a map if you held a knife to my throat. Where are we now?" he asked Thorn. "How many days' travel to Rashemen?"

"On foot, you could not arrive before hard winter. Follow me, and you'll see your homeland tomorrow by day's end."

He considered this. "I know but little of magical travel, but are not gates like doorways? One passes the threshold and stands at once in some distant place. Yet you speak of a day's journey."

"Distant places," Thorn repeated. "It is said that Rashemi on *darjemma* are fearless travelers. This is so?"

Liriel, who had been listening in uncharacteristic silence, let out a short laugh. "He's traveling with me," she pointed out.

"Well said," Thorn told her coolly. She turned her attention back to the human. "We walk," she told him, "through the lands of my people."

Fyodor jolted with surprise. Thorn noted the sudden flare of understanding, the way his eyes widened with wonder. Apparently this one had paid close attention to the old Rashemaar tales. More important, he believed them.

"Exile or silence," she reminded him.

"Your secret and my honor," he vowed, holding up two entwined fingers.

Liriel propped her fists on her hips and wheeled toward her friend. "What in the nine bloody hells just happened here?"

Thorn swung a sudden, roundhouse punch toward Liriel's face. Startled, the drow nonetheless managed to throw up both arms, wrists crossed, to block the attack. The elf's blow drove right into the parry and slammed Liriel's joined hands into her face with stunning force. The girl's amber eyes rolled up, and she slumped to the ground.

In a single fluid movement Fyodor drew his sword and stepped between the elf and his fallen friend. "No one harms Liriel while I live," he said quietly.

The elf lifted one ebony brow. "If I wanted her dead, I would have permitted Dolor to finish the task."

"Then why?" he demanded, nodding toward the unconscious girl.

"You know what I am," Thorn said, "and therefore you should not need to ask. You are not like this drow with her talk of 'fairies' or 'gray elves.' You are Rashemi, and you have heard tales of the lands through which we must walk. My people's lands are in this world and yet not. I do not know for certain whether the eyes of a drow goddess can follow us there. I have seen Lolth gazing through Liriel's eyes. I will not take that risk."

The Rashemi accepted this development with a wince and a sigh. "Liriel will not sleep long. Even now she stirs," he pointed out.

The elf took a spring of dried herb from a bag at her belt. "This is from my homeland. The scent of it is very powerful and will hold her deep in slumber."

"You couldn't have mentioned this before?" Fyodor demanded.

"It will *hold* someone in slumber," she said pointedly. "The amount needed to *place* someone in a deep sleep is much greater and can be dangerous. Knowing this, would you have chosen the herb?"

A soft groan came from the wakening drow. Fyodor put away his sword. He stooped and gathered Liriel into his arms. He rose and met Thorn's gaze.

"It was not my choice to make," he said softly, "nor was it yours. You do not wish to invite the Goddess of Spiders into your people's lands. I understand what you did, but I do not like it. Next time we come to a crossroads, speak of the paths we might walk, and let Liriel chose the way she will go."

"Fair enough."

The elf twined the stem of the herb through the weave of Liriel's cloak, so that the dried herb rested against her cheek. Instantly she went limp in Fyodor's arms.

"It will not harm her," Thorn said testily, noting the flash of alarm in the Rashemi's eyes. "Nor will it cause you to be drowsy or forgetful. Keep your wits about you, and come."

She turned and strode into the forest. Fyodor followed with the drow girl in his arms and his blue eyes alight with excitement and anticipation. He would have to reckon with Liriel come tomorrow, but in his heart burned the Rashemi's restless eagerness to see and know.

All young people in his homeland, male and female, devoted a year or more to the wandering they called *darjemma*. None of them had been permitted to see the place to which Thorn promised to take them—or more accurately, of those few who had stumbled into Thorn's homeland, none had returned. Or perhaps some *did* return, without memory of the places they had been or the wonders they had witnessed. The herbs of the Moon Hunters were powerful indeed.

A sudden doubt assailed him. Despite Thorn's measures, what if Lolth's power extended into this distant place? He doubted that it could, but then, Qilué and her priestesses had been surprised by the Spider Queen's invasion. Was it true that where Liriel went, conscious or not, Lolth would follow?

If so, he was not likely to see Rashemen again. Thorn and her kind were fierce people. They would not forgive any who endangered their homeland.

For that matter, what of Fyodor's people? What was he bringing their way, and how would they respond?

Find the Windwalker, Zofia Othlor had told him. Bring her back. She will bind and break, heal and destroy.

Fyodor gazed down at the drow in his arms. For the first

time he fully understood why the witch had spoken of the amulet as "she." Somewhere along the way, his quest had changed. He would bring the ancient artifact back to Rashemen, but in some mysterious but important way it was no longer the Windwalker of legend. Liriel was.

Zofia's grandson knew this to be true through the Sight that was his heritage and his curse.

A sad smile touched his face. It was a blessing that Liriel, for all her power, could not know the destiny ahead.

A day passed, and twilight was drawing near as Sharlarra pulled up to a small cluster of stone-walled travel huts located a hard day's ride from Waterdeep. She swung down from her horse and grimaced in distaste at the latest collection of skulls displayed on the stone plinth outside the caretaker's hut, an expression she quickly replaced with a smile when a bandy-legged old man hurried out to greet her.

A few dull strands of once-red hair clung to caretaker's pate, and his teetering gait was reminiscent of a sailor pacing the deck of a storm-tossed ship. The sword resting on one still-powerful shoulder gleamed in the fading light, and the carefully displayed remains of would-be bandits and horse thieves gave grim testament to the old man's ability to hold this outpost.

The elf's host squinted at her for a moment. His rheumy blue eyes lit with pleasure.

"Well, if it isn't Lady Judith, come to call on her old swordmaster! Come in, girl, and it's heartily welcome you are."

It took Sharlarra a moment to tune her ears to the thick North Moonshae burr. Shaymius Sky had been swordmaster to the Thann family. He remembered Judith's red-gold hair, all his eyes could pick out from the blur that people had apparently become. As far as Shaymius was concerned, Lady Judith remembered her old tutor. The aging warrior took so much pleasure from these visits that Sharlarra hadn't the heart to rob him of his fond notion.

She remembered something Danilo had told her at Galinda Raventree's last soiree and said, "The Westgate caravan was to pass through this way. I trust all went well and that you received the box of new wines and harvest cakes?"

Shaymius patted his belly contentedly. "That I did. The mead was as smooth as an elfmaid's arse. Already there's a nip in the air come nightfall, and nothing's better to push back winter aches than a flagon of mead heated with spice bark. The horses come first, o' course, but you'll have a mug?"

"If the horses leave any for us, certainly."

"Don't be daft, Judy girl. Horses don't—" The old man broke off, caught the jest, and cast his eyes skyward. He unhooked a hoof pick from his belt and flipped it to the elf. "For that, you'll help putting these three fine stallions to bed. Concerning that, what are you needing with three horses? By the looks of them, you haven't been riding hard enough to require a change of mount."

Sharlarra lifted a front hoof and began to scrape away the bits of crushed acorn clinging to the shoe. "The mares out at Ethering Farms are in season." That was true, as far as it went, and Shaymius would draw his own conclusions.

The old man grunted in agreement and patted the glossy black flank of the horse Liriel had ridden from Waterdeep. "Aye, these are well-chosen sires. The Lady Cassandra still keeps the stud books, then?"

"It wouldn't surprise me in the least." The Thann matriarch controlled every other aspect of the family businesses, and from what Sharlarra had observed she attempted to do the same with each member of the family. Such was the force of Lady Cassandra's will that Sharlarra suspected every stallion on the outlying Thann farms would instinctively await her advice on this matter, stud book or not.

"Great lady, your mum," Shaymius said, eyeing Sharlarra as if daring her to contradict him. "Good eye for business."

"Posting you here was certainly a good day's work," the elf said, getting straight to the heart of the matter. "The horses left with you couldn't want better care, and not a single merchant who's slept under these roofs has offered a word of complaint."

The caretaker nodded, satisfied. Old though he was, his employers were content, and his post was secure. He set to work brushing down the black stallion, happily unaware of the real circumstances of his current position.

Sharlarra had heard the gossip, of course. That was one of the benefits of an apprenticeship in Blackstaff Tower. Ballads had been written about the exploits of young Shaymius Sky, and Lady Cassandra had gladly paid a high price to have the sheen of his ancient glories bestowed upon her firstborn son. For a time, she even overlooked her steward's regular morning-after trips to the Brawlers' Den, a chamber in the prisons of Waterdeep Palace devoted to those who grew bellicose in their cups. But the price of Shaymius's freedom, meted out after every tenday, soon came to overmatch his wages. That, and the crescendo of whispered rumor, ended the matter. No sordid little scandal dared touch the heir to the Thann title and estates.

It had been Danilo who'd persuaded the steward to buy Shaymius free one last time and to offer him this new employment. The old warrior, increasingly restless with city life and longing for adventures that would never come again, regarded this post not as banishment for brawling but as a reward for the skills he so routinely displayed. As far as Dan was concerned, Shaymius Sky deserved to believe this pleasant lie until the day he died.

Sharlarra couldn't have agreed more.

Once the horses had been tended and fed, the old man and the elf settled down by the caretaker's hearthside to chase tales and songs of faded glory with mugs of well-spiced mead. As much as Sharlarra enjoyed her occasional stolen moments with the old warrior, she was relieved when at last Shaymius's stories faded into silence. She sang one more ballad just to make sure and kept singing until the music was lost in the old man's grating snores.

She eased away from the hearth and crept out of the hut, making her way into the clearing behind the stables. She took from her bag a large, unset sapphire and the small vial of the Blackstaff's powdered magic she'd stolen from Danilo. She had one more task to complete before she slept, on behalf of one more misfit in search of a place in an oft-confusing world.

Back in Waterdeep was a sea elf awaiting help in his quest to become a mage. Though Sharlarra had not yet found a suitable teacher, she wanted to assure the elf that he was not forgotten—and while she was at it, reclaim the bag of gems she'd left with Xzorsh as surety. Since leaving Liriel and Fyodor, it had occurred to Sharlarra that if she and Khelben could trace the drow girl through possessions she had once held, it was likely that others could do the same. Xzorsh held a fortune in his webbed hands, but a dangerous one.

The young wizard's fingers sped through the arcane gestures, a difficult spell but nearly identical to one the Blackstaff had recently taught her. Sharlarra finished the spell and braced herself for the result. An invisible hand seized her and pulled her along a magical trail. For a moment, all the colors she had ever seen or imagined careened past like a rainbow gone mad.

She came to rest suddenly. Momentarily blinded by the brightness of the magical transport, she drew in a deep breath, fully expecting the tang of salt water and the complex stench of the Dock Ward. Instead, her senses filled with the coppery scent of fresh blood and the dank, dusty smell unique to places that had never known the sun. The sort of place that she knew far too well.

"*T'larra kilaj*," she murmured, speaking a simple elven cantrip Khelben had taught her, one from archmage's long-ago childhood. Her vision cleared at once.

She stood in a rock-strewn cavern, a rugged place dimly lit by the glowing lichen that clung to the stone walls, and she stared with dawning horror into the equally startled face of a drow warrior.

The drow, a male with close-clipped white hair and a dragon tattoo across one cheek, was crouched over the body of a large lizard, his knife poising in the act of cutting off strips of flesh. The creature was not yet dead. It did not move its stick-straight tail or rigid limbs, but its eyes rolled wildly.

A stray bit of information rose to the surface of Sharlarra's shock-becalmed mind. The Harple treatise claimed that drow preferred to devour living animals, believing that the mixture of pain and terror lent a certain piquancy to the meat.

The dark elf spat out a half-chewed morsel of raw meat and rose to his feet. A sword appeared in his hand so swiftly and smoothly that Sharlarra's eyes didn't perceive the act of drawing it.

The thief shook off the moment of shock and drew her own sword. She did so recognizing the futility of defense, even before she saw the shadows stir and shift. A circle of dark warriors broke free of the endless, underground night and began to tighten around her.

"*Zapitta doart!*" snapped the drow hunter. Instantly his cohorts' advance stopped. His red-eyed glare flicked to the sapphire still clutched in Sharlarra's hand.

"Are there more?" he demanded, lending the Common speech an accent that was at once harsh and musical.

The elf swiftly followed his line of reasoning. He wanted to know whether someone else might follow.

"More of these gems?" she said, and shrugged. "Three or four, I suppose. This is the only one in my possession, but there were several other uncut stones at the auction and a number of other wizards bidding."

"Give it to me."

Sharlarra's first instinct was to toss the gem to the drow, but she realized that such action could be perceived as an attack. It galled her that it would *not* be an attack and that she had no other spell prepared. She had stepped into a magical gate, one with a variable destination, without any defensive spell at the ready. It was a mistake no sensible first-year apprentice would make.

One of these days, she really had to start paying closer attention to detail. Demons hid in them, that she knew. Apparently drow did as well.

She stooped slowly, lowering the gem to the stone floor, holding her sword in guard position.

The drow closed the distance between them in a few swift, fluid steps. Before Sharlarra could respond, the dark elf dealt a brutal kick to the ribs that stole her breath and sent her sprawling.

"Lies," sneered the warrior as he stalked a circular path around his victim, "and clumsy lies, at that. Only one gem was missing. Do I think I would fail to learn exactly what price was paid to free the pirate's ship?"

It occurred to Sharlarra that the drow leader was speaking not to her so much as to the other elves. His words were a boast and perhaps also a defense. If there was discord in these ranks, perhaps stoking it might offer her a chance for escape.

She managed to suck in enough air to fuel speech. "Useful knowledge, provided you also know enough about gems to realize when a bit of colored glass had been substituted for a sapphire."

The expression of fury and hatred that crossed the drow's face chilled Sharlarra to the bone. She felt the effort it took the warrior to refrain from glancing at the other dark elves. If he had, he would have seen flashes of malicious pleasure in their crimson eyes and smirks on their dark faces. Even so, Sharlarra knew with cold certainly that she would pay dearly for the leader's embarrassment.

"Stand," the drow commanded.

She did so, ignoring the pain of bruised ribs as best she could. The drow came on, delivering a barrage of jabs and slashes that came faster than Sharlarra could block. When the drow stepped back, the elven thief was quite frankly stunned to realize that she was still on her feet.

"Your sword," the drow said, his eyes moving pointedly to the jeweled hilt.

Sharlarra glanced down. The gems had been pried from the hilt and pommel, leaving empty sockets. Her opponent opened one palm to show the small, glittering hoard—including the sapphire she had placed on the ground.

"Impressive," she said and meant it.

"To you, perhaps. I could remove your lungs and liver without leaving a scar."

The gleam in the drow's eyes revealed how eager he was to begin this new project, but as he spoke, he shifted his forearm slightly, a subtle movement that nonetheless drew the eye. Sharlarra noted the faint raised line that traced a path from elbow to wrist—a mark that the drow was obviously eager to keep from view.

"No scar?" she said, gazing pointedly at his arm. "Too bad your former opponent didn't have your skill."

Fury twisted the dark face, and Sharlarra knew she had struck the right chord. She would die—there was no help for that—but a least her fate would be swifter and kinder than that suffered by the half-slaughtered lizard.

The drow lunged and caught Sharlarra's now-unbalanced sword with his weapon's cross guard. A deft twist disarmed the elf, and another quick stroke slapped aside her attempt to pull a dagger. The drow leaped and spun, lashing out high and hard with his elbow, slamming into Sharlarra's face and following with a smash from his pommel.

There was a bright burst of pain, followed by the quick flow of blood. Sharlarra dashed it away as best she could, but her eyes stung and swam. Blinded, she was helpless to block or dodge the repeated blows from the flat of the dark elf's sword, the taunting, stinging cuts from its edge.

Dimly, as if from a great distance, the elf became aware of a great light dawning somewhere beyond the cavern. She felt herself falling and did not care.

A sense of peace came over her, an easing of pain that had little to do with the abuse meted out by a vengeful drow. Despite all she had done, all the mistakes she'd crammed into her life, a place of light awaited. Sharlarra had never dreamed that such a thing was possible.

So it was that when at last the darkness came, the elf went into it with a smile on her face.

Khelben Arunsun crouched in a deserted cavern a few leagues from Skullport, backlit by the fading remnants of his blinding light spell. He carefully split his attention between the battered elf female on the cavern floor and the silent tunnels beyond. The drow band had scattered like cockroaches before a suddenly lit lamp, but where dark elves were concerned, not even an archmage could afford a moment's incaution.

Sharlarra groaned and stirred. The wizard pinched her jaws open and poured another healing potion into her mouth, grimly vowing to make the apprentice work off the cost of all three of them. He mentally listed the most odious chores and invented a few more for good measure.

The elf's eyes flickered open and slowly took focus. For just a moment, their green depths held all the bleakness of a northland winter.

Khelben did not have to ask what that meant. There had been times when he, too, had been less than pleased to awake and find himself still among the living.

He banished these thoughts from his face and arranged his features in a fearsome scowl. "Stupid girl. What I have told you about fighting drow?"

Sharlarra struggled up, propping herself on one elbow and gingerly pressing the fingertips of her other hand against the large knot on her forehead.

"Don't?" she ventured.

"That, too." The wizard sighed and settled back on his heels. "*Lady* Sharlarra Vindreth—if that is indeed your name—have you any idea what you've done?"

"I thought I was helping two companions on their way."

"You didn't think at all! Liriel Baenre is not just any drow, although Mystra knows that would be bad enough. She opened herself to Lolth's power in a way few mortals ever have. She was, albeit briefly, an avatar of sorts. Some might call her a 'Chosen.'"

The returning color drained from the elf's face. "So

that explains what happened in the Promenade," she said slowly.

"Yes, we heard about that," Khelben grumbled. "Laerel has gone to Evermeet to try to recruit elven clerics to help shore up the Promenade's defenses. My lady has a fondness for the impossible challenge and the hopeless cause."

"True, but she's also attracted to your sunny disposition," she said, attempting a flippant tone and a wry little smile. Never before had she dared such a comment. Most likely she assumed her apprenticeship was well and truly over.

Khelben stared at her for a moment. "Aren't you going to ask about the sea elf?"

Her façade shattered, and her violet eyes were haunted. "No need," she said softly. "I looked for Xzorsh and found drow warriors instead. I'm not stupid enough to think that they might have thanked him for returning Liriel's gems and sent him on his way."

The archmage knew all too well the weight of this particular burden.

"Then nothing more needs to be said. You're done with this, and so am I. Others must follow Liriel to the end of her particular quest, and we must find a way to be content with whatever comes of it."

Khelben rose and traced a sweeping, circular path with his black staff. Several paces away a glowing arch appeared, mirroring the archmage's movement. When the circle was complete, the light spilled inward, filling in the darkness and forming a sheet of translucent magic. He turned back. "Are you coming, or not?"

Sharlarra rose slowly to her feet. "You want me back?"

"Not particularly, but Laerel does, and I find that my life is considerably more pleasant when she gets what she wants."

There was a glint of self-deprecating humor in his eyes and astonishing charm in the smile that thoughts of his lady inspired. Khelben was not unaware of this charm, and not above using it. He noted with satisfaction that Sharlarra stepped toward him before she realized that she'd decided to return.

Together they walked through the gate. Khelben noted the regret on the elf's face, regret that came with the acceptance that Liriel's fate was beyond her reach. Even so, he resolved to keep a closer eye on her in the future.

And in a distant forest, Liriel stirred in her sleep, troubled by one of the dreams that had begun filling her resting hours. In it, she wandered through a gray world, bereft of both the sun's warmth and the cool mystery of the Underdark—and she was utterly alone.

Half awake, half dreaming, she groped for Fyodor's bedroll and found it empty. For a moment her sense of isolation and abandonment was complete, then a strong hand closed around her seeking fingers. A warm presence filled her with reassurance and love.

She slept on, comforted.

Fyodor saw this from his perch in a tree a few paces away from the campsite where he kept the first watch. He noted the sudden restlessness that marred his friend's sleep and the soft smile that replaced her moment of turmoil. A shaft of moonlight touched the drow, lending cool blue highlights to her ebony features.

The Rashemaar warrior's eyes traced the soft light up into the forest canopy. He allowed himself a moment to envision the night sky of his homeland and to dream of the mysteries that awaited him beyond.

CHAPTER TEN

RUDE AWAKENINGS

Liriel stumbled down the tunnel's steep incline. For some reason that she could not understand, she was running backward. Her footsteps echoed throughout the tunnel like the pounding of a battle drum, reverberating endlessly through the thick gray mists. They marched on and on, unfading.

She kicked off her boots and continued barefoot, ignoring as best she could the knife-keen shards littering the stone floor, but she couldn't ignore her bloody footprints. The cold stone did not leech the living warmth from her blood. In fact the small prints steadily grew brighter, taking on a ruby glow that set the damp walls aglow and filled the misty tunnel with faint crimson haze.

The drow could smell the blood, too, as vividly as she saw it. The sweet-salty tang stirred some deeply primal part of her and beckoned like siren song to the predator within.

Liriel shook her head violently, trying to clear her senses and her mind, but another scent, a sharp woody fragrance as unfamiliar as it was powerful, hung over her like a cloud, holding the blood lure tantalizingly close. It would not leave her be.

The first footprint began to sing.

A tendril of crimson mist rose from the bloody print, and with it a clear soprano voice. Liriel recognized an invocation to Lolth, one sung each evening at the devotional services at Arach Tinilith. One after another, the bright footprints took up the song. An intricate counterpoint of chant and descant filled the tunnel, keeping time to the thudding echoes of Liriel's steps. The thin crimson mist-threads swirled and entwined in jagged, circuitous paths, forming a visual interpretation of the hymn—and sketching the leering visages and beckoning hands of demons and fiends, of monsters Liriel had never seen or heard named.

The drow thudded solidly into the stone wall. Horror filled her when she realized there was nowhere to go.

Suddenly a cold, sharp breeze slashed like a sword through the oppressive woodland scent. The red mists converged and streamed upward in a single swift rush. The tunnel itself dissolved, solid stone turning to haze then spinning off into thousands of thin, gray threads.

Liriel awoke gasping and flailing, still entangled in her nightmare. A few frantic moments passed before she realized that she was quite literally entangled. Thick layers of webbing covered her, binding her to the forest floor. A blood-red spider the size of a tunnel rat scurried just out of reach. It skittered around her, still spinning the binding webs and humming the hymn to Lolth.

A slim, booted foot came down, and the spider's song ended in a liquid explosion. Long-fingered hands thrust into the mess surrounding Liriel and seized hold of her.

She was dragged to her feet with a sharp tug and thrown violently aside.

For a moment the unmistakable whirl and tumble of a magical gate surrounded the drow. Before she could catch her breath, she was cast out onto leaf-strewn ground.

Liriel rolled to a stop, sat up, and raked some of the sticky strings from her face. Fyodor dropped to his knees beside her, and she dived into his open arms. They clung together until the wild beating of her heart slowed and the phantom sound of her own footsteps faded from her inner ear.

Finally she eased back and looked up into Thorn's grim face. The elf stood over them. Her hand rested on her sword as if she expected retaliation for her rough rescue, and her gold-green eyes regarded Liriel steadily and without expression.

"Thank you," the drow said fervently.

The elf made no response, turning instead to Fyodor. "That was a dangerous, foolish thing to do. That sprig of herbs was holding the drow in slumber. When you moved it off her, you allowed her to escape her dream."

"I should have left her alone and trapped?" he demanded.

"If that's what it took to keep Lolth's filthy fingers out of my homeland, yes!" the elf snarled. "Better to keep a dream inside Liriel's head than unleash it in the hidden homeland of my people!"

Liriel's swirling thoughts began to settle, and memory returned. She rose unsteadily to her feet and faced the elf. "You hit me. Why?"

"It was easier than arguing with you."

This response startled a deep bass chuckle from Fyodor, which earned him an incredulous glare from both females. He wiped the smile from his lips, if not his eyes, and gestured for them to continue.

"There is a shorter path to Rashemen, one no wizard can walk. I did not wish Lolth's eyes to behold that path. Where you go, she follows." The elf lifted one raven brow. "The dream that so disturbed you proved this, did it not?"

Liriel spun away and began to pace. "What does she want from me?" she said in despairing tones. "Why won't she leave me alone?"

Thorn's cool stare turned glacial. "Come and see."

She turned and strode into the forest. Liriel and Fyodor exchanged a puzzled glance, shrugged, and followed.

They came to a small clearing, a pleasant place near a deep, clear pool. Obviously it was a favorite watering place for the forest creatures. Well-worn game trails wound through the surrounding brush, tufts of fur clung to bent twigs. These details were swiftly noted and immediately forgotten, for at the far side of the clearing was a sight that struck the eye like a dwarven warhammer.

Two drow males had been tied to the trees so that their arms were held painfully high overhead. Each of them had one foot caught in a metal device that looked like a tightly clamped jaw with wicked teeth—a trap of some sort. They were dead and had been for quite some time, but judging from the deep wounds left by their struggle against the traps and ropes, they had not died quickly.

"Wolf traps," Thorn said coldly. "These drow are raiders, dwellers of the Underdark. They take joy in wanton killing. Elves, animals, humans—it matters not to them. They died the death they planned for others."

Liriel let out her breath in a long, slow whistle. "You don't take prisoners, do you?"

"At least I did not take their hides," Thorn pointed out. "Return to the matter at hand. These drow are not allied with Vhaerun's worshipers. Examine their insignia. They are of the Underdark."

"You said that before. Why is it important?" Fyodor asked.

"Cast a spell that reveals magic, and you will see."

The drow shrugged and cast the simple spell. Instantly an azure haze filled the clearing. Nearly everything owned by the dead drow glowed: boots, cloaks, weapons.

She looked up at Thorn. "These raiders have been dead for many days. All of this should have faded by now."

"It should have, yes."

Liriel shook her head in astonishment. "How is this possible? I haven't been away from the Underdark for very long. When I left, no one could fashion spells or magical items strong enough to withstand the sun. Is it possible that drowcraft has changed so quickly?"

"Something has changed," the elf agreed. "How this happened and what it means is not yet clear. Those who believe the gods know more than mortals, and who have observed the Spider Queen's interest in you, might conclude that you play some part in this."

Liriel sat down heavily on a fallen log. "What is going on?"

"That is for Zofia Othlor to discover." The elf's eyes went to Fyodor. "The witch who set me upon your path spoke of your quest for the Windwalker. She saw the drow in a vision."

"She saw Liriel?" he marveled, an edge of hope in his voice. "She saw what would be and approved?"

Thorn made a small, scornful sound. "You know better than that. Visions speak in symbols. The witch saw a raven with golden eyes wearing the amulet around its neck."

Fyodor turned to Liriel. "Zofia Othlor told me to find the Windwalker and return. Her very words were, 'and *she* will bring you home.' The Windwalker is my destiny, little raven. I would not say this if the name belonged only to a golden amulet."

The drow reached for his hand and laced her fingers with his. "So that's why you were so sure your people would let me into Rashemen," she mused. "You think this Zofia can figure out what's going on?"

He nodded somberly. "She is among the most powerful *wychlaran* in our land."

"Well, then let's pick up the pace. How much farther have we to go?"

Thorn dropped to one knee. She brushed aside some fallen leaves and pulled a knife from her boot. With a few quick slashes she drew a rough map in the sandy soil.

"We stand here, in the High Forest," she said, tapping a large gray pebble. "The seas are far to the east, and here lies the city of Waterdeep. On good horses, you could have ridden this far in two or three days. Here is Rashemen." She thrust her knife into the soil an arm's distance away.

Liriel's heart sank. "I have no travel spells that would take us that far. You spoke of a shorter path?"

"It takes us through my homeland. There are many gates there, and my people travel them easily, but we cannot risk what happened before." She sent a cool glance toward Fyodor. "I carry an herb that grows only in my homeland. The scent alone kept you from awakening. The taste of a single leaf will put you deep into slumber, deeper than dreams can go. This herb is not without risk—some who taste it never awaken—but at least your goddess cannot follow you through your dreams."

The drow abruptly withdrew her hand from Fyodor's. "She's not my goddess," she insisted. "Bring out your green stuff. I have nothing to fear from dreams, and nothing to fear from her!"

The elf shrugged and reached for her herb bag. "I'm not the one you need to convince of that."

☉

Shakti sat bolt upright, shaken from her slumber by one of her own guardian golems. She wriggled free of the construct's stone hands and rose from her bed. A fresh robe hung ready, left for her by the newly attentive Hunzrin servants. She slipped it on and belted it with her snakehead whip, then stepped into her slippers. A driftdisk floated in the corridor just outside her open door. There was no need to ask who had sent it.

She quickly removed a folded bit of parchment from a hidden compartment in her writing table. After tucking it in her sleeve, she seated herself on the disk and settled in for the ride across the Menzoberranzan cavern. The honor extended to her almost, but not quite, soothed her irritation over the lost hours of sleep. After her wakeful sojourn in the Abyss, even the uneasy rest to be had in the Underdark was a welcome and much-needed solace.

The magical conveyance took her once again to the door of Matron Triel's audience chamber. This time two priestesses awaited her. Quenthel Baenre stood to one side of her sister's throne, her head held high and proud. She was richly gowned in embroidered spidersilk robes, and her hair had been dressed in elaborate curls and braids, which were held in place with ropes of black pearls. Around her neck hung the medallion that proclaimed her Mistress of Arach Tinileth.

So that's the use Triel decided to make of her newly returned sister, noted Shakti. It was a wise move. The powerful and ambitious Quenthel would be a potent rival for the Baenre throne. By placing her in charge of the priestess academy, Triel gave her sister a queendom of her own. Few matron mothers wielded such power as did the mistress of Arach Tinileth, and what better way to flaunt Lolth's favor than to put a Baenre priestess, recently returned from the dead, at the very front and center of the cult's stronghold?

Shakti stepped down from the driftdisk and bowed to both priestesses. "Matron Triel, Mistress Quenthel. I am honored—"

"Silence!"

The command thundered from tiny Triel, resounding with a magical power that stopped Shakti in mid sentence. "I care nothing for your flatteries. Tell us of your meeting with my brother Gromph."

She told them most of what had passed between her and the archmage. "I had no choice but meet with him," she concluded. "He sent me after Liriel, and he expected an accounting of my time Above. I could hardly refuse the archmage of Menzoberranzan, a scion of House Baenre."

"True enough, but why would you promise him Liriel's amulet?" the matron demanded.

"Because he wants it," Shakti said. "He wants it very, very much. The search for the Windwalker will drain his resources and, more importantly, deflect his interest from more dangerous matters. There are whispers of rebellion among the followers of the Masked God. Sooner or later, these will come to the archmage's ears. Might it not be prudent to keep him busy elsewhere?"

This amused Quenthel. "A rat chasing its own tail! How very appropriate. Tell me, what resources is my dear brother committing to this endeavor?"

"He has hired a mercenary band. Quietly."

"It is hardly something he would wish to hear sung in the marketplace," Triel murmured. She rested her elbows on the arms of her throne and propped her chin on her hands as she thought this through. After a moment or two, a thin smile tightened her lips.

"I will discover this little plot, and to support my dear brother I will grant forces of my own to ensure a successful quest—or more accurately, a long one! It might be wise to have a copy of this artifact made. If he is ever in danger of finding Liriel's trinket, set him upon the scent of a false amulet. That will keep him chasing his tail a while longer. Meanwhile you will find the real one and bring it to me."

Shakti inclined her head respectfully. "I suspected you might say that, and have brought something that will enable you to begin this task at once. I took it from one of Liriel's books."

She passed Triel the folded parchment, a page torn from a human lore book. On it was a finely detailed drawing of small dagger in a rune-carved sheath. The matron gave a curt nod of approval.

"There is more," Shakti cautioned. "Gromph believes that Liriel is dead. I told him this to ensure that he seeks the artifact but not the *Zedriniset.*"

Zedriniset: Chosen of Lolth.

Her choice of words was deliberate, and effective. A murderous gleam flashed in Triel's eyes, betraying the ultimate reward awaiting her too-favored niece. Shakti tucked this realization away as if it was her greatest treasure.

"Devious, but shortsighted," observed Triel. "What will you do if the Lady of Chaos decides that Liriel must return to us?"

"If this is the will of Lolth, I will bring the princess back myself," Shakti said. She nodded toward Quenthel. "Considering past honors given to House Baenre, such a return would not be beyond belief. Until then, it is better that the archmage has no reason to seek out his daughter."

"You are loyal," Triel observed. The matron's tone held both irony and curiosity.

"Why wouldn't I be? House Hunzrin has long been allied with the First House. I have nothing to gain through your ill fortune but much to gain from your favor."

"Blunt as a dwarven axe," Quenthel murmured.

"For the moment, I am glad of it," Triel said. "Speak plainly once again, and tell us why Gromph cannot have this Windwalker amulet."

Shakti had contemplated this question at length, but the answer only now came to her.

It all fit: her unfading *piwafwi*, the survival of the soul-bubble spell on the surface world despite the coming of day, Quenthel's words of triumph upon her transformation from yochlol to drow.

"Liriel used this Windwalker amulet to take drow magic to the surface," she said slowly, "but she did not realize how powerful this human trinket was or that the consequences of her casting might be far more widespread than she dreamed possible."

Triel inclined her head. "That is our belief."

For several moments the priestesses held silence, each absorbed in her own thoughts.

Shakti's head whirled with the enormity of this revelation. The shift to strategic thinking was profound, the implications were staggering. She thought back to old Matron Baenre's attack on Mithril Hall and in particular the disastrous battle in a place the humans called Keeper's Dale. The drow had not been defeated by the combined forces of dwarves, human barbarians, and wizards, but by the coming of daylight. If such a battle were to be fought today, they could win it! Once the other drow knew . . .

That, of course, was why the two Baenre females had summoned her. Once the other drow knew, what was to keep them underground? Why would the males of Menzoberranzan submit to matron rule if they had other, more attractive options?

"Suddenly you have become very important to us," Triel said softly. "As traitor-priestess, you can walk in places none of us can go. You can ensure that no one knows of these developments. No one. You will be the ears that listen, and the sword that silences."

Shakti inclined her head in acceptance—she had no other choice—but she couldn't resist giving voice to her reservations. "Many eyes have seen me come to House Baenre. Other priestesses will wonder why."

"Of course they will, and we will give an explanation that all will understand. The wars have devastated our supplies of slaves and workers, disrupted our trade, slowed production of needed goods. When nobles and common alike are garbed in new woolen clothes and feasting upon rothé and cheese, they will look upon House Hunzrin as Baenre's faithful stewards. See to it."

This, even more than the death of her hated rival, was Shakti's dearest dream! She could not quite keep the joy from her face. Finally, an acknowledgment of her gifts and talents! She was ambitious as any other drow, but she did not want to rule. She could manage affairs and processes in an orderly, precise fashion that eluded most of her chaotic kin. She could excel at the task Triel put before her.

Shakti bowed low. "All will be done. I should, however, point out that trade with the surface may be disrupted for some time to come. Some of our merchants are Vhaerun worshipers. Any Underdark magic they carried with them has long since vanished, and so they are no immediate threat, but they must be kept from returning, lest they discover this secret."

"I agree," Matron Triel decreed. "The wisest course would be to seek out and destroy these merchants. This secret must not spread beyond this chamber."

"What of Liriel herself?"

The matron was slow in answering. "Bring her back if you can, kill her if you cannot. Above all else, we must have the Windwalker. If it effected so profound a change, who knows what else it might do?"

The appearance of a human wizard and his damnable light spell left Gorlist in a foul mood. He stalked back toward the Dragon's Hoard camp in silence. Brindlor offered no comment, largely because the dark glares Gorlist sent him from time to time warned against any comparison with Merdrith.

Gorlist stopped at the edge of a ravine. Brindlor kept a judicious pace back. The stench of city sewage and rotting bodies rose from the foul water, and the deathsinger had no desire to contribute his mortal remains to this unpleasantness. The warrior selected several gems from Liriel's bag and tossed them into the sludge.

"Understandable," Brindlor observed, "but a shame nonetheless."

The warrior's glare snapped toward him. "Have no fear. I've saved the choicest gem for you."

He reached into a hidden pocket and took out a large, red stone. This he placed in Brindlor's hand. Before the deathsinger could step back, Gorlist gave his wrist a vicious twist, sending him to his knees and forcing his arm behind his back. He reclaimed the gem and lowered it purposefully to the deathsinger's face.

Brindlor struggled as the sharply pointed gem pressed against his forehead. The ruby flared with brilliant red light and began to sear its way into the deathsinger's skull.

Brindlor awoke on his pallet, although he could not recall making his way there. Nor could he guess how much time he had spent in oblivion. In fact, nothing seemed certain except the throbbing, burning pain just above his eyes.

He carefully touched his forehead and felt the hard, flat surface of the ruby embedded there.

The gem responded to his touch with a flare of searing heat. A vivid image leaped into his mind: a drow priestess with an angular, feral face and a voluptuously full mouth. She stared forward intently, her crimson eyes moving as if she scanned a room.

Nisstyre? she inquired. The words sounded in the deathsinger's pain-benumbed mind like the clanging of bells.

"Speak softly or kill me now," Brindlor mumbled.

"Ah, both the deathsinger and the ruby have awakened," Gorlist said in tones rounded with satisfaction. He came into Brindlor's field of vision and seized the deathsinger's tunic. With ungentle hands he hauled Brindlor into a sitting position and propped him against the wall. That accomplished, he squatted down to eye level and stared intently into the deathsinger's face.

"Just repeat what she says. She will hear my words well enough."

Nisstyre? the priestess inquired, more emphatically. Still dazed, Brindlor echoed the question.

"He is dead. Gorlist, son of Nisstyre, now commands the Dragon's Hoard."

You would be this Gorlist, I suppose?

Brindlor relayed the words if not the sneering intonation drow females typically employed.

Who is the stone's new host?

Brindlor decided it was time to speak for himself. "I am Brindlor Zidorian of Ched Nessad, a deathsinger famed for songs of dark glory."

"He will sing of the downfall and death of Liriel Baenre," Gorlist added. He paused, then inclined his head in a small, reluctant bow. "If that is still your wish."

Your purpose and mine are in accord.

Brindlor related this response. Gorlist smiled. "I thought they might be."

Bring your full forces to the troll caves near the Glowing Dracolich Cavern. I will meet you there.

The gleam in Gorlist's eyes abruptly dimmed when he heard these instructions. "You will join us? There is no need for you to endanger yourself in a long tunnel march, much less in the Night Above! The ruby gem will enable you to see all through a deathsinger's eyes."

In time I might find his particular vision useful or at least amusing. Until then, you will both do as I say. Gromph Baenre himself will see that you are well paid.

A searing heat flared high and hot in the ruby, then the painful presence receded.

"She's gone," Brindlor said with relief, speaking his own words at last. He turned furious eyes on Gorlist. "What is this about? The gem, the female? The *archmage?* I am to sing a Baenre princess's deathsong to an audience of her own blood? Why didn't you tell me we were working for Gromph Baenre? I could have cut my own throat and saved the great archmage the inconvenience of a bloodied dagger."

"Until this very moment, I didn't know about Gromph Baenre's interest," Gorlist said. "As to the other matter, this female, Shakti Hunzrin, gave that gem to my father, the wizard Nisstyre. They worked together until his death. My father's task is now mine."

"I'd prefer that your father's *gem* was now yours," Brindlor grumbled.

The warrior shrugged. "You chose to become a bard. Is it not said that all great art is born of suffering?"

CHAPTER ELEVEN

Merdrith stood on the docks of Kront, looking out over the deceptively calm waters of Ashane. A short, thick-bodied Ashanathi fisherman stood a few paces away, eyeing him with speculation. Despite the woolen cap concealing his head tattoos, the soot darkening his thin crimson beard, and his rough woodsman's garb, Merdrith had the look of Thay's wizard nobility. Red Wizards were slain on sight in Rashemen and were none too welcome in the bordering countries.

"You traveling alone?" the man asked.

"Passage for one," Merdrith confirmed.

"It'll cost you. I wasn't planning to dock in Rashemen and won't be coming near to any port town. I can set you ashore on the edge of the Ashenwood, about a day's walk south of Immilmar. Best I can do," he said defensively.

The wizard understood completely. While the fisherman didn't wish to lose a potential fare, neither did he want to risk angering his powerful neighbors. No doubt the wretch intended to stay overnight in Immilmar. He could sell the day's catch and warn the local *fyrra* of the suspicious outlander sighted walking northward along the shore. As it turned out, the proposed destination suited his purposes perfectly.

"Will ten Thesken gold suffice?" he asked, holding up a small deerskin bag.

The sailor's eyes widened with avarice. He snatched the offered payment and offered a gap-toothed grin. "Brunzel will stow your gear. Take a seat, get yourself a tarp cloak. In this season the winds coming off the Ashane could freeze the blood of a white dragon."

Merdrith already knew this. He had last stood on the banks of the Ashane in mid winter, as part of a band of Red Wizards charged with the suicidal task of attacking a witches' watchtower and keeping the guardians occupied long enough to distract them from the main invading forces. Contrary to all expectation, the magic of these few Red Wizards had prevailed over the tower's witches.

Even though it shouldn't have.

This unexpected success still puzzled and intrigued Merdrith. It had inspired him to commit the first truly impulsive act of his life. He had killed his fellow wizards and claimed the tower's treasures for himself. A treasonous act, to be sure, but had he succeeded in his purpose he could have returned to his homeland in triumph to claim a zulkir's honors.

It seemed eminently clear to him that the unique spirit-magic of Rashemen had faltered. That was the only explanation for this victory. If he could discover the source of this new weakness and find a way to exploit it, the conquest of Rashemen and the destruction of her much-hated witches would finally be within Thay's grasp. This particular watchtower was said to be a treasure trove of magic and lorebooks. Merdrith had not been disappointed, and he had left the tower confident that he would find the answers he sought.

His booty had included a witch's staff, this one a wish-staff fashioned from ebony and elaborately carved. With it he had secured one of the most powerful and well-guarded hiding places in all of Rashemen, a place filled with its own treasures and secrets. By now he should have been sitting in council with the greatest of Thay's wizards.

Then came two unforeseen complications: a band of drow thieves and an interfering Rashemi warrior. The drow had come upon Merdrith's hiding place—a legendary magical hut—when he was out walking the forest in search of talkative ghosts. The dark elves had done battle with Merdrith's gnoll warriors, the busybody Rashemi, and the hut itself. He had returned from his forest ramble in time to see the last flurry of battle as the berserker warrior was encased in an icy shroud. The Rashemi had escaped his prison, foolishly following the drow through a magical portal. The wounded hut had also disappeared, as it was said to do upon taking any hurt. No one knew where it went on these occasions, but according to the lore it would heal itself and return with the next autumn equinox to resume haunting the Rashemaar forests.

With nearly a year to wait, Merdrith found himself bereft of his quest, his magic, and his homeland. If he returned to Thay without the secrets he sought, he would be executed as a traitor and deserter. Lacking a better idea, he fled to the west and took up a hermit's life in the High Forest, a place notorious for the number of portals into the Underdark.

His first attempts to make contact with the drow raiders had proved disastrous. There were in the High Forest small bands of dark elf females, self-righteous priestess-warriors whose goddess apparently held a dubious view of Merdrith's character and motives. He'd slain one of the troublesome black wenches, and in conversing with her spirit he learned of a battle in the subterranean realms of Skullport between a band of drow thieves known as the Dragon's Hoard, and yet another group of drow females. One of these females was accompanied by a Rashemi warrior, and she was said to hold an artifact known as the Windwalker.

So Merdrith went to Skullport and sought the drow female, the Rashemi, and the band of thieves. The first two were long gone, but the new leader of the Dragon's Hoard readily agreed to form an alliance.

All was going well. Perhaps even a bit too well. The problem, to Merdrith's way of thinking, was in finding ways to delay the capture of the Windwalker until its current guardians returned it to Rashemen.

For it was there, and only there, that the amulet could release its full power.

The fishing boat made straight for the shore. Its captain sent out a small skiff and a man to row the passenger ashore. Merdrith gave the oarsman a silver coin for his troubles then obligingly headed northward, walking a careful distance from the lake's edge. As soon as the fishing boat was out of sight, however, he turned into the shadows of the Ashenwood.

He found a small clearing and took a bag of birdseed from his belt. This he sprinkled in a wide circle, all the while singing an old Rashemaar folk song he'd coaxed from the ghost of a slain berserker. They were plentiful, these Rashemaar ghosts, and still full of boasting insults and superstitious chatter. Some of them, however, had inadvertently aided his research.

The rustle of leaves and the creak of bending branches announced the success of Merdrith's summons. He backed into the concealing underbrush and waited.

A Rashemaar hut stalked cautiously into the clearing on legs resembling those of a giant chicken. Despite its startling mobility, the structure was otherwise unremarkable, with its dark timbers and wattle-and-daub walls, thatched roof, and brightly painted shutters. These shutters were closed, further proof that the hut's legendary occupant was not in residence.

The hut made its way into the center of the birdseed circle and turned around a couple of times, perhaps to survey the surrounding forest or perhaps in ritual such as that performed by drowsy hounds. Whatever the case, it seemed satisfied. The massive legs folded and the magical dwelling settled down like a brooding hen.

Merdrith began to sing the song that had proven so effective months before.

"While the mistress is asleep,
Chicken-legs a watch will keep.
When the mistress wanders off,
Chicken-legs will stand aloft.
When the mistress comes again,
Chicken-legs will let her in.
Stara Baba casts this spell.
Listen, hut, and hearken well."

There was a stirring at the door, where a small rug fashioned from many-colored rags softened the front stoop. The front edge of this rug rose into the air, fluttering rapidly as if vibrating in a sharp, strong wind. A resounding *phhhht!* filled the clearing.

The hut's response was eerily reminiscent of a child taunting a lesser playmate. Merdrith scowled and reached for his wand.

A pair of shutters crashed open, and a pewter plate

came spinning out of the open window. It struck his hand, shattering bone and sending the wand flying end over end. While Merdrith danced and cursed, one massive clawed foot reached out and snared the wand, drawing it under the hut. The hut settled back down and waited, as if inviting him to do his worst.

The wizard had seen enough. He had tried to broach the hut's defenses before using every spell at his command. It had finally been a combination of the witch's ebony wishstaff and the children's song that had gained him entrance. Without Rashemaar magic to aid him, he would never get past the door.

This knowledge only increased his determination to get his hands on the Windwalker. Even if his proud Thayvian brothers refused to admit it, the only way to overcome Rashemen and her witches was with their own magic.

Brindlor was the last to arrive at the Dragon's Hoard's hidden camp, a cave that still held the musky stench of the bugbear the drow band had forcibly evicted. He found his current master arguing heatedly with Merdrith, their human wizard. A half-dozen drow lounged against the far wall, sharpening weapons or tossing dice as they awaited the outcome. Brindlor, as was his habit, lingered out of sight to listen and observe.

Merdrith was not an exceptionally tall man, though he topped Gorlist by at least a hand's span. His bald skull was tattooed in bright red patterns, and his thin, braided beard had been dyed an equally garish shade of crimson. At the moment its straggly appearance was emphasized by what appeared to be soot, the removal of which had been attempted in desultory fashion. Instead of wizardly robes, Merdrith wore a doeskin tunic haphazardly bedecked with pockets and loose leather britches that hung like jagged stalagmites around knee-high boots. A rag bandage was wrapped around one hand, which was braced with a crude splint. At first glance, the human appeared to be nothing more than an eccentric hermit. Gorlist believed otherwise. Brindlor hoped that the warrior was right.

"We should go directly to Rashemen," the wizard insisted. "The drow and her Rashemi companion are headed in that direction. Your fighters can lie in wait for them without concern that the Promenade Temple priestesses will again interfere."

Gorlist's scowl deepened. He did not like to be reminded of past failures. "I know the area, and the tunnels between here and there. It is a very long walk."

"That, I had assumed, is why you employed a wizard," Merdrith pointed out.

"You are a means to an end, no more," the dark elf said coldly. "Do not presume to instruct a drow warrior in battle strategy. Once a course of action has been decided, you will use magic toward its implementation."

"What is this strategy that your deathsinger will render in immortal prose?"

"Use the gem. Trace the female. When we find her, we kill her."

"Ah, yes," Merdrith said with arid sarcasm. "The famed subtlety of the dark elves."

A knife flashed into Gorlist's hand, and he pressed the point between the wizard's eyes. "Do the magic, old man, or I'll peel off those tattoos, and your scalp with them!"

The wizard shrugged and held out his good hand. Gorlist tore the bag of gems from his belt and spilled two of them into the human's palm.

Merdrith tossed the jewels into a shallow, stagnant puddle. The green water steamed and swirled, then settled down into a crystalline blue sheen as smooth as polished glass. Merdrith leaned over the scrying pool. After a moment a sardonic smile curved his lips.

"All my recent travels, and where should I find them but on my back stoop?" he murmured.

One of the warriors, a young male known as Ansith, looked up from his whet stone and grimaced. "Days of travel. More time wasted."

"We follow a wizard," Gorlist reminded him, "and we follow as wizards do."

He turned an inquiring stare upon Merdrith. In response, the human pointed toward the pool. Gorlist nodded then glanced toward the watchful drow. "Ansith, Chiss, and Taenflyrr, follow me. You too, Brindlor."

With that, he leaped into the scrying pool. The serene blue circle swallowed him without splash or ripple.

Impressed, Brindlor left his "hiding place" and followed the warriors through the portal. He dropped through a short span of darkness and landed in a crouch on the forest floor.

The deathsinger scanned his surroundings, noting that the moon was past its zenith, that a river played softly nearby. At the same moment, it occurred to him that the river's voice sang alone.

The night was far too silent. No predators snarled, no nightbird keened. Even the chorus of night insects, usually lifted in a raucous farewell to summer, had fallen silent.

The other drow had already disappeared into the forest shadows. Brindlor crept away from the almost imperceptible portal, edging his way carefully into a tall stand of ferns.

A green glow caught his eye, a light so faint that it blended easily into the dappled interplay of moonbeams and forest shadow. The source was Gorlist, who was crouched behind the moss-covered truck of a fallen tree. The dragon tattoo on his face shone with subtle green light.

Wild elation swept through Brindlor. There would be battle at last, and with a green dragon! *That* would be a song worth singing!

Gorlist turned a stern glare toward a massive, vine-shrouded tree and the trio of warriors who hid among the shadows. His fingers danced through the silent drow cant, unmistakably warning them off.

Astonishment, anger, and suppressed mutiny darted across the warriors' shadowed faces. Brindlor recognized these emotions, for they closely mirrored his own.

Couldn't Gorlist see that his fellow drow were restless, itching for combat? It was not natural for them to go so long without blood on their hands!

To Brindlor's surprise, however, the young drow obeyed the leader and held their places. The deathsinger watched with wistful eyes as the dragon—a juvenile, not an easy kill but a rousing night's entertainment all the same—slipped through the deep shadows.

Its long, undulating form found pathways through the thick forest that even an elf might miss, and its bright green scales gleamed in the moonlight. The soft whisper of its passing called to Brindlor as a night breeze might beckon trysting lovers. Bloodlust burned in the deathsinger's veins, the fierce instinct that prompted predator toward prey.

With great difficulty Brindlor held his position, remaining silent long after the dragon had disappeared. The tentative chirp of scattered crickets resumed and melded into a steady chorus.

Ansith exploded from his hiding place with a sweep of his frustrated sword, severing a handful of vines. He stormed over to the place where his leader lay hidden and kicked viciously at the log.

Gorlist was already on his feet and several paces away. He drew his sword and met the young drow's rushing attack with a deft sidestep, followed by a quick spin and an answering lunge at his opponent's hamstring. Ansith half-turned back toward him, sweeping his sword down to block the diving attack. He completed the turn and kicked high above the enjoined blades.

As Gorlist leaned away from the attack, Ansith followed hard with his other hand, which held a curved knife.

The leader seized the mutinous drow's wrist and gave it a vicious, bone-cracking twist, but Ansith used his weight as a weapon, throwing it against Gorlist. They fell together, twisted away, and rose catlike to their feet. They circled each other, watching for an opening.

Gorlist made a quick, jabbing feint, drawing a high parry. Before the swords touched, he ducked and drove back in, harder and lower. The point of his sword dived between the laces of Ansith's vest and touched the rippling muscle the young drow so proudly exposed. Just as quickly he swept the sword back and up, swatting aside Ansith's sword before parry could become attack. It was an astonishing display of speed: three forays against a single response.

Gorlist stepped back, a cocky smile on his face and his blade held almost casually in low guard position. "Tell me why I shouldn't kill you."

"Because you can't," the soldier said bluntly, not at all cowed by the bloodless coup his leader had just scored. His head lifted in pride and challenge. "No scars mar these arms, this body. I have never been bested in battle. As the red-haired elf woman pointed out, *you* cannot make that claim."

The smile dropped from Gorlist's face, and with a howl of rage he hurled himself at the younger warrior. The two fighters set to in a frenzy of slashing blades. The others gathered around to watch, twisted pleasure shining on their faces.

"The dark eye in a whirling storm of steel," murmured Brindlor, watching his employer approvingly. He considered the phrase and nodded. It fit the general tone and tenor of the saga that was taking shape in his mind.

For many moments, Ansith managed to hold death at arm's length. Before he could falter, his brother Chiss joined the battle—not from any fraternal loyalty, Brindlor suspected, but from sheer frustrated bloodlust.

The drow bard frowned as he watched the uneven battle. He had no aversion to singing Gorlist's deathsong, but so far no one had offered to pay him for this feat. His own best interests lay in keeping Gorlist alive until the tale was told and the fees collected.

He glanced over at Taenflyrr and noted that the young warrior was considering him with cold, measuring eyes. Green dragon or not, it looked as if all of them would know battle tonight.

Before Brindlor could draw his sword, a soft, rising sound echoed through the trees, at first barely indistinguishable from the night winds. The deathsinger's trained ear divined its source at once.

"Hunting horns," he said, speaking just loud enough to be heard above battle.

The combatants immediately fell apart, panting and glaring at each other. They knew precisely what Brindlor meant, but the urge to fight and kill was not easily set aside.

"The hunting horns of Eilistraee," the deathsinger elaborated, "calling the Dark Maiden's followers to revelry or battle. I personally have no interest in the former, and I'm not sure whether the five of us would offer them much of a fight, either."

A second horn sounded, louder and closer. Two more answered, coming from each side of the small band.

Ansith backhanded a trickle of blood from his face and

sneered at Gorlist. "The priestesses saved your life," he taunted.

"We will see that they come to regret it."

The retort came quickly, carrying with it the unmistakable promise of torture and death. Ansith's sneer melted away, to be replaced by an eager, almost comradely grin. He obviously read in Gorlist's words a closing of ranks, a shifting of focus from the internecine quarrel to the foe shared by all.

Ah, to be young and stupid, mused Brindlor with malicious amusement.

The deathsinger noted Gorlist's answering scowl and marked how it faltered before the obvious delight of his soldiers.

Brindlor suppressed a smile. Perhaps Gorlist was beginning to understand how his father, the brutal and canny wizard Nisstyre, had held the band of renegade drow together. Perhaps all Gorlist required was a nudge, a suggestion, to help him understand what his followers needed.

He strode toward the fighters. "Can our human wizard change Ansith's appearance to that of a female?"

A dark flame leaped in Gorlist's eyes as he seized his deathsinger's suggestion. "If not, he will quickly learn how." His gaze shifted from Chiss to Taenflyrr. "We will take Ansith back to the Skullport caves, and there he will die as a wench."

Chiss was the first to shrug. After all, his sword had also been lifted against his leader, and he could more easily lose a brother than a hand or an eye. The two drow soldiers seized the impetuous youth and dragged him toward the return gate.

Gorlist rewarded Brindlor with a cold smile. "We will return to the High Forest, and soon. Slaying Ansith will whet their appetites for the Dark Maidens."

If Gorlist wished to claim this notion as his own, thought Brindlor, then all the better. The deathsinger gave a small, ironic bow. "I am a bard. What argument could I possibly make against the benefits of practice?"

Sunset colors stained the sky as Fyodor and Thorn paused at the edge of the forest glade and gazed out over the silver waters of Ashane. The elven warrior bent over the doeskin and birch litter upon which slept Liriel, surrounded by springs of potent herbs that grew nowhere in Faerûn. She busied herself with the herbs, removing them along with the protective enchantments that had held the drow in deepest slumber—and beyond the reach of Lolth's seeking magic. Fyodor, who knew better than to trouble magical folk at their work, turned his gaze toward the east.

Toward home.

The Rashemi drank in the familiar sights: the sharply sloping hills and the silver threads of rock-strewn water that stitched through on their way to Ashane. A shallow valley surrounded the lake. It was bordered by mountains, upon which grew a dense pine forest. Massive trees huddled so close together that from any distance at all they appeared to form an impenetrable wall. Near the edge of the forest grew smaller trees, their branches clad in the bright colors that spoke of coming winter. Falling leaves drifted and danced on the crisp evening wind.

Fyodor drew in a long, slow breath. The fragrance carried on the wind was unmistakably that of Rashemen, where even in summer the scent of coming snow seemed to linger. Though he could not see them from where he stood, bright crimson junipergia berries added their own distinctive spice. Even the pines smelled different here than in any other forest through which Fyodor had traveled. They were darker, more intense, and somehow melancholy.

His gaze rested upon the deceptively calm waters of Lake Ashane. The silver surface reflected the Rashemen sunset, which to Fyodor's fond eyes was brighter than any other sky he had seen. Certainly the sun's farewell this day reflected the tastes of his people. Gold, crimson, and purple swirled together in bold, bright patterns, a cheerful welcome that offered a powerful contrast to the stark stone tower at valley's edge.

A strong, slim hand rested on his shoulder. He turned to Thorn, noticing as he did that her pale gold-green eyes were on a level with his own.

"The drow will awaken soon. If all goes well, we need not meet again."

It was not the friendliest farewell that Fyodor had ever heard, but he understood why Thorn's ways were not his own. He extended his hand, one exiled warrior to another.

"If ever I speak of what I have seen this day, may my bones lie forgotten in a distant land."

"If I thought you would talk, they already would," the elf responded. She took his offered hand briefly then turned back to Liriel. A frown furrowed her pale face.

"She should have awakened by now. Get me several small, wet stones."

Fyodor quickly scooped up some pebbles from the water's edge and dropped them into Thorn's outstretched hand. The elf placed one on Liriel's forehead, another on each of her closed eyes, and several on her body. She held her hands over the drow girl, palms down, and let out a haunting, ululating cry. A bit of steam rose from the wet stones, and the pebbles turned several shades lighter as the water disappeared, but that was the extent of the spell's effect.

Thorn glanced up at the sky. "The only other things I might try involve moonmagic. It's a waning moon—not good for the needed spells—and at any rate it won't rise in time."

The Rashemi knelt at Liriel's side. Her face felt cool to his touch, and her breathing was nearly imperceptible. The deathlike slumber that had hidden Liriel's path from Lolth's prying eyes appeared to be deepening.

"Is there anything else we could try? Anything at all?"

"Throw her in the water," suggested Thorn. "The shock might wake her, provided it doesn't stop her heart first."

Fyodor sat back on his heels and thrust one hand through his hair. The Lake of Tears was bitter cold even in summer, but he'd seen Liriel swim and survive worse. He had little fear of her drowning. She still wore the ring of water breathing the illithid's minions had used during an attempt to kidnap her. "What of the guardians?"

"If the water spirits don't want your drow in Rashemen, you might as well know now as later," she pointed out.

There was reason in that argument, so Fyodor set to work. He quickly shed his boots, unbuckled his weapons belt, and stripped off his garments. No Rashemi entered the water clothed or armed. To do so was an affront to the spirits who dwelt in most rivers and streams, ponds and wells. The Ashane was the most haunted body in the land. As Fyodor peeled off the sleeping drow's garments and weapons, he marveled, as he always did in such circumstances, that so small a girl managed to hide so many blades about her person.

Finally he stood with Liriel in his arms. He waded a step or two into the water—the shore dropped off too quickly for him to go much farther—and tossed her into the lake.

Liriel came awake cursing and sputtering, her arms flailing the icy waters. She took in her situation almost immediately and tested the depth with her feet. The bottom eluded her, so she began to swim the few needed strokes to the shore.

Cold hands closed on her ankles, and suddenly she was being dragged deeper into the water. She heard Fyodor call her name, heard the splash as he dived after her.

Her captors were faster still. Liriel twisted as best she could and managed to catch a glimpse of them. Two elflike females skimmed effortlessly through the water, barely moving their naked green limbs. The drow snatched at the swiftly passing reeds, desperately trying to get a handhold.

When the nereids finally released her, she swam for the surface and took stock of her situation.

The nereids had dragged her well away from the shore. Moving steadily westward was a long wooden boat, its prow elaborately carved and brightly painted. The craft appeared to be unmanned, yet it changed direction and came directly toward the paddling drow. Liriel's mind raced. If she was awake, their journey to Rashemen must be completed—or nearly so. She racked her brain for information about boats in Fyodor's country. At once, there came to her the memory of the warrior's tales of the powerful Witchboats.

She snatched a quick breath and dived deep. The Witchboat came to a stop directly over her. She began to swim toward the western shore, glancing up frequently at the magical boat. It followed her but remained a length or two behind. There was room for her to come up for air when she needed to do so. Apparently the boat had no intention of drowning her.

Liriel considered her situation further. Fyodor had said that a powerful witch called Zofia Othlor had foreseen her coming. It was not beyond the realm of possibility that the witch had perceived their approach and sent both the nereids and the boat to bring them to Rashemen's shores.

The drow started for the surface. Suddenly her way was blocked by another elflike female, a familiar creature with a beautiful blue face and insanity burning bright in her sea-green eyes.

Liriel twisted in the water, but she was not fast enough to evade the genasi's leaping attack. The blue creature seized Liriel's hair and dragged her to the surface.

The drow fought with every ounce of ferocity she possessed. They tumbled and kicked and clawed, churning the water into foam.

Finally Fyodor made his way out to the battling females. He thrust his way between them and tucked one under each arm. He stood and made his way to shore in three quick steps.

Liriel wriggled free and lunged for her pile of weapons. She snatched up a long knife and whirled back toward her foe.

"Why did you fight me?" the creature demanded, her angry gaze fixed accusingly on Liriel and her blue fists propped on her hips. "You could have been drowned."

"You've just answered your own stupid question," Liriel shot back. "I was trying to keep you from drowning me."

The genasi looked genuinely shocked. "You thought I was trying to kill you?"

"Seems like a reasonable assumption, given our last encounter."

The genasi frowned as she struggled to sort through this logic. "Vestriss is dead," she said at last.

It was Liriel's turn to be puzzled. "Vestriss? The illithid?"

"I killed her," the genasi said proudly. "I, Azar, daughter of the Elemental Planes. The walking squid will never again enslave her betters."

This was starting to make sense—after a fashion. "Vestriss sent you out after me. We fought, you lost. So you traveled halfway across Faerûn to drag me ashore when you thought I was drowning. Why?"

"The illithid wanted you dead," Azar explained. "That is reason enough to want you alive. You inspired hatred in me, so of course I owed you a debt. It is no great matter for me to travel from one body of water to another."

With that "explanation," the genasi splashed back into the Ashane.

Liriel pursed her lips and shot an inquiring glance at Fyodor. "Is there lots of water around here?"

"Many streams and rivers, and hot springs as well."

She gave him a wry smile. "Chances are I won't be lonely, then. Rashemen's given me quite a reception so far."

"We haven't arrived yet," Fyodor said lightly, but there was something in his eyes that turned the words into warning.

The drow quickly dressed and armed herself. The Witchboat was making its way toward them at a slow, stately pace. As they waited, Fyodor took out a knife and began to chip away at a thick piece of driftwood. The wood was extremely pale, almost white, and marked by tightly-packed swirling patterns.

"Pretty," she observed.

"Rashemaar ash. There is no wood stronger."

Liriel recalled the cudgel he had carried when they first met. "Not a bad weapon," she said. "It's lightweight, hard, and strong."

"All that and more. Rashemaar driftwood holds the power of the land and water both."

"That's important?"

"It can be. There are strange creatures in this land. Some must be fought, others appeased, and some avoided.

Sometimes it is difficult to tell which is which or to know what is required," he cautioned. "It is best that you take my lead."

"I'll be as docile as a Ruathan maiden," Liriel promised, a demure smile on her lips and a wicked gleam in her eye. They exchanged a smile that was both teasing and deeply intimate.

Thorn rose from her place by the fire. Her stern face was softened by a faintly wistful expression. "The Witchboat's approach is slow, no doubt to give you two time to warm yourselves. For that, my presence is not needed." She lifted a hand in farewell. "Run swiftly, hunt well."

She turned away and with a few quick strides disappeared into the forest.

Liriel settled into Fyodor's arms and began to loosen the fastenings of his vest. "I could get to like that elf. Who would have thought?"

He chuckled and smoothed back her wet hair. "Docile Ruathan maiden?" he teased her.

"Why not? Anything's worth trying once."

The moon rose, the fire burned low, and the patient Witchboat waited at the water's edge to bring the warrior and the Windwalker home.

CHAPTER TWELVE

CITIES OF THE DEAD

One day in Blackstaff Tower was enough to convince Sharlarra of her error in returning. The round of lessons and chores seemed endless, the opportunities for mischief few. To make matters worse, the Lady Laerel had gone off to visit her sisters, leaving Sharlarra under the watchful eye of the archmage. Not that she was ungrateful—after all, Khelben Arunsun had followed her on her last misadventure and had appeared in time to save her from some very nasty dark elves.

He had followed her.

This thought stopped Sharlarra dead. The cauldron she'd been stirring bubbled over. Paying no heed to the spilled potion or the aggrieved complaints of her fellow apprentice, she spun on her heel and raced up the winding stairs to the small sleeping chamber assigned to her.

She threw open her trunk and rummaged. Sure enough, the faded satin lining had been peeled aside and her treasure trove plundered. Missing from it were the two perfectly matched bits of pale green peridot she'd appropriated from the bag of gems she'd lifted from Danilo Thann.

So that's how the archmage had been able to trace her steps.

Sharlarra bit her lip and considered her future in light of these new developments. The missing stones were not the only ones she'd taken as a private transaction fee. Several very nice diamonds had entered her possession. They were the perfect accompaniment for the obscenely huge ruby Laerel had left among the gems carelessly strewn across her dressing table. Even before Sharlarra had gone off in search of the drow's ship, she'd had the ruby and the diamonds set into a necklace. There was a dwarf down in South Ward who kept a variety of silver settings on hand, artfully tarnished to suggest vintage pieces. Setting the stones was a small matter of choosing a reasonable fit and pressing the silver prongs firmly around the gems. His services had come in handy more than once. Loose stones vanished into "family heirlooms," and jewelry was quickly recast into less recognizable form. In minutes after leaving the shop, she'd been on her way, and she hadn't taken the necklace off since.

Though the elf had few scruples, she did not steal from her friends. Borrow without permission, yes, but never steal. The necklace was a gift for Laerel, who loved jewelry but couldn't be bothered to shop for it. The beautiful mage would love this gift, not caring in the slightest that the ruby was already her own, but Sharlarra had not seen Laerel since the necklace's creation. She couldn't resist the temptation to wear the opulent piece herself, if just for a short while.

She reached under the collar of her shirt for the chain and undid the clasp. Wearing a fortune in diamonds and rubies had been a pleasant interlude but not one she could afford to continue. As long as she wore it, she was tethered to the archmage by invisible chains of magic.

The elf held the necklace up to admire it one last time—and let out a yelp of surprise and outrage.

The ruby was gone.

Sharlarra called the dwarf every foul name in her extensive repertoire and threw the silver piece into her chest. It landed with a clatter of metal on metal.

Her eyes darted to the chest. The jeweled sword she'd been wearing on her last misadventure lay at the top of the chest. She had not yet had time to replace the gems that the drow warrior had pried from its hilt.

"Damn," she said aloud.

So that was it. Her necklace must have swung free during the fight with the drow. He'd pried out the ruby as well as the ones in her sword. Now, *that* was a trick she wouldn't mind learning herself! Still, it was odd that he should take the ruby and leave the matched diamonds surrounding it.

If the drow simply wanted to track Liriel, there were enough gems left in the bag to accomplish that purpose. If his interest lay in the value of the stones, he would have cut the chain on the entire necklace rather than pry out a single gem. The ruby had some particular significance.

Well, so did the necklace. It was a gift for Laerel, and even if every god in the elven pantheon had ideas to the contrary, Sharlarra intended her mentor to have it.

She quickly dressed in her working clothes—dark green breeches and shirt, warm cloak and boots, bags to hold her picks and loot—and strapped on the despoiled sword. She strode out of Blackstaff Tower, setting a relaxed but purposeful pace.

It was late afternoon, and most of high society would be gathering in festhalls and taverns for tea, a meal usually eaten away from home while their servants prepared for the evening meal and entertainments. Most thieves preferred to work under cover of darkness; Sharlarra had better luck at teatime. Anyone caught sneaking around at night would be stopped and questioned, but those who went about their business openly and without fanfare were usually given the benefit of the doubt. Especially in Sharlarra's case. People saw her pretty elf face and red-gold curls and immediately concluded that she was on the side of angels and paladins.

In Sharlarra's opinion, people that shallow and stupid deserved to be robbed.

Within the hour she had completed her work and was leaning over the dwarf jewelsmith's shoulder.

"The new ruby is considerably smaller," the dwarf observed, his eyes shifting from Sharlarra's newly acquired gem to the damaged necklace, "and the prongs were dinged up something fierce. One of 'em's twisted so bad the metal thinned out some. Might not hold. Go to the kitchen and pour yourself some ale, and I'll have these sparklers in a new setting before you see the bottom of the mug."

"And the sword?"

"Easy job. Off with you, then."

As it turned out, the ale was surprisingly good. Sharlarra downed two dwarf-sized mugs before the job was finished and she was on her way. Perhaps as a result she was less attentive than she might otherwise have been.

She noted the long, black-draped carriage sweep toward her, the four matched horses setting a brisk pace toward the City of the Dead. It did not occur to her that the horses' trot was unseemly, given the usual somber pace afforded this last journey. Nor did she notice that the carter drove rather too close to the flagstone walk. None of these thoughts entered her mind until the curtained door swung open and burly arms reached out to seize her.

Rough hands dragged her into the hearse and threw her to the floor. Sharlarra's head struck the edge of an open coffin. She lay where she fell, too stunned to scream or struggle.

Two men, rough-bearded rogues whose dark garments were too coarse for any self-respecting member of the undertakers' guild, regarded her with sneering satisfaction. One of them seized her wrist and tugged her to her feet.

Her first impulse was to cast a spell. As the first word of the chant spilled from her lips, the other ruffian balled his fist and slammed it into her stomach.

The elf folded. Every whisper of air wheezed from her chest, leaving her too empty to draw more.

Dimly she felt rough hands paw aside her hair and rip the necklace from her.

"Got it!" exulted the smaller of the two. He nodded to the wooden coffin that stood empty and waiting. "Kill her, and have done with it."

"Not yet," the other replied. His voice hitched, sounding as breathless as if he, and not the horses, had been drawing the hearse.

A sick knowledge filled Sharlarra. She forced herself to focus on the man's face, and there she read the confirmation of her fears. His teeth were bared in a leer, and in his eyes was a terrible hungry gleam.

The man roughly lifted the elf and tossed her into the coffin. The sudden jolt forced a bit of air into her lungs, and the vise that gripped her chest relaxed just a bit. She could breathe now. She could live—at least for a little while.

Sharlarra did not breathe. Instead, the proud elf closed her eyes and willed herself to die.

Chadrik clambered out of the coffin, still fully clad and as pale as chalk. He tripped over the side in his haste and stumbled to the floor. The notion of taking the elf wench in her own coffin appealed to him. The reality of finding himself sharing a box with a corpse did not.

His companion hooted with raucous mirth and clapped him on the back. Chadrik threw off the man's hand.

"We've still to go to the City," he grumbled. "There's little enough to laugh about behind those walls."

The other man sobered abruptly. The City of the Dead, a large section of Waterdeep surrounded by walls and gates and magic, had been the city's cemetery since time out of mind. Many rich and ancient tombs lay behind those walls, walls that conspired to keep out all those who would despoil these tombs. The walls also served to keep the restless dead contained within.

The hearse slowed to a decent pace, and the creak of iron gates announced their arrival at the City of the Dead. The two men hopped down from the hearse and presented the gatekeeper with forged papers naming the dead elf and her intended tomb.

The official studied the papers, gave the men an odd, almost pitying look, and waved them in.

"Make it fast," he warned. "You've not much time before full dark."

All three men knew what that meant. The iron gates closed with nightfall and would not open again until dawn. The carter lashed his horses into action, and the carriage took off with a lurch.

They rumbled down the narrow, winding path, passing massive monuments and moss-draped trees. They passed the potter's field, where the indigent and the nameless took their final rest, and finally stopped at a stand of bizarrely twisted trees.

The carriage could go no farther, so the two ruffians slid the coffin out and shouldered it, going on afoot. Although twilight had not yet come, the shadows seemed deeper here, the night frighteningly close at hand.

They stopped before a small grassy mound and tapped out a rhythmic code on the ancient door. It swung open, unaided. A soft, phosphoric glow seemed to beckon them in.

The men exchanged a glance, shrugged, and started down the well-worn stone steps that led to a swiftly descending passage.

At the end of the tunnel was a circular crypt. Glowing lichen grew on the walls, and the soft light revealed a number of shelflike openings carved deep into the stone. They shoved the coffin into the first available place and eyed the several doors leading out of the room.

"Which one?" Chadrik wondered aloud.

The other man shrugged and settled down on a boxy stone tomb. "Don't hardly matter. The Serpent's man said the buyer would come to us. Break the summoning stone and let's get the deal done."

Chadrik removed a small, cloth-wrapped bundle from his bag and took from it an azure stone. It was a costly thing, but never once did he think to keep or sell it. There was money to be made in the Serpent's employ, but any man who thought to cross the moon elf ended up mysteriously and messily dead.

He tossed the stone to the crypt's floor. It shattered into sparkling bits of lights. They rose like a swarm of tiny blue bees and disappeared into a crack in the stone wall.

Chadrik sent a nervous glance toward the stone ceiling and thought of the coming night. "Let's hope they're quick about it."

His partner took out a small knife and began to carve the dirt out from under his nails. "Worse comes to worse, we spend the night here. I wouldn't wander the City, mind you, but what harm could come to us in here?"

"What about Dienter?"

The other thug snorted with laughter. "Think that corpse-hauler would risk his hide on our account? He's likely long gone, and the carriage with him. Might as well settle yourself down."

Not seeing an option, Chadrik took this advice and took a seat on an old marble sarcophagus.

The glowing lichen suddenly ceased to cast light, throwing the room into utter darkness. The two men leaped to their feet and dragged out their weapons.

"Put them away," suggested a sonorous male voice—a voice too deep for a halfling, too fluid for a dwarf, too musical to be human. "Drow can see quite well in the dark, you know, whereas you can see nothing at all. You can't possibly hurt anyone but yourselves."

Drow.

An invisible fist of dread clenched around Chadrik's throat. His companion started to whimper. The moss began to glow again, faintly at first and growing gradually brighter, pushing back the shadows at a tantalizingly slow pace—as if to grant the dark elves time to fully savor the men's misery.

Finally their doom stood revealed. There were four drow, all of them male. Two hung back, taking the unmistakable posture of subordinates standing guard. Of the other two, Chadrik was unsure which led and which followed.

One of them wore a warrior's leather armor and carried more fine weapons than Chadrik had owned in his most extravagant dreams. The drow's white hair was cropped close, probably to deprive his foes of a handhold, and a stylized dragon tattoo was emblazoned on one cheek. The other was clad in fine garments and gems, his long hair carefully woven into a multitude of braids. A large red gem was set in his forehead like a third eye. He regarded the men with a smile, the meaning of which was unclear to the terrific ruffian.

The warrior spoke first. "You sent word that you'd found the ruby."

Chadrik promptly handed over the necklace. "It's yours. No need to settle up; I'll get my pay from the man what hired me." His words tumbled over each other in their haste to be said.

None of the drow spoke. Chadrik dredged his fear-sodden mind for something to say. Remembering stories of drow hatred of surface elves, he manufactured a leer and a lie. "The elf wench was payment enough for me."

This did not seem to endear him to any of the dark elves.

"We have the ruby," the dandy said, gesturing to the gem in his forehead. "I can assure you that one is quite enough. Not a wise thing, to cheat the drow of the Dragon's Hoard."

"We didn't know! I swear," Chadrik babbled. "We took the elf woman just like the man said, got the necklace she was wearing. A mistake's been made, that's plain to see, but we stole the necklace in good faith. We're out the coin we paid the corpse-hauler to bring us in here, and the scribes who forged the burial papers. Not that I'm complaining! Take the gems for your trouble, and we'll be square."

The warrior listened in silence. When at last Chadrik's voice faded into silence, he tossed a glance toward the attentive guards. "Kill them."

"Not yet," said the other softly. "Many of the best tales have a circular form. The heroes or villains end as they begin. Justice is not always undesirable, provided the path it takes is sufficiently twisted."

"Meaning?" the tattooed drow demanded.

"You go along. I'll catch up in a bit."

The well-dressed drow turned to the captives, and the light in his eyes was horribly familiar. The warrior scowled but did not argue. He jerked his head toward one of the doors, indicating that the soldiers should follow. The door slammed shut behind the three drow. Somehow Chadrik knew that there would be no opening that door, or any of the others.

Chadrik had few morals and no illusions. Until this moment, he'd been certain that nothing could appall him.

He thought of the elf woman and envied her the ability to die at will.

Shakti Hunzrin ducked through of the low entrance leading to a small cavern on the outskirts of Menzoberranzan. The forces the archmage had promised her were assembled, and they stood awaiting her inspection in eerie silence.

She eyed her new command with dismay. The soldiers were not mercenaries, as she had expected, but undead drow. All of them were female.

For some reason that struck Shakti as deliberately offensive. Making matters worse was the fact that all of the zombies' heads had been shaved. Their lives gone, their names forgotten, even their luxuriant tresses stolen—reduced to this state, they were no better than males.

At least the fighters looked strong, and they were certainly well equipped. All were clothed in identical rothéhide armor, sturdy boots, and well-laden weapon belts. Most of the zombies were dark-clad, but a few wore crimson sashes to mark them as squadron leaders. Each of these leaders held a spear, and all the zombies carried swords that were plain but well made. A small crossbow hung on every belt alongside a quiver full of poisoned darts.

Shakti walked slowly down the line, a scented cloth pressed to her nose. One of Gromph's hirelings noted this.

"That isn't necessary," he said briskly. "These zombies are exceptionally well preserved and will keep indefinitely in the tunnels of the Underdark. Take them above ground as little as possible, for the spells will begin to dissipate."

She did not contradict this assertion. Now that she considered the matter, these fighters seemed ideally suited to her purpose. They would march without ceasing or tiring, and she needn't worry about organizing supplies or waste time hunting and foraging. Moreover, she was not unhappy to be spared the company of males.

"Will you be expecting their return?"

The young wizard sneered. "And waste magical resources laying zombie commoners to rest? Use them up, by all means. Here is the command key. They have been well trained—you shouldn't have any problem."

He handed her a small book bound in lizard hide. In it were a number of simple commands, most of them general enough to address a number of situations. Shakti paged through the book and found the needed command. She turned to the nearest crimson-clad zombie and issued the marching order. The zombie thumped the butt of her spear several times against the stone floor. An undead squadron wheeled smartly and headed for the eastbound tunnel. Other leaders took up the rhythm, and the zombie host set off with a seamless efficiency that no group of living drow could manage.

Shakti mounted a large riding lizard. She squared her shoulders and reined the beast toward the eastbound tunnel and the land known as Rashemen.

The spell Sharlarra had cast over herself gave way slowly. The sluggish whisper of her heart quickened and grew stronger, and the unnatural chill began to fade from her blood and flesh. Awareness returned first, and she lay in her coffin for many long moments while mobility returned to her frigid limbs.

There was no sound outside the wooden box. None whatsoever. Never had Sharlarra experienced such utter silence. The complete lack of sight and sound was profoundly unnerving. She actually took solace in the smell: mold, mostly, but also the musty, earthy scent peculiar to catacombs.

As soon as the elf could move, she braced her hands against the wooden lid and pushed, raising her knees at the same time. Fortunately the coffin was cheaply made of thin, light boards, and she was able to raise the lid.

A little.

Panic swept through her. She pushed the lid to one side and soon encountered solid stone. But at least a small opening had been created. She worked one foot out and braced it against the opposite wall, pushing the coffin as far as it would go. The top end was harder to move, but she finally managed to inch the box firmly against one wall. Then she pushed the lid back to the other side, creating the largest possible opening.

Fortunately, it was just enough. Also fortunate was the fact that the coffin had gone in feet first. She flipped over onto her stomach and then wriggled out into a round, faintly glowing room.

Her kidnappers were dead. Sharlarra glanced at the bodies and was just as glad that she'd slept while justice was being meted out.

It was easy enough to figure out what had happened. The thugs had been hired to find the necklace. They obviously didn't know that the tattooed drow had already found the ruby. When the two men tried to collect, they were accused of fraud.

An honest mistake, no doubt, but Sharlarra couldn't bring herself to shed tears over her fellow thieves.

One open door led out of the crypt. The elf ran up the swiftly sloping passage to the heavy wooden door. She threw her weight against it. It swung silently open, and she stepped out into a starlit night.

A copse of weathered trees surrounded the crypt entrance. They were of a type Sharlarra had never seen before. In the moonlight the leaves appeared to be an odd shade of blue, darkening with the coming of autumn to a deep violet. It was said that blue trees were common to Evermeet, but what were they doing here?

She ran her fingers over the faded inscription carved into the door. The curving marks were Elvish, a language she had never learned to read. She could make out only two words: "hero" and "Evermeet." A wry smile lifted one corner of her lips. Offhand, she couldn't think of any two words that were less applicable to her life.

Still, her hand lingered on the engraving that framed these words—a representation of the moon phases with a full moon framed by outward-facing crescents.

A faint whicker sounded behind her. Sharlarra whirled, then staggered back against the wooden door.

Before her stood a tall white horse, a beautiful creature with a luxuriant mane and tail so long they nearly swept the ground, and a face that was both intelligent and strangely expressive. The horse regarded her wistfully with long-lashed, silver-blue eyes that glowed like living moonstone.

These eyes were the horse's most substantial features. The rest of it was cloudy, almost translucent. Sharlarra could make out the shape of trees behind it.

"A ghost horse," she whispered.

Yet there was nothing of menace in the apparition's manner. If anything, it seemed delighted to see her. The ghost pranced a couple of steps closer, tossing its head in what looked suspiciously like a beckoning gesture.

Curiosity began to elbow fear aside. Sharlarra pushed herself away from the door and forced her shock-benumbed legs forward. She gingerly laid one hand on the horse's neck. To her vast relief, her hand did not sink into the insubstantial form. She stroked the ghostly horse. Its coat was silky, and cool to the touch.

The creature let out a soft whicker that sounded for all the world like a contented sigh. It nosed Sharlarra's shoulder and shifted around to present its left side.

"You want me to ride you," the elf woman said in disbelief.

The look the horse gave her left little doubt of its opinion of those who stated the obvious.

Sharlarra held her own hands in front of her face, turning them this way and that. Yes, they were still solid flesh. Her waking death spell had successfully faded. The horse was responding to *her*, not to a fellow ghost.

She considered the horse for a long moment. Curiosity defeated caution, and she vaulted onto its broad back. Immediately the ghost horse launched into flight.

After the first startled moment, Sharlarra realized that they had not actually left the ground. So swift and silent was the horse's stride that it had the sensation of flight. The elf relaxed one knee slightly, and immediately the ghost horse veered off in that direction.

A wild scheme began to take shape in Sharlarra's mind. "Can you jump?" she asked the horse.

In response, it soared over a mossy statue depicting a trio of long-dead soldiers. Sharlarra grinned and urged her mount toward the eastern wall.

A hollow, echoing battle cry sounded behind her. She shot a look over one shoulder. Her eyes widened in panic as three ghostly soldiers roiled out of the statue. They lofted swords that looked far too sharp and solid for her peace of mind and came after her at a run.

Sharlarra leaned low over the horse's neck, urging it onward. They dodged tombs and monuments, evading pale grasping hands that thrust up from the ground. Soon the east wall was before them. She urged the horse on, praying that the ghostly horse was equal to the eight-foot stone barrier. It might pass through unscathed, but she'd be left on the wall like a toad squashed by the wheels of a trade caravan.

An open grave yawned before them. Sharlarra screamed, and the horse leaped into flight.

Time stopped, and the moment between one heartbeat and the next seemed to last a Northman's winter. Then the horse's front hooves touched soundlessly down, and they began their eastbound flight across the meadows surrounding Waterdeep.

An inquiring whinny rose from the ghost horse and danced off on the rushing wind.

"I'm Sharlarra," she responded. "I don't suppose you could tell me your name."

The horse's pace slowed just slightly, and its head drooped. A pang of guilt assailed the elf. It was said that many ghosts did not realize they were dead. Some of these displaced spirits remembered pieces of their lives but were otherwise disoriented. A sure way to frustrate these ghosts was to ask them questions about themselves that they could not answer.

"Moonstone," she decided. "Your name is Moonstone."

Her mount bobbed its head in obvious accord, then it neighed again, louder and more insistently.

"Where are we going?" she translated and again received an affirmative response.

Sharlarra hadn't thought this far ahead, but the answer came to her quickly. What better destination than the adventure that had captured her imagination since the day she'd stolen Liriel Baenre's gems?

"You'll like Rashemen," she told the ghost horse. "I've heard they're fond of spirits there."

CHAPTER THIRTEEN

RETURN OF THE WITCH

Dawn was still hours away when the Witchboat's shallow hull crunched softly on the pebbles of the Rashemen shore. The two companions climbed out and gazed over the valley toward the somber tower. Liriel set off toward it at a brisk pace.

Fyodor caught her arm. "Before we go any farther, there are things you should know about this land."

"You've been telling me stories since we met," she pointed out.

"A drop in the ocean. Every place has its tales and legends. The valley between the shore and tower is known as White Rusalka Vale. We call this a silent valley. That means there are some places within it where no magic can be cast other than that which is in the land. The witches can use magic, but no one else."

The drow's eyebrows lifted. "Smart. In Underdark cities, we do much the same thing. It's like a magical moat around a castle."

"It is much the same idea, yes." He scanned the valley. "We should make camp."

They settled down in a small curve of the river and built a pair of fires. Liriel took the water skin Fyodor offered and made a face at the stale, musty taste.

"The water here runs fast and clear. Surely we could drink it."

"Tomorrow," he said firmly. "Tonight we must stay away from the river's edge. Promise me you will do this."

The drow bristled. "I know how to swim."

"If you meet a rusalka, you will learn how to drown," he responded. "Water spirits haunt this river. Some say that they are the ghosts of drowned maidens, and that may be so. Sometimes their attacks seem deliberate, but other times they cling to the living as if in remembered panic, dragging them under the water with them."

"You're just as dead, either way," Liriel concluded and eyed the darkening water with new respect.

"It would be well to stay within the circle of firelight, too," he added.

The drow acknowledged this with a curt nod. "I'll sit first watch. Thanks to that faerie elf, I've had enough sleep to last a tenday."

"Thanks to that faerie elf, you are alive," he pointed out.

Liriel puzzled over this. "Why would she bother?"

"Honor? Decency?"

"Not likely," the drow mused. "I suppose it's possible that she's honorable and decent, but she had to have a reason for what she did. Everyone does."

Lirel's stomach grumbled. She felt as hollow as if she'd gone a tenday without food, though she realized it had been only two days.

"Let's hunt." She rose and pulled a pair of throwing knives from her belt.

They had walked only a few paces into the forest when Liriel noted the rabbit emerging from the roots of an enormous fallen tree. It was beyond her accurate throwing range, but it seemed in no hurry to leave its den. She flipped her knife into throwing position and began to creep forward.

Again Fyodor seized her arm and indicated with gestures that she should wait. He unstoppered his *jhild* flask and took a swig.

Liriel's eyes rounded with astonishment. "A rage for a *rabbit?* How does one hunt Rashemaar *squirrels*—with summoned demons?"

"Check the rabbit for hidden magic," he told her. He began the chant that brought on the berserker rage.

She quickly cast the spell that revealed hidden magic. A soft aura surrounded the rabbit. Its head snapped up, and its long ears twisted this way and that as it sought the source of this disturbance. The creature bounded toward them, growing larger with each stride. Within a few paces it had changed form entirely.

A huge, hideous beast lurched toward them with the strangest gait Liriel had ever seen. The creature had two legs, but its powerful arms reached the ground, and it used them to pull itself along in an odd galloping motion. Matted gray fur covered the monster, and its face was like an orc's with its upturned snout and large, protruding lower canines. Most peculiar were the great black eyes—not just two, but a circlet of them that seemed to surround the creature's entire head like a string of enormous obsidian beads.

Fyodor lifted his cudgel and ran to meet the charge. He ducked beneath a vicious, swiping blow and lunged forward like a swordsman delivering a high jab.

The driftwood club smashed into the monster's face. The

creature swore with human fluency and spat out a mouthful of sharp, yellowed teeth. It swatted again. This time Fyodor blocked. The sharp crack of wood against bone rang through the air. Liriel winced, certain that the berserker had shattered his weapon.

The creature loped away, one arm hanging useless. As danger receded, so did the berserker rage. Fyodor seemed to slip down into himself, and he swayed where he stood.

Liriel ran forward and took the club from his slack hand. She pushed him down on the grass. He took the skin flask she offered and drank deeply of the stale water.

"How did you know?" she marveled.

He wiped the back of his hand across his mouth and pointed to the fallen tree. "See how the upturned roots make a small cave? That is too large a den for an entire warren of rabbits. The uthraki make their homes in such places."

"It's a shapeshifter, then. The spell should have shown its true form."

"Not the uthraki. The usual spells for such things show no more than the presence of magic."

Liriel pulled her knees up and wrapped her arms around them. "Well, clearly you're in no shape for hunting. Is it safe to pick mushrooms here?"

"If you know what to pick. There are many deadly mushrooms in these forests. Some will not kill you but will bring strange and terrible dreams. Better for tonight that we eat travelers' fare." He took from his bag some strips of dried meat mixed with what appeared to be berries and herbs.

The drow took one and nibbled off a corner. It was surprisingly good. "Where did these come from?"

"Thorn gave them to us, but we make something very similar in Rashemen. Let's get back to camp."

She rose and extended her hand to him. He accepted

without comment—another thing that still astonished Liriel. In her homeland, no one dared expose a weakness of any sort. An offer of help was the sort of insult that led to blood feud. Yet here between friends, this giving and accepting was a simple, expected thing.

Since even a short berserker rage was enormously debilitating, they didn't even discuss who should take first watch. Liriel sat beside her sleeping friend, watching the moon creep across the night sky and feeding sticks to the twin fires that framed their campsite. When she was certain that Fyodor was sound asleep, she rose silently and crept into the darkness.

It seemed to Liriel that Fyodor sometimes forgot the differences between them. The firelight was no advantage to her—quite the contrary. If there was any danger near at hand, she would be more likely to perceive it in the cool shadows beyond.

The drow began to explore the valley in ever-widening circles, avoiding the forest and keeping to the open grassy areas. The valley seemed deserted but for the singing insects in the grass and a small band of stout and shaggy wild horses. She noted with interest that they stood in a small circle, the young ones asleep in the center. All the adults stood, and while one was obviously a sentry, the others slept on their feet. Their heads drooped nearly to the meadow grass, but long velvety ears twisted even in slumber, alert to the slightest sound. The drow, of course, made none, and she was careful to stay downwind of the equine sentry.

She moved carefully, using the shadows and slipping between stony outcrops and small stands of brush. As she eased around a familiar-looking pile of boulders, she found herself face to face with a small, straw-thatched hut.

It had not been there before.

Instantly she froze, reminding herself that her magic was of no use in this place and that silence and stealth offered her best defense. Slowly she eased back into the shadows of the rocks.

The hut was silent, dark, and cold. No sound came from the open windows, no smoke curled from the small stone chimney. Yet Liriel could not rid herself of the distinct sense that here was a living presence.

It occurred to her that the hut itself seemed to be breathing. It leaned this way and that, almost imperceptibly, with a long, measured cadence that brought to mind a deep and silent sleeper. Curiosity overcame prudence, and she tossed a small stone at the hut.

Immediately the hut leaped into the air. Liriel's jaw dropped in astonishment as she found herself staring at a pair of enormous avian legs. Scaly limbs the size of young trees bent, and the huge, taloned bird feet flexed. The startled hut whirled and sped off into the night. This in turn alerted the ponies. Whickers of alarm and the swift-fading rumble of cantering hoofs filled the night.

Liriel sprinted back toward the campsite, knowing that these sounds, however faint and distant, would surely awaken the sleeping warrior. Sure enough, she saw Fyodor coming to find her, a make-shift torch in hand.

Her keen eyes saw the trap that he, entrapped in turn by his own circle of light, could not perceive. A drift of autumn leaves shifted, and the faint moonlight reflected off the teeth of a vicious steel trap.

She seized a fist-sized stone and hurled it toward him. It struck the trap, which sprang into the air like a striking *pyramo* fish. The warrior jumped back, and his quick glance traced the stone's arc to the place where Liriel stood.

"Don't move," he cautioned. "There may be others."

"It wasn't there last time I passed by. It was just set. I

don't think it's traps that we should be worried about."

Fyodor pulled his sword and continued toward her, probing the ground with the blade as he came. Another, smaller trap sang shut with a metallic clatter. He lifted his sword and showed her the steel maw clamped onto his weapon.

"Very well, it's not *just* traps," Liriel muttered.

He worked his way over to her without incident. Together they retraced their path toward the camp. To her puzzlement, Fyodor continued to test the ground, poking at the sod on either side of their path. Suddenly the sword tip sank deep into a narrow crevice. Fyodor yanked it free and put Liriel behind him.

A square piece of sod flipped open like a hatch, and several small creatures roiled out of their hiding place. They looked a bit like goblins, only smaller and brown of skin. None of them were above Liriel's waist in height, and all worn ragged trousers from which protruded long, hideous rat tails.

They were very like the kobold slaves who did menial chores in Menzoberranzan, but unlike the kobolds Liriel knew, and unlike the rats they resembled, these creatures did not attack in a swarm. They surrounded their larger prey, cutting off retreat but making no other move. Their round eyes caught the moonlight and reflected red.

"Traps and ambush pits," she said softly. "What other tactics do these things employ?"

"None," Fyodor responded, sounding genuinely puzzled. "They are sometimes mischievous but never do serious harm. I have glimpsed one before from time to time, but they are as skittish as deer."

"They're holding steady now," she pointed out, "and there's a lot of them. Right about now I could make good use of a meteor swarm spell!"

"It is bad luck to kill them."

"Let's hope they feel the same way about us," she said, eyeing the waiting hoard.

A creaking screech filled the air, like the sound of stormed-tossed tree limbs rasping together or the wooden hulls of two ships scraping one against the other.

Suddenly the creatures exploded into a gibbering chorus. Lofting small, dark knives, they hurled themselves into a running charge.

Fyodor batted aside the swiftest two, using the flat of his blade to lift them off their feet and hurl them aside. He spun to meet the next onslaught, carefully using his sword as a bludgeon to beat them back without killing them.

The drow had no such scruples. She drew her sword and ran it through the first squealing rat-thing that came at her. Tugging her sword free, she delivered a slashing backstroke that downed another and sent its companion darting back, jabbering in fear.

She stooped and swept up the knives all three of the creatures had dropped. To her surprise, they seemed to be carved of stone, but the edges were keen, the balance good. Liriel tossed all three knives into the air. She caught and hurled them, one after another, into a trio of attacking kobolds.

Another creak cut through the sounds of battle. Liriel glanced back in time to see a large limb sweeping toward her. Her quick glance took in the ropes suspending the projectile, and the huge tree to which they were attached.

A tree that simply hadn't been there a moment before.

Several kobolds stood in the branches, silhouetted against the night sky, hopping about and hooting with delight over their successfully launched trap.

The drow dived to the ground as the suspended limb swept over her. Immediately several of the creatures leaped onto her prone form. The very next instant, two or three of them were swept away, squeaking with surprise and pain, as the log pendulum swung back over them.

They were not very bright, Liriel noted. Not nearly bright enough to have planned any of this.

She bucked and heaved, trying to throw the remaining kobolds off. Fyodor fought his way over and began to peel the little beasts off her.

Finally he pulled her to her feet. She shoved a handful of disheveled hair off her face and took stock of the situation. Several of the kobolds sprawled nearby, senseless or dead, but most of the others had regrouped in a circle. The circle began to move as if following some well-rehearsed choreography, forcing the friends to keep moving in order to keep out of reach of those small sharp knives.

"They're herding us," Fyodor said in disbelief.

"Toward whoever planned this attack," the drow added.

He responded with a single grim nod. "They never gather in such numbers, never attack."

"So let's make their master come to us."

Fyodor flashed her a quick smile and a nod. Together they charged the swarm, swords leading.

The kobolds reverted to nature. Surprised by the sudden attack, they scattered, hooting in alarm. The friends broke through their ranks and kept running.

A keening shriek ripped through the night. Liriel shot a glance back over her shoulder, and her eyes widened in astonishment.

Gibbering in terror, kobolds sprang from the tree. The log still swung from the upper branches, which shuddered as if in a high wind. A ghostly form was pulling itself free, a treelike woman appearing nearly as large as its host.

The creature seized small, hard fruit from the tree and began to pelt the fleeing pair. The kobolds regrouped and roiled after them.

Fyodor seized Liriel's hand and pulled her along. "A thornapple haunt," he panted out. "Very dangerous. I should have remembered the story and checked the forest's edge for such trees."

"Where to?"

He pointed with his sword to the stone tower. "When we get there, I will talk for us both."

As it turned out, neither of them had a chance to talk. The massive wooden door swung open, and wall torches within flared into life. They ran into the tower and threw themselves against the door, pushing back the kobolds that hurled themselves with uncharacteristic determination at the door. Finally they slammed it shut and shot home the iron bolt. Small fists and stone knives clattered against the portal for a moment, then silence abruptly fell.

Before Fyodor could draw breath, a sharp *snick* above warned him of the coming trap. He seized Liriel's arm and spun her aside, leaping after her. The heavy iron chandelier crashed to the stone.

Dust filled the hall with choking clouds. Just as suddenly, the dust was gone. Fyodor spat out a mouthful of grit and regarded his grinning companion. She nodded toward the circle of fresh air around them.

"My magic's working again."

"So, drow, is mine," announced a stern female voice.

Dawn was breaking as Sharlarra cantered up to the travelers' inn outside Shadowdale. Smoke already rose from the chimney, and a lad busied himself hitching a pair of chestnut draft horses to a wooden cart. He caught sight of Sharlarra's mount, and his jaw dropped.

She stung off, painfully stiff and chilled to the marrow of

her bones. "What are my chances of getting a hot breakfast and a hotter bath? My arse is frozen solid."

He swallowed hard, and his mouth worked for a while before he managed to get a sound out. "Are you . . . "

"Alive? Yes, indeed. Better yet, I can pay." She jingled her coin bag, which held the money the dwarf jewelsmith had advanced her against the rest of her teatime jewel robbery.

She whispered a few words in Moonstone's ear. The ghostly horse inclined its head and trotted off toward the woodlands. Color began to return to the boy's face, and he beckoned the elf to follow him in.

Sharlarra was soon seated before the open hearth, a mug of hot spiced cider in her hands and a thick woolen blanket wrapped around her. A large haunch of venison roasted over a spit. The innkeeper, a round little woman with cheeks like rosy apples, sliced off a hearty slab and set it before her guest, clucking her tongue in motherly disapproval.

"Riding all night, and alone! A pretty girl like you. You should know better. It isn't safe, and it isn't respectable."

"The ghost horse tends to discourage unwanted suitors," the elf pointed out.

The woman considered this. "That it would. You keep strange company."

A fleeting smile touched Sharlarra's face. She wondered what her hostess would say if she knew she was on her way to meet up with a drow wizard!

Two hours later, after a good meal and blissfully warm soak in an oversized laundry barrel, Sharlarra went out in search of her horse. Moonstone was waiting for her in the place she'd named: a small copse of slender birch trees, silver-bright against the deep pines. One of the trees suddenly uprooted itself—or so it seemed for a single startled moment.

A ghostly woman emerged from the copse of trees and extended a slender hand to Sharlarra's horse. Fear shimmered through the elf, not fear of the spirit, but of the possibility that it might lure her horse away. She found her voice and let out a shout of outrage. Two ghostly faces turned toward her. The woman was somehow familiar, though Sharlarra could not place her. Then the ghost faded away. Moonstone did not follow.

The elf sprinted toward her horse and threw her arms around its cold white neck. "You stayed," she marveled. "You stayed."

Moonstone pulled away and gave her a disgusted look. A nudge of its head urged her to mount. Sharlarra swung herself up and set off on a brisk pace toward Rashemen.

With any luck, she's have a few miles between them and Shadowdale before anyone noted the missing venison.

Liriel peered into the cloud of dust. A black-clad figure took shape in the haze, her face obscured by an elaborate black mask. The woman lifted one hand, and tendrils of vines erupted from the walls and tangled around Liriel.

The drow spoke a sharp, sibilant word, and the vines withered and fell away. She seized a throwing spider from her belt and sent it spiraling toward the witch.

Fyodor let out a shout of protest and warning. The witch gestured, and the small weapon exploded into dust.

The pieces of the drow weapon were not content to lie still. They stirred, and grew, and each skittered on eight long legs toward the tower's guardian.

The spiders swarmed up the woman, under her robe and into the openings of her mask. She pawed at her face, screaming spell after spell that should have slain the attacking insects or at least turned them aside.

But the spells of a witch had little potency against the minions of a goddess. The Rashemi woman sank to the floor, thrashing in violent convulsions as the spider venom took hold. In moments, she lay still. The spiders skittered off, shrinking as they went and disappearing into tiny cracks between the stone.

Liriel stood as if frozen, her amber eyes darting here and there as she sought the next manifestation of the stubborn drow goddess. Moments passed, and none came. She rubbed both hands over her face like someone trying to awaken from a nightmare and walked over to the dead guardian.

Words Fyodor had spoken months before came back to her:

The penalty for killing a *wychlaran* is death.

She had barely entered the berserker's homeland, and already she had placed herself under sentence of execution.

There must be some way out, some way to accompany Fyodor on his journey to return the Windwalker and to see for herself the land of which he had spoken. Yet how could she do so when she had committed an unforgivable crime at the outset? Pleading that the witch's death had been the result of Lolth's will would do no good. The Rashemi, upon finding the body, were most likely to slay the drow on sight without waiting for explanations.

Mechanically her eyes roved over the witch's body, lying in a position of twisted agony on the ground. The mask covering her face was askew, her hair disheveled, her hands clenched in a rictus of agony from the poison the spiders had pumped into her veins.

As Liriel gazed at the corpse, an idea began slowly to stir in the depths of her mind. She was vaguely conscious of Fyodor moving toward her, his eyes large with horror as the full implications of what had just occurred became clear to him. She closed her eyes for a moment to shut him out. In that momentary darkness, the seed of a convoluted drow plot rooted and bloomed. Liriel's eyes flew open.

"I can become her."

"What?" The Rashemi stared at her in confusion.

"I can disguise myself as her. Here, help me." Liriel's hands were busy now, her mind made up. Swiftly she began to strip the garments from the dead woman.

Fyodor shook his head, like a man caught in the depths of a nightmare. "You cannot!" he said in an appalled voice. "The punishment for impersonating a witch is death."

"I just killed a witch," she reminded him. "You once told me that carries the death penalty. I don't see how things could get much worse."

Fyodor let out a long, frustrated sigh. "Even with the vestments, you would still be a drow. There are no dark elves among the witches."

"Not recently, no," Liriel argued. "But what about Qilué's sister?"

The Rashemi stared at her, not following.

"Don't you remember what Qilué told me? Her sister Sylune trained among Rashemen's witches."

His face cleared as he followed her reasoning. Liriel had assumed, logically enough, that since Qilué was a drow, her sisters would also be dark elves. Before Fyodor could disabuse her of this notion—and before he could mention that Sylune was not only dangerously famous, but dead—the swift clatter of footsteps from the tower's top room announced the arrival of reinforcements.

Liriel tugged the mask from the dead witch. The woman's appearance changed, instantly and drastically. She seemed to shrink, and her features softened and blurred into plump middle age.

Fyodor recalled what folktales said of the power of this mask. It was a Rashemaar artifact that placed a glamour over the wearer, allowing her to change her entire appearance at will. Liriel also made the connection. She quickly put it on, and suddenly a stranger stood before Fyodor.

The appearance Liriel assumed was reminiscent of Qilué: a tall and slender female with long silvery hair. Fortunately, with the mask covering her black face and her hands gloved against the chill night, the guise was a reasonable approximation of Sylune's appearance.

Liriel's hands sped through a spell. A small, flowing portal opened and drifted down like a sheet of silk to cover the dead woman. She disappeared as the magical fabric settled, then it, too, was gone.

A band of three masked, black-clad women burst into the hall. They regarded Liriel with narrowed eyes. "Who are you?" demanded the tallest of the three, a very slender woman with an abundance of dark brown hair.

"Leave this to me," Fyodor told Liriel softly. He stepped forward, sank into a low bow. "I am Fyodor of village Dernovia, recently returned from a task given me by women of your order."

"As I well know." One of the witches removed her mask, revealing a round, pleasant face. A web of lines radiated from the corners of bright blue eyes. She was old. That still surprised Liriel. Drow aged slowly, and few lived long enough to reach old age. Those who had the power to survive also possessed the means to prolong youth. In this woman, though, the mark of years seemed more an ornament than a deterioration.

"Zofia," Fyodor said. His eyes went to Liriel, and the old witch followed his gaze.

"We know Fyodor, but who is his friend?"

He seized upon that word. "A true friend, to me and Rashemen."

"Surely you haven't forgotten Sylune?" Liriel quickly supplied.

Fyodor suppressed a groan, and the two witches with Zofia exchanged puzzled glances. They both removed their masks, as if to better regard the stranger in their midst.

"Sylune, witch of Shadowdale?" demanded the slender Witch, who was clearly the youngest of the tree. "Sylune is dead."

Liriel glanced at Fyodor. He gave her an almost imperceptible nod. "Ah, but Sylune has had a rather active afterlife," Zofia put in with a faint, dry smile.

"This is no ghost, and no witch," the young woman insisted.

She spun toward Liriel, her fists clenched and her face white with rage. "I demand that you remove *my mother's mask*, and submit yourself to truth-testing!"

CHAPTER FOURTEEN

TRUTH TESTING

Zofia held up her hand. "All in good time, Anya. First we should learn what became of Fraeni and how this silver-haired woman came to wear our Sister's mask."

"We fought a swarm of kobolds who had fallen under the spell of a thornapple haunt, and ran into the tower for refuge," Liriel said honestly. "There were other monsters, as well, and they followed us in. The witch was overcome. I took the mask from her after she fell." She looked toward Anya. "Your mother died bravely, fighting an evil foe."

Fyodor winced at this painful truth. The fallen woman had believed she was trapping and attacking a drow and a traitorous human. He wondered briefly if this was not the simple truth. If he had not brought Liriel to Rashemen, the shadow of Lolth would never have fallen on this tower.

"Where is she now?"

"I do not know," the disguised drow said. "She disappeared. I don't know where she went."

"She speaks truly," Zofia said. "Your mother's body will return to us, young Ethran, and her spirit has never left. As for this outlander, perhaps she is who she claims to be. Who among us has not seen stranger things?"

Anya scowled. "We will see."

"I have seen the truth-testing done," Fyodor said quietly. "It can be a terrible thing. I will not permit it."

The young witch looked at him in disbelief. "What could you possibly do to stop me?"

"I could take her place." Fyodor shook his head, cutting off Liriel's protest. "It is my right to do so. I am pledged guardian to a powerful and honorable *wychlaran*. This much I will swear, on my sword and on my life."

"That is not needed," Zofia said gently. "You have the name of an honest man. What of the battle frenzy? You have mastered it? And you have found the Windwalker? Of course you have, or you would not have returned."

Liriel quickly removed the gold amulet from her neck and held it out. "We have no further need of the Windwalker. Fyodor's rune is carved upon Yggdrasil's Child."

The old woman's eyes lit with interest. "A tale I await with interest. Well done, Sister. No, you keep the amulet. I suspect that it is yours to wear."

"Zofia, are you very certain?" The third witch, a thin woman of middle years, spoke for the first time. "It has been many years since Sylune walked among us, and your eyes—"

"I am not yet blind," Zofia said firmly, "and I am the only one yet alive who knows the witch of Shadowdale."

She tipped her gray head to one side as she regarded Liriel. "Do you still wish to be called Sylune? Perhaps there is another name that you have come to prefer?"

It occurred to Liriel that the old woman had never actually endorsed her claim. Zofia awaited her response, her canny blue eyes giving away no secrets.

"Liriel," the drow offered.

The old witch nodded. "So be it."

Anya sent her a fulminating glare. "She still hides behind the mask. Does no one think to ask why? Perhaps she is *durthan,* an evil witch. If her intentions are good, let her remove the mask."

"I can only suppose that Sylune did not wish to appear before us as a ghost," Zofia said mildly. "Or are we mistaken about this, Sister? Are you still numbered among the living?"

Liriel inclined her head, not only to signify agreement but to hide the amused admiration in her eyes. The old woman was as adept at partial truths and misdirecting questions as any priestess in Menzoberranzan.

"She has the right to wear it, Anya," the witch continued. "Sylune was one of many witches to wear this mask on her face or on her belt. The mask remembers her. It forgets none who wear it."

The drow heard the hidden message. She surreptitiously brushed her hand against her skirts, moving the glove aside enough to afford a glimpse of her skin. It was not black, but a creamy pale hue only a shade or two darker than Thorn's white face.

So the mask *did* remember! She had imagined Sylune as a tall, beautiful drow with silvery hair. The mask, fortunately, had a more accurate version in its memory.

Now, she thought, comes the real test of its power. She tugged off her gloves and raised her long white hands to the mask, which she carefully removed. Judging by the astonishment on Fyodor's face, her magical disguise held. She gave him a reassuring smile and tied the mask to her belt.

"May I keep the mask while I am in Rashemen?" she asked belatedly.

Zofia gave the drow a sweet, benevolent smile. "You will, of course, guard it as if your life depended upon it."

"Of course," Liriel echoed. She and the witch exchanged a look of perfect understanding.

They spent that night in the tower, and in the morning left Anya behind to take up her mother's post. The remaining four boarded a Witchboat, the same sleek little craft that had brought them across the lake. They glided smoothly northward, stopping at midday at a small fishing village.

The journey was a revelation to Fyodor, and a disturbing one. He had never traveled with *wychlaran* before—at least, not with any but Liriel, and not in his own land. He was accustomed to the deference given them but had never given much though to the practical details of their lives.

Neither, apparently, did they. The Witchboat was met at the dock and the travelers ushered to the village tavern. There they were served a midday feast of rabbit sausage and rothé cheese with bread still hot from the morning baking. Riding ponies were brought to them without question. Fyodor took note of their brands and privately vowed to ensure their return to their owners.

"I can see why there's such a strong penalty against impersonating a witch," Liriel told Fyodor in a joking whisper. "If there wasn't, every lazy halfling pickpocket would be walking around behind a black mask."

The witches rode astride their animals, and Liriel was pleased to note that her black gown had a split skirt, covered with a long tabard. It was all she could do keep her seat on a horse with both knees clamping the beast's sides.

"Come, Wanja," the old woman said, speaking to her companion. "These young people have things to say to each other, things our old ears have long forgotten."

"Speak for yourself," the other witch responded with a grin, but she clapped her heels to her pony's sides and took off after Zofia.

"The old one is clever," Liriel observed. "She sees more than most and says much without giving away secrets. This might actually work!"

"It cannot be done," Fyodor said in despair.

"Why not? Zofia is the only one who actually knew Sylune. For reasons of her own, she is willing to let things stand. What I would like very much to know, however, is what these reasons might be."

"She is an Oracle. No one in Rashemen sees the future as clearly as she."

"And?" Liriel pressed, sensing more.

"She is my grandmother."

The drow nodded, encouraging him to continue. After a moment, it occurred to Fyodor that she didn't automatically make the connection.

"Family is considered of greatest important in Rashemen. We form close bonds, we stand for each other. You remember when the gods walked and magic failed?"

"Yes."

The answer was terse, closed. Fyodor did not press the point, not sure he wanted to know the kind of turmoil this had caused in Liriel's home city.

"When the berserker warriors go into battle, the natural magic of our battle frenzy is strengthened by ritual. For some reason, no one could say why, this magic twisted in me. In this I was not alone," he added softly. "A few witches were never right again. All were slain.

"It was deemed necessary," he said hastily, though Liriel

had not condemned this harsh verdict. "The witches bond together in circles to cast their magic. One person's weakness endangers all. Some thought warriors should receive the same sentence."

"Zofia didn't agree."

"No, and because she sees more than most, the others listen when she speaks. She entrusted to me the Windwalker, one of Rashemen's great treasures, and gave me a chance to find my way home."

"Because she is your grandmother." Liriel spoke the words aloud as if she thought the exercise might help her understand what they meant. Coming around full circle, she added shrewdly, "And because she is an Oracle. Maybe she foresaw some great destiny for you."

The young man shook his head. "She told me only that I would find my own destiny, one that could change the course of Rashemen's history."

Liriel quickly made the connection. "That would be me?"

"Zofia is willing to wait and see."

They fell silent as the drow thought this over. Fyodor, too, had his own thoughts to consider.

Despite Zofia's tacit approve, he was dismayed by the deception in which he found himself. Though no untrue words had actually been spoken, a lie had been crafted, and both he and Liriel would have to live it as long as they remained in his homeland. This galled him. He himself believed in speaking simple truth, but he had seen enough of subterfuge to know that truth has a way of coming out. Attempts to conceal it usually made matters worse.

"Don't think that I'm unaware of the risk," Liriel said softly, uncannily echoing Fyodor's thoughts. "If this little game goes awry, you should call *xittalsh*."

She noted his puzzled expression and struggled to

explain the drow concept. "In my homeland there are contests of arms, fought in special caverns to entertain those who watch. Do humans have such things?"

"We do, yes."

"Some of the fighters are slaves, others monsters, some are professional fighters who thrive on the battle, but sometimes fighting can give a drow a second chance. Let's say that two drow are caught in a conspiracy. One is undoubtedly guilty, but the other's involvement is not so clear. That drow can call *xittalsh*, and claim the right to establish her innocence."

"They fight in the arenas. If they win, they live," Fyodor concluded.

Liriel nodded.

"Even though they may be guilty. Even though everyone knows that they are guilty."

"They live," she said bluntly. "If we are caught, you must tell them you knew nothing of my true identity. Go on as you did before we met. Fight for Rashemen. That will make most people believe in your innocence. Win enough battles, and in time even the doubters will cease to care."

They rode for a long time before Fyodor trusted himself to speak. "Do you think so little of me to believe that I could do such a thing? There are pledges between us—pledges of honor and promises of the heart. These things I should throw away so I can keep breathing a few years more? I should betray you so I can grow old alone and die in dishonor?"

"Dishonor? Why so?"

In response, Fyodor pointed to a small, rounded hill beside road ahead. Behind it, the village of Dernovia was visible on the horizon. Smoke from the hearth fires spiraled up from behind a high stone wall. Neat fields surrounded the walls, and shaggy rothé cattle gleaned the harvested grain fields. Smoke rose from some grass-covered knolls just outside the walls. One side of the hill was flat, and a door and shuttered windows had been cut into it.

"That is the home of Stanislor the butcher," Fyodor said. "It was learned that he had deliberately weighted his scales to cheat his customers. He has lived here, apart from other villagers, since I was a boy."

"Why?"

"It is said that a man is known by three things: his sword, his children, and his word. Deception of any kind is not lightly treated."

"Then don't get caught!"

"That is not the point," he said heatedly. "Even if no one else knows of this lie, I do. It is in that knowledge that dishonor lies."

The drow shook her head in befuddlement. This was new to her—dangerously new. One thing was clear: Fyodor had risked much to throw his lot in with hers. If she were ever found out, Fyodor would be considered a traitor, and she did not fully understand what this would mean to him.

They stopped at the gate, a large arch framed by massive wooden doors and more of the fanciful carving such as had decorated the Witchboat. Liriel noted common patterns: unicorns, deer, and hunting hounds formed borders, and scenes of mountains and village were carved in manner that created an illusion of great depth. The heavy doors were closed, as were the shuttered portals near the top of the wall.

"Stay here," Fyodor murmured to Liriel. "Do not dismount, whatever happens. Cast no spells, draw no weapons. There is no danger here."

He cupped his hands and took a deep breath. "I had heard there were *men* in Dernovia!" he bellowed. "Who cowers behind these walls like chickens in a coop?"

Liriel's jaw fell. Despite Fyodor's warning, her hand went to the dagger tucked in her boot.

Carved shutters flew open with a crash, and a black-bearded young man thrust his head out of the portal. A fierce grin split his face.

"Walk into the Black Bear's den, will you? Come, and welcome! We're fattening for the winter sleep, and you look soft enough to eat with a spoon."

In response, Fyodor pantomimed ringing a dinner bell. The portal slammed shut, and the door flung open. The bearded man hurled himself at Fyodor like a charging bear. Several other men, all of them garbed in rough wool breeches and leather or fur vests, boiled out of the walled town close behind him.

They surrounded Fyodor's pony and pulled him down. To Liriel's astonishment, the bearded one pulled him into a fierce, back-slapping embrace. After several moments of this they thrust each other at arm's length and grinned like fools.

"You look well, Kaspergi," Fyodor said. "Imagine my surprise."

The other man snorted. "I was always the handsome one. If not for this beard, the women would stare all day long, and who would do the baking?"

Fyodor glanced back at Liriel, as if he feared this observation might raise her ire where the friendly mayhem failed. The bearded man followed his gaze. A look of puzzlement crossed his face when he noted the silver-haired woman Liriel appeared to be. He touched his forehead in a gesture of respect.

"This is Liriel, who once called herself Sylune, witch of Shadowdale," Fyodor said carefully. "She has come to learn from Zofia."

It occurred to Liriel that the men still blocked the gate.

Any males who showed such disrespect to the priestesses of Menzoberranzan would be summarily slain. The witches, far from taking offense, smiled tolerantly at this strange • reunion.

"We will talk later," Fyodor said, clapping Kaspergi on the shoulder.

More of the same awaited them as they made their way through the town. Fyodor pulled up at a snug cluster of buildings. He slid down from his horse and whistled a few sharp, high notes. Several children abandoned their play and swarmed him with a fervor that reminded Liriel uncomfortably of the recent kobold attack.

A sturdy young woman came from the cottage to investigate. She let out a glad cry and ran to Fyodor, her black braids flying. She wrapped him in a fierce hug while the children hopped around and loudly demanded attention.

Fyodor turned to face Liriel, his arm still around the woman's waist. "My Lady, I present to you my sister Vastish. Some of these children are hers. I forget which," he said with a somber face and laughing eyes. The small humans' delighted howls of protest brought a puzzled smile to Liriel's face.

The woman dropped into a low curtsey. "*Wychlaran*," she said politely, speaking to all three of the mounted females.

It occurred to Liriel that this was only introduction expected or needed. Fyodor's sister saw only the black gown, the mask hanging on her belt, and believed that all was known.

Zofia placed a hand on Liriel's arm. "You must greet your Sisters, then I will show you where you will stay. No outlander can enter the witches' longhouse. You will have your own hut outside the walls. That has not changed since Sylune was last among us. Fyodor will stay there, as well, but he must spend this night with his brothers. There is a new *fyrra,* and they have much to discuss."

Fyodor hoisted one importunate imp and propped her on his hip. He came over to Liriel and took one of her hands. This he raised to his lips. "You have only to call, and I will come."

His sister's winter blue eyes, so like her brother's, widened in astonishment. "You have become a guardian?"

He nodded, and Vastish sighed happily. "Then you will not be going to the barracks with the other men! That is wonderful news. Since the midsummer moon, I have bribed the children into bed with promises of your stories."

"I must report to the *fyrra* and will most likely stay the night. There will be time for a tale or two first. The others will keep for another day."

"Petyar will be pleased to see you in the barracks. He received his sword while you were gone."

"Petyar my cousin?" Fyodor echoed incredulously. "Little Petyar?"

"He is taller than you now, and eats as if he means to be every bit as broad before the tenday is done."

Brother and sister continued to chatter happily as Liriel rode off. She was intrigued by this strange reception. Fyodor had told her that in Rashemen family was important. That was clear to see. In a few moments, she had added as much to her knowledge of Fyodor as she had learned through months of travel, shared battle, and an intimacy deeper than the drow had ever dreamed possible.

His roots ran deep in this land. He had enough family to fill the Baenre stronghold, friends who welcomed him with foolish joy, and a place in the community. Clearly he was a favorite among the children. From a distance Liriel could hear his deep bass voice lifted in a silly song.

She could see him growing old here, becoming the much-loved village elder and storyteller. And family. . .

For the first time she considered this particular implication. She and Fyodor were lovers, yes, but children did not necessarily follow. Every drow female with any access to magic at all chose when she would conceive. This was a choice Liriel had never considered. There was nothing in her own family to make her look back with pleasure on childhood or anticipate parenthood with longing. What life could any child born to her and Fyodor know? Half-drow children would never find a place here or anywhere else that she could imagine.

Her pony lowered its head and plodded up the increasingly steep street. Liriel put aside these strange thoughts and focused on her surroundings. At the top of the hill was a large, long building of unpainted wood, a simple design made elaborate by huge carved panels. A steeply slanting roof crowned the building.

"The barracks," Zofia said softly, pointing to a long, low building to the left of the witches' longhouse. "The berserkers form groups known as *fangs*. Each has a name. Fyodor belongs to the Black Bear lodge."

"That's appropriate," Liriel murmured.

In the courtyard were a dozen or so warriors, stripped to the waist despite the chill air. Some of them wrestled, while others shot arrows at targets propped up against bales of straw. There was much laughter and loud boasting, but none of the men drew steel or turned their bows upon each other.

"I suppose you have questions?" the old witch prompted.

Thousands, Liriel thought, but she began with one of the newest. "The males . . . " She caught herself and corrected. "The men of Rashemen amaze me. How can they compete so vigorously without creating blood feuds?"

Zofia chuckled. "You have been too far to the west, and too far to the south. The hot sun addles the brain. Too much is made of too little. Here we know what is important, yes?"

The drow nodded sagely. In truth, however, she had never heard a question spoken whose answer seemed so far beyond her grasp. How could she possibly know what was valued in this strange place? It was not a question she had asked herself under familiar circumstances!

That realization hit her like a stone dropping into the pit of her stomach. How odd. She had lived for more than forty years—probably longer than the careworn Wanja—and it had never occurred to her to wonder what was truly important.

Oh, she'd privately scoffed at the constant striving and plotting that was Menzoberranzan. The intrigues that so absorbed her fellow drow held little interest for her, but what *did* matter?

Survival, obviously. Magic, certainly. Life without adventure was unbearably dreary. Power . . .

Her mind slid uncomfortably away from that notion. She'd had enough of that on Ruathym to last her a dragon's lifetime. Fyodor set great store by honor, and she had to admit that her faith in his steadfast ways had become a touchstone in her life. Liriel treasured the unexpected joys of friendship. These things she knew. What else could there possibly be?

"There are many kinds of truth-testing," Zofia said softly, breaking into Liriel's thoughts with uncanny timing. "Sometimes the answers matter less than the questions."

This was too much for the pragmatic drow. She threw up her hands in disgust. "Life was less confusing when I was dead."

For some reason, this amused the witch. "Welcome back, Sylune," she said with a wry little grin. "I suspect that this visit will be as interesting as the last!"

CHAPTER FIFTEEN

BLACK WOLF

Later that evening, when Vastish's brood had been spoiled by one too many stories and far too much honeycake, Fyodor made his way up the hill toward the residence of the witches and berserkers. His progress was slow for at nearly every house he was stopped by neighbors he had known since childhood. All celebrated his return with rough embraces and affectionate insults. All produced flasks of *jhuild* or mugs of scrump—a fermented cider that was nearly as potent as the Rashemaar liquor—in hope of prolonging Fyodor's visit and coaxing from him news of the wider world.

There was news to be had, as well. The old Iron Lord had stepped down. Word was that he had taken ill and that he was being cared for in the forest retreat of the witches. In his place ruled Thydrim Yvarrg. A good choice, most agreed, provided that he did not expect his impulsive, hard-drinking son Fyldrin to succeed him. There was lesser news, too, ranging from tales of hauntings and monster attacks to the happy birth of twin boys to the village cooper and his wife.

With one thing and another, the evening swiftly passed. By the time Fyodor reached the barracks of the Black Bear lodge, a waning moon peered over the summit of Snowcat Mountain.

It was custom for any returning warrior to report to the village *fyrra*. Fyodor made his way to Treviel's cottage. The door stood open, revealing a blazing fieldstone hearth before which sat a stocky but powerful man of an age and size that Fyodor's father might have known, had he survived the Tuigan hoard. The old warrior hummed to himself as he polished his boots with goose grease. His feet were clad in stockings of a highly singular nature. They had been knitted to look like gloves, with each toe a different bright color. Narrow bands of the same colors marched up the man's thick legs, and matched the bright embroidery on his boiled wool vest.

A faint smile touched Fyodor's face. Few men dressed in clothing that so clearly proclaimed their nature as did Treviel. The man was as cheery as his garb, and Fyodor had long considered him a valued friend. Yet the young warrior stood where he was, deeply reluctant to begin this interview. *Fyrra* had been his father's title and these his rooms. Treviel was a good man, but it pained Fyodor to see another in Mahryon's place.

Certain proprieties must be observed. Fyodor cleared his throat and delivered the expected insult. "How can a warrior be a leader of men when he cannot persuade his own toes to agree upon a color? Is Sashyar angry with you, or did you knit those yourself?"

The graybeard looked up from polishing his boots. Pleasure lit his eyes, swiftly followed by caution.

Fyodor understood the man's concern. His last memory of the new *fyrra* was colored by the haze of uncontrolled battle frenzy. He was not certain, and no one would tell him yes or no, but he suspected that he might be responsible for the deep, puckered puncture scar on the old man's brawny forearm.

"Sashyar is *always* angry with me," Treviel said complacently, "and that is a good thing for a warrior. You could do with such a wife. Too many hours spent dallying with sweet-tempered maids softens a man's spirit and leaves him unprepared for battle."

An image of Liriel in full dark-elf fury came vividly to mind. Fyodor chuckled. "I have become guardian to a *wychlaran* outlander who possesses the temper of a drow and the sweet reason of a pack mule. Will that suffice?"

"A guardian, eh?" For a moment the *fyrra* looked sincerely impressed, then he shrugged. "This woman might be all you say and more, but she's still a pale shadow of my Sashyar," he said proudly. "Even so, I will allow myself to hope that she may yet make a fighting man of you."

"As to that, I am not such a fool to challenge a yeti to snow racing or think I might wrestle the wood man into submission," Fyodor said dryly.

"Then I am hopeful indeed, for I could say as much about Sashyar," Treviel confided in a droll whisper.

The men shared a chuckle. Treviel beckoned Fyodor into the room and pointed to the chair opposite him. His keen-eyed gaze noted the dark sword at Fyodor's side, and his face grew serious.

"It is said that Zofia Othlor sent you after a great magical treasure. You found this?"

"That and more," Fyodor said.

The man's face brightened with the expectation of grand tales to come. One shadow remained, however, and they both knew it well. "You are whole, my son?" ventured Treviel.

"I am."

"Then all is right with Rashemen," the older man said briskly. He nodded to the porcelain samovar on the nearby table. As befitted its owner, the tall, lidded pot was brightly painted: Red and yellow unicorns cavorted on meadows of emerald green. Lid, rim, and base were ringed by entwining runic designs rendered in unsubtle shades of blue and purple.

"The tea is hot and nearly strong enough to strip the hide from a bear. You will drink?"

There were things that must be spoken, and Treviel's choice of words provided as good an opening as Fyodor expected to get. "Perhaps I should save some of your tea in a flask. If the change is slow to pass, it would peel off the bearskin swifter than a hunter's knife."

Treviel gaped, then his smile stretched his thick gray mustache nearly from ear to ear. "Is it so? You have become *chesnitznia*?"

This was an accomplishment sought by all of Rashemen's berserkers and achieved by few. Although the title "berserker" came from an ancient word for "bearskin," the literal transformation of human warrior to bear was in these days more a legend than a reality.

"They call it *hamfarrig* on the island of Ruathym. Shapestrong."

The village lord grunted with satisfaction. He was something of a scholar as warriors went, and Fyodor could see him tucking these new words away to savor at a later time.

"Word of the battle there has reached us. A sea battle," he added wistfully, this warrior of a land-locked nation. "Your *darjemma*, it would seem, was more interesting than most."

He poured tea into wooden cups. Fyodor took one sip and understood why. The acidic brew would no doubt eat right through pewter. He threw back the contents of the little cup and accompanied his swallow by slamming his fist on the table. This ritual completed, he set the empty cup down. Treviel refilled it and nodded expectantly at the young man, clearly waiting to hear the story of this wondrous battle.

"I have just come from my sister's home," Fyodor said apologetically.

The commander threw back his head and let out a deep, belly-shaking roar of laughter. "No need to say more! Even the village storyteller must rest his voice, yes? Sit, then, and drink your tea. Your story can wait until after the Mokosh games. You will go to the mountains with the others?" he asked, noting the strange look that crossed the young man's face.

"In truth, I had forgotten." The thought of leaving Liriel alone so soon after their arrival left him profoundly uneasy. Who knew what sort of mischief she might achieve in his absence? "Perhaps I should wait for the next holiday."

Treviel snorted. "You will go, and you will win. See to it!" he said with a teasing wink.

Fyodor knew an order when he heard one, and a dismissal as well. He managed a wan smile and rose. "No stories, no tea," he surmised.

The older man let out a guffaw and slapped one beefy thigh. "You should live to be so lucky. Drink!"

Fyodor obligingly downed the rest of the bitter brew and took his leave.

A chorus of grating snores greeted him at the barracks. As was custom, most of the warriors had retired early in anticipation of the grueling holiday ahead. Fyodor toed off his boots at the front door and studied the parchment tacked to the doorpost. With sorrow he noted the names no longer listed: Mahryon, his father; Antonea, the sword-smith with whom he had apprenticed; several cousins and boyhood friends. Some of them had been alive when Fyodor had entered his last berserker frenzy against the Tuigan. He hoped that none had died following him on his suicidal charge.

His cousin Petyar's room was toward the end of the barracks. He made his way quietly down the long wooden hall. A thin ribbon of light underlined the door. Fyodor tapped the door faintly then pushed it open.

Two cots filled the room with the scent of fresh hay and dried angelica flowers, excellent for repelling both insects and unwanted dreams. One of these cots was filled from head to foot—and beyond—with the longest, skinniest excuse for a Rashemi warrior Fyodor had ever beheld.

A face still soft from yesterday's childhood regarded him with a mixture of hero worship and welcome. The boy's upper lip was decorated by a faint shadow that looked more like a smudge of axle grease than a mustache. Fyodor sternly resisted the urge to tousle his young cousin's hair. Instead he seized one of the oversized feet that hung over the edge of the cot and raised it for closer scrutiny.

"If you were a pup, I'd suspect that your mother befriended a bear," Fyodor said. "Of course, if you *were* a pup, I'd have to drown you or risk weakening the kennel. Who would have thought my Uncle Simaoth's litter could produce such a runt?"

Petyar grinned and tugged his foot free. "The cobbler complains that if I grow any more I'll be wearing boots of unmatched leather. He'll have to slaughter two rothé cows to get enough for a pair!"

"If you wish to provide the cobbler with a single piece of leather, there is an easy solution," Fyodor teased. "Those feet were made for dragonhide boots."

The boy chuckled delightedly. "Easy enough, now that you're back home! You'll go snow racing with us tomorrow?"

"Why? Does a white dragon await us in the mountains?"

The gleam in the boy's eyes darkened. "Worse," he said flatly. "A black wolf."

Fyodor received this news in silence. Petyar had been born the same spring as Vastish's firstborn, and the boys had grown up like brothers. The death of his favorite cousin had cast a deep shadow over young Petyar's life, and left him with an indelible and unreasonable hatred of wolves.

"Has this wolf done any harm?" Fyodor asked at last.

"Not yet. It has been seen lurking near the village."

"How near? The refuse hill? The fields?"

"The forests," the boy admitted.

"Petyar."

The young man responded with a defiant shrug. "Do not say you haven't been warned. The snow race should be a contest, not a hunt! If you are content to be a wolf's prey, so be it. I at least will keep close watch."

"That you will watch closely I do not doubt," Fyodor said somberly, "especially if Treviel's daughters join the race."

A grin edged its way onto Petyar's face. "What of it? There is no harm in looking."

"I will pass that thought along to the *fyrra*," Fyodor suggested. "Perhaps he will have it carved upon your coffin."

The boy chuckled and reached for the oil lamp. "Time for sleep, or tomorrow morn we won't know whether we're looking at wolves or women."

Fyodor settled down on his cot and sent a wry smile into the darkness. "Sometimes it is difficult to tell."

"Aye," Petyar agreed, in a tone that suggested he had vast experience in such matters. After a moment's silence, he added, "You have met many such women in your travels?"

The wistful tone in the young man's voice was familiar to Fyodor. He had heard it this night from his sister's children, fully two-score neighbors, and even the *fyrra*. Now he had no heart for more stories and scant voice left to speak them. Instead he offered, "I have known Sashyar all my life."

Petyar let out a hoot of amusement. "Now I have no fear of the *fyrra*'s wrath! Go on, tell Treviel that I admire his pretty daughters. I have a weapon to match yours."

Fyodor thought of the blunt, black sword resting against his cot and prayed with all his heart that the boy's words would never come to pass.

Liriel's tour of the Witches' Lodge was not quite what she had expected. For one thing, the complex was more extensive than she'd gathered from first impression. It went on and on, covering the top of the hill that crowned the village and stretching down much of the back slope. In addition to the great hall and the warriors' barracks, there was a temple to the Three, the goddesses who formed the center of Rashemi worship. The temple was a lovely thing, with a rounded domed roof guarded by a trio of towers. Still, how was such a thing possible?

"One temple for three goddesses?" Liriel demanded.

"One goddess, if you prefer. We worship the triple goddess: maiden, mother, and wise woman," Zofia explained. "They are called by other names in other lands. We of Rashemen also have our names for them, but these are our own and must not be spoken to outsiders. Come – I will show you the bathhouse."

This proved to be a small, round, windowless building constructed of stone and roofed with slate. The old witch pulled open the door. Steam escaped, along with a sudden, rushing energy that was more than air.

Liriel peered inside. In the center of the room was a well filled with rocks that glowed with heat. A large bucket had been suspended over it with ropes running from it to the wooden benches built against the walls. Liriel saw the purpose of this at a glance. Anyone desiring a steam bath would pull a rope and tip a bit of water onto the hot rocks. The drow had similar steam houses, albeit magical ones, in Menzoberranzan.

Fyodor's sister sat on one of these benches, a linen sheet wrapped around her. She gave them a pleasant nod—and vanished.

"The *Bannik*," Zofia said casually. "A spirit of health and divination. Most bathhouses have one. If you see a familiar person in the bathhouse who should not be there, do not take alarm. It is only the *Bannik*."

"If I see a familiar person, I'd be a fool *not* to take alarm," Liriel muttered.

The witch gave her a curious stare. "It is so? You have many enemies?"

"I'm not sure what a Rashemi means by 'many' enemies," Liriel prevaricated.

Zofia let out an amused chuckle. "Well said. It would seem that Fyodor has told you some of our tales. What a storyteller he would have made!" she said wistfully.

Liriel considered these words and discarded them as unimportant. Most likely Rashemi storytellers devoted their lives to this art, as did human bards or drow deathsingers. Fyodor had taken a warrior's path instead.

"I felt something leave when we entered. What was that?"

"Who can say?" Zofia responded. "The Bannik sometimes invites friends to the bathhouse. Forest spirits, water spirits, demons."

The drow took a cautious look over her shoulder. "This doesn't bother you?"

"Do you think that one spirit has the power to heal or to divine?" Zofia demanded. "The *Bannik* are powerful because they *have* friends. It is a lesson we Rashemi have learned well."

They closed the door and moved on to the main building. Zofia shook her head. "None but a witch may enter. No outlander is permitted within, not even one with a *wychlaran*'s training. Even if you were who you claim to be, you could not pass this door." Zofia held up a hand, silencing Liriel. "That will keep. Come, I will show you to your hut."

The two females walked in silence down the long road leading to the village wall. Liriel's new home was surprisingly pleasant, a small hillock crowned with meadow grass still studded with summer flowers. Smoke rose from the small circle of stones, giving evidence of the dwelling within.

The single round room was heated by an iron stove. A large fur-covered bed filled one side, a small table and chairs the other. Pegs provided places for clothing. A wash-tub stood next to a shelf holding dishes and pots.

Zofia took down a samovar and set to work making tea. She also took from her bag a small loaf of bread, a salt cellar, and a white cloth.

"You will need these to befriend your *domovoi*. A house spirit," she explained, responding to Liriel's inquiring stare. "They are helpful and kind, and as long as you do not offend them they will protect your house and do some of your chores."

"What am I supposed to do with these things?"

"Wrap the bread and salt in the cloth and stand in your open doorway. Invite the *domovoi* in with kind and pleasant words, then leave the gift under the threshold stone. There is a special hollow there, of course."

"Of course," Liriel echoed, feeling slightly dazed by this recitation. "What does a *domovoi* look like?"

"Oh, don't expect to see it. You will hear it from time to time. It will hum when content and sigh or even groan when sad. Now, let us speak of you," she said. Her keen blue eyes regarded Liriel steadily. "Tell me why you have come to Rashemen."

"I came for Fyodor and to bring back the Windwalker."

"Nothing more?"

The drow hesitated, not sure how far to trust the witch. She decided that she had little choice. Without Zofia's patronage she would not have been allowed into this land at all.

"Another task was entrusted to me," she said slowly. "I was given a tapestry in which are imprisoned the spirits of slain elves. I promised to free them."

A light swept over Zofia's face. "Now I understand. You are a morrigan!"

Liriel lifted a skeptical brow. "I wasn't the last time I looked."

The witch chuckled. "A raven, then. A being who moves between two worlds, between starlight and shadows. It is your task to see lost spirits home."

This notion was entirely new to Liriel, and yet it had the uncomfortable fit of newfound truth. "Between starlight and shadows." Fyodor had used that very phrase in a story he told her. Still, this morrigan business was too much to absorb.

"Who decided this?" she said heatedly.

Zofia shrugged. "Who knows? Is our fate written on the day of our birth, or do we choose our paths?"

"You tell me."

"Neither," the old woman said, "or perhaps both. The future is not ours to know."

"Fyodor has the Sight. He says you're an Oracle."

The witch inclined her head. "We see what might be, just as the fisherman sees the darkening clouds and knows that rain might fall. He also knows that a strong wind might come and blow the storm far from the Ashane, or that the song of the bheur—the blue hag, the bringer of Winter—might change the rain to snow."

Liriel took this in. "What do you see for me?"

"Let's have a look."

Zofia took a bag from her belt and spilled several small, rune-carved stones onto the table. "These were made from bones left by creatures no living eye has seen. The ancient power of the land is in them. Gather them up and strew them on the table."

Liriel did as she was bid. The old woman studied the result for long moments. At length she lifted her eyes to the waiting drow. "You will bind and break, heal and destroy. What you sought, you have found. What you love, you will lose—yet your heart will sing and not alone. You will make a place for those who walk between the starlight and the shadows."

The drow considered these cryptic words. "At least rain clouds eventually get to the point."

Zofia shrugged. "The wind will blow where it will. Keep the stones. Learn to listen to them, but do not seek to know your own future. That is courting ill fortune."

She rose to leave. Liriel stepped caught the witch's sleeve. "Do you know what I am?" she asked softly.

"Oh yes," Zofia said. "You are a black wolf."

The drow blew out a long breath that was part relief, part resignation. At least her deepest secret—or nearly so—was on the table.

"There are black wolves among every kind of creature," the witch went on, "who are different from their kin, outcasts either by choice or birth. Perhaps both. For whatever reason, they have no place among their kindred. They walk alone. I say black wolf because oftentimes a rogue wolf has a dark coat. Is such a beast shunned by its kind because of its hide, or does it hunt alone because of differences hidden beneath?"

This explanation struck Liriel as ambiguous as her "fortune." Did Zofia know that her guest was a dark elf or didn't she?

"I'll try not to keep the village awake with my howling," she grumbled.

The witch chuckled. "Sleep, then. Tomorrow you take the next step on your path."

She went her way. Liriel gathered up the bread and salt and stood in the open door. "This is for the *domovoi*," she said, feeling rather foolish. "You're welcome to come in." No further pleasantries came to mind, though she tried to think of some.

"Hang old shoes in the yard," called Zofia without looking back. "The *domovoi* like that."

"Kill me now," Liriel muttered. Resolving that the house spirit would have to make do with an evening snack, she put the gift under her stone and closed and latched her door. She fell facedown into the fur coverlet and was asleep almost at once.

Some time later, she became aware of a most peculiar feeling, a sensation so subtle that that it belonged neither to dreams nor waking. Her feet were suddenly cooler, as if some highly skilled servant had managed to get her boots off without waking her.

Liriel cracked open one eye and instantly came fully awake.

A peculiar creature leaned over her. It looked human but for the silky fur covering its face and limbs. Most likely male, it appeared quite old and was clad only in a long-tailed red shirt. Long, gnarled fingers reached for the strings tying the witch mask to her belt.

Liriel exploded from the bed, her back to the wall and her daggers in her hand.

The creature stared at her in open-mouthed astonishment. "*Domovoi* to the drow I have become?" it moaned. "A bad hut, this is! Better a *dvorovoi* it should have!"

Only then did Liriel notice the mask in the house spirit's hand and realized that she wore her true face. A glance at her black hands confirmed this.

Thinking fast, she responded firmly, "No *dvorovoi*. I mean no harm to Rashemen and want nothing to do with bad spirits."

This apparently was the right approach. The furry being nodded approvingly. "Better in the yard they should stay. You can cook?"

"Not if my life depended on it."

The *domovoi* brightened. "Then no dishes I must wash, no pots scour! But there will be milk?"

"If you want it, I'll have someone deliver it."

"Rothé's milk, or goat?"

Liriel shrugged. "Whatever you want."

"Eggs?" the spirit inquired hopefully.

The drow extended her hand for the mask, indicating a trade. The *domovoi* handed it over and faded from sight, but a contented little melody rose from the stove. The drow tied the mask firmly to her belt and went back to bed.

Yet sleep eluded her. Liriel opened her door and gazed toward the mountains, drinking cold tea and watching the sky brighten to silver. A single howl wafted down from the forested slopes, a wild voice that sang alone. Liriel remembered the witch's words and lifted her mug in silent salute to a kindred spirit.

The sun was well past its zenith by the time Fyodor stood near the top of Snowcat Mountain. The young people of Dernovia had left before dawn to make the long trek up the mountain. He sought the small smudge of brown and gray far below that marked the village walls and wondered how Liriel fared.

She would love this, he decided, glancing back at the band of men and maidens he had known all his life. They laughed and teased, flirted and boasted, reveling in the fine day and the bracing shock of wind-blown snow against their skin.

Fyodor had already stripped down the traditional doe-skin loincloth and strapped the racing shoes to his boots. He helped Petyar stuff the discarded clothes into sacks and load them onto the pack animals—sure-footed, shaggy little ponies that seemed more goat than horse.

Everyone was dressed in similar fashion, men and women alike. All of them, even young Petyar, were well accustomed to this. There was little shame in Rashemen regarding the body, and none of the Rashemi confused sport with courtship.

Even so, Fyodor couldn't help contrasting the sturdy Rashemaar women with the tiny drow and envisioning Liriel's lithe black form against the setting of white snow.

Petyar elbowed him sharply in the ribs. "Now who's watching?" he said with a grin.

The warrior chuckled and tossed his head toward the ribbon that last year's winners held between them. The starting line could not be tied to trees, as they had left the tree line behind perhaps two hours ago.

They joined the group and waited for the ribbon to drop, then all of them hurtled down the mountain in huge, sliding steps. A fast start was important. Once they reached the forest, the paths narrowed and the lead was difficult to take.

Frontrunners could be expected to protect their positions with their fists and staffs. Competition among the swiftest racers often developed into impromptu duels, which opened the door for less-favored contestants and added the possibility of an unexpected win. It was this that lent the race much of its excitement. All shared the likelihood of friendly battle. Any man or maid might win honors.

Petyar shouldered his cousin out of the way, sending him into a tumbling roll. Fyodor found his feet and took off after the boy, loudly promising vengeance.

They would neither of them win this way, but the young man's playful mood suited Fyodor. Better this than a senseless quest for a black wolf that had harmed no one and was best left alone.

Fyodor scooped up a handful of snow and slung it at the boy. It slapped into the back of his head. He turned and hurled a missile of his own. Fyodor leaned away from the snowball and quickly closed the distance between them. He stooped as he neared the boy and grabbed a handful of snow. With this he briskly washed Petyar's face.

The boy yelped and gave pursuit. Fyodor leaped over a snow-covered boulder and slid along the trunk of a fallen log. The younger warrior, though, had the longer legs, and on this steep slope his stride was nearly the match for a hill giant's.

They raced only each other, leaving the prize to others. After a time, however, Petyar seemed to lose interest. He did not increase his speed when Fyodor drew abreast with him, did not return his cousin's cheerful insults. As they neared the tree line the boy lengthened his stride and veered off the path. He disappeared into the trees.

Fyodor set his jaw and followed the big-footed trail.

Suddenly there were two trails.

He did not see the second trail at first, for Petyar's prints had obscured the delicate markings. No doubt he had done so deliberately, in an attempt to hide his true purpose, but as the boy's excitement drew, his caution ebbed. The marks of large but delicate paws, front and back feet falling into the same straight line, wove through the trees.

Petyar followed.

Fyodor found his cousin in a small clearing, not far from the runner's path. The fading voices of the runners proclaimed that they had been left far behind, but Petyar did not seem to notice. He stood at the base of a snow-frosted pine, staring in puzzlement at the snow. Tracks circled the tree, but the thick white blanket beyond was marked by a single pair of tracks: Petyar's. The wolf prints had completely disappeared.

The warrior clapped the boy on the back. "You would not be the first Rashemi to lose a trail. Forget it."

"I didn't lose the trail," Petyar insisted.

"Perhaps you didn't," Fyodor agreed. "Perhaps this wolf should not be found."

The boy scoffed. "I'm not such a fool as that! If you think to frighten me with tales of werewolves, you'd do better to wait until the night has come and the moon is full."

"True enough," Fyodor admitted. He nodded toward the path. "However it happened, your quarry is gone. Let's join the others."

Petyar grumbled but fell into step. "It will be back," he insisted, "and it will cause trouble before it's finished. That is its nature. A wolf is always a wolf."

His words drifted through the crisp air. Thorn heard them, albeit somewhat muffled by the thick branches that shrouded her hiding place. The familiar Rashemaar saying prompted a wry, humorless smile.

A wolf will always be a wolf. It was strange they should think so when so many of their old tales said otherwise.

CHAPTER SIXTEEN

THE WARRENS

Liriel eyed the clearing uncertainly. It was a desolate little spot, ringed and roofed by tall trees. A small spring bubbled and spat, sending sulphorous steam into the air. She whirled toward the witches who had accompanied her. Zofia had brought along all of Dernovia's witches—thirteen of them—to meet their guest and to escort her to a sacred place. To the drow's eyes, this little excursion was most likely a means of getting her out of the way.

"Here?" she demanded, eyeing Zofia with mingled outrage and incredulity.

"The witch of Shadowdale has been too long away," Zofia told her. "This is a haunted land. To know it, you must know and respect the sacred places. We will return before the sun sets."

The old woman nodded to the others. They turned and left the clearing.

Liriel glumly surveyed her surroundings. She

walked over to the spring and peered into the bubbling water. She could not see the bottom and did not expect to. There were hot springs like this in the Underdark, and even those came from deep, hidden sources.

When she was certain that she was alone, she untied Sylune's mask from her belt and sighed with relief as she slipped back into her own form. She kicked off her boots and removed her clothes and weapon belts, leaving on only the knives strapped to her arms and calves.

She dipped one foot into the water and found it pleasantly warm. Carefully she climbed over the rocks and lowered herself into the pool.

The steam rising around her coalesced into a strange form—a dragonlike head sculpted from mist.

Liriel scrambled out of the pool, eyeing the ghostly thing.

Yet it was not a ghost. She was sure of that, though she could not exactly say why. She felt none of the instinctive sick dread that dead things inspired.

She remembered the lore books that she had plumbed in her attempts to learn about the Windwalker. Her hand went to the hollow of her throat, the place where the amulet rested. "Place magic," she whispered, "and place spirits."

The misty reptilian inclined its head and waited. Liriel remembered how the villagers on that remote Moonshae island had honored the sacred river. She wore no ornaments, but she took a small, jeweled knife from a wrist sheath and dropped it into the water.

The misty dragon favored her with a toothy grin and sank back into the pool. Liriel smirked. Dragons were the same all over, no matter what form they took. She'd be willing to bet that this one had amassed quite a hoard.

She remembered the White Rusalka Vale, and a grim possibility occurred to her. Perhaps some of those drowned maidens had been greedy in life, determined to loot a sacred spring or river. She didn't suppose the guardian spirits took kindly to that.

"Or so people would assume," she mused, adding a layer of drow logic to this unfamiliar place. "What better place to dispose of a rival or victim? What better explanation than 'the Rusalka did it' when a body washes ashore?"

Liriel felt the ghost before she saw it. Cold fingers, no more substantial than wind, brushed her shoulder.

The drow whirled and stared into a pair of empty white eyes. No delicate maiden, this. The ghost was white but appeared far most solid than the wispy dragon spirit. Liriel got a quick impression of muscle under sodden leather armor and noted the empty scabbard. The odd cant of the colorless head suggested a broken neck. A warrior, perhaps, slain during one of Rashemen's many invasions.

All this Liriel took in with a glance. She sprang to one side and rolled away. The ghost lunged and seized her ankle.

The drow kicked out with her free foot, lashing out repeatedly at the surprisingly solid spirit. The dead warrior woman headed for the pool, dragging the drow with her.

Liriel seized a rock. It came loose in her hand, and she let it go. The fingers of one hand dug furrows in the ground as she flailed about with the other, seeking something to halt her deadly progress. All she needed was a moment or two, long enough to cast a spell.

She remembered suddenly that she knew no wizard spells that would protect her against the determined rusalka. Learning them had seemed foolish, when a simple clerical spell worked just as well.

And clerical magic was dependent upon the favor of the goddess.

Even as the thought formed, Liriel's hand closed around something slender and strong. She seized it and looked up into a pair of multi-faceted black eyes. With a shriek, she released her hold on the giant spider's leg.

Ask, suggested a silent voice, one Liriel had hoped never to hear again. Lolth's power had followed her even into this alien place, tempting her, haunting her.

The rusalka dragged her inexorably toward the pool. Liriel twisted onto her back, trying to break the dead warrior's grip. That failing, she lashed out repeatedly with her free foot, connecting with the solid form again and again. None of her efforts had any effect.

Mist rose from the pool and surrounded the dead warrior. Before the drow's frantic eyes, it took the shape of an enormous dragon's head. The misty jaw gaped wide and lunged for the ghost. The rusalka let go of her prize and reached for her empty scabbard. A startled expression crossed the ghostly face. Liriel got the distinct impression that this was not the first time this warrior had been surprised by the lack of this weapon. Frozen once again in its moment of death, the rusalka offered no resistance to the dragon. It was swallowed by the spring's guardian and, strangely enough, disappeared into the less substantial form.

The dragon sank back into the stream, leaving Liriel on the bank. For just a moment, the drow caught a glimpse of her jeweled knife below the bubbling surface and understood that the impulsive tribute had saved her life.

Perhaps more than her life. The giant spider, the minion of Lolth, had also disappeared.

Liriel rose and dressed herself. She tied the mask back to her belt. Changing her appearance back to that of the human Sylune did not make her feel much better. Lolth had found her, and the stubborn goddess would be less easily fooled than the villagers of Dernovia.

Zofia had been right, she thought grimly. This was indeed a haunted land, and if it truly was her destiny to see the spirits to their rightful homes, where in the nine bloody hells was she supposed to start?

Gorlist glanced up sharply as the sound of scuffling feet approached the cave's opening. His mercenaries had finally captured something of value, or at least, of interest! By the Masked Lord, it was a feat long overdue!

One of his mercenaries broke free of the small battle and saluted his commander. "We have captured an elf. A female."

Well, that was something. "Bring her in," Gorlist ordered.

Three of his soldiers dragged in a tall faerie elf. Even bound and gagged, form half shrouded with the remnants of a canvas sack, she put up an impressive struggle.

Gorlist strode forward and seized a handful of her disheveled black hair. He jerked her head back and noted the distinctive light streak that framed one side of her face. With a start of dark pleasure, Gorlist recognized this elf. It was she whom he had fought on the deck of his lost ship!

With his free hand he fingered the silver braid. "Clever, that little shapeshifting trick. What would this braid become if I ripped the entire thing from your scalp?"

The elf spat a mouthful of blood at his boots. "Try it and see," she invited.

"Another time," the drow said coldly. "At present, I am more interested to learn why I see you in Skullport when fighting Liriel Baenre there and find you in Rashemen near the village of her pet human."

She sneered and started to work up another wad of spittle. Gorlist backhanded her hard, sending her head snapping to one side.

"Bring the irons," he commanded.

The elf spat out a jagged shard of tooth and laughed in his face. "I counted almost a hundred dark elves in and about these warrens, and I am one alone. Am I not bound tightly enough for you?" she snarled, holding out her bound wrists.

Gorlist nodded to Chiss. The young drow bared his teeth in a fierce smile and set to work. He snapped iron manacles on the faerie elf's wrists. Deftly climbing the stone wall, he threaded the attached chain through hoops embedded high overhead.

Gorlist nodded to his cohorts.

Two drow pulled swords and slashed away the ropes binding their captive. As she lunged at them, Chiss yanked the chains back, pulling her arms out wide and stopping her charge.

Gorlist strode around her, eyeing the marks that drow swords had left in leather and flesh. The female's toes barely touched the ground, and the angle of her arms suggested that they had been pulled from the shoulder sockets, yet her green-gold gaze remained steady and implacable.

"Cut off her armor and garments," he told the two drow. "Don't be too dainty about it."

His soldiers went about their work with obvious pleasure. Gorlist picked up a length of severed rope and knotted it. He handed this to one of the drow and a vial of salt to the other.

"Enjoy," he said as he settled down to watch. He smirked at the elf woman. "I certainly intend to."

The torture went on longer than Gorlist would have thought possible. In time, pleasure became tedium, but nothing they inflicted upon the faerie elf induced her to speak.

"Get Brindlor," he said at last.

One of the drow—a young female who had been born to Nisstyre's first mercenaries—went in search of the deathsinger. They returned shortly. Brindlor sent a quick look of distaste at the faerie elf that had nothing to do with her condition and little to do with the color of her skin.

"Merdrith is not here. You know more magic than any of us. Strip her secrets from her mind," Gorlist demanded.

The deathsinger sniffed. "Small wonder she did not talk. Didn't you know that iron draws the life force from some faerie creatures as a rag soaks blood from a wound? Perhaps this elf is one such creature. Cut her down."

Reluctantly Chiss lowered the chains and snapped off the manacles. What happened next took them all by surprise.

There was no spellcasting, no slow metamorphosis, no warning at all. One moment a battered elf woman lay at their feet, the next, a large black wolf regarded them with gold-green eyes. Her lip curled back in a snarl, her hind feet tamped down, and she leaped.

Chiss went down under her before he could draw a weapon. The wolf's teeth sank into his shoulder, and the massive head gave a savage shake. Then she was up, dodging this way and that as she evaded the swords of her tormenters. She darted out into the cavern with preternatural speed and was gone.

"Find her," snapped Gorlist, but he already knew that the effort would prove futile. He kicked in frustration at the fallen soldier.

"Drag him out under the sky and watch him until the moon rises," he commanded. "Perhaps adding a drow werewolf to our band will inspire the rest of you to act like hunters!"

They did as Gorlist commanded. Under the night sky they drew swords and waited, some with fascination and others with almost-concealed trepidation, for the transformation to come and their former comrade to rise.

Hours slipped by, marked only by the steady dripping of water in some nearby tunnel.

"The moon has long since risen," Brindlor said at last. "Bury or burn him or leave him to rot. It matters not."

"Not a werewolf, then," Gorlist mused. "What was she, to change like that? A druid? A sorceress?"

"Worse," the deathsinger said grimly. "The wench is a lythari."

The sky was thick with stars before Liriel finally made her way to her little hut. Fyodor was already there and was busy stirring herbs into a stew.

"You're cooking," she observed. "The *domovoi* isn't going to like this."

He looked up sharply. "You've spoken with one?"

"We came to an understanding." She shut the door and untied the mask from her belt, sighing with relief as she slipped back into her own form. Even more pleasant was the way Fyodor's eyes filled with the sight of her.

"Songs and stories claim that the Seven Sisters are the fairest among women," he said quietly. "Have the bards all gone mad, or are they merely blind?"

She ran into his arms. For a long moment they clung together, then she led him to the rumpled bed. They settled down side by side, her head nestled against his broad shoulder.

"Rashemen is an interesting place. I was undressed by a *domovoi,* inspected by a coven of witches, and attacked by a dragon-shaped water spirit and a muscle-bound Rusalka. How was your day?"

"Much the same."

"Hmmm."

She lifted her face to his, and for quite some time there was no need for other words. The stewpot scalded, the *domovoi* sighed, and neither warrior nor Windwalker cared in the slightest.

Much later, Fyodor took her into the courtyard and pointed to the stars. "Do you see that small cluster there, shaped like a crossroads? We call it the Guardians after the spirits who watch the four corners of the year. The bright star there is Mokosh, named for the spirit of the harvest. A similar star pattern marks each turning of the year. Soon we will celebrate the Autumn Sunset, the time when night and day stand in balance and the wheel of the year turns toward winter."

The drow pulled her cloak closer. "I have heard of this winter. Does it get colder than this?"

"Much, but there is a chill wind tonight. We should go inside."

She turned wistful eyes toward the forest. Fyodor caught her look and shook his head. "That is not wise. This is a haunted land, and the nights are filled with ghosts. More so in these days than in times past."

"Zofia said that I should get to know the land's spirits," Liriel argued. "What better way?"

He relented with a sigh. "We will break fast with Vastish and her children. Perhaps we could bring a rabbit or two for her pot."

"Or an uthraki," she said with a grin, referring to their recent misadventure.

Fyodor's eyes twinkled. "Why not? Everything Vastish cooks ends up tasting much the same."

They set a brisk pace down the rutted dirt road that wound through the fields. Liriel heard a faint rustle to her left. From the corner of her eye she noted a squat, malformed dwarf scuttling through the ripened grain, keeping pace with them. Strings of green hair sprouted from its head like tall meadow grass, and a thick green mustache bristled under a vast beak of a nose. Its large eyes were deeply set and shadowed by beetling green brows, but even at a glance Liriel could see that one was a light green shade and one a brilliant orange.

"A *polevik*," Fyodor said in a troubled tone.

"Dangerous?"

"Only if you fall asleep in the field or follow it into the grain. What troubles me is the hour. Usually the *polevik* only wander about at highsun."

"Maybe it had a cup of Zofia's tea and can't sleep."

He chuckled briefly. The troubled look returned to his face. "You know I have a bit of Sight. Before I left Rashemen, I started to see things that should not be there. Ghosts, spirits, even heroes from tales my father's father heard from *his* grandsire. They wander about like drunken men locked out of their huts by angry wives, uncertain of where they are or where they should go. It has been so since the Time of Troubles. The magic of Rashemen lies in the land itself and in the spirits of the land. It is not like wizards' spells, which once cast and forgotten can be learned again. No witch will say so, but I suspect that this magic did not heal as it should have."

She considered his words, wondering if this was part of the confusing destiny Zofia foresaw.

Before she could give voice to this thought, a bitter wind ripped through the trees with a shrill, almost metallic shriek. Branches rustled sharply. The singing insects went silent, and a small bird fell from its perch. Liriel stooped and picked it up, marveling at how light the little thing was. How cold.

Fyodor seized her arm and pulled her to her feet. "Hurry," he urged. "We need to be within walls before the *bheur* song strikes again."

The urgency in this voice convinced Liriel to run now and ask questions later.

They raced through the forest, retracing their steps. They were almost free of the forest when they saw the old woman. She stood on the path ahead, leaning on a tall wooden staff. Her long, wild hair was as white as a drow's and her wrinkled skin nearly blue from cold. Barefoot and clad only in rags, she looked as if she would fall if not for the staff in her gnarled hands.

The Rashemi skidded to a stop and put Liriel behind him. "Lightning magic," he said tersely. "The most powerful you know, and quickly!"

She dug into her coin bag and took out an emerald—the last gem from her share of the deepdragon's hoard. With one hand she tossed this toward the hag, with the other, she gripped the Windwalker and called forth the spell she had stored within.

The gem disappeared. In its place stood a half-elf female, taller by half than the wizard who had summoned it. Her sharply sculptured body was translucent as glass and green as fine emeralds, and in her hands was a jagged bolt of white fire. The golem drew back her arm and threw the lightning as a warrior might hurl a spear.

A shriek like the clash of elven swords tore from the hag. She lifted her staff and sent a spray of icy crystals flying to meet the oncoming lightning. The bheur's blast spread into a lethal cone, which flared into brilliant life as the bolt passed through. It hit the hag and sent her hurtling backward. She hit the base of a pine, hard, and sank to the forest floor.

With astonishing agility the hag was up and running, fleeing back toward the mountains.

Liriel started toward the staff.

"Don't bother," her friend told her. "It only is magical in

a *bheur's* hands. Even if you *could* use it, some magic is best left alone."

She caught the grim note in his tone. "I did something wrong?"

"The spell was wisely chosen," he said carefully, "but you must not summon a golem in Rashemen. Many such creatures were brought against us by Thay's Red Wizards. Any who see you cast such a spell will wonder where you learned it."

She shrugged. "There was a book of Mulhorandi magic in the Green Room. I had a lot of gems left over from the deepdragon's hoard, and this seemed a good use to make of them."

"Even so, such magic can be deadly in Rashemen. No outlander wizards of any kind are permitted here. Because Sylune was a friend to Rashemen and trained in some of the witches' minor arts, and because Zofia has taken you under her wing, my people accept you. If they saw you cast such a spell, neither of us would live to see the next dawn."

Liriel received this news in silence. "No such spells," she repeated, as if saying that words aloud would make them sound more sensible.

"Only to save your own life. Promise me this."

The words came quickly to the drow's tongue, but she found she could not speak them. She shook her head, unwilling to make a promise she doubted she could keep. To her astonishment, Fyodor looked oddly gratified by this.

"The day dawns," he said softly. "Vastish will expect us soon."

He took her hand, and they walked to the cottage where his sister's family lived. Already smoke rose from the chimney, and a kettle of boiled grains mixed with what appeared to be dried berries bubbled on stove.

Two small boys hurled themselves at Fyodor and

attached themselves to his legs. A taller girl, one close enough to maidenhood to be mindful of her dignity, hung back, eyeing her brothers with disdain.

Vastish shook her wooden spoon and gave one of the urchins a light swat on the rump with it. "Do your manners fail you, or just your eyes? Can't you see that there's a *wychlaran* present?"

The children fell back, abashed, and dipped into jerky little bows. "You bring grace to this household," the trio chanted.

Liriel smiled uncertainly. Drow children the size of these males were still being word-weaned and were seldom seen except by the one or two people who oversaw this training. She had never had anything to do with anyone so small.

She gave her name and received the children's names in turn. Lacking other ideas, she suggested, "Perhaps a story before we eat?"

The boys greeted this with great and loud enthusiasm, Vastish with a grateful nod. Fyodor settled down and pulled a nephew onto each knee.

"Long years ago, a hero known as Yvengi walked the land. Times were troubled, and many brave men fell in battle. Yvengi's father was a great warrior, a berserker equal to any man alive, but one day he faced a foe that had neither blood nor breath."

"The demon Eltab!" the younger boy put in excitedly.

"None other," Fyodor agreed. "Yvengi knew that his strength and his sword would be powerless against the demon's armored hide, so he prayed to all the spirits of the land and was granted a magical sword. Not even a demon could stand before *Hadryllis*. Eltab fled to Thay—"

"To walk among mortal demons!" the child chimed in.

"You know the tale," observed his uncle with a smile. "Then you know that in each turn of the family wheel—

from father to son, mother to maiden—another great sword will be raised for Rashemen."

"Like yours," the boy said in worshipful tones.

A deep silence fell over the room. Judging from the stricken expression on the females' faces and the red flush staining the older boy's cheeks, Liriel surmised that some important taboo had been broken.

The little one glanced from one face to another, looking as puzzled as Liriel felt. "There is magic in this sword," he insisted.

Fyodor looked to his sister. An expression of mingled pain and pride crossed her face. "Thrisfyr has the gift," she said simply. "It is already decided that he will join the *vremyonni*. He will go to the Old Ones for training before next winter's snows."

"A great honor," he said softly. Vastish smiled but not without irony.

The morning meal passed swiftly with nothing more serious to mar it than a mug of spilled milk. They thanked their hostess and left to tend to the day's business.

"What was all that about?" Liriel asked softly as soon as they were beyond hearing's range. "What did the little boy say that made your sister turn pale?"

Fyodor's shoulders rose and fell in a heavy sigh. "When we first met, you commented on my blunt sword. I told you that it was thus fashioned so I would not cut myself. You thought I was merely being foolish, but I spoke the simple truth. A warrior who cannot control his battle rages is given such a sword, and for several reasons. First, so he is less likely to harm his brothers. Second, so he does not cut himself and die by his own hand. There is no greater disgrace to a Rashemi than this. Finally, so he will die with honor and purpose. The berserkers go first into battle. Any man with a blunt sword leads the way."

The grim truth came to Liriel slowly. "It is a sentence of death."

"Yes. Zofia lent this sword magic so that it might cut those not of Rashemen and that I might stay alive long enough to complete my quest."

"Throw it away," she said passionately. "Get another sword. Your battle rages are under control—you don't need a blunt sword anymore."

"That is not our way," he said softly. "This is the last sword I will wield. That is our law and custom. I must die with this sword in my hand."

Liriel's first impulse was to protest this new example of human stupidity, but memories flooded her mind and stilled her tongue: Fyodor facing drow and Luskan warriors, fighting sea ogres, slaying a giant squid—by cutting his way out from the inside. She relaxed. He had won many battles with that blunt, black sword. Why shouldn't he continue to do so?

A tall, gangling youth trotted toward them, his arms full of what appeared to be a bundle of black sticks and his shaggy brown hair falling into his eyes. He pulled up short and bobbed his head to the "witch" at Fyodor's side. Fyodor quickly completed the introductions and asked what Petyar was about.

"We're to scout the Warrens," the boy said without preamble. "Treviel's orders. The others are waiting at the west gate." He grinned broadly. "There will be a lightning wand for each of us. The *vremyonni* sent them."

Liriel noted the grim set of Fyodor's jaw. "The male wizards?" she asked.

"Yes," he said shortly. "They live and study and create in a hidden place."

"These Warrens," she concluded. "These are caves?"

The look he sent her confirmed her unspoken concern.

Where there were caves, there were tunnels. Where there were tunnels, there might well be drow. She did not doubt that Gorlist would catch up with her sooner or later. This was not, however, the time she would have chosen.

"I'll come with you," she stated.

The boy's face fell. "With all respect, Lady, this is a simple scouting expedition."

Fyodor claimed one of the ebony wands. It was about the length of a big man's forearm and the thickness of his thumb. It had been intricately carved with a tiny design that spiraled up the length of the wand. It was a priceless work of art, created to be destroyed in a single moment.

He lifted this pointedly and raised one brow. "For a simple scouting expedition we need such a thing? Speak truth, Petyar. We are hunting. Not your black wolf, I hope."

Liriel blinked in surprise to hear this term.

"The beast does not travel with any pack," the boy said, his tone defensive, "and a lone wolf often seeks easy prey, becoming a danger to livestock and children."

Fyodor hefted the wand. "Even if you convinced Treviel of that, this was not meant for a wolf."

"I followed it into the Warrens," the boy admitted. "I was hoping to find her lair. What I found instead was a dead drow."

Fyodor glanced at his friend. "This drow was killed by the wolf?"

"Who cares?" Petyar retorted. "A dead drow is a blessing, however it came about, but yes, it appears so. His shoulder was torn open, his throat savaged."

Fyodor drew him away from Liriel and placed himself between the two—whether for Petyar's protection or hers, Liriel couldn't say. Fyodor glanced back at her.

"It is best that you stay close to the village today. Promise me this."

She did and was rewarded by the glad flash in her friend's eyes. His word, his honor—these were no small things to Fyodor. Apparently he considered her refusal to give her word, unless she meant to keep it, a good thing.

For the first time, she wondered how he felt about the deception she had forced them both to live. Perhaps Zofia's word might have been enough to gain cautious acceptance for a drow, but the lie had been told. To the eyes of the truth-loving Rashemi, concealing her nature most likely confirmed it.

"We will talk when I return," Fyodor said gently. He took her hand and raised it to his heart then turned and strode off beside his lanky kinsman.

They met the other warriors at the west gate. Horses awaited them, and they rode hard toward the Running Rocks.

The scouting party stopped at the mouth of the caves and lit small torches. They waved these overhead as they ducked into the tunnels, warding off a sudden rush of startled bats.

Petyar led them down to the narrow passage where the dead drow lay. Fyodor crouched beside the body for a closer look. After a few moments he glanced up.

"He did not die here. Something dragged him to this place, and not the wolf."

Treviel sneered. "What else should we expect? Of course there are more of these two-legged vermin. The drow do not hunt alone."

"They leave their dead in a tunnel for the rats?" Fyodor asked.

"What else would they do? It is difficult to bury or burn in a cave."

Fyodor had had enough experience with dark elves to understand that their thinking was seldom so simple. He lifted his torch high and surveyed the tunnel. Though the passage was narrow, the ceiling soared overhead. Fyodor made out odd shadows and impressions in the uneven rock that might be nothing or might be passages into unseen tunnels. The drow had moved their dead comrade for a purpose. Bait for a trap, perhaps?

The warrior lowered his torch. "No wonder Petyar chose this tunnel. The ceilings are high enough to keep the cobwebs from tangling in his hair," he said lightly. He made a show of sweeping the torch low to check the floor. "No sign of wolf scat. She hasn't been back to feed yet, and from the looks of things the rats will polish these bones within a day or so. I warrant that we'll find no wolf in these warrens today."

Petyar looked puzzled, but before he could speak Treviel gave him an ungentle shove. "Move it, boy, and hold your tongue," he said in a stern, soft voice.

The men fell into step, moving swiftly toward the open cavern beyond. They were almost there when the drow attacked.

The Rashemi scouts reacted at once. Swords hissed free, and the warriors ran eagerly to meet this much-hated foe. Men near the rear of the party gave shouts of warning as more dark elves clambered down the stone walls and into the torchlight.

A drow female, small, lithe, and clad in scant leather armor, leaped into Fyodor's path. She leveled two weapons at him: a broadsword and a coldly beautiful smile.

Fyodor hesitated just for a moment. Even this small delay was too much. The female lunged, her sword seeking his heart. He gathered his wits and used his best weapon—his size—against the smaller and more agile drow.

He leaned away from the drow's attack then lunged at her, pinning the small female to the wall. She writhed and thrashed but could not bring her weapon to bear. Knowing Liriel's penchant for multiple weapons, he immediately seized the drow's wrists and pinned them high over her head.

"Go!" roared Fyodor, waving the others to pass as he struggled to hold onto the drow. Treviel repeated the command.

The female wriggled away and climbed the wall. Fyodor let her go, suspecting that he might yet have cause to regret this. He took the ebony wand from his belt and took stock of the battle.

Most of the men had retreated down the exit tunnel. Bright lights flared suddenly, driving the drow back and providing an escape for the Rashemi. Only Petyar and Treviel remained in the cavern. Side by side, the two warriors backed down the narrow tunnel, holding off the cat-quick swords of several attacking drow. Fyodor made a quick count and came to an unanticipated conclusion:

There were not enough drow.

The irony in that observation did not escape him, hard-pressed though he was. But it was better to see one's enemy than to wonder when a hidden foe might strike. The drow for whom he could not account had probably taken the same route as the female, nimbly climbing the walls along paths only they could see.

Again Fyodor lifted his torch high. This time the light was reflected back by several pairs of red eyes and small, gleaming knives.

Fyodor tossed his wand straight up, sending it spinning high into the cavern. It struck the ceiling and shattered. He shielded his eyes for the resulting blinding flash.

Instead, the tunnel filled with a faint, deep purple light. Clearly revealed in it were the mocking faces of the drow warriors—and the smug countenance of a bald human not more than ten paces from where Fyodor stood. He shoved young Petyar out of the way and moved to block the tunnel himself.

"You go no farther," he told the lurking drow.

Soft, mocking laughter bounced along the high ceiling, and the dark elf warriors swarmed down the rock wall toward him.

Fyodor slammed his black sword back into its sheath. He would not need it. His eyes drifted shut for a moment, and he swiftly reached back into a place deep within, seeking a force that was both ancient and newly discovered.

The change hit him like a panicked stallion. Power surged through him, knocking him to the stone floor, but when he struck the ground, it was not with his hands. Enormous black-furred paws slapped down against the stone, claws clicking like ready daggers.

The power flowed on and on, bursting from him in a roar that shook the tunnel and froze the attacking dark elves where they stood.

Or so it seemed.

It was always so when the berserker frenzy came. Time slowed around him, giving Fyodor room to observe, to respond. To attack.

One paw lashed out, lightning quick, and slashed the nearest elf across the throat. Fyodor caught the falling body in his jaws. With a toss of his massive bear's head, he threw the dead elf onto the swords of two attacking dark elves. Both went down under the weight of their comrade. The berserker kept coming.

Fyodor felt the sting of nimble swords, but his thick fur and tough hide proved more effective than leather armor. The human hurled sizzling balls of light at him. These singed and stank, filling the tunnel with rank smoke, but the berserker felt no pain. He never did, until after.

Roaring with battle fever, he charged past the last of the drow in the tunnel and hurled himself at the bald wizard.

A sharp crack, like the flap of an unsecured sail in a gale wind, announced Fyodor's newest foe. A terrible creature dropped from a high perch, an enormous birdlike monster with a bat's leathery wings and a long, pointed beak lined with needlelike fangs. It hurtled down, seemingly intent upon stopping the berserker's charge.

In the part of his mind that was still human, Fyodor recognized the handiwork of a Red Wizard. The avian spread its massive wings and leveled its beak at Fyodor in a bizarre parody of a knight's charge. Fyodor reared up and charged right through the monster's path, his claws slashing and his fangs snapping at that dangerous beak. His onslaught shredded the thick membrane of the wings, and the pointed beak snapped between his jaws. The berserker spat and came on.

The wizard was not yet finished. He threw a handful of powder onto the floor and stepped into the rising cloud. For a moment he was obscured by the thick mist. When he stepped out, it was on two strong, furred legs. A fierce gray cave bear waded toward the berserker, its powerful upper limbs spread in preparation for a lethal hug.

The two combatants tangled and went down, snapping and rolling. In the cavern beyond, flares of light flashed and waned, and the sounds of fierce battle rang through the warrens. Fyodor clung to the transmuted wizard, worrying him with fang and claw, determined to keep him from joining the drow band.

He did not know how much time passed or how long he fought. After a while Fyodor noticed that the tunnel had gone dark and that his opponent no longer struggled.

No longer breathed.

The warrior pushed himself away and padded on four

feet into the cavern. Two torches were still burning faintly. Someone among the fighters had had the presence of mind to wedge them among the scattered rocks.

The scene revealed in the dim light was a grim one. The Rashemi band had won but at a high cost. Three men lay dead, and most of the others had taken wounds.

Petyar noticed the bear and let out a yelp of alarm. The older warriors went alert at once, swords ready.

The *fyrra* held up a hand to keep them back. "*Chesnitznia*," he said wearily, explaining Fyodor's altered form.

The survivors eyed him with awe and respect. This was nearly too much for Fyodor to endure. His borrowed form slipped away, and he slumped against the cavern wall.

Someone wrapped a cloak around his naked shoulders and pushed a flask into his hand. He took an obliging sip and found that it contained strong tea thick with honey. The sweetness sickened him, but he remembered the old tales that spoke of shapeshifters who were ravenous after a change. Perhaps the thick liquid would restore his strength. It was too much to hope that it might quiet his thoughts.

His stomach roiled, and a bit of the tea washed back. Fyodor wiped his mouth, and his hand came down smeared with a viscous red. The realization of its source sent him staggering off to be sick in earnest.

"Better?" inquired Treviel when at last he returned.

Fyodor nodded, not able to bring himself to meet the *fyrra's* eye, but the older man seized his chin and forced it up.

"What you did was well done," he said firmly. "While the wizard lived, the lightning sticks could not do their job. Without them more of your brothers would have died."

"If anything, the wizard died too easily," one of the other men spat. "He was the worse kind of traitor—a human who sided with the drow against his own kind."

The others murmured a vicious assent. Fyodor noted the hatred on their much-loved faces, and his heart broke. It was all too easy to imagine it turned upon him. He was not certain that he did not deserve it.

The Rashemi gathered their dead and walked in silence through the warrens. Fyodor was glad for this silence. He had much to think about.

He had always tried to be an honest and honorable man. Many times he had warned Liriel away from the goddess of her childhood, challenging her to consider if any good could come from a union with evil. Perhaps he should have more closely heeded his own advice.

On the surface of things, this thought was unfair to Liriel, and he knew it. She was no more evil than a snowcat. On the other hand, she had no more morals than the same wild cat. Without guides or restraints, how could anyone safely chart his way? The result of this lack was the tangled deception they now lived. Any lie was difficult to sustain, and Liriel's was especially dangerous.

Fyodor regretted also his naiveté in thinking that his people might come to accept Liriel, perhaps even to see her as he did. The Rashemi hated the drow, and he could not fault his people for their deeply ingrained prejudice. Their history bore this out—as, he had to admit, did his own experience.

He loved Liriel, deeply and completely. More importantly, however, he knew her. It was not without reason that Lolth wove Her webs around the errant drow princess. Liriel battled a dark nature, and she never seemed quite sure of the line between right and wrong. Sometimes she didn't seem to realize that such a line existed or even that it *should* exist.

These troubling thoughts followed him through the winding caves and tunnels of the warrens. By the time the silent band stepped into the light, Fyodor had dragged himself to a painful but inevitable conclusion.

He had done his people a disservice by bringing Liriel among them. If he had not done so, these drow would not have followed her here. These men would not be dead. For the sake of all concerned, he would take Liriel far from Rashemen as soon as he returned to the village. Even if this meant abandoning his duty as a warrior. Even if it meant committing what his people would certainly regard as an unforgivable treason.

Even if it meant leaving his homeland forever.

CHAPTER SEVENTEEN

CIRCLES

Within the Witches' Lodge was a large courtyard walled by vine-draped trees. In the sheltered circle within gathered several of Dernovia's witches. For the first time Liriel was permitted to observe their spellcasting.

In her now-familiar guise of the tall, silver-haired Witch of Shadowdale, she watched intently as the circle of black-clad women moved through their dance, hands joined and voices lifted in chant. The pattern was intricate, the magical language unknown to her. What puzzled her most was the ability of these many women to unite not only their strength but their purpose.

Power rose from each of the masked women like steam—not quite visible, but tangible all the same. The object of the witches' focus and the recipient of the power they raised was a carved wooden staff. It bobbed gently in the air in the precise center of the circle.

One of them would wield it. Oddly enough, no one seemed concerned over who might eventually claim the prize.

Liriel imagined, briefly, how this decision would be made in Arach Tinileth, the priestess school in Menzoberranzan. Several females would die before such a treasure came to rest in one pair of dark hands.

When the casting was completed, the staff glided over to one of the masked women. The witch took it reverently in long, slender hands. When she took off her mask, Liriel bit back a curse.

Anya, the young witch who had challenged her at the border watchtower, had come to Dernovia.

The disguised drow quietly slipped out of the clearing and made her way back to her hut. She would have to deal with Anya sooner or later, but better not to do so when she was backed by the full might of the village witches.

Fyodor had not yet returned. She paced the small room and bitterly regretted the promise that bound her here. The sleepless night before finally overcame her, however, and she curled up under the fur coverlet and sank into deep slumber.

She came awake suddenly, alerted by the soft creak of the ropes holding the mattress. To her surprise, the person sitting at the edge of the cot was not Fyodor but Thorn.

The elf woman gestured her to silence. "I come with a warning," she said softly. "The Dragon's Hoard band has come to Rashemen. They seek you."

"I know," Liriel replied in the same tone. "Several of the village warriors have gone looking for them."

"There is one you should beware. He had in him enough hatred to fill seven lives." Thorn touched her left cheek. "He has a dragon tattoo here."

"Gorlist," the drow said with disgust.

"Don't dismiss him," the elf warned. "More things have been accomplished in this world by persistence than by wisdom."

"I'll keep that in mind. Thanks for the warning." Liriel swung her legs off the cot and stretched. The elf did not move.

"What?" the drow demanded.

Thorn hesitated. "I have spoken with Zofia. She told me of the tapestry you carry. I wish to see it."

Liriel grimaced. "It's not a pretty thing."

"Nevertheless."

The drow shrugged and rose. She took the tapestry from the chest at the foot of the cot and unrolled it carefully.

For a long moment Thorn studied the terrible scene. "What have you done about it?"

The accusation in her voice stung Liriel. "It's elf magic. You'd probably have better idea what to do with it than I would."

Thorn considered her for a moment. "Perhaps I do," she said slowly and rose from the bed. "Come."

The drow hissed in exasperation but fell into step behind the much-taller elf. She followed her out of the hillock—

And into a small meadow on the side of a mountain.

Liriel pulled up short and looked around in astonishment. She had studied magical transport with some of the best minds in Menzoberranzan for a period of over thirty-five human years, but she could not begin to conjure so smooth and spontaneous a gate.

She looked around. The air was thinner here and cold. A lone raven crawled across the sunset sky, and its plaintive call rang out over the valley below.

Another raucous voice took up the cry, and the message worked its way across the trees. That it *was* a message Liriel did not doubt for a moment.

"They are carrion eaters," Thorn explained. "They have found a dead or sickly animal, and are calling the others to the feast."

"Generous of them."

"It is what they do. It is one of the things they do," the elf added pointedly. "Sometimes a raven is just a bird. Sometimes it is far more. Do you understand this?"

Liriel remembered Qilué's avian messenger, and nodded. "They carry messages."

"And more," Thorn said softly. "My people believe that the ravens carry the souls of the dead to their afterlife."

The drow began to understand where this was going. She tucked the tapestry more firmly under her arm and strode off in the direction the birds had flown.

They came to a clearing and saw the ravens were not alone. A circle of large gray beasts gathered around the carcass of a boar. Wolves. Liriel recognized them from the pictures in one of her lorebooks.

Thorn held out a hand to warn the drow back. "The ravens called the pack," she said softly. "They do that, sometimes."

This made no sense to Liriel. It was strange enough to share with their own kind, but to call large predators?

However, as she watched the wolves, she began to sense the pattern they followed. The largest male and the sole pregnant female ate first. All the others did homage to the royal pair and were in turn allowed their chance at the wild pig. The ravens ate, too, hopping forward to snatch at a morsel of meat then leaping away. No other bird was allowed. An inquisitive hawk settled on too low a branch. One of the smaller wolves jumped at the bird, which lifted off, squawking in protest.

Liriel noticed that Thorn was her regarding with speculation. "I'll try," she said testily, "but there's nothing I can do until nightfall."

"Understood."

They settled down to wait, watching as the wolves ate and slept then ate again. Little was left but the bone, and the pups carried many of those off as toys or trophies. The ravens, no nightbirds, winged off to their hidden place of rest.

Liriel spread the tapestry out on the ground. She tipped her head to the rising moon and listened for the song of distant places.

She heard first the faint music of Ysolde's drow, singing a welcome to the coming stars. Farther away was Qilué, and still farther other drow whose names she did not know. Even in the depths of her magical trance, Liriel was stunned by the number of drow who walked beneath the stars. They were not many, certainly not enough to fill an Underdark city of any size, but it was amazing that even a handful survived.

Liriel touched her palm to the tapestry and listened. There, too, was music, a terrible cacophony of sound punctuated by the shrieks of the tormented elves. Beyond that, like the edge of light around a storm cloud, was another sound, another place. The beauty of it filled the young drow with awe and desperate longing.

Tears ran unchecked down her face. Liriel was not sure whether she wept for the horror the elves experienced, or the beauty that she herself would never know.

Still in trance, she began to sing. Without thinking what she did, she tugged a dark thread from the edge of the tapestry. She twisted the Windwalker open and threaded the wool through a loop in the hilt of the tiny chisel. Using this as a shuttle, she began to weave. Her fingers, though unschooled in this art, moved unerringly through the unfamiliar dance.

She was faintly aware of the circle of ravens gathering

around her. A similar circle was taking shape on the tapestry, forming a ring of power around the tormented souls. One by one, the ravens took wing. The tapestry counterparts did likewise, and she imagined that the elves slowly began to disappear from the tapestry.

Liriel slowly eased back from her dream, her mind and heart still filled with the silvery light of it. She turned to the elf, blinking in surprise at the look of awe on Thorn's stern face.

Thorn pointed to the tapestry. There was nothing left upon it but a fine-woven cloth, the pale dull color of unbleached flax.

"They're gone," Liriel marveled.

"They are free," the elf woman said softly.

A quick, furtive skittering filled the clearing. Liriel glanced up sharply. Beyond the circle of light was another, darker circle, one that seethed with movement. Countless spiders, minions of Lolth, had felt the touch of Eilistraee's magic and had come to assert another deity's prior claim.

Liriel felt no fear. So great was her joy that there was no room in her heart to provide a foothold for Lolth's call.

Thorn seemed to understand this. Her face was softer than the drow had ever seen it, and the silver braid that hung over her shoulder gleamed with reflected moonlight.

And in the nearby shadows, beyond the loathsome circle of spiders, a young witch with a new-made staff watched and wondered.

News of Sylune's return did not long remain within the walls of village Dernovia. All across Faerûn there are those whose business it is to know of such wonders and portents, rumors and lies. Chief among them were the fey women known as the Seven Sisters.

Six silver-haired women gathered in a small cottage just outside the village of Shadowdale. Their host, a tall, athletic woman with long-fingered hands seemingly fashioned to dance upon harp strings, unstoppered a bottle of new wine and poured it around.

"She's not here, I tell you," Storm Silverhand asserted. "Not at her cottage, not in mine. Not anywhere in Shadowdale."

The other women exchanged worried glances. "She" was of course their sister Sylune, who had died years before in a battle against dragons and their dragoncult followers. Sylune lingered about her old home in the form of a spectral harper—an intelligent ghost who, unlike most, remembered almost all of her life and had actually managed to put much of it into perspective. The possibility that Sylune was no longer present filled them with loss and also with hope.

"Perhaps the rumors hold truth," suggested the sister who appeared to be the oldest of them. Her face was gentle and careworn, but her silvery gown was suited for royalty

Impatient energy crackled audibly around a tousled beauty in a wind-rent robe. "Be sensible, Alustriel. This so-called witch is an imposter and a dangerous one. Others will hear the rumors and come to investigate. Rashemen lies very close to Algorand's borders."

"No one doubts your ability to protect the lands you rule," Qilué Veladorn said quietly.

The other women, with the exception of Laerel Silverhand, cooled visibly when the drow spoke. Qilué was their sister but in a manner almost too fantastic to credit. She was a stranger to most of them, and not many years had passed since Laerel first ferreted out their ties.

"I must agree with the Queen of Algarond," the drow sister continued, addressing the stormy woman with formal respect. "In all honesty, I confess that I feel somewhat responsible for this misunderstanding."

She told them about Liriel and Fyodor and their determination to carry the Windwalker amulet back to the witches of Rashemen.

"I'm afraid that I might have mentioned that my sister Sylune studied among the witches. What else would Liriel assume from this, but that Sylune was a drow? And what better way for a drow to gain a foothold in Rashemen than to take Sylune's place?"

The other women groaned and nodded. Dove Silverhand, a well-muscled warrior in dark green leathers, spoke up. "She will be found out, of course. The important thing is to end this drow's charade before Sylune's enemies come calling on Rashemen. What I want to know is, will this drow gather these enemies and turn them to some dark purpose of her own?"

"I have no reason to believe that she will," Qilué said firmly. "That said, although I like Liriel and believe her to have vast potential, I'm afraid that nothing good can come of this situation. I'll send my daughter Ysolde, a priestess of Eilistraee, to get Liriel out of Rashemen before matters get completely out of hand."

The women murmured their agreement. "We're forgetting one important thing," Storm reminded them. "If Sylune is *not* in Rashemen, where is she?"

CHAPTER EIGHTEEN

THE WITCH OF SHADOWDALE

Sharlarra rode into village Dernovia beside the silent, unsmiling young witch. The latter had eventually appeared when the elf came to the city of Immiltar and asked to speak to the witch of Shadowdale.

The elf was still surprised by her own request. She had come to find Liriel, not chase a legendary ghost. Oddly enough, the Rashhemi did not seem to find her question strange. The first response to her query had been an outpouring of old stories—there was apparently no shortage of these in Rashemen—but eventually someone got around to contacting one of the *wychlaren*. They in turn had made inquiries, and Sharlarra's current escort was the result. The young witch didn't seem at all put out by Sharlarra's ghost horse. She demanded to know the story behind it. When the elf described what had happened in Waterdeep's graveyard, the woman nodded as if this made perfect sense.

They road in silence for over an hour before Sharlarra made another attempt at conversation. "So tell me, Anya, are there many elves in this village Dernovia?"

The witch sent her an incredulous look. "Few outlanders are allowed this far into Rashemen. You are permitted only because Zofia Othlor says you may come."

"I hope I'll have a chance to thank her."

"That is unlikely. You have asked to see the witch of Shadowdale. You will see her, and you will go."

Friendly sort, mused Sharlarra. "There's been some talk of drow sightings hereabouts. Tavern talk," she said, in response to Anya's narrow-eyed glare. "Have you seen any drow around?"

"Perhaps."

The cold answer found the edge of Sharlarra's patience. They didn't speak again until the village walls came into sight.

"That is the outlander's hut," the witch said, pointing to a small hillock. "The woman who calls herself Liriel is there."

Sharlarra sent her a curious look. "How do you know that?"

"There is a tripod of sticks on the roof. The *Domovoi*— the house spirits—like such things. They only put them on the roof when people are within and take then off when they leave. If they are upset about the people leaving, they throw the sticks at them." There was a slight warning tone in Anya's voice.

"So visitors tend to leave in a hurry," the elf said.

"That would be wise."

Sharlarra swung off the horse and tapped on the door. A tall, silver-haired woman answered the door. Her eyes widened in recognition and astonishment. Sharlarra had her own moment of recognition. This, in living form, was the ghostly woman she had seen with Moonstone.

Which meant that the ghost she'd seen had truly been Sylune, witch of Shadowdale.

"Oh gods," Sharlarra moaned.

The woman seized the elf and dragged her into the hut. She slammed the door and pulled a black mask off her belt. Before Sharlarra could blink, the "woman" had changed form into a small, slender drow.

"What are you doing here?" Liriel demanded.

"To be perfectly honest, I came looking for trouble." The elf grinned. "Looks like I found it. Impersonating Sylune! You've got more brass than a cheap dagger. Tell me all that happened since you left the ship."

Liriel took out a bottle of wine. They shared it as they pieced together their stories. News of Xzorsh's death brought a sharp pang to Liriel. He was the first elf she had met, the first who taught her that not all faerie elves were to be feared, that some could perhaps be friends. This odd female, in Liriel's opinion, was another such oddity.

They talked until nightfall. Finally Sharlarra rose. "I'll be off. The stiff-necked witch who brought me here made it very clear that I was to leave as soon as we spoke."

The drow felt a pang of regret. "I would like to talk again sometime."

Sharlarra winked. "That's not likely to be a problem. I said I'd leave the village, not the area. Moonstone and I will camp out in the forest for a few days. I'll see you again, little doubt of that!"

"Moonstone?"

"My horse. Come see."

Liriel followed her to the hillock's courtyard and started in surprise at the sight of a ghostly horse. This set the elf off into gales of laughter. She swung into the saddle and urged the strange mount down the forest path.

The drow glanced up at the moon and wondered if she might be able to find Sharlarra's song in the moonmagic of Eilistraee. She thought briefly of the lurking spiders, but the lingering echoes of the freed elves' joy pushed aside such grim considerations. Liriel had made her choice: surely even the persistent Lolth must know that by now. So she went back into the cottage and sat at the table, leaving the door open to let it the moonlight.

She closed her eyes and listened for the song. After a time she found the elf woman – but the song seemed a strange fit for the merry, pretty female. A surging sound like dark waters warred against a constant, valiant struggle of a spirit determined to keep afloat. There was also a chorus of elf voices, a faint echo that seemed to go back and back to its source in the distance past. Connecting the disparate themes was the rhythmic clatter of a horse's hooves.

Liriel sought farther for Eilistraee's own. She sensed the music unique to many distant places. Each had small, hidden groups of drow, their power humming through the moonlight that bound them. Liriel could sense that many were dancing, too full of joy to hold still.

She rose and began to dance to the silent music in perfect accord with the scattered priestesses. Even the candle she'd lit at dusk seemed to move and sway in time.

The candle.

Liriel stopped short and stared at the candle. It had melted into a large formless glob, a strange thing that looked like a lumpy pillar. Then the eyes opened, fastened on her, and shone with malevolent intent.

There was no mistaking its identity. "A yochlol," Liriel breathed, staring into the tiny creature's eyes.

The handmaid began to grow, and the young drow snapped into action. She leaped forward and smashed her fist down on the candle. Half-melted wax splattered. Again she struck the candle and dashed the remaining puddle and the stand that held it to the floor.

The girl sank down onto her chair and covered her face with her hands, oblivious to the burn and the painful-looking blisters already starting to rise.

"I renounce you," she whispered, rocking in her seat. "I am your child no more, your priestess never again."

In the courtyard beyond the open door, the spectral harper watched with narrowed eyes. Her translucent hand moved suddenly to the place where an ancient amulet had rested over her once-beating heart. The drow now wore the amulet. More than that—she had *awakened* it!

The Witch of Shadowdale nodded slowly as many small mysteries converged into one. She who had battled evil in so many of its forms, she who should by her very nature be beyond all fear, knew a moment of pure mortal terror.

Shakti Hunzrin worked her way steadily eastward, following the unrelenting zombie hoard and the vision granted her by the ruby embedded in the deathsinger's forehead.

This male intrigued her. He did not protest the pain of contact, did not respond to her mental questions. He simple allowed her to see what he saw. To Shakti, this was a revelation.

The deathsinger's keen eye picked up nuances she would never have noted on her own, and his keen sense of irony was a piquant frame for the grand tale of revenge that Gorlist intended to weave. For days Shakti was puzzled by the image that Brindlor showed her, but she began to suspect his purpose. He would tell a tale, but his current master would not be the hero of it.

Shakti spent many hours on the long trek thinking of ways to use this.

She and the undead finally reached the meeting place, a series of caverns deep below a mountain ridge humans called Running Rocks.

The deathsinger came to meet her, extending his hand to help her down from her lizard. Ordinarily she would have declined with scorn, but the long ride had left her stiff and sore.

"Where is Gorlist?" she demanded.

Brindlor nodded his head toward a side cavern. The warrior stood there, his narrowed eyes taking in the orderly ranks of female zombies.

In turn, Shakti inspected his forces. A score or two of drow stood behind Gorlist. "This is all?" she demanded.

"We had an unfortunate encounter with some berserker warriors," Brindlor said.

The warrior strode forward. "You took your time getting here," he snarled. "We will attack the humans tonight."

"What are their numbers? Their defenses? What magic have they?"

Gorlist laughed scornfully. "They are human. What magic could they have?"

"These human wizards can be surprisingly resourceful," the priestess said coldly.

"I have seen little evidence of this. We had one of the famed Red Wizards with us. He was killed by a bear."

Shakti looked past the truculent warrior to his troops. Some had been wounded. The bandages were still new, the blood that stained them still bright. "How many humans did you fight, and where are they now?" she said briskly. "If we take their raiding party now, we will decimate their numbers and weigh the final attack in our favor."

"A good strategy," Brindlor observed. He shrugged aside Gorlist's warning glare.

"Come," Shakti said and strode toward her silent army.

She took only a score of them—more to provide protection against possible drow treachery than to bring against the humans.

They made their way though a series of tunnels and emerged on a narrow walkway overlooking a high-ceilinged passage. A small band of humans walked along, carrying their dead and wounded with them.

There was something familiar about one of them: the black hair, the breadth of his shoulders, his way of moving. A slow, feral smile lit Shakti's face as she recognized Liriel's pet human.

She began to chant a prayer to Lolth. In response, thousands of spiders emerged from their hidden places and swarmed toward the warriors. They launched themselves from the walls, trailing silken threads. For several moments the air was dark with leaping spiders and thick with the startled curses of the Rashemi and the futile clang of their swords against the stone. Spider web was strong at any time, and the blessing of the goddess rendered it impervious to all steel and most spells.

When the humans were firmly enmeshed, Shakti made her way down the narrow walkway. She walked around the netting, observing the struggling humans within. She took a small silver cuff from her pinky and slid it onto the curve of one ear. This, a magical gift from the illithid Vestriss, enabled her to speak and understand the humans' coarse language.

"I have no use for you," she announced. "You will be set free, unharmed, in exchange for a small fee."

"Pay ransom to a drow?" snarled a thick, gray-bearded man. "Not a single coin, on my life!"

"Did I mention money? How very vulgar of you." Shakti smiled coldly. "I will trade many lives for one. Bring me the drow wench known as Liriel, and you will go free."

"Liriel?"

A long, skinny young man repeated the word incredulously. He twisted in the web as best he could, turning to face the warrior beside him. "Fyodor, is not Liriel your *wychlaran*? What does she mean by calling her 'drow'?"

"Oh, but she is," the priestess said with cruel pleasure. As an extra little sadistic twist, she added, "Who should carry this message but Fyodor, who knows this drow so very, very well?"

The boy looked to Fyodor with shattered eyes. "You would not do such a thing, bring a drow into Rashemen. Tell me she lies. Tell me you would never betray us so!"

For a long moment the warrior held the pleading stare. Then he turned to Shakti.

"Send the boy with me," he said in bleak tones, "and I will go."

Fyodor and Petyar did not speak until they were free of the Warrens. At last the older man spoke. "Go back to the village to warn the others. The drow are likely to attack."

"I have heard they can be treacherous," the boy said coldly. "Apparently the whole of *that* story has not been told."

The warrior caught his arm. "Petyar, there are things you do not understand. Zofia herself foresaw Liriel's coming. I am not happy that Liriel chose to present a name and form not her own, but that was her choice, not mine. She made it according to the light she had."

"The drow have precious little of that."

"I have watched Liriel's journey into the light," Fyodor said. "She is not what you think she is."

Some of the fury slipped from the young man's face, leaving only the hurt and worry. "I hope, cousin, that you are right."

Fyodor hurried to the hillock hut he shared with Liriel. The burden of his task lay heavy on his heart.

It was an impossible dilemma. In sending Petyar to take the message to the village and bring fighters to battle the drow, he was almost certainly letting his people know who and what Liriel was. If he did not, a band of his countrymen would die at the hands of Liriel's enemies.

He found the drow sitting at the table peeling what appeared to be melted wax off her hands and arms. She looked him over from head to foot. Only then did Fyodor remember that he was naked except for his boots and the borrowed cloak. Her eyes registered what that meant. There had been a battle, one fierce enough to require transformation to berserker form.

"Gorlist?" she asked.

Fyodor nodded. "There are others, too. Undead drow, female warriors all, and a priestess with red eyes and a whip of undead snakes."

"Nice touch," Liriel muttered. "If that's who I think it is, you're not here because you managed to escape."

He told her the story in quick, lean words. "You must flee Rashemen at once."

The drow dismissed this with an absent wave of one hand.

"I'll just give Shakti what she wants."

"Little raven, we can't know what forces they command!"

"Who said 'we'? I've faced Shakti before and defeated her. I can do it again." Her gaze dropped to her hands, and she flicked off a bit of wax.

"You are being arrogant."

Her eyes flashed to his face. "I have reason to be. I not only survived in Menzoberranzan but thrived. I have seen the worst life has to offer, and I'm more than a match for anything Shakti has in store."

He let out an exasperated sigh. "Do you say that because you believe it or because you think I'm stupid enough to?"

Her eyes narrowed. "Not very flattering."

"You know what I mean! If you are determined to go, I go with you."

He went over to the chest and dug out some clothes. He dressed quickly, and they stepped out into the night.

Beyond the door, Anya stood waiting for them, her staff pointed accusingly at the pair. Behind her stood a circle of witches. Anya stepped forward and with a twitch of deft fingers tore the mask from Liriel's belt. The drow's true appearance flooded back like a dark tide.

"There is your 'witch of Shadowdale.' Now you know what she truly is," Anya said with cold fury. "You know what *he* is as well! I demand the penalty of death earned by all traitors to Rashemen!"

CHAPTER NINETEEN

YESTERDAY'S PROMISES

"You are wrong," announced a musical, strangely hollow voice. "*Here* is the witch of Shadowdale."

A pale glimmer appeared beside Liriel, spreading into a misty cloud then taking a familiar form—the tall, silver-haired woman whose face Liriel had worn since the battle of the watchtower.

The ghostly woman turned to Liriel's accuser. "Anya, daughter of Fraeni, your mother was my friend, and in her name I invoke the oath. All vows made in shared circles must be kept, all secrets hidden. The drow who claimed my name has been accepted among us by the witch who knew me best. Do you not think Zofia had good reason for this?"

The young witch's lips set in a tight line, and she sent a glare toward the old woman. The Othlor inclined her head in confirmation.

"I must do as you bid," Anya said grudgingly. "But we Rashemi have a proverb: What good can come of alliance with evil?"

"An excellent proverb, and an even better question," Sylune said. She rested a ghostly hand on Liriel's arm. "I have many questions about you. I will stay with you until I find answers. With Zofia Othlor's permission, of course."

"You will ever find a welcome here," the old woman said softly. "You have been too long away, my sister. You must find me much changed."

Musical laughter spilled from the spectral harper. "The dead do not age, dear Zofia, yet I suspect you would not change places with me."

"True enough, and truer now than in days past. It is no easy time to be a spirit in Rashemen," Zofia warned.

"Even so, I will not regret what comes of it. It will be good to see battle again," she said wistfully. She turned to Liriel. "Do you agree, drow?"

Liriel gave an ungracious shrug. "I'm none too happy about being haunted, but I suppose enduring a ghost is better than becoming one."

Fyodor looked to Zofia. "The witch of Shadowdale spoke of battle. Did Petyar bring the message?"

"And came with it," the boy said. He stepped from behind the hillock. His defiant glare challenged the older man to condemn what he had done.

"I am proud of you, cousin," Fyodor said at last. "The first duty of a Rashemi warrior is to the land, his first loyalty to the *wychlaran*."

Some of the ice faded from the boy's eyes. "What will you do now?"

"How well do you know the Warrens?" Liriel asked him.

Petyar found it easier to regard the toe of his boots than the face of a drow. "I often go there," he mumbled. "Why?"

"Are there back tunnels to the place where the hostages are held?"

He glanced up, and nodded cautiously. "Yes, but they are narrow. No more than one can pass at a time."

"Perfect," she said. "Fyodor and I will go with you. I have spells that can counter the spider trap. Once the men are freed, you can lead them back to the clearing outside the Warrens. That's as good a place for battle as any."

"That would be my choice, as well," Zofia agreed. Her gaze swept the circle of witches. "Go, and prepare."

The three young people set out for the Warrens at a run. When they were still some distance away, Petyar stopped beside a large dead tree stump and threw his weight against it. The log fell with a crash, revealing a dark hole beyond.

Liriel's hands flashed through the gestures of a spell, and a sphere of blue light bobbed into existence. This earned her a wondering stare from the boy. She scowled and shoved him into the tunnel, tilting her head to listen to the clattering sound of his fall.

"Not a bad drop," she concluded. "It's safe to jump."

"Little raven!" protested Fyodor.

"It wasn't that steep," she said defensively. "Even if it was, he deserved it."

The Rashemi merely shook his head and followed his cousin into the cave.

The trio rose and regarded their surroundings in the light of Liriel's azure globe. They had emerged in a large cavern. Water dripped from jagged spires of rock high overhead and ran in rivulets toward a deep ravine. Two tunnels led out of the cavern, a broad passage leading westward and a narrow opening leading to the south.

A sound like a rushing wind swept toward them from the larger tunnel, and a full battalion of drow warriors roiled into the room.

Fyodor and Petyar drew their swords, but Liriel stepped between them and the drow. She flung up one hand and issued a sharp, staccato command—a word known only to the nobles of House Baenre and the forces under their command.

The warriors came to an abrupt halt. The leader recovered his surprise first and sauntered forward.

"That's close enough," Liriel said coldly. "You have not been granted permission to approach me."

She spoke in the drow language, dropping back into her old, imperious ways with terrifying ease. Something in her manner gave the warrior pause. "By what right do you command me?" he demanded.

"You wear the insignia of House Baenre. Therefore you are mine."

His thin, cruel lips curled in a sneer. "Triel is matron mother of the First House. Who are you?"

Liriel responded by hurling a gout of magical fire at his boots. The drow danced nimbly back. "Someone who does not care for your insolence," she snarled.

"A female wizard," he muttered. "A Shobalar, then."

Liriel sent him a venomous glare. "Triel didn't pick you for your intelligence, that's clear enough, nor for your knowledge of the House you purport to serve. I was trained by House Shobalar, yes, but I am Liriel Baenre, daughter to Menzoberranzan's archmage."

The male's smile returned in full. "You have made our hunt all the easier. It is you we seek."

As if a signal had been given, every drow with him drew a weapon. They moved as one, swiftly and silently. Not a single sword hissed as it came free of its scabbard, not a single tiny crossbow clicked as its wielder snapped it into firing position. The silence was eerie, but no less so than the precision. Liriel had almost forgotten the preternatural skill of her people's fighters. She had not, however, forgotten their subtle and devious ways.

She threw up an arm to hold Fyodor back. "As I have sought you," she retorted. "Triel took her time in sending help! Or perhaps it is you who took your time in getting here?" she added pointedly.

Uncertainty flickered in the leader's eyes. "We were told to meet Gromph's forces here."

"Zombies," Liriel said with disdain. "So like my dear father, to use expendable troops." Her gaze swept the battle-ready warriors, and she lifted one eyebrow pointedly.

"We are Matron Triel's," the leader said stiffly, "and as loyal to her as any zombie to its master."

"I don't doubt Gromph's zombies. He only purchases the best of anything, but they have a commander, yes? A high priestess?"

The drow nodded cautiously. "A high priestess of Lolth?" Liriel persisted.

"Who but?" the male said, obviously puzzled by this line of reasoning.

She let out a small, scornful chuckle. "You've heard the stories of Vhaerun, the Masked God. No male in Menzoberranzan hasn't heard them, and many dream that the rumors might be true. Some dare to do more than dream," she said meaningfully.

"We are faithful servants of Matron Triel and followers of the Spider Queen!" the soldier protested.

Liriel nodded crisply. "Good. Then you will stand with me against Shakti Hunzrin, traitor priestess to Vhaerun."

"This is not possible!"

"Then why does she travel with Gorlist, the leader of a band of drow outcasts known as the Dragon's Hoard? They are known followers of Vhaerun who make their living trading on the surface, slaving and stealing."

The drow snapped a look back at his second in command.

"I have heard of this band," the warrior replied. "Their name is sometimes spoken when the stories of Vhaerun are told."

Drow steel flashed, and the speaker's head tipped slowly to one side. The leader turned back to Liriel. "He should not have listened to such tales," he said grimly, "but before we seek out these traitors, perhaps you would be good enough to explain the strange company that *you* keep."

"These two?" Liriel said dismissively, switching to Common and flicking one hand toward the watchful Rashemi. "They are my slaves."

A howl of protest burst from Petyar. Fyodor slammed one fist into the boy's gut, and the cry ended in a wheezing gasp. "A thousand pardons, princess," he murmured. Fyodor spoke to Liriel, but his eyes never moved from the young man's face. "This one does not yet know when to speak and when to keep silent."

"You have dealt with him properly," Liriel said. "Tell these warriors what we will face."

Fyodor gave a concise, accurate field report.

When he was finished, the drow commander shook his head. "Too many."

"We have a wizard with us," the Rashemi pointed out.

"They have a priestess," the drow shot back, "and apparently their priestess can call upon two gods. We do not know what magic this Masked Lord may grant!"

"We Rashemi also have magic," Petyar said stoutly. "There are no male witches among us, but those men who have the gift craft wondrous magical items, powerful artifacts that any warrior can wield in battle!"

Liriel gritted her teeth and glared at the boy. Where drow was concerned, information like this was the equivalent of throwing blood in shark-infested water!

"I have seen no magic of consequence in this land," she

said flatly. "Hold your lying tongue, boy, or I will cut it into three strips and braid the pieces. You," she said to Fyodor. "If he speaks again, see to it."

She turned back to the drow warriors. "You will wait here and engage in battle any drow soldiers, alive or dead, who come through that tunnel," she said, pointing. "Leave none alive. Destroy the zombies."

The drow snapped a quick salute, and Liriel waved Petyar toward the tunnel. As soon as they were beyond the range of hearing, she seized the hem of the boy's vest and pulled him to a stop. "Is there another way out? A way that doesn't go through the cavern?"

Petyar spat at her boots. "So you can escape now and abandon my comrades?"

Fyodor backhanded the boy across the face. "Think before you speak, fool!" he said softly, his voice more angry than Liriel had ever heard it. "You will lead the others to the surface, and Liriel and I will draw the drow warriors and their zombies to fight this new force. That will give us some time and decimate their numbers."

"Exactly," she agreed.

The young man did not look convinced. "And if there was no second way?"

"Then we would have to fight our way clear," the drow told him. "It could be done, but I'd rather save the men for the battle to come. There *will* be a battle if even one of the drow remains standing. You've made sure of that. Now go!"

The boy looked uncertainly to his cousin. "Fyodor?"

"Do as she says, and hurry!"

Petyar took off at a run. Liriel followed close behind. Her mind raced as she sped along behind him, planning strategy, listing spells.

"These newcomers might join the other drow in battle," Fyodor said.

She shot a glance back at him. "It is possible, but they belong to House Baenre, and they are accustomed to following the orders of Baenre priestesses."

"Even if the battle is won, any surviving drow will have learned much about Rashemen's defenses and magic."

Petyar came to an abrupt stop and whirled to face the others. "Now I understand what you meant," he said in an appalled whisper. "I should not have said what I did about Rashemen's magic. From my words they might conclude that Rashemen is worth pillaging, perhaps even conquering!"

"We can't let them return to Menzoberranzan," Liriel acknowledged.

The boy's consternation turned to puzzlement. "You would lead them into battle, knowing that you must later slay them?"

"They won't take it personally," she said. "They're drow. They expect allies to turn on them."

Petyar turned helpless eyes to Fyodor. The warrior reached over Liriel's shoulder and gave him a shove. "Remember the men held by these drow, and go!"

The moon was high when Liriel and Fyodor climbed out of the tunnel. Petyar and the freed Rashemi warriors awaited them. All stared at her for a long moment before the *fyrra* ordered them to join the forces gathering in the clearing.

Treviel fell into step with the pair. His gaze flicked from Liriel to Fyodor, and he shook his head.

"She'll turn, my son. No doubt the others already have. There are more drow down there than rats in the sewers of Immiltar."

"She will stand," Fyodor said firmly.

There was no more time for talk. The mountains were suddenly alive with dark forms. A silent army marched from the mouth of a nearby cave. Drow females, larger and stronger-looking than the males who had ambushed the scouting party, advanced in grim precision. Moonlight gleamed on their bald pates and ready swords but found no answering glimmer in their dead eyes.

"Zombies," Fyodor whispered. The memory of his last battle on Rashemaar soil flooded back in full.

A sharp pain exploded in his thigh and jolted up his spine. He dived forward and rolled to one side, coming up with his black sword in hand.

The drow female whose life he had spared regarded him with contempt. The point of her long, slender sword was wet with his blood. She snarled something at him and beckoned him to come closer.

He glanced around for Liriel, but she had already been swept away by a fierce battle with two of the males.

The drow female advanced on him quickly, Her sword slashed the air in a dazzling display of speed and grace, taunting him with her superior skill, flaunting the promise of death.

Fyodor waited, hating what he must do. The beautiful drow lunged at him. He blocked the drow's attack with a slow, clumsy parry, one that drove her sword down toward his thigh. Contempt flared in her red eyes, and she leaned into the stroke.

Fyodor was no longer there. He spun away from the contrived blunder and swung his sword in a circle—a move many times faster and more fluid that his first. He smacked the drow hard with the flat of his sword and sent her sprawling.

An arrow sang past him and buried itself in the base of the fallen drow's neck. She twitched once and went still.

Thorn ran past him, nocking another arrow. This she aimed at one of the drow males who fought Liriel, backing her away from battle and toward the caves. Liriel dodged his falling body and tore the arrow free. This she plunged into the throat of her second opponent. With a quick nod of thanks, she raced off toward the hillside where the witches stood.

Another male stepped into her path. Liriel kept running, casting a simple heat-metal spell as she went. The drow dropped his sword and reached for his dagger. Consternation flooded his face when he realized it was not there.

"Looking for this?"

An elf woman with red-gold hair stood several paces behind him, a smirk on her face and a drow dagger in her hands. Sharlarra gave the dagger a mocking little shake and tossed it to Liriel.

In one smooth movement Liriel snatched it from the air and sent it spinning back toward the male. It slammed into his throat. His mouth moved around a drow curse, but only blood emerged. As the light faded from his eyes, he lifted one hand and in silent drow cant jerked out the curse he could not speak:

Lolth take you.

A shiver went through Liriel. She tossed her head, shaking it off, and looked for the elf, but Sharlarra was already off. She ran like a deer, weaving among the roiling throng with a small, hooked knife in one hand and a sword in the other. Wherever she went, hamstrung zombies toppled and fell.

Over the sound of battle came a terrible sound, a keening wail that would have given pause to a banshee. The cry grew in power, taking on the harsh, irregular rhythm of a drow chant. It was like no song Liriel had ever heard, but she recognized the power of a deathsinger's magic.

Dozens of zombies that had been reduced to a crawl by Sharlarra's knife stood up and resumed their advance. Those that had been cut apart by Rashemi swords retrieved their limbs—or someone else's—and pressed them back into place. They came on, moving inexorably toward the place where the witches stood.

Geysers of steam burst from the soil in the midst of that orderly advance. The rock itself stirred, flowing upward into a roughly human form—or at least the top half. A crudely hewn head, massive chest, and long, thick arms rose from the stone. A rocky fist hurled forward and shattered a zombie skull. Other, similar constructs took shape, and soon a score of stone warriors battered the advancing army.

A shout of triumph rose from the Rashemi warriors, greeting the appearance of the rock elementals.

Liriel could still hear the deathsinger's chant. So, apparently, could the zombies. They rose, and healed, and came on. Deathsingers did not just celebrate death: they commanded it!

Liriel looked around for the source of the song. On a nearby ledge stood a male drow, flanked by two fighters. His many braids swung this way and that as he swayed in time to his own chant. A large ruby gleamed in his forehead like a third eye.

On impulse, Liriel reached for the Windwalker and called forth the powerful spell stored there—a spell that required as its material component a large and valuable gem.

The deathsinger's wail rose to a shriek of mortal agony. He clawed at his head, raking furrows in his own flesh. Suddenly he went rigid, and his form began to expand like that of a berserker entering frenzy.

The drow exploded in a spray of gore, shattering from within. A large ruby statue stood in his place. The golem backhanded one of the guardian drow and seized the sword hand of the second. It casually threw the dark elf from the ledge and made its descent with a crashing leap. The golem waded into the zombie throng, pushing them back toward the land-bound rock elementals.

Fyodor saw this from where he stood and fought, and a faint smile touched his face. It was well that Liriel had not promised to refrain from raising golems.

He caught her eye and raised his sword in a quick salute. She gave him a brilliant, fierce smile and continued fighting her way toward the witches.

From the vantage of a nearby cave, Gorlist watched the course of the battle. Jerking himself back from the sight, he paced and snarled like a caged cat. He slammed a hand into the stone wall, ignoring the blood that flowed from his torn knuckles.

"Damn her!" he snarled. "Damn her to the deepest depths of the Abyss!" Foam flecked his pale lips, and Shakti, watching him closely, realized that his mind had slipped the last leashes of sanity.

Gorlist drew his sword, preparing to leap into the combat. Shakti started forward.

"No! Wait! Wait for—"

Her words were cut off as something hard slammed into the back of her head. Her red eyes glazed and rolled up.

Thorn stepped from the shadows and shoved the stunned priestess aside. Shakti hit the wall hard and slid down to the damp stone floor.

"Now," snapped the elf fighter, "let's continue the discussion we were having earlier."

Liriel raced toward one of the elementals. The stone guardian began to shiver, vibrating faster and faster. The drow took refuge behind a rock just as the creatures shattered. Shards of rock soared over the battlefield as if they had been shot from a trebuchet, arching toward the witches. The women met them with a single soprano shout. Stone clattered against an invisible wall and slid down to form a rough stone wall around their position.

Liriel scrambled to her feet, staring in disbelief at the place where the elemental had stood. She *knew* that spell! She had studied it as a girl with the Shobolar wizards. A relatively simple spell, it was the sort of thing that one of Triel's warriors might know.

She glanced toward the eastern sky. The crimson rim of the sun edged over the mountains, turning the snowy peaks into a silent tribute to the night-spilled blood. Day had come, and yet the drow fought on undeterred, *and their magic still held.*

Drow magic on the surface. This wasn't possible!

Oh, but it is, my little Windwalker.

The drow stopped dead. Her hand went to the Windwalker amulet, the magical trinket that allowed her to bring her magic to the surface.

A terrible possibility began to burn into Liriel's mind. "No," she whispered.

Oh, yes. The amulet is more powerful than you dreamed. It can hold the power of this land, and the spirits who act in league with these witches. The spirits are scattered, sundered. Yield to me, as you did before, and we will command them with a single voice!

Even as Liriel shook her head in vehement denial, she knew what must be done. Once before she had called a wandering spirit into the Windwalker and sent it safely home. In doing so, she had healed Fyodor of his uncontrolled rages.

If the amulet was truly that powerful, could she do this on a greater scale?

And more important, could she keep such power from Lolth's hands?

She ran toward the witches and vaulted over the tumbled stone wall. Two groups of six stood in linked spellcasting, commanding airborne whips that lashed at Triel's forces. Zofia stood between the two groups, directing their efforts.

Liriel hurried to the old witch, holding out the Windwalker. "What one witch knows is known to all. You said that I would bind and break, heal and destroy. Help me!"

The witch took Liriel's small black hand without hesitation. "One circle," she said, reached her free hand out toward her friend Wanja.

The hathran gripped the old woman's hand in her own. One after another, the witches joined hands. The circle went around and stopped with Anya. The young witch hesitated only a moment before she reached her hand out to the drow.

The moment their fingers touched a surge of power went through Liriel, a magic as great as any she had known under Lolth's sway. She opened her mind to the Windwalker and the drow magic stored within.

A frigid wind buffeted her, whipping her hair around her and chilling her until she felt certain her skin must be a gray as a bheur's. None of the witches was touched by the storm. All its fury was focused on Liriel as the goddess tried to claim her and take for herself this power.

This land.

But Liriel was not alone. The will and power of the witches lent their strength to hers. Their collective will thrust the goddess aside, as a circle of lamplight pushes back the darkness.

Liriel shook off the debilitating chill and formed in her mind an image of Yggdrasil's Child, the mythic tree whose roots ran deep, whose branches were broad enough to encompass all life.

There was magic deep in the bones and marrow of this world, magic she knew well. She reached down to it, strengthening the ties she had inadvertently created when she carved her own destiny on the Ruathym oak.

Next Liriel reached for the heart of Fyodor's homeland. The song of Rashemen began as a whisper, swelling to a mighty chorus that filled her mind with its powerful cadences. She saw the recognition on the faces of the witches, and the wonder. For the first time these women heard the song of the land they served.

A small whispery soprano took up the melody. Liriel's gaze went to the singer and linked to Anya's awestuck eyes. The young witch squeezed her hand, and her heart—as open to Liriel's gaze as her own—welcomed her one sister to another.

Other witches joined in the song. Still in a handclasped circle, they began to dance, and the ancient spellcasting they had learned as maidens kept perfect time to the song.

The waning moon had not yet set despite the coming of day. Using the magic that Qilué had taught her, Liriel reached out into the moonlight, listening for the song that was unique to each place.

A silvery glow surrounded her as she reached out with the moonmagic of the Dark Maiden. She heard the song that was Ysolde, daughter of Qilué, and the priestesses with her. To her surprise, they were very close. Liriel reached out into the forests and sent out a silent summons.

The winding of a hunting horn rang out from the wooded slope and bounded from mountain to mountain. The remnants of Gorlist's band fought with renewed ferocity.

Silver arrows streaked down from nearby trees, and a ringing chorus of female voices rang above the sounds of battle. Ysolde ran down the slopes with her sword held high. Behind her raced several of her maidens, all lofting bright swords and emitted the eerie, ululating cry. Their hair shone silver-bright in the dawning day.

"More of the demons coming!" roared Treviel, pointing with bloodied sword toward Ysolde's band.

Fyodor seized the *fyrra*'s shoulders and spun him about. The older man went rigid with shock at the sight before him.

A drow danced among the circle of spellcasting witches.

"That dance is a summons to the guardians of the land. This—*this!*—is what Mother Rashemen sends?" Treviel murmured.

"Tell the men not to attack any of the silver-haired drow women. Tell them!"

The *fyrra* hesitated. This advice went against everything he knew as truth or even sanity. Yet he could not deny what his eyes told him.

"This drow is truly *wychlaran?*" he asked.

"That and more," Fyodor said softly.

He looked toward his dearest friend, her small hands entwined with the pale fingers of Rashemaar witches, her eyes fixed upon things he could not see, and a vision of his own came to him. Through the Sight that was his heritage he glimpsed a golden-eyed raven—the spirit form of the girl his destiny and heart had chosen.

The raven-spirit sent forth a call, a mighty summons as familiar to Fyodor as the sound of his sister's voice. He felt the power of that summons, for once his own wandering spirit had followed it to the Windwalker. He was not at all surprised when the ghosts that haunted the edge of his vision stirred and moved toward the raven's call. He did not marvel when spirits rose from the trees and rocks and waters to join in the powerful spell of binding.

"She is *wychlaran* and more," he repeated firmly. "She *is* the Windwalker."

"You're Zofia's kinsman," Treviel said, accepting Fyodor's vision. He lifted his voice and began to roar out the song that sped the berserker transformation. Here and there the warriors took up the ritual.

The entranced drow heard the familiar song and drew it into the dancing circle. Fyodor's quest had been tied to the Windwalker, and echoes of his own spirit journey lingered in the mighty artifact.

The witches took up the song that was begun on Ruathym, when Fyodor unleashed the *hamfarrig* magic within, and the sea-going fighters of Ruathym became once again the legendary wolves of the waves.

Power flowed from the witches into the singing berserkers. The rage came over them swiftly. Fyodor was the first to throw down his sword and rear up on two strong, black-furred legs. A blue-eyed bear roared into the thick of battle, tossing aside zombies and living drow alike with swipes of his massive paws. Petyar changed, and a long-limbed brown bear galloped toward a beleaguered Rashemi. The clatter of Rashemaar swords against stone echoed through the clearing as one after another the men dropped their weapons and took on their true berserker forms. Before long every man of the Black Bear lodge fought with the form and fury of his totem animal.

In some corner of her mind, Liriel was aware of Sharlarra darting through the battlefield, collecting the discarded weapons. These she took to the edge of the battlefield where grim-faced women took up swords their husbands and brothers had dropped, and children stood waiting to leave childhood behind forever. The elf handed out the weapons, and all Rashemi who could hold a blade went to fight beside their berserkers.

The drow reached out to Thorn, felt the powerful dual nature of the elf-wolf—and a depth of pain she would not have thought the stoic hunter capable of feeling. A lone voice, a wolf's plaintive howl, rose to the moon in unwilling solo. With all her heart, with all her being, the exiled hunter longed for a pack.

Liriel brought to mind the sundering of the tapestry and the healing circle of ravens that had guided the spirits of the captive elves home. Little raven, she thought. Fyodor had named her well. Following the example of her namesakes in this world and the one beyond, Liriel called the wolves.

With one voice, the witches and drow sent Thorn's plaintive wolfsong out into the surrounding mountains. Lithe, silvery creatures slipped from the forest as the lythari came to battle. Thorn's people, if just for this one time, would fight with her as a pack.

Packs of natural wolves came as well. With intelligence remarkable for forest creatures, they fell upon fallen zombies, dragging them toward the ravine.

A booming crackle came from the forest, and the thud of titanic steps. Cries of mingled fear and triumph rose from the villagers as a fifty-foot monster burst from the trees. Feet the size of hillocks slammed down as it stomped the zombie army, crushing the undead creatures into the soil. The wood man, legendary protector of Rashemen, had answered the song. The battle was over, and the surviving drow fled into the forest.

Power flowed through Liriel, burning her as if somehow the blood in her veins had turned to the acid venom of a black dragon. She began to sway on her feet. One task remained, she told herself.

But the song began to slip away, driven off by the terrible fire kindling over Liriel's heart. Time stopped, caught and immobilized by the searing agony. The stone beneath Liriel's feet seemed to turn molten and drift away. Vaguely familiar shapes took form in the dense gray mist, but Liriel was beyond knowing or naming them. Power swept through her, terrible power that merged the sun's fire, the crushing weight of stone, the screaming force of wind, and the immortal anguish she had sensed in the displaced elven souls woven into the tapestry.

She could not say when the agony peaked or when she could no longer bear it. It washed over her like waves of the sea or echoes in an Underdark cavern. Eventually she began to sense that the waves were receding, the echoes drifting into silence.

Someone slapped her awake none too gently. Liriel cautiously opened one eye. The sun was fully risen, and her chest burned with heat every bit as fierce. She looked down. The Windwalker hung over her heart, its gold blackened and its magic silenced.

Zofia took Liriel's hand in both of hers. Her aged face was radiant with joy. "The ghosts are free. The link between spirits and land is healed."

Liriel thought of the drow magic and the horror she had inadvertently unleashed upon the surface. "What about the other link?"

"Strong," the witch said somberly.

The drow buried her face in both hands. "I thought only of myself. I never once thought *this* could come of it!"

Zofia reclaimed Liriel's hands in hers, and her blue eyes gazed earnestly into the drow's. Her face showed deep concern but no condemnation.

"What you did was not done alone. When one thing is bound, another is broken. When one thing is healed, another is destroyed. This is the nature of magic and of all life. Your sisters know this."

She looked up at the black-robed women. They nodded silent agreement.

Liriel sat bolt upright, ignoring the wave of vertigo the sudden movement caused. "Lolth spoke to me of this. If she would speak to one, why not another?"

She pushed herself to her feet. "There was a priestess with the drow, a female who fought me before over the goddess's favor. If Lolth speaks to this priestess, the drow of the Underdark will know everything!"

"Have you any reason to think that they don't already know?"

Liriel nodded grimly. "These warriors were sent by my father and his sister. They are among the ruling elite of the city in which I was born. These warriors were their personal troops," she stressed.

"So they wish to keep this secret to themselves," Zofia reasoned.

"It will come out in time," the drow said with the surety of long experience. "Sooner, if Gorlist and his band learn of it."

She looked around for Fyodor. A black-furred bear paused in the act of savaging a drow warrior, looking up as if it sensed her seeking thoughts. She gestured and headed for the forest, her legs becoming steadier with each step.

An unseen presence went with her. The ghostly woman whose form Liriel had worn for many days walked beside her, and her gait was no steadier than the battered drow's. Sylune was deeply shaken by what she had witnessed. In many ways she deeply regretted her impulsive journey to

Rashemen. She'd reconciled herself to her death, but it was difficult to walk unseen through a land she had known as a living woman, to see Zofia, who had been like a sister, as a powerful but aging woman.

Sylune had never been an ordinary woman, and she was no ordinary ghost, but she, too, had felt the call of the Windwalker and the cool brush of ghosts and spirits as they passed her on their way into the powerful circle.

She could have been part of that. Perhaps her magic would have changed the outcome, shattered the link between the Underdark and the surface rather than strengthening it.

Perhaps. Even one of Mystra's Chosen did not know all of magic, nor did a ghost understand all there was to know of the Afterlife. If Sylune had heeded the Windwalker's call, what might have become of her?

The ghosts and spirits released with the Windwalker's greatest and final task had dispersed, each going to the place it belonged, the place it most wanted to be. Where would she, Sylune, have gone?

Most likely she would have returned to Shadowdale and resumed the existence she'd known for years: a spectral harper, more solid and sentient than most ghosts. Perhaps she would have returned to life. Or would she have moved on at last?

For a moment Sylune allowed herself to hear the poignant call of her goddess, to feel the warmth and healing that would change this half-life into something immeasurably better. Joy and pain filled her in equal measure as she contemplated what might have been and what might yet be.

At the end, Sylune did what she had always done. She chose duty.

With a sigh, the witch of Shadowdale turned her silent steps homeward, and left Rashemen to the living, and to the spirits who were as much a part of this land as stone and sky.

Sharlarra saw the drow girl leave the battlefield, walking unsteadily at the side of an enormous black bear. Her first impulse was to follow, then she remembered her own guardian animal.

The elf sprinted toward the place where she'd left Moonstone half-hidden among the trees. Dread filled her. She'd heard the swift-spreading stories about the Windwalker and the powerful magic it had drawn from summoned ghosts and spirits. What if Moonstone had been among them? The thought was beyond bearing. There was more than a comrade's bond between her and her horse: there was a soul-deep recognition. Sharlarra remembered little of her early life or her people, but she knew in her blood and bones that the ghost horse was a link between her and her forgotten ancestors.

She whistled for the ghost horse and was rewarded with a crescendo of cantering hoofs. Sharlarra watched in puzzlement as a tall, silver-gray horse, its black mane and tail nearly sweeping the ground, came running toward her.

Realization struck the elf like the effects of too much bad brandy. Her legs gave way, and she sat down hard on the forest floor.

"Moonstone?" she breathed.

The horse's strangely expressive face registered mild exasperation, as if to say, "Who else?" He bobbed his head, inviting her to climb onto his back. The elf scrambled up. Together they cantered off in search of trouble.

Liriel caught sight of a tall, slender drow female ahead, running lightly through the underbrush. She cupped her hands to her mouth and called, "Ysolde!"

The drow turned toward Liriel's voice. "We pursue a priestess of Lolth," she called. "Join us."

With that, she turned and disappeared into the shadows. Liriel heard the unmistakable hiss and crack of a snakehead whip and the ululating cry of the Dark Maiden's warriors as they ran to aid one of their own.

She glanced down at Fyodor, still in bear form. He had taken advantage of her stop to rest, settling down on his haunches and panting like a hound run too long and hard. His muzzle was stained with blood, his thick fur damp and matted.

Deep foreboding filled the drow. She ran her hands over her friend's bear form and found the gashes where drow steel had parted the thick hair-and-hide armor. Berserkers never felt their wounds during battle frenzy, never felt cold or thirst or weariness. The fact that Fyodor needed to rest told her he would soon change back to his own form. Weakened by the frenzy, wounded as he was, he would need healing.

"Go back with the others," she told him. The berserker rose, responding instinctively to a *wychlaran*'s command.

Liriel watched him plod off, noting the weary, limping shuffle. Her heart ached for him, but there was nothing more she could do. She turned and ran along the path Ysolde had taken.

The sounds of a whip led her to the bank of a stream. She skidded to a stop.

Shakti Hunzrin stood over the body of Qilué's daughter, wielding her whip. A trickle of blood ran down her face from a wound on her scalp, but her mouth was twisted in malicious triumph. Skeletal snakes rose and fell, their bony jaws and blood-soaked fangs diving again and again.

Liriel called the priestess's name. The beating stopped—too late for Ysolde—and malevolent crimson eyes settled on Liriel's face.

The surrounding underbrush parted, and several dark maidens stepped into the clearing. Shakti gave a shriek of frustration and struck the ground with the whip. The pebble-strewn soil parted, and she disappeared into the small chasm. Just as swiftly, the escape tunnel closed, and a thin trickle of Ysolde's blood collected in the fissure.

Two of the priestesses knelt beside Ysolde's battered form. One of them looked to Liriel with hate-filled eyes. With a start, she recognized Dolor, the priestess she had battled in the High Forest.

"I should have killed you then," the priestess said coldly. "First Elkantar, now Ysolde. How much grief must Qilué bear on your behalf?"

Liriel had nothing to say. Unshed tears burned in her eyes as the drow priestesses shouldered their slain leader and disappeared into the trees. Grief filled her: for Ysolde, the first priestess of Eilistraee she'd ever met, and the first living being to welcome her to the surface world. For Qilué, who would live on without the joy and comfort to be found in the company of those she loved. More unexpected was grief for a dream that had died before Liriel understood that she harbored it: the dream of finding a place for herself among the priestesses of Eilistraee.

The followers of the Dark Maiden might revere Eilistraee, but they were still drow. No one could hate more bitterly, or cling so persistently to a grudge. Liriel suspected that she would find no welcome from Qilué and her followers.

Perhaps Eilistraee herself would accept her. The goddess had shown her favor to Liriel more than once. And what of the moonmagic Liriel had cast, the sound of moonsong that echoed through her senses still? Surely that was sign that the goddess had not turned away! Perhaps she could live as Thorn did and find a solitary, goddess-blessed purpose of her own.

As if in response to her thoughts, a wild cry rose from among nearby trees, a voice that was not quite elven. She took off toward the sound and soon picked up the clatter of steel.

She leaped the tangle of roots that stood in her way and burst into the clearing. Her eyes took in Thorn in battle against Gorlist. The drow warrior caught sight of her and stopped in mid-lunge. He quickly recovered and stuck aside Thorn's riposte with a brutal slash. He shouldered past the elf woman and lifted his blade overhead to catch and parry the strike she aimed at the back of his neck.

Liriel thrust out one hand, warning Thorn back. "Go hunt down some of the others," she said. "This battle is mine to fight, and it has been long in coming."

"Too long," Gorlist snarled. He crossed the distance between them in a running charge, holding his sword high overhead and screaming with a fury too long repressed.

She got her sword out in time to haul it overhead with both hands. The blades met with a force that sent her staggering backward.

Gorlist pressed his advantage. He thrust in hard with a high lunge, deftly disengaged from Liriel's parry and struck again a few inches to the side. The tip of his sword thrust hard against Liriel's breastbone, where the Windwalker rested over the mark it had burned deeply into her skin The amulet saved her, but she gasped in pain.

Wild, triumphant laughter burst from the warrior. He slashed his blade across one shoulder, cutting through her shirt and tracing a long, stinging line across her shoulder.

"Now *you* are marked," he gloated. "Your first scar. Let's see how many more you can bear before you die." Spittle flew from his lips.

His sword flashed up toward her face. Liriel managed a high parry that turned his blade aside. It skimmed through her hair. Gorlist wrenched it free, tearing a lock from her scalp.

"That's another," he said as he came in again.

The two drow danced along the stream bed, their swords clattering in a deadly duet, but the long night and the powerful spellcasting had drained Liriel's strength. She felt as if she were moving through water or slowed by a nightmarish lethargy. More than once the vengeful warrior got past her guard.

His blade skimmed the knuckles of her sword hand, opening a long red line. Blood poured over her hand and the hilt it gripped.

Gorlist leaped into a deep, lunging attack. Liriel parried, knowing what was surely to follow. As she expected, he moved his sword in a small but powerful circle, twisting the sword from her wet hand. He kicked the falling sword and sent it spinning into the stream.

Liriel dived under his next attack and rolled aside, reaching for the throwing knives in her boot. She threw these at the advancing drow. He batted them aside and kept coming.

Again she rolled, grabbing and throwing whatever knife came to hand. Gorlist struck them down with contemptuous ease. The cold waters of the stream closed over her, shocking her into full awareness of her situation. Her weapons were gone, her spells all cast.

She leaped to her feet and faced her enemy with defiant pride. It was all she had left.

An enormous black bear paused at the forest's edge, gazing out over the battlefield with pain-clouded eyes. The rocky ground was littered with the bodies of the slain, and the wheeling multitude of ravens formed dark clouds against the morning sky.

The bear's wounded paw gave way, and he stumbled to the ground. Fyodor felt the chill embrace of Rashemaar soil against his skin.

Naked and bleeding, chilled to the very bone, he pushed himself away from the ground and looked about for something to cover himself. Not a difficult task, since the berserkers' clothing had all torn away with the coming of the change. He found a pair of boots—judging from the size, his cousin Petyar's—and a shirt and breeches. The lacings along the front of the shirt and both sides of the breeches had been torn away when their owner took on bear form, but that presented no problem. By Rashemaar custom, all warriors' garments were fashioned with a second pair of laces just below, in honor of the time when berserkers changed form at will.

Fyodor threaded and tied the second laces as quickly as his shaking hands would allow. He pulled on Petyar's boots and looked around for his sword.

A few weapons littered the ground, Rashemi and drow alike, but he reached for none of them. According to tradition, the black sword would be the last he wielded.

He looked for Liriel, his gaze following the black-robed witches as they moved with the other women around the field. She was not among them.

As the haze of his battle frenzy receded, he remembered when and where he'd last seen his friend. A priestess of Lolth awaited her, and so did a deadly drow swordmaster. She had bidden him leave her.

And he had left.

Fyodor turned and stumbled into the forest. He had no strength, no sword. There was nothing left to him but the drow girl he loved and the knowledge that he need never leave Rashemen again.

The water beside Liriel exploded upward, reforming in the familiar blue shape of the genasi. Azar gave the drow a fierce smile, and the light of insanity burned bright in her eyes. She showed Liriel the sword Gorlist had tossed into the water.

"The illithid wanted you dead," she said. "Live to spite her!"

Liriel had no time to respond, no time to claim and lift the blade. Gorlist's running charge was almost upon her. She did not see Fyodor streaking toward her, moving with the preternatural speed granted by his berserker frenzy.

The young Rashemi thrust himself between the girl and the warrior, accepting the thrust meant for Liriel. Drow steel sank deep and true. Fyodor fell heavily to his knees, and the strength of his final frenzy slipped from him like a sigh.

Liriel's keening wail tore through the clearing. She hurled herself at Gorlist, tearing at him with her nails and teeth like a wild thing. They fell together, but the stronger male quickly rolled her beneath him.

He captured her furious hands and pinned them above her head. Holding her captive with one hand, he reached in his belt for a knife and raised it for the killing stroke.

He froze, hand uplifted and neck chorded with an unvoiced scream. A crimson fountain spilled from his open mouth, and the light of hatred at last faded from his eyes. He fell slowly to one side and lay with Liriel's sword impaling his throat.

Azar stood over him. "The illithid wanted you dead," she explained to Liriel, "and so did this dark male." She extended a slim blue hand to the drow girl.

Liriel took it and allowed the genasi to pull her to her feet. She ran the few steps to Fyodor's side and fell to her knees beside him. Dimly she was aware of the clatter of horse's hoofs, and of Sharlarra's bright head close to her own. "What can I do?" the elf said softly.

The drow met her eyes. "He had a sword—a black blade without an edge. Find it and bring it here."

The elf woman leaped to her feet and onto her horse's back. Moonstone raced toward the battlefield as if sensing the time for this task was swiftly running out. Sharlarra backhanded tears from her face and scanned the field.

Finally her eyes settled on a sturdy woman of about thirty years of age. The woman's black braids were unraveled, her kirtle stained with blood. Two small boys clung to her skirts, and a black sword rested on her shoulder.

Sharlarra pulled up beside the woman. "Liriel sent me to find Fyodor's sword. Don't ask me why. Is that it?"

A bleak expression filled the woman's winter-blue eyes. "It is, and I don't need to ask why. A warrior of Rashemen always dies with his sword in his hands."

CHAPTER TWENTY

RAVEN ASCENDING

Fyodor stirred in Liriel's arms. His eyes opened and met hers.

There were so many things she wanted to say, but all she could manage was, "I sent for your sword."

A faint smile touched his lips. "Windwalker," he said. "The heart and strength of the land. Of course you would understand such things."

His words shattered her. She rested her cheek on his head and struggled to hold back a different kind of darkness—a wave of grief and despair unlike anything she had ever known.

"Listen to me, little raven," he said in a fading voice. "I was a dead man the day I left Rashemen. What adventures we have shared since then, and what wonders I have known." He found her hand and raised it to his lips. "You have brought me home, as Zofia foretold."

There was peace on Fyodor's face, utter content-ment in his eyes, but for Liriel, this was not enough.

"You told me that truth would always find its way out, that good is stronger than evil. We've come so far together. Why must we lose now?"

"Dying is not the same as losing. What we were meant to do, we did. What we are, we became."

His breath hitched then released on a soft rattling sigh.

Liriel's tears fell freely as she rocked him in her arms. "Not yet," she pleaded. "Wait for the sword. Just wait a little while more. Don't leave. Don't leave me alone."

Thorn and Sharlarra found them there. The drow's cheek remained pillowed on Fyodor's head. Her eyes were closed, and her small frame shook with her anguished mourning.

The elf's horse whickered softly and nosed Sharlarra. The elf following Moonstone's pointed gaze and noted the translucent form of the young Rashemi, standing near the grieving drow.

Sharlarra walked over to Liriel and laid a hand on her shoulder. The drow looked up with dull eyes. Sharlarra held out Fyodor's sword.

Bitter laughter spilled from the drow. "It's too late. He's gone."

Thorn seized her chin and turned it toward the watchful spirit. "Not yet, he isn't. I know this land. It is not an easy place to leave. Did you bid him stay?"

The drow nodded silently, her eyes fixed on her friend's face. "I didn't want to be alone," she whispered, "but I didn't mean this."

Sharlarra knelt beside Liriel and eased the Rashemi's body from her arms. She lowered Fyodor to the ground then placed the black sword on his chest and folded his hands over it. She and Thorn helped Liriel to her feet.

For a long moment Liriel stood between the body and the spirit of her beloved friend.

It was Thorn who finally broke the silence. She looked to the lingering spirit and said firmly, "We will hunt well, and run swiftly. We three."

Fyodor's ghostly eyes shifted from Thorn to Sharlarra. The elf nodded. Finally he looked to Liriel, and there was both a farewell and plea in his eyes.

An image came vividly to Liriel's mind: the battle for the island of Ruathym, when Fyodor took on yet another transformation, sending his spirit in animal form to take Liriel from the very hand of Lolth. She nodded and closed her eyes, listening for the music of the place to which Fyodor belonged.

The song of Rashemen filled her mind, growing louder as new voices joined the chorus. A familiar deep voice, as like to Fyodor's as shadow to source, took up the song. Entwined with it was a woman's voice. Fyodor's parents. She knew this with absolute certainty.

The voices of friends whose names she did not know filled her mind, shouting cheerful insults over the background of song. The faces began to take shape in her mind. There was the bearded visage of the friend who had welcomed them to Dernovia. There was young Petyar. There was a wild snowcat awaiting Fyodor with the calm air of a beloved pet expecting her master.

There was Home.

Liriel felt her spirit tear free, saw her small dark form sag between the two elf women who had thrown their lot in with hers.

Then she was soaring away, the cold Rashemaar wind beneath her black wings. Strong arms encircled her neck, but she felt her friend's weight only in her heart. The flight was over too soon, and the raven spirit that Liriel had become came to rest on a strong perch—a limb, perhaps, of the mythic tree that held all worlds in its branches. Fyodor's spirit filled hers with a final embrace, and then he was gone.

Her golden eyes sought him, but she could go no farther that this. Neither could she bring herself to leave. What was there left for her in the world she knew but elusive starlight and lingering shadows?

A sharp slap dragged her suddenly back into her body.

Liriel's eyes flew open. The lythari leaned over her, hand upraised for another of her trademark "rescues." The drow caught Thorn's wrist.

"Do that again and you'll be running on three feet instead of four," she warned.

"What's this?" Sharlarra said warily.

The drow dragged herself to her feet. "Explain it to her. I've got something to do."

Between the three of them they managed to lift Fyodor's body to the back of a beautiful gray horse. Liriel stood and watched them go with dry eyes. The farewell that mattered had been spoken.

One more battle awaited her. She would have this done today, one way or another.

She turned around, not at all surprised to see Shakti Hunzrin waiting for her. Her gaze dropped to the skeletal whip writhing in agitation by the priestess's side, and she gave a resigned sigh. "Let's get this over with."

"Matron Triel wants you back in Menzoberranzan," Shakti announced.

This information stunned Liriel into silence. After a long moment, she asked, "You would take me there? Alive?"

"If that is what Triel wants, yes."

It was on the tip of Liriel's tongue to ask what Gromph wanted. Since the day she'd left the Underdark, she'd never been certain whether the forces he'd sent after her were trying to find her or kill her.

In truth, it did not matter. As far as Liriel was concerned, her father was dead. Hrolf, the pirate who had loved her, who had wanted nothing from her but her happiness, had died on Ruathym.

She managed a contemptuous half-smile. "Would you be shocked if I told you that Triel's desires are not first thing that come to mind when I awaken?"

"So you will not return?"

"No. Kill me now, or try to."

Shakti nodded as if she had expected this. "If the drow of Menzoberranzan learn that you live, they will never stop seeking you. You know this."

Liriel nodded.

"There is another way." Her crimson eyes dropped to the mask that still hung from Liriel's belt.

She understood at once and tugged the mask free. Shakti tied it to her belt. The mask remembered its former wearer, and the priestess took on Liriel's form—and something more.

A measure of Lolth's dark glory shone through the priestess's borrowed amber eyes.

"This is what you have lost," Shakti proclaimed in a voice filled with power. "In choosing service over power, you have made your choice. Yet what has it profited you? You have lost the favor of Eilistraee. You are alone. You are nothing."

Dark laughter rose on the wind, and the insane light faded from Shakti's eyes. The satisfaction there was entirely her own.

"Matron Triel might claim otherwise, but she wants you dead. You have lost Lolth's favor, which is even better. I think the archmage will quickly accustom himself to his daughter's loss, but if Gromph comes to suspect that you are alive and becomes troublesome in his demands to have you back, we will have a means to quiet him. Better yet, he would view *this*—" Shakti broke off and gestured contemptuously to her borrowed form—"as a pawn to use in his pathetic little intrigues. Triel will know of these games, and, through me, will be able to thwart the foolish male at every turn."

"Gromph is not easily fooled, and you have no wizard's spells. I suppose you've thought of a solution to that, too."

Shakti's eyes dropped to the Windwalker.

Liriel handed it over without hesitation. It had purchased Fyodor's freedom. Now it would purchase hers. Its power was spent. It had done all the damage it would do. Let Shakti discover that some other time.

"What of the mercenaries?"

Shakti followed her reasoning at once. "They cannot return to Menzoberranzan, of course. What has happened here and what it means to the drow is a secret that must be kept for as long as possible. I will return to the city alone."

"You want to kill me. Why don't you?"

The priestess's eyes moved to the place where Gorlist lay, a sword through his throat. "This male wanted to kill you. He wanted that more than anything else. That wanting made him blind and stupid."

"Not to mention dead."

"That is the logical consequence of blindness and stupidity." Shakti untied the mask. In her own form, she looked upon Liriel for the last time. Her eyes held all the endless hatred of the Abyss.

"You bested me once. I learned from that. The curse of the drow is uncontrolled hatred. If I can walk away and leave you alive, I will know I am equal to any challenge."

Liriel received this pronouncement in silence. Apparently she was not the only one who had changed profoundly over the past few months.

"You will become a great matron mother," she told Shakti.

The drow's smile was cold and supremely satisfied. "I know."

A raucous cry sounded overhead, and a dark shadow winged across the clouded sky. Its flight took a circling path that spoke of hidden enemies—most likely one of the drow males who had fled the losing battle.

Thorn reflected that she would have to teach raven lore to her new pack sisters. There was much she could learn from them, as well. She had taken the drow's measure and seen her power. As for Sharlarra, any elf who rode with a *teu-kelytha*—one of the legendary moon horses of Evermeet—must have depths worth exploring. The story of how such a horse came to leave the sacred island would surely be one worth hearing.

A deep contentment filled the lythari, such as she had never expected to feel. She slipped into her lupine form and followed the hunt.

CHECK OUT THESE NEW TITLES FROM THE AUTHORS OF R.A. SALVATORE'S WAR OF THE SPIDER QUEEN SERIES!

VENOM'S TASTE
House of Serpents, Book I
Lisa Smedman

Serpents. Poison. Psionics. And the occasional evil death cult. Business as usual in the Vilhon Reach. Lisa Smedman breathes life into the treacherous yuan-ti race.

March 2004

THE RAGE
The Year of Rogue Dragons, Book I
Richard Lee Byers

Every once in a while the dragons go mad. Without warning they darken the skies of Faerûn and kill and kill and kill. Richard Lee Byers, the new master of dragons, takes wing.

April 2004

FORSAKEN HOUSE
The Last Mythal, Book I
Richard Baker

The Retreat is at an end, and the elves of Faerûn find themselves at a turning point. In one direction lies peace and stagnation, in the other: war and destiny. *New York Times* best-selling author Richard Baker shows the elves their future.

August 2004

THE RUBY GUARDIAN
Scions of Arrabar, Book II
Thomas M. Reid

Life and death both come at a price in the mercenary city-states of the Vilhon Reach. Vambran thought he knew the cost of both, but he still has a lot to learn. Thomas M. Reid makes humans the most dangerous monsters in Faerûn.

November 2004

THE SAPPHIRE CRESCENT
Scions of Arrabar, Book I
Available Now

FROM *NEW YORK TIMES*

BEST-SELLING AUTHOR

R.A. SALVATORE

In taverns, around campfires, and in the loftiest council chambers of Faerûn, people whisper the tales of a lone dark elf who stumbled out of the merciless Underdark to the no less unforgiving wilderness of the World Above and carved a life for himself, then lived a legend...

THE LEGEND OF DRIZZT

For the first time in deluxe hardcover editions, all three volumes of the Dark Elf Trilogy take their rightful place at the beginning of one of the greatest fantasy epics of all time. Each title contains striking new cover art and portions of an all-new author interview, with the questions posed by none other than the readers themselves.

HOMELAND

Being born in Menzoberranzan means a hard life surrounded by evil.

March 2004

EXILE

But the only thing worse is being driven from the city with hunters on your trail.

June 2004

SOJOURN

Unless you can find your way out, never to return.

December 2004

Two new ways to own the Paths of Darkness by *New York Times* best-selling author

R.A. Salvatore

GIFT SET

A new boxed set of all four titles in paperback

September 2004

Contains: *The Silent Blade, The Spine of the World,
Servant of the Shard, Sea of Swords*

Wulfgar the barbarian has returned from death to his companions:
Drizzt, Catti-brie, Regis, and Bruenor. Yet the road to freedom will
be long for him, and his path will lead through darkness before he
emerges into the light. And along the way he will find old enemies,
new allies, and someone to love.